Ronan Ryan is originally from Clonmel in Ireland. At thirteen, he moved to Nagoya, Japan. He was educated in Dublin and studied psychology at university before embarking on an MSc in neuropsychology. He completed an MSc in Creative Writing at the University of Edinburgh, and lived in New Zealand, where he completed an English Literature PhD. Returning to Dublin, he worked on *The Fractured Life of Jimmy Dice*, his first novel. He lives in Dublin, still.

Praise for *The Fractured Life of Jimmy Dice*:

'An Irish epic with a potent post-millennial hum and a wave-like momentum that becomes insidiously addictive'
Irish Independent

'Expertly experimental. Ryan has talent to burn'
Irish Examiner

'Brimming with affection, wisdom and texture, this coming-of-age saga announces [Ronan Ryan] as one of the more accomplished newcomers in Irish fiction' *Sunday Independent*

'Hugely engaging . . . warm, sincere and big-hearted. A wonderful debut from an Irish talent' *Image* Magazine

'Ryan's imaginative novel is full of adventure and told with compassion . . . a compelling account of a family's fortunes'
Irish Times

RONAN RYAN

THE FRACTURED LIFE OF JIMMY DICE

TINDER
PRESS

First published in Great Britain in 2017 by Tinder Press
An imprint of HEADLINE PUBLISHING GROUP

First published in paperback in 2017 by Tinder Press
An imprint of HEADLINE PUBLISHING GROUP

1

Cataloguing in Publication Data is available from the British Library

ISBN 978 1 4722 3725 5

Typeset in Sabon LT Std by
Palimpsest Book Production Ltd, Falkirk, Stirlingshire

Printed and bound in Great Britain by Clays Ltd, St Ives plc

MIX
Paper from
responsible sources
FSC® C104740

HEADLINE PUBLISHING GROUP
An Hachette UK Company
Carmelite House
50 Victoria Embankment
London EC4Y 0DZ

www.tinderpress.co.uk
www.headline.co.uk
www.hachette.co.uk

For Anne-Laure Richert

I ask what is involved in the condition I recognise as mine; I know it implies obscurity and ignorance; and I am assured that this ignorance explains everything and that this darkness is my light.

Albert Camus, *The Myth of Sisyphus*

I realised that the world does not represent a struggle at all, or a predaceous sequence of chance events, but the shimmering bliss, beneficent trepidation, a gift bestowed upon us and unappreciated.

Vladimir Nabokov, 'Beneficence'

PART ONE

Identity Knocks

Chapter One

Death

July 1980

I was alive once, briefly. I'm just not sure if it counts – it was thirty-five years ago, and I was dying at the time. I closed my tiny eyes against the slicing light. I attempted to gasp, choking deeper instead. My purple body shook and something crumbled inside me. I faded into darkness, receding from screams.

I remember being born again, but it's not quite real. It isn't my birth. The screams are the same, so is the room, and the panicked flurries of activity. And the baby I think is me, my vibrantly healthy twin, is pushed and pulled into the world in my wake, then lifted into gentle but unyielding hands, and we are carried into a corner, away from where our mother lies. She has been gutted of life. Not hers. Mine. My husk has already been taken away, but I remain with my twin. We are one with each other now, with the solid arms of the nurse holding us, and with the people behind her: the stern-faced obstetrician, whose composure slips – he yells, 'Shit!' – when he hits his elbow against the corner of a silver tray and a bloodied forceps is sent crashing across the floor; the other nurse, a young student, who, as she lunges to retrieve the forceps, is silently praying that she'll never again witness a

3

birth as shocking as mine; our father trying, and failing, to soothe our mother by telling her how much he loves her. We are one with her too. Our mother is the room's epicentre. Her wailing ends abruptly, her eyes are moving but vacant, and she's too distraught to feel her husband gripping her hand. She'll never know that I'm still here. I'm with the living baby, who gurgles to the nurse's humming and her rocking arms. In the midst of this wreckage we feel peace.

We are betrayed. We are lifted and the remainder of the umbilical cord is cut from our belly. We are slapped. We yell. The nurse swings us around to face our mother. 'Grace, you have a beautiful baby boy!'

Our mother squeezes our father's hand and she almost smiles, before anguish clouds into her eyes and, in her confusion, she mistakes the saved baby for the lost one. 'Get him away from me! He's dead! Get him away!'

As the obstetrician prepares a sedative, the nurse pulls us to her warm breast and retreats. We are carried through the doors, as our father bites his tongue; as our mother, Grace, screams over and over.

We are cleaned, weighed, wrapped in a snug white blanket, sheltered in a glass box, goggled at. The world floats around us, vague colours blurring together.

We meet our father. He has a crooked smile, sad but genuine. His finger touches our palm and we clench it, marvelling at the existence of our hand and what we can do. We gurgle. His eyes well up. A tear splashes on our nose. Our father laughs. He wipes his eyes with his trembling hand, then runs it through his thick coal-black hair. It sticks up in odd-angled tufts. He extricates his finger from our grip and dries our nose by pressing it. 'Hey, fellow, my name is Eamon. I'm your dad. When you grow up, I promise the world is all yours.'

My twin, unimpressed by the prospect, falls asleep. Our father, Eamon, leaves us, stepping outside the room ever so quietly.

I'm incapable of creating my own dreams, but I enter those of my twin, believing that they belong to both of us. I'm too new to realise the truth yet. As I said, this all takes place a long time ago. I won't form an understanding of my nature until years later, but I'll give you a head start.

My twin and I are bound. I've some capacity for movement, a leash permitting me a short radius in any direction. I can see everything in his line of sight, but his eyes are not mine. I can see when his are closed. I can see above, below, and behind him. When focused, I can see it all simultaneously, but I can also look away.

And I have a talent: if someone is in our proximity, I can look them in the eye and go deeper. I can sift through their memories and feel what they feel. The things they've forgotten are inaccessible, but the experiences that make them who they are – these are open to me. They never sense my presence. Whether I'm journeying through a single memory, or combining multiple points of view – and I admit to bridging the gaps with informed guesses from time to time – I see it all like it's happening before me. I'll get to the 'real' now in due course.

As a conscientious narrator, I'll try to keep embellishments to a minimum, but I make no promises. My twin is your tragic protagonist. His name will be James, but to me, and perhaps to you, he's Jimmy Dice. This is the edifying tale of his fractured life.

EAMON STEALS A FEW MOMENTS IN THE GENTS'. HE WASHES his hands in the sink until they're nearly raw. Closing his eyes, he washes his face blind. He feels two days' stubble, rough against his fingertips. His eyes feel large and heavy. He opens them, staring down his reflection. Water drips from his bushy eyebrows and his chin, as if his face is dissolving. He spits into the basin. There are flecks of blood in his saliva from biting his tongue earlier. He had forgotten, but now he flexes his tongue against his teeth and palate. The ache brings relief.

Eamon's other children – Tighe, Elizabeth, and Paul – are in the waiting room, guarded by his parents, Arturo and Maggie, known to the kids as Abuelo and Granny. Apart from the Diaz family, the room is empty. It's after midnight and, with the one exception, there's a minimum of commotion in St John's maternity ward.

Paul, at four, is the youngest. He's asleep on Maggie's lap, his legs sprawled, his head resting in the crook of her arm. She brushes his mop of brown hair from his eyes. From how she looks at him, with a doting tilt of her head, it's clear that he's her most precious grandchild. His chest shudders, he releases a *humpf* noise, then he eases out of his nightmare and his body stills. Maggie smiles.

Elizabeth, aged six, has energy to burn and so she's pacing around the coffee table. Her Barbie lies on top of a stack of magazines, balanced close to the table's edge. If Elizabeth bangs into the table, which looks possible, Barbie will plummet off it, but the doll's days are numbered anyway – her plastic feet are bent and worn and her arm is disjointed from being dragged along too many floors by her owner, who would welcome a brighter, and more interesting, favourite toy. Elizabeth increases her speed, her hips listing from side to side; she has auburn hair and her long pigtails harmlessly whip her shoulders.

Tighe, aged nine, stands gazing out of the window, his eyes darting from star to star. He's connecting the dots, imagining lasers shooting from one to another, if only for the purpose of channelling his powers of concentration. His game doesn't

6

have any greater meaning for him, but, on hearing Elizabeth giggle as her runners screech against the waxed floor, he turns and glares at her. When Tighe was born, his parents endowed him with his name because there was something tiger-like in his expression whenever he was about to really let loose with a howl, and there's a flash of that ferocity in his eyes now. 'Don't be so annoying!'

Elizabeth comes to an abrupt halt, steadying herself with both hands gripping the side of the table. Her lips are aquiver and she turns to her grandmother for help. Maggie looks up from Paul and obliges with a disappointed 'Tighe.'

Attempting to keep his voice sarcasm-free, Tighe tells his baby sister, 'I just don't want you to run around like an annoying person because I don't want you to fall over and hurt yourself. We all love you.'

Arturo 'Art' Diaz sits a seat away from his wife and Paul, a hand squeezing each kneecap. His moustache twitches as he surveys his charges. He doesn't have much hope for his granddaughter. Elizabeth seems to have inherited her parents' worst characteristics: Eamon's timidity and Grace's eccentricity. Tighe, meanwhile, is a different type of child. He's confident with his peers and adults, and rarely causes trouble. He's the one whose looks are most permeated by his one-quarter-Argentine lineage, so he has some of his grandfather's dark handsomeness. But – and Art isn't sure about this – there's something about him that's a bit off; it's harder to love a precocious child, and maybe Tighe is too smart for his own good. Then there's Paul, who alternates between being a boisterous boy and being a needy one who cries easily. It's too early to tell which temperament he'll lean towards when he's older, but, if given the choice, Art would rather he be a bully than a wimp.

Art notices his son watching them all from the hallway. On

recognising that he has been spotted, Eamon approaches with reluctance in his step. Art stands. 'Well, Eamon? What is it? Boy?' His gruff voice still has an Argentine inflection, even though he hasn't returned home in more than forty years.

Eamon begins, 'Papá . . .'

'Spit it out!'

Maggie, shifting Paul so his head rests on her shoulder, stands. 'Art, can't you see something's wrong? Eamon, did Grace deliver?'

'Mam, she's resting. If we could step into the hallway. The children can wait here. Okay, Papá?'

Art nods, takes Paul from Maggie's arms – he stirs from his doze, with a left-nostril snort – and deposits him on a chair. Elizabeth sits beside Paul and puts her arm around his waist, for her comfort more than his. Her mouth is down-turned, her eyes expectant. Art turns to Tighe, who is already awaiting instruction. 'Keep an eye on your brother and sister. We'll be a moment. Grown-up stuff.'

'Yes, Abuelo.'

'Good boy.' Art squeezes Tighe's cheek, quickly ruffles Paul's hair, and smiles at Elizabeth without meeting her eye. To Eamon he says, 'C'mon, son.'

Maggie puts her hand on Eamon's shoulder and they follow Art out. Tighe turns his back on his siblings.

Down the hall, Eamon, his hand entangled in his hair, says, 'We never had an ultrasound. You see, Grace thought we should leave it to fate. Either a boy or a girl would've been fine, as long as they were healthy, and the others were all easy births compared to most pregnancies. I don't know that we could have seen the problem coming, but we'd have seen she was expecting twins.' He smiles at the shadow of how this news could have been joyful. 'I'm sorry. It's been a long . . .'

Maggie says, 'It's okay, dear.'

Art says, 'Just tell us what happened.' He means to sound sympathetic but it comes across as impatient.

Eamon says, 'We have a son. Perfectly healthy. He's beautiful.'

Maggie covers her mouth. 'The other?'

Eamon shakes his head. 'No.'

'How's Grace?'

Eamon knows he stinks, of his own sweat and Grace's. As he thinks of that strangled baby, heat courses through him. He closes his eyes and breathes deeply to diminish his nausea. Opening his eyes, he says, 'They put her asleep. It's devastating, but when she wakes tomorrow and sees her boy, that'll restore her. It would've been much worse if we'd expected two.' He grits his teeth, then says, 'We've been lucky.'

Maggie squeezes his arm. A reflex concern flashes through her mind: there's no meat on his bones; does Grace never think to feed him? 'It's best to look at it that way. Think of the blessing not the . . .'

'Curse?'

She winces. She would have said 'misfortune'. 'Come home, get some sleep. Look at the bags under your eyes. Sure, you can barely stand.'

'I'm fine, Mam. I need to be here when Grace wakes.'

Before Maggie can respond, Art shoots her a let-him-be glance. He says, 'We'll take the children, but first you should tell them they have a brother, that their mother is resting, that she's well.'

'I will.'

'But don't tell them about the other one.'

'Of course not.'

They return to the waiting room. Elizabeth still has her arm

9

around Paul, and she's holding his hand now as well. Her doll is discarded on the floor, one leg pointed up. Paul looks grumpy and Elizabeth, her smile frazzled, doesn't let him pull his hand away. Tighe is back standing by the window, staring out to space. He's thinking about how far away he would like to get. To Eamon, he looks like a young philosopher or a potentially groundbreaking scientist. Art guesses he's incredibly bored. Eamon says, 'Tighe,' and motions him to sit with his siblings, then crouches in front of them, on the tips of his toes, his forearms on his knees. 'Kids, Abuelo and Granny are taking you home, but first, would you like to meet your new brother?'

And so, for a few minutes, the senior and junior members of the Diaz clan are allowed to see their grandchild, their brother, through the window of the nursery.

Tighe is indifferent, but pays attention anyway. If he shows some interest in this sleeping mini human, as he's expected to, he might get home earlier. Paul is less concerned with appearances. He presses his forehead against the glass. His eyes are half closed. His hand is limp in his sister's grasp. Elizabeth is sincerely enthused. 'Dad!'

'Yes, honey?'

'What's he called?'

Eamon puts his finger to his mouth. 'It's a secret. We'll all know soon.'

Elizabeth catches an irritated look from Tighe. She responds with a defiant glance, then ignores him, knowing that he won't snap at her in front of their father. She says, 'Daddy! What's his name? Please?'

Eamon, who missed the exchange between Tighe and Elizabeth, presses on his daughter's nose with his thumb and shakes his head. 'Not tonight. Soon.'

Grace believed it was bad luck to pick a name in advance

of a baby being born. Her smile self-deprecating, she had told Eamon, 'It's like counting chickens.' He does have a name in mind though – James – but he wants to discuss it with Grace before saying it aloud to anyone else.

Art and Maggie exit with their grandchildren. Eamon continues to watch over his newborn son. He feels happiness, fragile as that is.

Chapter Two

Dancing with Grace

Before I share more about Jimmy Dice with you, I'm taking a detour. It's okay; trust me. To understand my twin, it will help to know more about the people around him, and I want to tell you the story of how Eamon and Grace met.

August 1969

SIMON FITZGERALD LEANS BACK IN HIS SWIVEL CHAIR, his elbows on the arms, holding a pen horizontally with an index finger and thumb pinching each end. His smile shows a touch of amusement. 'Will you or won't you?'

Sitting on the opposite side of the desk, Eamon is dumbfounded. He's twenty-seven but has yet to fill out much, and while he can grow a beard, whenever he's clean-shaven he looks like he can't. His oversized shirt, rolled up at the elbows for a contrived newspaperman effect, and his wide black tie, at an oblique angle to his collar, emphasise his discomfort. 'Me? Really?'

'Some initiative, Diaz!'

'Mr Fitzgerald, I'll do it.'

'Finally.' Simon throws his pen on the desk. 'Get out. You're not paid to sit on your arse.'

'Sir.' Eamon hustles to his feet.

'And Eamon?' Simon's smile grows shark-like. 'If you call me "sir" or "Mr Fitzgerald" again, I'll fire you. I'm not your schoolteacher or your damn father. Call me Simon.'

Eamon attempts to smile. 'Yes. Simon. Thank you.'

When Eamon slumps into his cubicle chair, he's being watched by the *Rathbaile Chronicle*'s primary sports correspondent, Harry Burke, who stands propped against his office door jamb. With his tie at an obedient angle to his collar, his shirtsleeves naturally rolled up, and casually holding a lit cigarette, he perfects the newspaperman look. An ex-GAA hurler, a star in his own mind, Harry has been at the paper for five years. Despite a fondness for binge drinking, he has maintained a trim physique. Sometimes he pats his stomach and says, 'It's all about the right metabolism.' His friends call him by the ironic nickname of 'Fatman'. By the time of Jimmy Dice's birth, eleven years later, this nickname, while still used, will have ceased to be ironic.

Harry calls to Eamon, 'What did the boss want with you?'

Eamon blushes. 'Oh, it was nothing.'

Harry comes and sits against Eamon's desk. 'Diaz, you're one of the boys now. 'Fess up.'

Eamon isn't really 'one of the boys'. He's new to the paper and, as an arts correspondent, his work isn't taken too seriously. It's not real news, like politics or sport. On Fridays he goes to Keogh's with the others, but he isn't much of a drinker and he isn't permitted to call Harry 'Fatman'.

'It was just, ah, Simon wanted to know if I'd take his niece to the ball.'

'Grace! You're taking Grace Corcoran to the ball?'

'I am. What of it?'

Harry has a puff of his cigarette and slaps Eamon on the

back. 'Hey, boy, it's just someone should warn you.' As he saunters back to his office, he smirks over his shoulder. 'Good luck, though.'

Even before meeting her, Eamon deduces that Grace must feel like an outsider in Rathbaile. There's that inevitable comparison to her mother, Simon's sister Dorothy, currently a resident of St Augustine's Mental Hospital, who, according to various know-it-alls, went mad from too much sex – after chasing off her no doubt exhausted husband, she carried on with numerous men, all of them so anonymous that no one has confirmed any of their identities. And then there's the predicament that, when she was twenty, Grace left for America, 'thinking she was too good for the rest of us and abandoning her poor mother in her time of need'. After four years of getting up to 'God knows what', she recently returned to live with her uncle and his wife – 'remembering where the money in the family is; that's what that was'. Eamon, though, has the good sense to pay no heed to gossip, and as far as he's concerned, Grace's outsider status isn't a cause for reservation. In fact it adds to her appeal because it means they have something in common.

The suspicion he's subjected to isn't only due to his lack of interest in local sports, his rare use of off-colour language, or his college education and the fact that it was gained in Dublin – granted, Dublin is significantly closer than America, but it's still the best part of a three-hour drive away, and it's well known that Dubliners look down their noses at people from anywhere else in the country. These are all factors, but a bigger reason is having an Argentine father. Like most Irish towns of this time, and especially true of one located in an inland county like Tipperary, Rathbaile is about as homogenous as can be. Ninety-five per cent of its population is Catholic, and the majority have never even seen a black or Asian person in the flesh, so here Eamon is as exotic as they come, and he's exotic before it's popular. Having spent his entire life in Ireland is insufficient. With his surname he should be going out of his way to live and breathe Rathbaile, but instead he appears aloof. His older brothers do a better job of fitting in. Luis and Manny are loud and hard-drinking, and their tendency to act without thinking can be relied upon.

Eamon isn't too bothered by his lack of popularity. He likes the space he's afforded. What makes him anxious is interacting with attractive women, and so the real problem with escorting Grace to the ball is unconnected to her mother or that she's the boss's niece. It's that he expects to fancy her. He has observed the black-and-white photo on Simon's desk of her and her mother on a pier bench. Dorothy stares into the camera, her long hair unencumbered by a hat and her eyes cunning. Grace, appearing to be about sixteen, wears a straw hat. Her eyes are on her mother's hand on her right shoulder, pulling her closer. Grace's hand is over her mouth and chin, and she might have succeeded in looking indifferent if, beneath her fingers, her lips weren't curved upwards.

Eamon realises that having been pretty in a photo as a teenager doesn't necessarily mean that she's now a beautiful woman. His expectation is more down to a hunch, and as pronounced as this is, boring into the see-saw base of his stomach as he waits on the Fitzgeralds' doorstep after ringing the bell, it offers little guarantee. But when the door opens, he turns out to be right. To others, her jaw might possibly be too square, her nose too narrow. These criticisms are below Eamon's attention. He marvels at her brilliant sea-blue eyes, her cascading-curl hair, and how her face is so clearly capable of a multitude of vivid expressions. He marvels as her features unite to form . . . disappointment?

'I presume you're Eamon?'

He blushes. 'Yes. Yes, I am. You're Grace.'

She steps aside for him to enter. 'I suppose you'll do.'

She leads him into the drawing room, where Simon and his wife are sitting on one of the couches. They stand, exchanging an excited glance with each other. Simon fervidly shakes Eamon's hand. 'Eamon, lad, you didn't have any problems getting here, I hope?'

'Oh, no. I . . .'

'This is Sarah.'

They shake hands and she kisses Eamon's cheek. Aiming to reciprocate, he misses the mark, kissing air. Sarah is frail of build, without looking unhealthy. Her smile bursts from cheek to cheek. 'Such a pleasure, Eamon. Simon has only good things to say about you.'

Simon slaps a hand on Eamon's shoulder. 'And the brains this boy has, I'm telling you – watch out.' He says this to Sarah, but it's intended for Grace, who has settled into a plush armchair and is making a show of examining her finger-nails.

Eamon tries to process being in a house that's more than double the size of the one he grew up in, and with a shine on every surface; the first praise he has ever received from his boss; and how Sarah, who looks about thirty, is perhaps fifteen years younger than Simon. Facing his hosts' hopeful stares, he recognises the need to speak. 'This is a lovely, lovely house, Simon, Sarah. Lovely. I love it.'

They thank him in unison. Grace suppresses a laugh. Sarah asks, 'Can I get you a drink, Eamon?'

'God, yes! Thank you, Sarah. That would be . . . lovely.'

The drink – he has what Simon's having, a brandy – helps his nerves, and they sit around the antique coffee table with

Simon and Sarah attempting to initiate talking points between Eamon and Grace. After hitting a few dead ends, Simon says, 'Eamon's a lover of the classics! Aren't you?'

'Oh yes. I am. Dostoevsky's a master. Did you know his father was murdered by his serfs? And, ah, Tolstoy too, of course. Not that he or his father was murdered, but he's another master. Had thirteen children, I believe, and they all hated him. But I don't mean to spread rumours.'

Sarah says, 'Fascinating! Grace always has her nose in a book as well. Don't you, dear?'

Grace leans forward, picks up her glass from the table, and sips. 'Sure.' She sits back in her seat and has another sip.

She doesn't acknowledge Simon and Sarah glaring at her. Eamon, steeling himself, says, 'So, then, what writers do you like?'

She turns to him with eyes that are not unkind, and he manages to hold her gaze. 'Too many to list really. I suppose Camus isn't bad.'

'Camus! My favourite of his is *The Fall*. The point of view is so unique and there's a wonderful line about charm. He defines it as "a way of getting the answer yes without having asked any clear question".'

It occurs to Eamon that he might have erred by highlighting a quality he feels devoid of, but Grace is smiling at him. 'I haven't gotten to that one, but maybe I will.'

When she observes a measure of smugness in Simon and Sarah's expressions, she banishes her smile. 'We should get going. Shouldn't we?'

Trailing Simon's Jaguar in his Morris Minor Traveller, Eamon finds that talking to Grace is easier one-on-one. Well, the small talk is easier; saying what he wants to say is as difficult. Previous to ringing the Fitzgeralds' doorbell, he had been planning on paying her a compliment on her appearance – his mother had told him that was the done thing – and he'd hoped to think of a specific and sincere one, but when he saw her, his mind blanked. Now, listening to her speak about her travels, he knows that to assail her with hyperbolic adjectives wouldn't be too suave.

'You should see the Californian beaches. They stretch on, feels like forever, and then there's the ocean. Have you ever been to a really great beach?'

'I've been to Tramore.'

'It doesn't compare. It's always so overcast here. And the sand shouldn't actually feel like sandpaper against your skin. It should be soft. In Cali, when you lie down, the sand moves to your body's contours and it's like the sun gives your body a massage. All your worries go, like you never had any. The people aren't like the prudes we have here. Why are people so shocked if a girl shows some skin? I mean, it's the twentieth century. Irish people need to loosen up, drop their holier-than-thou attitudes. Y'know?'

'If it's so much better over there, why did you come back?'

Appraising him, she says, 'Why do *you* think I came back?'

'I honestly wouldn't know.'

She looks out the window, while Eamon's stomach constricts at the possibility that he may have upset her. She finally says, 'Why should I have to live somewhere else? Even if I was more accepted over there, this is my home. But that doesn't mean I should force myself to fit other people's expectations. If you do that, nothing ever changes.'

They arrive at Ashburnham House, an immaculately reno-vated castle hotel that serves as the venue for the annual ball for some select local businesses. When the car is parked, and Grace has her fingers on the door handle, Eamon says, 'Wait.'

He gets out, goes around to her side, opens the door, and offers his hand.

Normally she disdains chivalry, but she decides to make an exception. Putting her hand in his, she says, 'You're a gentleman, Eamon.'

'You look stunning tonight. You're very stunning, Grace.'

They both blush. 'Let's just go inside, shall we?'

Upon finding Simon and Sarah in the reception area, Grace releases Eamon's hand, but not swiftly enough for it to go unnoticed. Sarah nudges Simon and says, 'C'mon, you two. You can wait until we've all been fed before you start idling about.'

Sharing their table are Harry and his wife, plus two other veteran correspondents for the *Chronicle* and their wives. As Eamon, Grace, Simon, and Sarah sit, Harry halts mid-anecdote to say, 'Diaz, boy, you must be nervous. If you play your cards wrong tonight, you might not have a job on Monday!'

Everyone except Grace laughs.

Over dinner, Nixon and Vietnam are discussed, then Teddy Kennedy driving off Dike Bridge, poor Mary Jo, and how much he was to blame. The comparison is predictably made to his assassinated brothers, and Harry merrily expounds on a conspiracy theory. Talk of American politics shifts to Irish politics, and old debates of Fianna Fáil versus Fine Gael are rehashed. The relative manliness of Michael Collins versus Eamon de Valera becomes a sticking point. When voices rise, Simon suggests changing topics, so they chat about the moon landing just under two weeks ago – 'The fucking moon! Did you ever think we'd see the day?' – and projections are made about the future of space travel: a moon colony and astronauts on Mars before the new millennium seem like sure bets. The conversation somehow segues to Harry telling stories about his playing days – mostly funny, though never at his own expense. Eamon had expected to be the target of slagging from Harry, but, other than the odd sly comment, he's spared, probably out of deference to Simon.

After dessert, the band, Richie Sullivan and the Shakers, start up. The lead singer, with his imitation hairstyle and sideburns, wants to be like Elvis, but he does at least have a decent voice and the band is adequately rocking. Simon takes Eamon aside. 'Listen, lad, Sarah has a bit of a migraine so we're going to have an early night.'

'I hope she's all right.'

'Nothing to worry about. I trust I can rely on you to get Grace home safe and sound?'

'Of course.'

'Good. Watch how much you drink. You're driving.'

'I will. I've only had two glasses.'

'I know. You've been acquitting yourself well. Keep it up.'

After Simon and Sarah have left, Grace takes Eamon's hand. 'Let's go.'

'Wh-where? Don't you want another drink?'

'There'll be time for that.' She nimbly guides him away from the table. 'I need someone to dance with.'

'I don't know how. I mean, I've never really . . .'

'You'll pick it up.'

He's already on the dance floor before he can further object, and all around them people are dancing, poorly but joyously. Grace places Eamon's free hand on her waist and whispers, 'We'll look sillier standing here doing nothing. What have you got to lose?'

Her strawberry-smelling perfume is dizzying, and the sensation of her waist against his hand, the thin silk a flimsy barrier to really touching her – it all threatens to overwhelm him, and he can't bring himself to meet her eyes until she takes a step back. He says, 'Let's do it.'

They dance and he's awful at it, but his efforts are earnest and Grace likes him for that. In contrast to his fish-out-of-water sputter-shuffling, she possesses a symmetry of co-ordination and rhythm. There's something sexual about how confidently she moves, and this isn't lost on Eamon or on others.

Over the music, Harry shouts, 'I see wedding bells in your future!' He's dancing nearby with his wife, Sylvia, or rather he's swaying drunkenly against her shoulder and she's helping him keep his balance. Her expression pleads with Eamon and Grace to take no notice. Eamon, his blush hidden by the dimmed lights, smiles at Harry. Grace ignores him, and that slight prompts Harry to say, 'But she won't be wearing white on her wedding day. That's for certain!'

Eamon and Grace stop dancing. Sylvia starts to push Harry off the floor. Grace says, 'What did you say to me?'

'Sorry, darling. Slip of the tongue. Pay me no mind.'

Eamon blocks Grace's way, whispering, 'He's just acting the maggot. He's not worth the attention.'

Sylvia pulls Harry away by the elbow, berating him as they go. Grace says to Eamon, 'How could you allow that disgusting man to talk like that? It's an insult to you too, y'know.'

'I'm sorry. There's a time and a place for confrontation, and he barely knows what he's saying.'

'He knows exactly, believe me. Just take me home. I've had enough.'

'If you're sure that's what you want, I will. Look, if there's anything I . . .'

'It's what I want.'

They don't speak as they retrieve their jackets and walk

out to the car, or as they drive. Once they pull into Simon and Sarah's driveway, Eamon says, 'I'm really sorry.'

Grace briefly squeezes his hand. 'It's me who should be, and I am.'

'I'll say something to Harry on Monday, I promise. Tonight, with his wife there – I didn't want to embarrass her further, but I should've said something.'

'No, I shouldn't have cared. Small-minded men like Harry Burke . . .' With a hollow laugh, she says, 'From now on, it's water off a duck's back. You kept your head, handled it right. And you don't need to say anything to him.'

'I will anyway.'

She smiles appreciatively, but it's sympathetic too. 'Y'know, that's why my uncle thought of you to set me up with. It's because you're very . . .' He refrains from squirming while she chooses her words. 'Very good and sensible and safe. You always do the right thing because you're such a gentleman.' She doesn't intend to be patronising, but her comments on his character sound like the diagnosis of a fatal illness. 'You're the person least likely to . . .'

With an emphatic absence of inhibition, he kisses her. And she gives as good as she gets. When they disentangle themselves, he's proud of her surprised look. He says, 'I want to see you again. Tomorrow.'

She laughs. 'Then you will.' She puts her hand on his knee. 'Unless you want to be really risqué and sneak inside?'

She's smiling wickedly and he can't tell if she's serious. He hesitates, then says, 'I'd better not.'

She laughs again and quickly kisses him once. 'Don't worry about it. Tomorrow, then.'

Chapter Three

Heartbreaker

July 1981

A year to the day after Jimmy Dice was born, and I lived and died, the Diaz family are gathered in Crann Dubh Park, celebrating my twin's birthday but declining to commemorate me. Jimmy lies in the basket of Grace's arms. She's sitting at a picnic table. Maggie is facing her and Eamon and Art are at the other end, a chessboard between them. Tighe is standing to the side of his father and grandfather, watching them play. His hands are in his pockets and a folded-over comic, The Amazing Spider-Man, *is wedged under his arm. Great-uncle Simon and Granny Dorothy are sitting at the adjacent table. Simon is keeping one eye on the game of chess and the other on his sister, who is across from him. Dorothy doesn't appear to be paying attention to anything. Over in the nearby car park, Elizabeth and Paul are playing together: she chases him around the three parked cars, catches him, releases him, then chases and catches him again. He squeals each time.*

Jimmy is normally a placid baby, rarely crying, but on this summer afternoon he's bawling. Grace accents her mechanical rocking of him by repeating 'hush'. She doesn't say it to gently coax her son; she uses it like a magic word that will make his voice disappear.

Looking back at this, I foolishly imagine that when she stares at him the way she does, she can sense I never really left, that I'm hidden within him. She's aware of this before even I have figured it out, because she carried me inside her too, and she's wise and won't abandon me in this nothingness. Allowing myself this fantasy is masochistic. She may frequently ponder what I would have looked like, and how I'd have felt in her arms, but she hasn't retained any hope of ever finding me. I'm truly dead to her.

GRACE HASN'T NOTICED THAT ELIZABETH AND PAUL HAVE run over from the car park, and that Elizabeth is now standing impatiently at her elbow, with Paul a few steps behind, giddily smiling and bouncing on the balls of his feet. Elizabeth quietly says, 'Mam,' then louder, 'Mam!'

Maggie, with more authority, says, '*Grace*,' and, when Grace looks up, Maggie nods at Elizabeth.

Grace turns to her daughter and, over Jimmy's cries, says, 'What is it? Can't you see my hands are full?'

Unapologetically Elizabeth says, 'Me and Paul want to explore the woods. Can we go?'

'If your father says so.' Grace returns her gaze to Jimmy.

Elizabeth gives Eamon a look that says, *See?* She only asked her mother because he has told her that she shouldn't always come to him first. 'Dad? Can we?'

'If Tighe promises to go with you.' Eamon playfully jabs Tighe in the belly with his finger, and his son, unprepared for it, laughs. 'Well? Can you tear yourself away from high-stakes chess?'

Art doesn't look amused. To him, any game where you can

win or lose is high stakes. Tighe says, 'Will you buy me a comic if I do?'

Eamon laughs. 'Do a good job and we'll talk about it.'

Maggie gestures to Paul with a come-here wag of her index finger. He obeys and she hugs him to her. 'You're going to be such a heartbreaker when you grow up! All the girls will want to run away with you!'

'No they won't!'

Hugging him even harder, Maggie glances at Grace – *this* is the kind of affection a child should be showered with – then laughs and tells Paul, 'Just you wait and see!'

Elizabeth is annoyed that her fun with Paul is being delayed, but she gets a smile from Simon and he makes her laugh when he rolls his eyes. Dorothy, suddenly alert, turns her head and smiles at Elizabeth too, but her smile is scary. Elizabeth looks away from her – worried that her grandmother, the crazy one, might want to receive a hug now too – and, taking a step towards the woods, says, 'Paul! Come *on!*'

As soon as Maggie lets go of Paul, he and Elizabeth run off towards the nearest line of trees. Tighe follows them, in no hurry.

Jimmy wails all the more. Maggie is trying not to offer advice to Grace as her daughter-in-law rocks him, with her dour countenance and how she's barely supporting his neck. Why should Jimmy have to suffer because his mother is slow to get over things? Maybe that's unfair. It's progress, of a sort, that she's touching him at all. For months he had been essentially motherless. He hadn't even been breastfed, all because of Grace's depression. Luckily Eamon is the man he is and he filled both parental roles for his children – with the aid of Simon, a saint of a man, who allowed him to cut back on assignments and to work from home. It's thanks to their father that the other children are sound: Tighe is mature beyond his years; Paul is an ever-more happy boy; and Elizabeth, well, she has become less clingy. Their ability to thrive has been *despite* their mother, and so Maggie is angry with Grace for all of it. Yes, angry! But she's also willing, and resolved, to forgive. And so she continues to watch Grace, to pull on the loose thread at the elbow of her cardigan, to wrap that thread around her finger, to say nothing.

Grace knows she's being scrutinised. It's why she'd rather fixate on her son's sobbing little face instead of meeting the eyes of someone who doesn't understand. While Art is ignoring Jimmy's acting up, his eyes on the chessboard, Eamon reaches out and rubs Grace's back. She stiffens at his touch, then relaxes and they share a small smile. The intensity of Jimmy's crying lessens, and soon he's only sniffling.

Art coughs and Eamon returns his attention to the board. Art seems to be winning; nevertheless, his scowl is entrenched. After each move – all of his are deliberate, Eamon's more casual – he swigs from his beer can, a reward for the frustration of playing his son. Eamon has a beer too, but only sips it after long pauses. Art had handed it to him from the cooler without asking if he wanted one. Eamon is lifting his black knight, about to put his queen in jeopardy, when he notices that Tighe has only gone as far as the outskirts of the clearing, and is leaning against a tree and reading his comic. He calls, 'Tighe! You're supposed to be keeping an eye on your brother and sister!'

Irritation passes over Tighe's face. 'Dad, they're just around the corner, down the hill! They're fine. They're laughing. I can *hear* them!'

Now that Eamon listens for it, he hears the distant laughter, so he shrugs and deposits his knight on the board. Art clenches his jaw in reaction to both his son's lackadaisical parenting and his poor move. Eamon isn't intentionally losing, but he's careless and doesn't possess a killer instinct. Art attacks with his bishop. Eamon will have to sacrifice his queen to save his king. While Eamon searches in vain for another option, Art shouts at his eldest grandchild, 'Tighe! Come here to me!'

Tighe rolls up his comic as he jogs over. His expression becomes serious when he sees Art's chastising look. 'Yes, Abuelo?'

'What did your father ask you to do?'

Eamon says wearily, 'Papá, it's not a big thing.'

With forced good humour Art says, 'I never claimed it was.' To Tighe he says, 'Well?'

Tighe, feigning disappointment with himself, says, 'To watch Elizabeth and Paul.'

Art nods at Tighe's comic. 'And what've you been doing?'

'I'll do better.'

'Good lad. Between you and me . . .' Art drops a squashed-up note into Tighe's open palm. 'There's a pound for you. Don't spend it all in one go.'

Eamon sighs as Art waves Tighe off. Turning to Simon at the other table, but ignoring Dorothy, Art says confidently, 'Kids need to be told things with infallible conviction. Am I right?'

Simon, who has been observing all of this with a muted expression, says, 'It's one way of doing things.'

Accepting that as approval, and oblivious to how over-bearing Simon considers him to be, Art returns to the task of defeating Eamon in their game.

Simon finishes off a can of beer, his second. He'd like to get another from the cooler, but he's driving so he exercises restraint. There are two butter-and-jam sandwiches left on the plate before him on the table. He devours one of them, in three bites. It provides him with scant satisfaction.

His wife, Sarah, is dying. No one else here today knows. When he eventually makes it public, plenty of people will be shocked, but when the prognosis was confirmed, it hadn't come as a shock to him. She had long been punishing her body.

When you last saw Simon, at the Ashburnham Ball, he was forty-five and had the vitality of a man half his age. He thought Sarah was just a social drinker who found it hard to stop. He didn't see the dependence yet; besides, they were in love and surely that was enough to withstand what was on the face of it a minor problem. That has been the worst part: discovering love was only a speed bump compared with her susceptibility for self-destruction. He hadn't been the only one fooled. Did people not think to question it when so many nights ended early with 'headaches'? And Sarah had fooled no one as much as herself.

Simon is fifty-seven now; his face is etched with many lines and the spark in his eyes doesn't come without a struggle. He has no time for people who give up, but as for having hope, he keeps going despite having run out, because others need him to be strong.

Dorothy, Simon's little sister by two years, looks a decade his senior. Her hair, a source of pride when she was young, was groomed and tied in a bun by Grace this morning, after they took her out of St Augustine's on a day release. She's neatly outfitted, her blue dress buttoned tight at the back, the sleeves buttoned tight at her wrists. Occasionally she tugs at her sleeves, but mostly she doesn't appear uncomfortable. However, no one would need to spend much time with her to realise she isn't all there. She's talking today, but her responses are limited to 'yes' and 'no'. With either word her lips form an extravagant smile. After speaking, her smile loiters. Whenever she starts scratching her palms, Simon holds her hand and this calms her. This is one of her good days. Earlier, Eamon and Grace even allowed her to hold Jimmy. They stood on either side of her, ready to catch him if Dorothy relaxed her grip. She didn't.

Simon lifts the last sandwich from the plate. He's about to take a bite when he notices that Dorothy is eyeing it. He gives it a hungry look and passes it to her. She holds it in her hands as if it's something extraordinary, before bringing it to her mouth and nibbling at the crust.

Art narrows his eyes, then slides his bishop forward and says, 'Check,' but Eamon is marvelling at Jimmy, who has quit all of his sniffling, as if nothing had ever been wrong.

Grace raises her eyes and meets Maggie's stare. 'Don't look so worried. He was just trying out tears, but he's fine now. He's a cheerful boy.'

Maggie breaks off the hanging thread from her cardigan and lets it float to the ground. 'Of course he is. Of course.'

Out of the grown-ups' sight, Tighe trudges down a mud-and-gravel path, through the pine trees, and goes deeper into the woods. Always having to be the responsible older brother is tiresome. Whether he likes it or not, they will expect it of him with Jimmy as well, but it's to his advantage, he decides, to pretend not to mind too much. He'll get more credit that way.

Finding Elizabeth and Paul is easy. They're noisy as they weave among the trees playing tig. He doesn't have much of a chance to evade her – she's bigger and faster. She strides after him as he scurries towards his brother. Hiding behind Tighe's legs, and pawing his trousers, Paul says, 'Don't let her get me!'

Tighe leafs through his comic. 'She'll get you no matter what.'

Elizabeth catches up and feints in each direction without leaving her feet. Paul squeals. Bending her fingers like claws, Elizabeth growls. Tighe increases the violence of his page-turning. Elizabeth, with cautious enthusiasm, says, 'Want to play?'

'Definitely not.'

She makes an exasperated face, then acts like she has lost interest in the game too by dropping the claws and staring at her feet. When Paul lets go of Tighe's trousers, she lunges and tugs a lock of his hair. 'You're it!'

Then she's off like a bolt, with Paul doing his utmost to match her pace. Tighe shouts after them, 'Keep off the main road or Mam and Dad will kill me!'

Content with his command, he sits at the base of the nearest tree. Despite Dr Octopus's dastardly trap, he knows Spider-Man will find a way.

Elizabeth never goes very far ahead. When the gap between her and Paul widens, she slows. When he stumbles, she waits. As she races down the incline she's constantly looking over her shoulder, and this is reckless because she's pelting forward – they both are – and she could smack into a tree. The threat of cuts and bruises is so remote it doesn't register as a possibility. The thrumming of car engines, the roar of the occasional fast one as it takes the sharp corner on the road she and Paul are moving towards, are mere blips to her senses. This is almost how one would wish children to be: ecstatically in the moment, and yes, even a bit reckless because they shouldn't be afraid of life.

At the last row of trees, Elizabeth jumps. It's only a short drop to the road and her shoes slap loud against the tarmac. A reverberation shudders through her – she's suddenly aware of the entirety of her feet – but she doesn't stop to think and she has already made it across the road when she hears Paul behind her and turns her head to check he's still playing. Their eyes meet. The car smashes into his side, breaking his arm, hip, and leg and flinging him into the air. He comes down on the other side of the road with a thud and a snap, as his temple hits the tarmac, as his neck breaks.

In the clearing, Art checkmates Eamon, but takes little joy in it. Grace hands Jimmy over to Maggie, who hugs him. Simon wipes butter and jam from Dorothy's hands with a napkin. Later on, there'll be a remembrance of *someone walking on my grave* before hearing Elizabeth's forlorn scream, but the truth is the cold-sweat dread comes just after the realisation of what it could mean. Not that it matters. They hear her and most of them run, but it's too late.

Chapter Four

Blessings

I
October 1970

'YOU'RE SURE?'

In his parents' guest room, previously his childhood bedroom, Eamon stares at his oldest brother, Luis, who, despite his on-the-fence smile, isn't joking. He reaches out to adjust Eamon's tie when it's his own that's askew. Eamon swipes his hand away and says, 'Absolutely.'

Sitting on the chair behind Eamon, Manny, the middle brother, laughs. 'C'mon, Luis, what sort of question is that? At best, it's a little late.' Realising he's not being listened to, he adds, 'You're not fucking jealous, are you?'

Luis and Manny are hefty men, with curly black hair. Luis's face is like a stretched-out version of Manny's, with his wider cheekbones, flatter nose, and larger mouth. Discerning a resemblance between either of them and Eamon, however, would require squinting. To Manny Luis says, 'Shut up, you.'

Manny smiles and drinks from his hip flask. Like his brothers, he's wearing a suit. His collar is undone. His hangover is leisurely levelling off. He'll be ready when he needs to be.

Luis says to Eamon, 'Look, if you were thinking of

backing out, this would be the time. You've got to ask yourself: is this the woman you want to have children with, to spend fifty years with? Making a commitment like this requires a tremendous amount of trust, a really tremendous fucking amount, and hey, I'm not one to interfere, but if your own brother can't tell it like it is, well then, he's not much of a brother, is he?' He looks at Manny for support, only Manny's attention has turned to admiring his reflection in the smudged silver of his hip flask. Luis slaps his hand down on Eamon's shoulder, accentuating his relative shortness. 'The last thing I'd want to be is insensitive, but if you feel you owe her a marriage because you've already slept with her, I'd think . . .'

'Luis, I love her.'

Luis sighs. 'I know you do.' He shrugs and punches Eamon's arm. 'I'm sure you'll be very happy together.'

II
August 1969

Let's go back another year. It's four a.m. on Sunday night, or Monday morning, and we're in Grace's bedroom at the opposite end of the house to Simon and Sarah's room.

The cream-coloured walls feature a collage of posters – one is of the Beatles in their matching suits, another is of a many-limbed tree bathed in psychedelic colours – and photos of bronzed and long-haired American friends idly posing on a Californian beach. The floor is strewn with clothes, and rock-and-roll records plus their sleeves. In one corner is a guitar, its strings cobwebbed. On her desk, a fresh rose is upright in a glass of water, sitting on the record player, and there are

33

dog-eared books with broken spines. Her coat and Eamon's are flung over the chair.

In her double bed, Grace is looking up, past the yawning skylight, to the cloudless sky. Eamon reclines next to her. They are naked and he's covering himself from the waist down with the sheet. Grace doesn't need to catch his eye to know his thoughts are sizzling. This deflowering – his, not hers – has been startling.

He's three years older than her, yet he's so young. She likes showing off her body to him, knowing he admires her self-assurance, that he thinks she's beautiful and they haven't been fucking or screwing or even having sex; they've been making love. How can he not see that just because something is sublime, it doesn't mean it isn't sordid too? And that latter aspect, she feels, should be treasured.

Eamon cherishes the silence because it slows time, making these moments malleable to sight and smell, touch and taste – her kiss lingers, luscious in his mouth – so he can store as much of this as possible in his memory. He understands that experience is transitory, but you should still try to hold on when something's perfect. He's unbothered that she may think he's foolish or by how she has looked at him throughout this night with an expression that's both amused and mocking. This is just her way.

He lies, jaw in one hand, the other flat on the mattress halfway between them, and contemplates where to touch her. Her chest rises with listlessly exaggerated breaths. Her lips are curled into a sly smile. He reaches out. His fingers stretch across the soft expanse of her stomach, palm and thumb dragging closely behind. His hand stops as his thumb meets her navel's concave resistance. She laughs, not meanly, having anticipated a more erogenous foray, but she's aware he's taking

34

his time, savouring touch. She closes her eyes as his fingernails graze along her ribs, lightly, inciting goose bumps, to her breast, where his hand massages her, if not adeptly then with eager tenderness. They kiss and she takes his hand, gently to begin with, then with gathering momentum, back across rib and curve, down through thatch of hair, taking two of his fingers inside her. With her free hand, she disregards his modesty, the cover of bed sheet. She takes hold.

Twelve hours earlier, Eamon had phoned Simon to gain permission to take Grace out for a late dinner, followed by a surprise trip to the pictures, a midnight showing for just them. Simon said, 'Was the privilege of escorting her to Ashburnham last night not enough for you? You wouldn't want to give her some time to recover?' When Eamon began to stammer a response, Simon quickly ended his suffering. 'As long as you're in work first thing in the morning, I don't have any objections. And you didn't need to ask.'

Getting exclusive access to the Supreme, the town's only cinema, meant calling in a favour from the proprietor, Eddie. In his teens, Eamon had worked there as an usher. Originally he'd been terrified of Eddie, even though the older man was five feet tall and his face seemed to have as many wrinkles as years he had been alive, and he was in his seventies. He deemed anyone who didn't revere cinema to be a 'fecking heathen', and so he disliked most people, but when Eamon mentioned being a fan of *Citizen Kane*, it led to a lengthy dialogue about the film's ahead-of-its-time tracking shots. Eddie revelled in Eamon's disbelief when he imparted that the word 'rosebud' really referred to a prized part of William Randolph Hearst's mistress's anatomy, and since then, Eamon has had his feet planted on Eddie's good side. They still see one another regularly. On Wednesday mornings, Eamon is treated to advance screenings of new films before they open on Fridays, and afterwards they have coffee and he defends whatever he's planning on writing in his review.

On the phone, after Eamon had made his request, Eddie said, 'You know you'll be keeping an old man from his much-needed sleep.'

'Why don't you get Rory to change the reels? I'll pay the overtime.'

'That moron? If the job's going to be done, it might as well be done right.'

'He does the job well enough for everyone else.'

'"Everyone else" doesn't mean he does the job well enough for everyone.'

'You'll do it then?'

'Looks like it. Does this mean you're going to write something favourable? I hear this film's controversial.'

'It'll probably get a decent review by itself.'

'Hmm. This lady friend, is she a Monroe? A West?'

'More of a Dietrich.'

'I always liked Dietrich.'

'I know. Me too. Thanks, Eddie.'

'Yeah, see you later.'

So everything was in place and Eamon was hoping that at the end of the night he might, fingers crossed, kiss Grace again. However, shortly into the evening, catastrophe loomed. They were in the Hogan's Hotel restaurant, which was only slightly fancier than the average Rathbaile pub. As they waited for their starters, Eamon was rambling about his respect for Simon and how lovely he thought Sarah was. Grace was nodding and smiling, but she kept looking over his shoulder; then, cutting him off, she said, 'I recognise some of these people.'

She focused on him. 'Ever get the feeling you're being talked about?'

Misinterpreting her tone, he said, 'I don't think anyone's even noticed us. There's no need to worry about it.'

'You think I'm paranoid?'

'I . . . I don't.'

'Well I'm not. This is a gossipy town. You should hear some of the things they say about my mother. You probably *have* heard them.'

'Grace, of course you're not paranoid, and people around here can be ignorant and cruel – I haven't forgotten what Harry said to you. I didn't mean to suggest anything negative at all.'

She covered her eyes and he thought he'd botched his chance with her, but then she removed her hand and meekly said, 'Sorry, Eamon, really. You must think I'm nuts. I wanted this to go well and I guess it's brought out my high-strung side. If you want to cut it short . . .'

'Listen, I'm on edge too. This is going well. We're finding our way.'

'I'm not normally so oversensitive.'

'Even if you are, I like you anyway.'

She laughed. 'You're a kind man, aren't you?'

'I don't . . .'

'It's rhetorical. Anyway, when are you going to drop a clue about that surprise you said you have?'

Eddie, wearing a grey-and-gold uniform complete with a box hat and white felt gloves, welcomed them into the Supreme's foyer with a grand gesture of his arm. 'Madam, Mr Gentleman, tonight's feature is *Easy Rider*, a journey into the depths of America's heartland.'

He kissed Grace's hand, produced a red rose from behind his back, and lied: 'Eamon asked me to give you this as a token of his affection.'

To Eamon Grace said, 'Charmer.'

When, half an hour into the film, he finally put his arm around her, she rested her head on his shoulder and wrapped her arm around his waist. She whispered, 'Took your time.'

About forty-five minutes in, after numerous sighs failed to rouse Eamon into making a more daring move, she leaned into his ear and said, 'Just so you know, I like you too.'

When he turned his head to respond, she kissed him. Most of the remainder of the film was missed – he won't learn the machete fate of Jack Nicholson's character until he returns for an undistracted viewing on Wednesday – and while his own groping was perhaps overly respectful, she pressed her hand to his thigh and brushed against his groin. Eamon, bless him, assumed this was inadvertent.

Later, his car parked around the corner from Simon's house, he pulled away from a long kiss and said, 'I want you to know how taken I am with you.' Grace leaned back against the passenger door, studying him. 'Did I say the wrong thing?'

She smiled. 'No. I'm just realising how dangerous you are for me.'

'Dangerous?'

'Your sweetness and honesty are disarming. But I'm dangerous to you too.'

'Why?'

'Because I want you to come inside so I can see what you're made of.'

'I'm not . . . I don't . . .' He took a breath. 'You're serious.'

'I think you want to.'

'I want to more than I've ever wanted anything, but there are other things to consider.'

'You mean like what would happen to your reputation, and mine, if we were caught? Things like what would Simon do to you?'

'I guess so, yes.'

She folded her arms. 'Well, he'd probably fire you. And if the reason why got out, I'd be called a slut. In some quarters you'd be respected more but trusted less. You'd bring shame to your mother. So you have to ask yourself: is what you have to gain by coming in worth what you'd be risking by getting caught?'

We know his choice. If he had rebuffed her, she wouldn't have given him another opportunity, but he passed her test and sleeping together that first time felt momentous to both of them. They didn't admit it aloud, not then, but they were quick to embrace the knowledge that their lives would never be the same. Looking back at this saddens me, because they had no idea of all that was to come. How could they have? They held each other and fell in love, and the consequences of that were set in motion, domino tapping domino.

III
October 1970

Eamon leaves Luis and Manny in his old room and heads downstairs. Standing outside the door to his parents' kitchen, he tugs with one finger at the knot of his tie then reproaches himself to let it be – it had looked all right in the mirror. He hears his parents bickering, but their voices are too low to distinguish their words until his father says, 'Sit down, will you?' There's the screeching sound of a chair being pulled back against the floor.

Eamon goes inside. Art and Maggie are sitting at the kitchen table. Art is in his suit, with a mug of steaming coffee between his planted elbows. Maggie, sitting opposite him, has her hands clasped together on her lap and a full cup of tea in front of her. The colours of her dress – navy and purple – are just a few shades light of being funereal. Eamon reckons he has likely interrupted his parents debating their prospective daughter-in-law's virtues and faults, with the emphasis on the latter. He doesn't care, though: they'll come around when they've had the chance to see how good she is for him; failing that, she'll win them over once she has borne them a grandchild or two.

Maggie hops up and points at her tea. 'Have that, dear.'

Eamon laughs. 'I don't want to drink your tea, Mam.'

'But you must! You can't have your mouth going dry when you're standing up there with everybody watching.'

Eamon is about to protest further, but he receives a look from Art with a clear import: that it'll be easier for all of them if he drinks the damn tea. He sits in Maggie's chair. 'Thanks, Mam.'

'What else can I get you? A sandwich? Biscuits?'

'It'd be better if I didn't risk getting crumbs on my suit.'

Before she can suggest an alternative snack, Art says, 'There'll be plenty of food at the wedding. He doesn't need you mothering him any more. That'll be his wife's job now.'

Eamon isn't sure if Art has just made a rare joke, so he smiles politely instead of laughing. Maggie definitely doesn't see any humour in what Art said. She doesn't spare him a glance as she lifts the teapot from the table and brings it to the sink, where she pours out the dregs, then dumps the tea bags into the bin.

Eamon casts his eyes to the ceiling. His brothers can be heard thumping about in his room and laughing disparagingly at each other. 'They sound like a pair of elephants and a pair of hyenas all at once. Was I ever so loud?'

Art sips his coffee, pauses, and says, 'No, you were a quiet one. We hardly knew you were there.'

Throughout Eamon's childhood, Art had wanted him to be more like his older brothers. Luis and Manny were foolish and stubborn, as boys were supposed to be. When they were eight and seven, Art remembers banning them from climbing trees after they suffered broken noses in separate incidents: Manny pushed Luis out of the tree in the back garden; a week later, after they'd both climbed to a higher branch, Luis took his revenge by heaving Manny out of the tree, laughing as the branches knocked him senseless on the way down. Predictably, they continued to climb trees, and Art caught and belted them. This pattern was repeated until they either learned discretion – and they most certainly didn't do that – or grew bored of that particular game and found a new outlet for risking their necks. With Eamon, though, there was never a need to ban him from climbing trees – heights made his knees shake – or to even discipline him harshly. Art doesn't have a single fatherly memory of having to take a belt to him.

However, more recently Art has begun to question his own judgements, and it has occurred to him that Eamon has always been stubborn too, just not in the reliably pig-headed manner of his brothers. No, he has been stubborn in how he has sought out and maintained his independence. While Eamon went off to college when he was eighteen, without receiving any encouragement from Art or Maggie on that decision, Luis and Manny stayed put until they were twenty-six and twenty-five. Then they moved into a badly kept bachelor pad together, but they still bring their laundry over for their mother to do, and most evenings she feeds them dinner as well. Time and again, when they tear through their wages from the pram factory with a few days still left in the month, it's to Art, who is also their foreman, that they come asking for money. Eamon is well used to living alone and taking care of himself, and he hasn't borrowed a penny since he first moved out. Far more than Luis or Manny, he is his own man.

After rinsing out the teapot and putting it aside to dry, Maggie checks the clock on the wall behind the table. 'Would you look at the time. What's taking them two so long?'

Without waiting for a response from her husband or her youngest, she goes out into the hallway. Art says to Eamon, 'Are you ready for this?'

'You mean for my big day?'

'I mean for your marriage. The wedding is the easy part.'

Eamon smiles. 'I can't wait. For all of it.'

Art nods, a glint in his eye. Eamon was right that his parents were discussing Grace before he entered the room, but he doesn't know that Art is in favour of her, that he thinks she has spirit and will bring out the best in him, and that Eamon will do the same for her too. Art could, of course, say all of this, but there'll be enough sentimentality throughout the day ahead, so he doesn't want to overdo it. He drinks his coffee and settles for 'Good for you, son.'

They can hear Maggie calling out, 'Luis! Emanuel! Where are you? We have to go!'

And then there's the banging of shoes on the stairs, and Luis telling Manny, 'Put on your tie and stick in your shirt, yeah? Christ, this is a wedding we're going to.'

* * *

In her elegant white dress Grace walks down the aisle of St Mary's, a typically majestic Irish church with an arched ceiling, dense marble columns, and vivid stained-glass windows. Her arm is locked with Simon's; there's no one other than him she would have considered walking beside. Her uncle has been her true guardian. Even if she knew where to look for her father, and presuming he's still alive, she wouldn't have allowed him to attend. In fact, she's determined to purge the memories of him from her mind for good, along with those of everyone else who has ever wronged her. After all, today is the day that delivers the culmination of her life's relationships, the ending that forgives the mistakes made during the thorny process of getting here.

Up ahead, Eamon is standing so proudly. At his side are his brothers, both of whom repulse her – they act as if she must find them doubly attractive as their younger brother but, unfortunately for her, she met him first. So never mind them as well, and that also goes for their disapproving mother.

Simon squeezes Grace's arm and she pats his hand. When he squeezes again, she looks at him and he tilts his head in the direction of Dorothy, sitting at the corner of the front pew, where she's smiling pleasantly and trying to get Grace's attention. Grace returns her smile, then looks away. She proceeds slowly to the top of the aisle, aware that not only is her mother continuing to stare, but that every pair of eyes here is on her; yes, wishing her joy, but judging her too, wondering if she deserves that joy. She concentrates on meeting Eamon's gaze, and that steadies her. When she sees how he's struggling to restrain his smile, she reminds herself of how right they were to choose each other. It will be enough, surely, to fill her thoughts with the future they will share together.

The wedding's conductor is Father Theodore, a caring man

beneath his fondness for Old Testament rhetoric. He lets his parishioners know that St Mary's is God's house, but if you're in a back pew, the reason you don't speak to your neighbour isn't because God is everywhere; it's because you suspect Father Theodore is. Eamon remembers, aged ten, being called forth to the pulpit and, with Father Theodore's hand clamping his shoulder, having to apologise to the congregation for his 'chattering' – all he had actually done was to snap at Luis to stop poking him in the nape of his neck with a saliva-tipped finger, but he wasn't granted an opportunity to explain that. Before he had returned to his seat, he could hear the oration continue and he didn't dare look behind for fear of seeing demonic eyes with flame-consumed irises. And yet today he doesn't feel afraid of Father Theodore or of anyone, or anything, else. This sense of fearlessness is new to him and he knows he has Grace to thank for it. He's prepared to spend the rest of his life trying to make her as happy as she can be. That's the least he can do to pay her back for liberating him.

Father Theodore baptised Eamon and Grace. Both of them wailed, which he approved of, as it suggested that they felt some of the gravity of having their souls saved. Looking at them now, standing together as adults and sharing surreptitious glances, he's perplexed by what a match they appear to be. He would have pictured Grace with someone flashier, a bit of a cad, and he would have put Eamon with someone a little more demure. Evidently he'd been mistaken, but when it comes to predicting love, that's easy to do.

Eamon's parents sit in one of the front pews. Art is taciturn, while Maggie is crying – it's unclear to Father Theodore whether this is out of elation or misery. He'd been barely out of the seminary when he presided over their wedding, but he recalls what an unlikely couple they were. Art was a foreigner and a soldier who had seen war. There was something hard about him. Maggie was only seventeen. She was caught up in the romance and had no grasp of what a marriage really entailed. Yet it worked. They had three sons together. They still hold hands.

And then, across the aisle, there's Grace's mother Dorothy, her hand being held by her stalwart brother Simon on one side of her and his winsome wife Sarah on the other. Apparently Dorothy is recovering well from an 'episode', one of many she has had, but who knows if her demons are at rest? When she married Peter Corcoran, Father Theodore thought that was a fine match. She appeared sane, and he appeared to have fortitude, but just because you have sanity or fortitude one day doesn't mean you'll have it the next. It's an arrogant man who thinks he can predict God's plan. All one can do is have faith and pray for good fortune.

Father Theodore doesn't hurry, or tarry either. He knows a wedding is all about its climax – the vows – and as soon as the ceremony is over, the celebration can begin.

Eamon and Grace each say 'I do' with a cadence indicative of butterflies in their bellies, but neither hesitates. They are pronounced man and wife, and kiss to their audience's approval. Eamon whispers in Grace's ear, 'I love you.'

Louder, she says the same.

Manny nudges Luis, who nudges him back harder. Maggie cries on Art's shoulder. Dorothy exclaims to Simon and Sarah, 'My Grace is married!'

Throughout the day, the sky had been lowering and growling, threatening to weep. When the congregation spills out of the church, the weather has cleared up. There are still a few innocuous clouds scattered around, and there's a bite in the air, but the consensus is that the sky is empty of clouds and there's no breeze. The change in the weather is taken to be a good sign, a blessing. I would tell these people if I could: signs are always either coincidences or something stamped on to memories in hindsight; blessings never have merit.

Chapter Five

Clarity

January 1985

JIMMY IS FOUR, AND OF ALL HIS RELATIVES, INCLUDING the dead, he looks most like Paul. While he's bigger than Paul was at the same age, and also quieter, he has the same mop of brown hair, pudgy cheeks, and sleepy eyes. If they didn't look so similar, his eyes wouldn't be stinging now.

Grace stands behind him, her hands in his hair, kneading dye into the roots. They're facing a mirror so she should see that oily tendrils are soaking his forehead, passing through and going around his eyebrows, veering towards his eyes in their hollows. Too late, he battens down his eyelids. He could rub his eyes or call out, but he's trying to be still. His hands clutch the arms of the chair. Within his shoes, his toes curl inwards.

Grace's shoulders quiver, as if they're receiving little electric shocks from the loose twine of her hair. Her fingers press on his reddening scalp. Then larger hands cover hers and bring them to her sides. Eamon whispers, 'Grace. What are you doing?'

She blinks and tears escape, locating her mouth. She releases

47

a breath and tilts back unsteadily against Eamon. 'I wanted to make him different, to be an individual.'

He turns her around. 'He already is.'

'I know. I do.'

Standing in the doorway, Elizabeth, her voice breaking from both fear and anger, says, 'This wasn't my fault. I didn't think she'd do anything.' She has only just stopped crying, and some damp strands of hair are pasted to one side of her face.

Eamon, with one arm gripped around Grace, looks over at Elizabeth and insists, 'I know, honey. This wasn't anyone's fault, least of all yours.'

Elizabeth doesn't say what she's thinking: nothing ever happens by itself and someone is *always* to blame, especially when another someone gets hurt.

Eamon says to her, 'Bear with me.' Then he gently kisses Grace. 'Why don't you go wash your hands in the kitchen? I'll clean up here.'

Her expression becomes frighteningly casual and she doesn't argue. Elizabeth steps back into the hallway to give her mother a wide berth as she leaves, but Grace doesn't even acknowledge her presence.

Jimmy hasn't moved yet. Eamon turns the chair around, puts a cloth under the tap, dabs his son's eyes, and wipes his forehead. 'Jim. Open your eyes.' The light is sharp. 'That's it, as much as you can.' Eamon hides his dismay as he sees those bloodshot eyes. For Jimmy, his father's face is a blur of mismatched features. 'Can you see all right, Jim?'

'Almost, Dad.'

'We're going to fix you up. Hold on here for a bit, okay? Elizabeth will stay with you.' Jimmy nods stoically, and this is more upsetting to Eamon than if he was throwing a fit. 'Just don't rub your eyes while I'm gone.'

Eamon gives Elizabeth an entreating look and she comes closer. He hands her the cloth. 'Hold on to that. I'll be right back. Can you watch over your brother for me?'

She hears an accusation in his question, even though it's not there. 'Yeah, I can. Why wouldn't I be able to?'

He'll reassure her of his trust in her later. For now, he says, 'Good girl,' and walks out of the bathroom.

Alone with Jimmy, Elizabeth notices a black streak along the bridge of his nose. She reaches out with the cloth to wipe it off. He flinches and, squeezing his eyes shut, says, 'No, no, no.'

She sits on the edge of the bath, her back bending forward, and folds her arms into her stomach. 'You let *her* do that to you, but you won't let *me* help.'

Keeping his eyes closed, he doesn't reply.

This mess is the last thing Eamon needs. He hasn't been sleeping well for a long time. He can't even try until Grace falls asleep. Then he finds himself watching her – sometimes it's like she's sleeping with an anvil on her chest – and he deliberates over whether to wake her as she slips into nightmares. He hopes her groans are a sign of her subconscious working things out, but maybe it's easier not to rescue her rather than coping with her when she does wake and she's distraught. Maybe, instead of having any restorative value, her nightmares are where she loses herself. Rather than take the wrong action, he lies there.

Today was another difficult day at the *Chronicle*, not due to his workload, but because his colleagues kept talking to him, and smiling and laughing in response felt gruelling. Harry, as usual, was the worst, telling the same old stories, beating the same punchlines to death. Eamon had come home hoping to vegetate in front of the telly and found his ten-year-old daughter weeping by herself in a corner of the living room. When he calmed her down and asked what had happened, Elizabeth said that Grace had been 'really sad' and ignoring her all day and that she just wanted to get her to say something. 'I only told her that Jimmy looks like Paul, and he didn't understand but he thought it was funny so I kept calling him Paul, and then Mam said that he couldn't look like Paul because he was dead, and that she wouldn't *let* him look like Paul. She was being weird and *laughing* about it, and she told Jimmy they were going to play a game in the bathroom and *I* wasn't allowed to come with them. So she took him away from me.'

Eamon knocks on Tighe's door and, as he turns the knob, says his name aloud to give him a moment to object if he's interrupting anything – his son is thirteen, after all. He hears, 'Come in!'

Tighe is cross-legged on the floor, playing *Pac-Man* on his Commodore 64, the volume turned up loud. He's wearing a grey shirt and grey trousers – his school uniform minus the red-and-black-striped tie and the wine blazer. Noticing Eamon's anxiety, he gathers his gangly mantis limbs and stands. A ghost touches Pac-Man, taking his last life and ending the game. Tighe says, 'What's wrong?'

Eamon is gradually getting used to Tighe's deeper voice. His escalating height is even more peculiar. He's thin, though, and still very boyish, ruddy and soft-skinned. Eamon manufactures a faulty smile. 'I need your help. Jimmy got something in his eyes. I'm going to run him over to the hospital so the doctor can check him out. A precaution.' He knocks on the wooden door for luck.

'What do you want me to do?'

'Your mother isn't feeling the best. You could keep her company. Have you and Elizabeth eaten yet?'

'No.'

'Could you rustle something up? Even toast, until I get back?'

'I'll make beans, too. Some for Mam as well.'

'Thanks. You're a good . . . young man. Don't tell Grace where we've gone, okay? There's no need to concern her. And listen, this is going to sound odd, but don't leave her alone with Elizabeth. I'll explain when I get back.'

Tighe is curious, but senses that this isn't the right time to ask what's really happening. 'No problem.'

Eamon steps over a long extension cord, twisted in multiple places, without catching his foot in one of the perilous loops. He hugs Tighe and his son returns it. Tighe is already planning on delegating either the beans or the toast to Elizabeth. It's good for her to have something to do and for him to have less. She can set the table, too.

On the way to the hospital, Jimmy sits in the passenger seat. Eamon knows they could be in trouble if they're pulled over, at least until he shows the guard his son's eyes, but he wants to keep him close. He repeatedly asks how he is, strenuously maintaining a relaxed tone. When they come to a red light, he turns on the overhead light and tells Jimmy to follow the movement of his finger. He appears to be able to see, but his eyes are so bloodshot, his pupils balanced on crimson spider webs. A driver behind them beeps his horn, prompting Eamon to drive again.

An interminable fifteen minutes later, they arrive at St John's. Before going inside, Eamon says, 'Jim, when we meet the doctor, we have to play an important game of make-believe. This might be confusing, but no one in there is allowed to know it was Mammy who hurt your eyes. If we tell them that, they could get angry with her. We don't want that, do we? Because if they think she's bad, they could take her away. Now, you don't . . . you don't want them to take her away, do you?'

Eamon feels like the most useless father in the world as tears stream down Jimmy's cheeks and he says, 'Nooo . . . Daddy, no.'

He presses Jimmy's face to his chest. 'Shushhh . . .' The pungency of the dye assaults his nostrils. Normally Jimmy's hair smells wonderfully fresh. Now it smells like roses mixed with petrol. Eamon strokes his hair. It's hard and sticky at the top, but downy behind his ears. He embraces him one more time, then pulls back. 'We'd better go in. Can you be brave for me?'

Jimmy sniffles himself under control.

'Mammy isn't going anywhere, but remember our game?'

Jimmy swabs away his tears with his sleeve. 'I promise to be good.'

Eamon kisses his forehead, wanting to smooth out the corrugations.

To Eamon's surprise, the doctor who sees them is German. Dr Schrempf is balding, and perm-like hair springs from the sides and back of his head. He smiles toothily at Jimmy, pulls up a stool next to where he's sitting on a bed, and briefly examines his eyes with a torch. His manner is almost lazy, as if he has already seen a dozen boys today with bloodshot eyes. After doing the same follow-my-finger routine that Eamon did, he says, 'How did this occur, little man?'

Eamon says, 'Kids, y'know? He and his sister were playing

dress-up. They found a bottle of hair dye and got carried away.'

'It happens. Are your eyes sore . . .' Schrempf glances at his clipboard. 'James?'

Jimmy looks at his father, who nods. Jimmy says, 'A bit. They're more itchy, yeah, than sore. They're only a bit sore.'

Schrempf stands. 'Good, good.' He reaches to tousle Jimmy's hair, but, upon noticing its gummy tangle, his hand freezes, hovering an inch above Jimmy's head, before he pats his shoulder instead. He scribbles on his prescription pad, then tears the leaf off and hands it to Eamon. 'Eye drops. They'll clear it right up. Easy to administer. Any problems, don't hesitate to return.' He takes a lollipop from the pocket of his white coat and holds it out to Jimmy. 'For you, little man. Little . . .' Clipboard. 'James.'

Jimmy takes it while Eamon says, 'What do you say, Jim?'

'Thank you, Dr Shrimp.'

Schrempf smiles and strides away.

'So he's all right then?'

'He is. He was scared by the whole thing, although he tried not to show it. When I woke him this morning, his eyes were almost completely cleared up. Well, they had a pinkish tint, like an Old English Sheepdog's eyes. Have you ever pushed back the hair over the eyes of one of those dogs? They were kind of pink like that. Maybe I looked too hard. Maybe the whites of his eyes were perfectly white.'

Eamon and Simon are in Simon's office. The black-and-white photo on the desk of Grace and Dorothy at the pier is yellower than it was back when Simon asked Eamon to take Grace to the ball, but she's timelessly young in it, and Dorothy's sanity is preserved. There are other photos too.

53

One is of Simon and Sarah's wedding. Some of his higher-ranking employees used to slag him about his mutton-chop sideburns in the shot. They'd never do that now, not with the bride dead. With her sanguine complexion and the I-know-something-you-don't twinkle in her eyes, she looks like she couldn't be unhappy even if she tried. Another photo is of Simon's great-nephews and great-niece on the family couch. Tighe is on the left, Elizabeth is in the middle, holding Jimmy, and Paul is on the right. They're laughing, except for Jimmy. He's stretching his limbs in four directions in a bid to break free of his sister's grasp. The photo was taken less than two months before Paul died.

Eamon hasn't been telling Simon the hair-dye story to relate a close call and say, 'It's all over with now.' They've been dancing around the implications and this conversation has long been coming. Simon's expression is supportive, but he can't be the one to suggest the next step. Eamon pulls on his hair and says, 'I love Grace. I want what's best for her.'

'There's never been any doubt on that score. None what-soever.'

'Until she's better, she shouldn't be looking after the kids. She needs help. I don't know what else to do.'

'Grace is like a daughter to me.'

'She *is* a daughter to you. To all intents and purposes, you've been her father.'

'Look, I'm behind you on whatever you feel needs to be done. I know how difficult this is.'

Eamon nods. 'When Dorothy had her stays at St Augustine's, did they ever make a difference?'

His mouth slouched, Simon says, 'St Augustine's isn't what it used to be. The care of people suffering from . . . emotional problems has improved by miles since Dorothy was first committed. There's a reason it's called a psychiatric hospital now instead of a mental one.'

'Other than image?'

'Yes. Really. It's not *One Flew Over the Cuckoo's Nest*. The doctors know what they're doing.'

'You didn't answer my original question.'

'It seemed like it made a difference. I mean, I liked to believe she was being helped because you have to have hope with her kind of illness. But obviously Dorothy has never gotten well. It was always one step forward, two back, until about ten years ago, when it stopped getting worse and it just became the status quo. By then, the person she used to be was gone. Maybe with fewer drugs or better ones she could've come back from it. Maybe with earlier treatment. To be honest, I try not to spend any more time on the what-ifs than I can help. Maybe there was never a possibility of her getting better and it was hopeless from the start.'

Simon wishes he could suck the toxicity of his last sentence back down his throat, but it has already settled in the air. Eamon stares at his hands. Simon says, 'Don't forget that Grace is stronger than Dorothy ever was. It's understandable that Paul and the stillbirth have taken their toll. She'll overcome this.'

'Of course she will. I'll do whatever needs to be done and she'll be well again. I know it.'

Eamon will convince Grace to check into St Augustine's – it wouldn't have to be for long, and if it doesn't help, she'll have the autonomy to leave whenever she wants. Initially she'll curse him for suggesting it. Then she'll plead. What happened was an aberration. She's fine. He will play his ace: he'll ask her to do it for their children's sake. Ultimately she'll give in.

The hair-dye incident aroused my suspicions. I saw Eamon outside the bathroom door before he entered, but Jimmy was unaware of him until he spoke. Jimmy's vision became blurry; mine was always clear. But we were supposed to be the same. In my confusion, I still didn't realise that I wasn't him. Not yet.

Chapter Six

Recognition

February 1985

Tomorrow, Grace, having served her six-week voluntary sentence, will leave St Augustine's and come home. She'll get her family, most of us that is, back: an adoring husband and three out of five children still physically intact.

Today is one in a line of family 'fun' days: Eamon, joined by Art and Maggie, has taken the kids to the Rathbaile race-course to watch the horses. Tighe, Elizabeth, and Jimmy detect that time spent as a family has a solemn undercurrent – it's just so important that the fun part comes off – so they are well versed in dutifully fudging enthusiasm, then hoping that it develops into the real thing.

Art and Eamon have gone to place bets. Tighe is off having a look around. As a teenager, he's allowed to have reprieves from the proper children and the boring adults.

In the nosebleed section of the grandstand, Elizabeth, Jimmy, and Maggie are sitting along a row of blue seats – they're in the least crowded area because Maggie is conscious that large groups of people make Elizabeth more skittish. Elizabeth is resting her head on Jimmy's shoulder and her arms are around him, her fingers locked against his ribcage. He wishes she wouldn't hug him so often. He's not a baby, or a teddy, or Paul. But he doesn't complain. While he isn't able to articulate it, he can sense her neediness and doesn't want to upset the equilibrium that is her peace of mind; constructed, everyone fears, from gossamer threads.

Maggie anxiously says, 'Oh look! The horses are lining up at the gates.'

Elizabeth raises her head and surrenders Jimmy from her grasp. They see that their grandmother is right. The horses are in the stalls, snorting and clomping under the jockeys, who are stroking their muscular necks.

Throughout the stands, the anticipation is palpable as noon is struck. The shot is fired. The horses are off, their hoofs thundering along the track. The clamouring gamblers rise to their feet like they've just realised they've been sitting on hot coals. They're happy because they haven't lost yet. They've taken a leap of faith that they can will their chosen horses to victory. They'll believe it until finish-line reality kicks in.

Down by the track, Tighe is standing back from the mob of people who are mashed against the railings and each other. He appears to be searching for a gap to squeeze his skinny frame through for a better view. He's not, though. He sees what he's looking for. She's blonde, about twenty-one, wearing a figure-hugging milk-white dress and rose-red high heels. One of her hands is pitched into the mass, attached to a boyfriend. The other one is holding a black hat with an unfortunately wide brim to her head. She can't move nearer without simultaneously clocking two other spectators with her fashion weapon, and it doesn't seem to occur to her that she could just take it off. Tighe checks her out with an efficient glance and beelines. Pretending to be another race-lover, he presses against her, copping a feel of her ass, and when she turns her

head, he bumbles an awkward-teenager apology about acci-
dental contact and moves off, grinning to himself.

Standing over on the tunnel steps, there's a man I want you
to meet: he's wearing a tattered paddy cap and a black coat,
the thick collar hiding almost all of his neck, and his name is
Terry Walsh. He's only in his early thirties, but his deep-set
green eyes are framed by conspicuous crow's feet. His face is
so gaunt that if you stared long enough you might swear you
could make out his teeth through his cheeks. Incongruous to
the rest of his features, his colourless lips are full Humphrey
Bogart lips, and he unintentionally endorses the likeness with
the slow-burning cigarette balanced on the lower one. Every
now and then ash breaks off from the tip, falling on to his
coat and shoes.

When he notices what Tighe is up to, he smiles subtly,
without disturbing his cigarette. It's more reflex amusement
than anything else, for Terry isn't a man with much of a
capacity for enjoyment. He wasn't always this way. It's the
result of a cause, an effect. He mostly hates everything now,
including all people. They seem rat-like. Himself too. He's the
biggest rat of all.

He might not deserve it, but I feel sorry for him.

A HORSE NAMED FOUR-LEAF WINS THE RACE, SENDING
ripples of cursing, and some sporadic cheers, through the
crowds. Terry remembers the cigarette on his lip. It's gone out.
With yellowed thumb and index finger he chucks the butt to
the ground and wipes ash from his chin. He turns and enters
the tunnel, wanting to find somewhere less people-infested to
watch the next race from.

Inside the stadium, he walks towards Art and Eamon, who
are walking away from the bookies. As he passes, Terry's elbow

brushes lightly against Eamon's, but neither of them glances at the other.

Art and Eamon go to the bar, and there they stand arguing over who'll pay for the beers Art has insisted they have. 'If I feel like buying my son a pint, I have every right . . .'

Eamon, seeing he's going to have to concede, interrupts, 'Okay, Papá. I appreciate it.'

Art smiles, his moustache shimmying. Once he has paid the bartender, he gives Eamon his beer and says, 'To Grace.'

'To Grace.' They press their plastic cups together. 'Cheers.'

The day at the races was Art's idea. Sharing something he has a passion for is a way to show he cares. When he asks how Grace is, he listens attentively to the reply and doesn't offer an opinion on how he views the situation. To his mind, that would be disrespectful. As for Paul, Art hasn't mentioned his name to Eamon since the accident. He knows he should say something about it, but it feels close to impossible. Maggie can talk about Paul and has cried often for him. Art hasn't. At the funeral, he had tears in his eyes. He just didn't shed them. In fact, in Art's adult life, the number of times he has cried could be counted on one hand and you wouldn't need every finger. Since he moved to Rathbaile, you wouldn't need to be able to count.

The races remind Art of his father, Andreas, who never would have taken him to a place like this, as he saw all gamblers as immature, wanting something for nothing, though he did own and breed stallions. He shared his love of horses with Art, teaching him how to gain their trust and how to ride. While they used to argue about almost everything, around horses they were patient father and deferring son. When Art bets on races, however, there's still an element of pleasure in doing something his long-dead father would disapprove of.

Art and Eamon didn't have time to put bets on the race that has just been run, but they have money down on the next five, for themselves and for Tighe and Jimmy too – marking this occasion as Jimmy Dice's first-ever taste of gambling action. Eamon gave five pounds each to Jimmy and Elizabeth, and twenty to Tighe – the extra amount being a bonus for the responsibilities he took on while Grace was 'getting better' – and told them they could either pocket the money or gamble with it.

Elizabeth immediately chose to hold on to hers. Eamon said, 'You know you could end up with more than that if you bet it wisely.'

She replied, 'Yeah, Dad, but I could lose it all too.'

Eamon, amused by and appreciative of her logic, didn't attempt to persuade her otherwise.

Tighe and Jimmy were also quick to decide, both of them keen to risk it all. For each race Tighe bet four pounds on the horse with the longest odds, because if he was going to take a chance, he wanted the highest possible pay-off. Jimmy, uninterested in listening to any advice on the matter, picked his horses based purely on whether he liked their names, going with Mighty Beast, Speed Demon, Razor's Edge, Lightning Strikes, and Horse on Fire.

Without much hope of it, Art suggested to Maggie that she might want to 'get in on the action', but she said, 'If one of you wins, that's all I care about.'

She didn't explain that she felt it would be hypocritical of her to bet seeing as how she had rebuked Art for doing so in the past, or that she suspected all gambling might be sinful so she feared she might like it. She learned a long time ago that sometimes sinful acts can be gratifying.

Art claimed to Eamon that he made all of his bets, twenty

pounds apiece, based on a combination of factors – tips, track records, what he knew of the owners, what he had gleaned from studying the horses in the mounting yard – all calculated against the given odds, but in truth, for a couple of the races he ignored his own system in favour of hunches. Eamon, knowing nothing about horses, and not wanting to outdo his father, even accidentally, made the same picks, but for half the money down.

At the bar, Art has a gulp of his pint. He's getting excited. For him, the most fun part of the races isn't actually the gambling; it's the bellowing without restraint as the horses gallop. Life rarely provides such a good excuse. With some froth sprinkled on the tips of his moustache, he tells Eamon, 'I'm glad you said yes to today.'

'Me too, Papá. Maybe we'll make a habit of it.'

Above Art and Eamon's heads, near the top of the grand-stand, Terry sinks into a plastic seat, which creaks as it accepts his weight. A cigarette already hanging on his lip, he rummages in his pocket for his Zippo lighter. Success. Flick of the wrist and deep first drag. The smoke wafts over his shoulder, snaking up the incline of rows, three back, to Jimmy and Elizabeth's expanding nostrils. Maggie would like to scold this man for his poor appreciation of the fragility of children's lungs, but he has an unsavoury air and looks best left unprovoked.

She didn't enjoy the first race. The state the horses were worked into suggested a sort of lunacy, and there was some-thing ugly about the people as they cheered and jeered. Jimmy and Elizabeth had ballooned with excitement, leaping on to their seats and exhibiting their tonsils. Maggie suspended her tentative clapping to jerk on Jimmy's trousers and entreat him to refrain from bouncing on his seat, so he wouldn't fall and scrape his knees, or worse. Now he and Elizabeth are sitting subdued, recharging their energy for the next race. Jimmy has shifted over so that there's an empty seat between them.

Despite the vague promises made by the clear sky and luminous sun, the wind has an icy touch and Maggie tugs on her woollen shawl. Jimmy and Elizabeth don't look bothered. They're not wearing jackets, but they're young and their bodies are probably cold without their minds even realising it. Maggie doesn't know if this is an advantage. There are so many things she's unsure of now, especially when it comes to Eamon's family.

Paul's body on the tarmac will forever lurk in her nightmares. After he was killed, she prayed every night for God to change what had happened: *take me instead; take me.* Eventually she quit this particular prayer. Her temptation to despair was sacrilegious. She asked God for forgiveness and has been trying hard to forgive Him. She keeps believing because she needs to know Paul is in heaven while the rest of the family are in this world, doing what they can to pick up the pieces, but it's like putting together a jigsaw made of shattered glass.

The only choice is to keep going. Tighe, Elizabeth, and Jimmy must overcome the loss of their brother, and their mother's madness. They can still have happy futures. Well, Maggie hates to admit, Tighe and Jimmy can; the odds are against Elizabeth. She has an intimidating legacy to contend with: a schizophrenic, subsequently catatonic, grandmother; a possibly schizophrenic, at any rate depressive, mother. And as if her cursed blood wasn't enough, she has *that* memory. It wasn't her fault, and especially not Tighe's, but she did run too far and Paul followed her to his death. When the rest of them rushed towards her screams, they found her standing over him. She was bleeding from her cheeks, where her nails were digging in. When she stopped screaming, you could tell from her bulging eyes that the dirge had merely been suppressed. She was seven then; she's ten now and still seeing a therapist. Maggie knows she takes sleeping pills, and Eamon hasn't said, but it seems likely that she's on antidepressants too.

While Jimmy thought the first race was great fun, he knew he couldn't win anything on that one. In the next race, he'll be able to win loads of money and he's daydreaming about how he'd like to spend it. He loves Transformers and he already owns Optimus Prime and Megatron, but maybe now he'll be able to buy Prowl or Soundwave.

Registering Jimmy's distracted expression, Elizabeth switches her attention to the man sitting three rows below. She discerns something ominous about him – unrelated to the vice that elicited Maggie's cursory judgement – even though she can't see much of his face from her vantage point. There's only a pink ear and a hint of jowl in sight. His cigarette isn't visible to her, but the cloud of smoke it's producing is. If logical inferences couldn't be made, the impression would be that his hidden face is on fire. Elizabeth wants to see his face in full. She stands and steps away from her seat, moving out of the row.

When his cigarette goes out, Terry turns from the wind and leans over the back of his seat, elbows out, to light a new one. His cap casts a shadow over his eyes, but it's not dim enough to conceal them from Elizabeth. Her own eyes widen, her jaw slackens, and the blood retreats from her cheeks.

It takes Terry a few attempts before his sputtering lighter works and the cigarette is lit. Satisfaction breezes over his face. Then he looks up. After his mind processes his initial glance, his eyes are wrenched back to the girl with the frozen expression. The cigarette drops from Terry's fingers to the stone floor.

He thinks of that sleek red sports car he bought, a Ferrari

Dino, and how he drank a few whiskeys to celebrate. He remembers laughing to himself as he took that corner, although he has no idea what it was that he could have found so amusing. He just knows he was going far too fast.

The small brown-haired boy was in the middle of the road, knees bent and about to burst into a run. There just wasn't any time left. He was as good as dead before the car hit him. Terry swerved, rolling the wheel. The collision came anyway, before the car skidded into a U-turn halt. Ten feet from his cracked headlights and dented bonnet, the debris of the dead boy lay in the other lane, the white stripe marking the churning absurdity of before and after. The girl in the flower-patch dress materialised next to the boy, her shadow draping over him. Her face was contorted into the expression of a scream for the longest time before it emanated from her mouth. Or maybe that detail is wrong. Maybe she was screaming all along, but he was deaf to it. They stared at one another through the windshield, sharing their terror as he turned the keys in the ignition. Meaninglessly he said, 'I'm sorry,' reversed the car, U-turned it again, and sped away.

Elizabeth has grown a lot in the last three and a half years, but they recognise each other. He stands; he would drop to his knees and beg her to stop looking at him like he's a monster if only his need to escape her stare wasn't stronger than his need to repent. He flees and his lighter falls from his grasp, scuttling down the steps ahead of him. Instead of picking it up, he barrels past Art and Eamon as they come up the stairs, almost knocking the beers from their hands. He's gone.

Jimmy says, 'Daddy! Abuelo! We saw the horses race!'

No one is listening to him. His father and grandfather are looking at Elizabeth.

Eamon hands his beer to Art and, approaching his daughter slowly, says, 'Elizabeth? What's wrong? You had an accident.'

Maggie, just noticing what has happened, says, 'Oh, Elizabeth dear. You should've said something. You should've told me you had to go.'

Elizabeth sits, shaking, her face ashen, her dress wet at the crotch. Urine is sliding down her leg to her sock and shoe.

The day at the races is cancelled – Eamon says it's postponed, but it's cancelled really. Maggie cleans Elizabeth up in the toilets, then when they get home she gives her a bath. Her family tiptoes around her, speaking to her quietly. She'll never tell them who she saw and she'll convince herself that he wasn't who she thought he was. He may even have been a phantom she conjured from thin air.

Elizabeth isn't the only one who has suffered a profound shock. I have too. While Jimmy was imagining what Transformers he would like to collect, I became bored and, without even being self-conscious enough to realise what I was doing, drifted away from him. Sensing that something unsettling had caught Elizabeth's attention, I watched her watch that man, and then I watched him too. At first I couldn't understand why they were staring at each other the way they were. And it just happened. I met his eyes and plunged into his mind.

I saw the accident in all its vivid details, how horrifically permanent it was, and its aftermath for Terry, how he put his Ferrari at the bottom of a river and the Gardaí didn't come knocking at his door. He could have moved far away and tried to never look back, but his guilt has compelled him to stay put, waiting for someone to punish him.

Back at home, Jimmy is content to play with his toys and to accept what he's told about his sister having had an 'episode'.

With Elizabeth in denial, I'm the lone family member who is aware of the truth, and I'm frantic. Everyone needs to know that was the man who killed Paul! I can't help anyone understand, but I finally know I'm not Jimmy Dice, an insight that bestows both freedom and imprisonment on me. Alone in my vacuum, I exist.

Chapter Seven

The Importance of Flesh and Bone

April 1988

THAT'S SEB QUINN SITTING UPSIDE DOWN ON AN ARM-
chair in the Diaz living room. It's not the scruffy one matching
the three-seater couch – both are blue-grey, freckled with black
dots. No, it's the good, creaking leather one, 'Dad's chair'.
Seb's seven-year-old feet extend to the chair's apex, gravity
pulling on his shoelace loops and on his turquoise tracksuit
bottoms, revealing his hairless forelegs. His arms and head
droop off the seat. His mouth agape, the heavy rush of blood
to his skull is pleasant. His perspective doesn't seem all that
untenable: the beige carpet has become a ceiling, showing no
indication of jettisoning the furniture to the white floor; only
the inverted door looks properly confused. He's enjoying
himself, but needs more. 'Jimmy! I'm so bored!'

'Shut up. I'm almost done.' Jimmy says this without looking
up from the *Transformers* comic he's reading while lying on
the couch – until the Decepticons are defeated, he feels justified in ignoring Seb.

'C'mon, Jimmy.'

Jimmy flips to the last page. 'Almost there.'

Seb springs off the armchair. Too fast. His legs buckle as

the surplus of blood in his head whooshes through his body. He says, 'Whoa, wobbly.' Hamming it up, he collapses.

Jimmy says, 'Done!' He sits up and sees Seb starfish-like on the carpet, his eyes staring at a spot on the ceiling. 'You'll have to blink sometime. Loser. Dipshit.' On reflex, Jimmy looks left and right for anyone resembling an authority figure, then says, 'Dipshit-loser.'

Now that blinking has been mentioned, all Seb can think about is the tears building up in his eyes, and he's forced to blink. 'I could've been dead right there and you'd have had to come to my funeral and my dad would've strangled you because everyone would say it was all your fault. And the devil would've gotten you, while I'd be in heaven laughing my socks off.'

'If you were dead, there wouldn't be a funeral. Your parents would put you out with the rubbish and there'd be a massive party and I'd be given all your stuff.'

'No way.' Seb pulls himself back on to the armchair, sitting more traditionally this time. 'So what're we going to do?'

Jimmy tosses the comic at Seb's head, but it misses and disappears over the armchair. They laugh. Seb doesn't retaliate. Jimmy says, 'Want to see my neighbour's dogs?'

'Yes. Why?'

Jimmy grins. 'They're mean sons of bitches. Plus . . .' He lowers his voice. 'We're not allowed.'

'Cool.' Seb beams; three of his teeth are missing.

This weekend, Eamon and Grace are staying at a cottage in Waterford. In the three years that have passed since she was a patient at St Augustine's, Grace has been a model of mental health, or nearly. She rarely gets too excited or upset, and it would be unfair, perhaps, to focus on her worried eyes instead of her effortful smile.

Now that they have gone away, they intend to simulate being happy, and if that works, maybe it'll be time to move on to the real thing. But for their holiday to be successful, nothing can go wrong at home. Elizabeth is staying with Art and Maggie and they will monitor her for signs of disturbance. Tighe's instructions are to not let Jimmy set foot past the front gate, and to make dinner for him and Seb. Eamon also warned Tighe not to have his new girlfriend over.

All that's expected of Jimmy is to be good, putting him in a bind. If he tells Seb they should stay at home, that will turn his proposal to go see the dogs into a lie, and his father has always said those are very bad things; except white lies, which this wasn't. However, Old MacGrath's is just down the road, so they could go there and back quickly. Could an action really be bad if no one ever found out? Jimmy decides that no, it would only count if they were caught. There's still a problem, though. Even if Tighe doesn't hear them leave, all it would take to notice their absence would be for him to poke his head into the living room and Jimmy's room. Jimmy makes a plan: he'll ask for permission. Tighe isn't particularly unreasonable, but if he says no, they can just wait an hour or so. Then, when his guard is relaxed, they can take their chances and sneak out.

Jimmy goes down the hall to Tighe's room. Before he can knock, the door swings open and Tighe appears. 'Jimmy! I was about to summon you.'

Encouraged by that, he enters. Tighe sits sideways on his chair, with one elbow on the back of it and the other on the open Rowntree maths book on his desk. Jimmy remains standing. 'I have a question.'

'I've something to ask you too. You first.'

Jimmy explains how he and Seb want to go on an adventure, omitting any mention of potential danger, and feels quite clever when he remembers to add, 'Dad always says it's better to play outside and not watch too much TV.'

Tighe looks receptive to the pitch, nodding throughout, but as soon as Jimmy stops talking, he says, 'Sorry, but no.'

'No?' A lump consolidates in Jimmy's throat.

Tighe is amused by his brother's inability to repress the smallest disappointment. 'Not unless you return the favour and keep a secret for me.'

'I'm great at keeping secrets!'

'Good. Isabel's about to call over, but as far as you and your buddy are concerned, if Dad or anyone else asks, she was never here. Got it?'

'No problem! I don't even care!'

Tighe thrusts his hand out. 'Shake on it.' His grip is steely. 'You know what it means if you break your word? You go straight to hell when you die, but that's nothing compared to what I'd do to you.' Jimmy pales and Tighe laughs. 'You've nothing to worry about. Go have fun. Tell Seb what we agreed and be back by six. I'll make pancakes.'

As Jimmy is passing by the front door on his way to the living room, the doorbell rings. He stops and looks back down the hallway. Tighe comes out of his room. 'Well? Get it.'

Jimmy opens the door. The caller is a girl with shoulder-length black hair, wearing ruby-red lipstick, inexpertly applied. Her jean shorts show off her thighs and she has a padded bra on under her low-buttoned shirt. The ankle-length dress and regular bra she was wearing when she left her parents' house are in the brown leather bag slung across her shoulder. Despite her efforts to appear older than she is, she only succeeds in looking like a fourteen-year-old who is trying

71

too hard, which is exactly what she is. Tighe is two weeks away from turning seventeen and she doesn't want him to feel like a cradle-snatcher – a needless concern because he's unbothered. She says, 'Ah, do you know who I am?'

'You're Isabel and I'm Jimmy. You're allowed in. I won't tell.'

She comes inside and spreads her arms wide. Jimmy looks at her without comprehending what she wants, until she says, 'You're adorable. Can I have a hug?'

Jimmy glances at Tighe, who ushers him forward with a nonchalant motion of his hand. Jimmy steps closer and lets Isabel squeeze him tightly to her. He's surprised by how much he likes the smell of her perfume.

Tighe pushes him aside. 'Enough of that.' He takes Isabel in his arms and kisses her, with tongue. When he begins to feel her up, she slaps his hand away. 'Tighe, don't destroy your little brother's innocence!'

Tighe smirks at Jimmy's obvious embarrassment. Jimmy says, 'I'm going now,' then goes.

In the living room, he pulls his *Transformers* comic out of Seb's hands and chucks it on the couch. 'I forced Tighe to let us do whatever we want!'

The Diaz house is on the outskirts of town, surrounded by countryside. The most direct way to MacGrath's is out the front gate, on to Lyons Road, then take a right and go down the hill until you come to the rusted gate leading to a nameless dirt road. MacGrath's house is at the end, out of sight from Lyons Road. But it's more adventurous to scale the back-garden fence, then tramp through some mucky fields, passing the oblivious cows and the odd rotted tree-stump, so this is what they do.

As Jimmy leads Seb, he shouts at a cow in their way, giving her a start. She sidesteps, then returns to chewing the cud. Seb is impressed by Jimmy's apparent fearlessness and the dogs have grown in his mind. They probably have red eyes, claws like knives, and teeth like a tiger's.

As they stride through their third field, Jimmy says, 'See that fence? The yard is on the other side. We can get a look at them from up that tree.'

The eight-foot-high fence looks sturdy, but the boards are rattling. Seb says, 'Eh, Jimmy, that's the wind, isn't it? The dogs aren't *right there* on the other side, are they?'

Jimmy, noting that Seb is slowing down, picks up his pace so that Seb has to as well to keep up. 'I dunno. Could be the wind, or maybe it's one of the dogs and he's smelled you already.'

'But I mean, have they ever gotten out? I guess not. Like, they're chained up and stuff, yeah?'

Jimmy doesn't look back as he says, 'They've broken out a couple of times, and when they have, some sheep have disappeared. There was a kid that went missing too, Larry something. No one's ever proven anything and the Gardaí are too chickenshit to X-ray the dogs' stomachs, y'know, to check for remains.'

'No way? Really? You're a liar.'

Jimmy stops and turns. 'I'd never lie about that happening to a kid. No one likes to mention it. Larry's parents pretend he never existed. I've heard my parents talk about it and they never saw anything, no one did, but they believe it must be true. Everyone does.' He's, surprise, making this up as he goes along, but he's convincing himself of the story too and can vividly see his parents having a muzzled night-time conversation about poor Larry.

'Maybe we should go back. We could wait until another time, when your dad's around and we're allowed to go exploring.'

'You're not scared, are you?'

If Seb answers this truthfully he'll be branded a coward or, even worse, a girl. He blows air out of the side of his mouth. 'No way. I was just thinking about, like, respect for the dead. But I don't care. They're only dogs. Let's go look.'

They climb the sycamore abutting the fence, perching on two tentacle branches overhanging MacGrath's property. Both boys position themselves within arm's length of the huggable trunk.

They spot the dogs. One is rubbing his flank against a ramshackle shed. Snarling half-heartedly, his foam-coated tongue lolling out of his mouth, he doesn't appear to be alleviating his itch, yet he persists. He isn't a large dog, but he's built block upon block with compact muscle.

Across the yard, past the path to the back door of the house and the weed-plagued garden – which is littered with bones and inert gardening aids: a shovel, an upturned wheelbarrow, a bucket with a dislocated handle – are two doghouses. One is empty. The other is occupied by the second dog, who is gnawing on a bone. Like the first, he's a pit bull terrier. Although he's lying down and half in, half out of his house, he's clearly a stouter dog. He has picked his bone clean of meat, but it still serves as a teeth sharpener.

Seb says quietly, 'I thought they'd be bigger.'

Jimmy puts his finger to his lips. 'We don't want Old MacGrath to know we're here. He's usually in his house. They say he hates children and has a shotgun.'

'A shotgun?'

'Yeah. And the dogs may not be huge, but they're fierce as

hell. Do you see how many bones are down there? Who knows where they all come from? I mean, do you know what the dogs are called? The one by the shed is Manson. The one eating the bone is Ripper.'

'Because he rips people?'

Jimmy rolls his eyes. 'No, idiot. They're named after Charles Manson and Jack the Ripper, the cannibal serial killers.'

'Oh, right. Which one got Larry?'

'Probably both, but I'd say Ripper was in charge. You can tell he's more dangerous if you look at his neck.' Jimmy points at Ripper's red collar and the attached chain, trailing into his house. He's about to expound on a gorily detailed theory of just how Larry must have met his end when Manson erupts with a barrage of barking. Seb wraps his arms around his branch, digging his fingernails into the bark. Jimmy is startled too but masks it, keeping his hands lax on his thighs. Manson bounds over to the fence. Ripper's eyes are also on them as he continues to grind on bone.

Seb edges back towards the trunk. 'W-we'd better get out of here.'

'It's okay. We only need to do a legger if Old MacGrath comes out, and he's used to his dogs acting up for no reason. They can't get us here.'

Seb halts his retreat, but doesn't return to his previous place. Manson stops barking. He bares his teeth, then trudges back to the shed, flopping down beside it. Even if he still has an itch, he has resigned himself to the futility of scratching.

Jimmy laughs. 'You almost pissed your pants!'

'No I didn't! So what, anyway? You said these dogs are killers. You're scared of them too and you know it.'

'They *are* killers and they can smell fear. They'd kill you if they got the chance. They wouldn't tangle with me because they know I don't get scared by anything. You're scared of shadows.'

'You think you're so great, don't you?' Jimmy shrugs, doing it to goad. Seb says, 'If you're so macho, why don't you jump down? Show those mutts who's boss.'

Jimmy looks at Manson and Ripper. They stare back, perhaps benignly, perhaps not. 'I could if I wanted, but it'd be trespassing and breaking the law, y'know? What's the point?'

Seb smiles. 'You're full of it. I *dare* you to go down there.'

'And do what?'

'Get from here to the gate and I'll believe you're as hard as you want to be.'

'What if the gate's locked?'

'Climb it. The dogs can't follow then. You don't have to if *you're* scared.'

Jimmy gazes down at the grass. He almost makes the right choice, before looking at Seb's triumphant expression. 'I'll do it.'

Seb momentarily feels bad. 'Really? You don't have to.'

'I'm not chickenshit like you.'

Seb gestures below. 'Go for it.'

The yard is about fifty feet by a hundred. The gate, leading to the front lawn, is at the furthest corner with, from clockwise, the doghouses, the tree, and the shed marking the other corners. Jimmy's challenge is to cut diagonally across the yard without Manson catching him. Ripper's reach appears limited by that chain.

He tries to create a diversion by throwing a twig in the direction of the shed. It sails over Manson's head as he remains focused on Jimmy, who dangles from the branch with his arms elongated, then drops to the ground. His ankle turns on landing. Somehow it's fine, only a jolt. He's in. Now it's time to get out.

He runs faster than he knew he could. Looking to his left would slow him down, so he keeps his eyes on the gate, but he's aware Manson is incoming – with his bobbing eyes and hanging jaw and his gluttonous load of teeth – because of his low grunts and Seb's rising shouts: 'Run! Jimmmy, runnn!' Manson is clever enough to run not to where Jimmy is but to where he's going. Seb yells, 'Watch out!'

It's enough of a warning that when Manson careers in front of him, Jimmy is able to react astoundingly and leap over him, nearly clipping the open maw underneath with the sole of his runner. Manson slows to turn around while Jimmy is accelerating, his hand stretched out. He's so very close to escaping when he feels Manson bite his calf, pulling his leg out from under him. He loses control of his spinning body and it's his forehead, and not his hand, that meets the gate with a clang. The pavement at the base delivers the knockout punch, a stinger to the chin and cheek.

Jimmy is in the dark as Manson nudges him with his paws and snout. He presses his face to Jimmy's and there's something intimate about how their moist breath mingles. He takes a last sniff of his prey, then leaves him be, trotting back to the patch of grass by the shed, where he lies with his head on his paws, his eyes only half open.

Seb shouts, 'Jimmy, get up! Help! Somebody help!'

Manson silences Seb with a bark and a sinister look. Seb doesn't know what to do. Jimmy's chest looks like it's faintly quivering, but it's hard to tell for sure. What if he's dead? Oh God. Oh God. Stop. Don't be a baby. Seb wants to be brave and do the right thing, but if he jumps down to save Jimmy, Manson will probably get him too and they'd both be goners before anyone could discover it. Like Larry. Finding adult help means leaving Jimmy behind, and if Seb does that, he may never see him again and it'll be all his fault, and even if he never tells anyone about the dare, they'll know.

Manson is disregarding Jimmy at the moment, so maybe there's time to get Tighe if he goes right away. He has to. 'Jimmy, I'm sorry! I'm getting help! I'll be back!' Seb shoots Manson a bitter look, mutters, 'Son of a bitch,' and scrambles down the tree to the field on the safe side of the fence. Then he's off, running back towards the Diaz house.

As I wait, I become restless. I'm curious about where Old MacGrath is. There has been no sign of him despite Seb's shouting and all the barking, suggesting he's not in, but then MacGrath doesn't get out much. There's a window within my reach. I take a look. It's the living room. Then I'm inside, as far as I can go, and through the doorway there's something that explains the grimy film floating on the cup of tea cobwebbed to a tray, and the plate of mouldy toast.

I see tartan slippers, socks that look like they're made from Brillo pads, grey-and-blue-striped pyjama pants, and a russet bathrobe that isn't in full view because it's obstructed at the chest by the door frame. I see his withered hand, thick-veined and purple, his gnarled fingers and yellowed fingernails. This is the first dead body I've seen since Paul, though Paul doesn't really tally as an experience of the dead because I was too young and didn't know who I was yet. I want to get closer to see what happens if I try to go into MacGrath's eyes, but I can't.

I pull back. A dead Old MacGrath bodes badly because it means Manson and Ripper haven't been fed any time recently, and there lies Jimmy, practically on a platter. But it seems to be okay. Manson's eyes are closed now, and even if he isn't asleep, he doesn't look like he's readying to chow down. And Ripper . . . Damn. Jimmy, Seb, and I, we made a mistake. We saw one thing and presumed another. The chain attached to Ripper's collar doesn't mean he's chained up. He isn't. He's approaching now, bone discarded, his teeth sharp enough; the two-foot chain, broken off at one of its links, drags flaccidly beside him. On further inspection, there's a metal pole embedded in the ground not far from the doghouses, and the other end of the chain is tied to it. I realise I saw this earlier. I just didn't grasp its implications.

Ripper is a brute. The silver hairs on his chin and on his ears may mean he's old, but he's also eighty pounds of bulk. His mangy coat is like a layer of leather armour. Those croco-dile eyes of his, those bone-pulping teeth, shimmer with malice. If only I could shout at Jimmy to wake up, there'd still be time to escape or put up a fight.

Closer, closer, then Ripper is here, spittle dripping from his mouth. He demonstrates none of Manson's unhurried curiosity as he bites hard on the heel of Jimmy's shoe. Snorting at the disagreeable taste, he releases and reassesses for a new point of attack. He picks Jimmy's calf, where there are two punctures in the jeans from Manson's effort. He tears strips of denim off the leg until the soft flesh is exposed. Manson's bite hadn't even pierced the skin. It was a love bite compared to what Ripper is about to do as he opens his jaws wide and crunches them around Jimmy's leg. Blood sprinkles the dog's white head and back, inciting him even more.

Jimmy opens his eyes. The pain is so much more severe than any sensation he has ever experienced before that for a moment he doesn't understand that this is his *pain. He looks up. 'Tighe . . .'*

His brother is there, watery, behind the bars, prising the bolt from the hole in the wall, shoving the gate open. As he rushes forth, fists clenched, his face comes into focus. His expression is one of both revulsion and resolve. He roars. Jimmy smiles, sickly, and blacks out.

I watch the killing.

Chapter Eight

Bravery and the Freak Show

April 1988

THE BIGGER DOG, THE ONE CHEWING ON JIMMY'S LEG, Ripper, needs to be dispatched before the second can attack. Tighe is confident he can take on either of them, but if they gang up, the odds will turn. He charges, yelling at Ripper, making him look up – a morsel of meat is jammed between his teeth – and kicks him in the side of the head, toppling him on to Jimmy's body. Before Ripper can rally, he kicks him again, in the ribs, knocking him off. Seeing out of the corner of his eye that Manson has gotten to his feet, he turns and runs in the direction of the doghouses, where there's a shovel lying in the mud. He grabs it. The head is warped and the wooden handle badly chipped, but it'll serve his purpose. He spins around. Ripper is back up and stepping over Jimmy. Manson is also moving closer.

Suddenly Ripper growls and hurtles at him. Manson is dashing now too, so Tighe only has seconds to incapacitate Ripper. Once he's near enough, Ripper leaps and Tighe times it just right, bashing his face in mid-air with the shovel's blade. Ripper crashes to the ground and Tighe brings the shovel down on the top of his skull, splitting it open.

Manson, almost within reach, slows. Tighe springs towards him and Manson snarls, then flees. Tighe chases him to the shed, where the dog is compelled to turn. Tighe hoists the shovel behind his head and is about to swing but Manson pounces, chiselling teeth into his left forearm, forcing him to drop it. With his right fist he punches Manson in the throat. As the dog collapses, gagging and rasping, he picks up the shovel and delivers three hard blows, only the first of which is necessary. Gazing down, he sees slivers of bone and a section of blood-soaked brain, and he feels powerful.

He hears whimpering. Seb is standing over Jimmy. Afraid to touch him, he cries, 'Jimmy, I'm sorry!'

Tighe approaches, his heart hammering and his aching hands still clutching the bloodied shovel. Seb steps back – he arrived in time to see the second slaying, and Tighe is now scarier than the dogs. Tighe drops the shovel. Aggravated by Seb's weakness, he says, 'Stop your weeping. I need to get into the house to call an ambulance. Can you stay here with Jimmy?'

Still sniffling, Seb says, 'This is all my fault.'

'Worry about that later. For now, shut up and do what you can for Jimmy. Try and keep the bleeding under control. Got it?'

Seb nods. Tighe goes through the gate and around to the front door. There's no point in ringing the doorbell – if there was anyone to answer it, they would have come out to see what was happening by now. On either side of the door are columned frosted-glass panels. Tighe curses himself when he realises that he should have brought the shovel. He picks up a rock and smashes the panel closest to the lock, slashing his hand in the process. He reaches in, unlocks the door, and shoves it open, sweeping back a pile of post.

Inside, the stench is appalling. With his hand covering his

mouth and nose, he guesses, before turning into the hallway, what he's about to find.

He doesn't flinch when he's proved right. Instead, he gets down on his haunches to observe how bloated and bug-eyed Old MacGrath's face is. His coal slug-tongue protrudes from between his teeth, and whatever his cause of death, he possesses a look of great shock. Tighe puts out his hand to touch him, but stops short. Best not to get blood on the corpse, and he doesn't have time for this anyway. He stands up and sidles past.

In the kitchen, he discovers the phone. He dials emergency services and coolly tells the operator about Jimmy's condition. He'll wait for the ambulance to arrive before he explains about the dead dogs and the dead old man.

Seb has taken off and balled up his T-shirt, and he's using it to press down with both hands on Jimmy's butchered leg. There's just so much blood, so he's looking away to Jimmy's eerily peaceful face; his closed eyelids have no wrinkles.

I'm terrified that he's about to die, but to be honest, I'm also intrigued about what will happen to me if he does. Will I be condemned to sharing a coffin with his corpse as he rots until he's dust? Maybe we're bound until that dust is scattered, dispersing my consciousness with it. Maybe we would get to meet, two ghost wisps conversing, and I won't be alone any longer. It might be simpler than that: if he dies, I might be erased too. This could be my demise I'm observing, my prolonged accident of an existence on a precipice not of my choosing. And there's the possibility I may become free; I may be able to cleave myself from my ball and chain – I'm sorry to use this phrase, but it's what Jimmy is – and soar in any direction. I could leave this town and this island, and journey

into the stars. I'm getting carried away, but here's one more
selfish thought: maybe I would get to be reborn in an actual
heart-beating, hungry body, and it would be my turn to live.

But if I could have a say in it, I would choose for him to be
saved. Let's face it: his life is fleeting. Eventually I'll have my
questions answered. If I had palms to place together, and a head
to bow, I would pray into the void. Don't let him go. Please.

'There you are. That's it. Open your eyes. How are you feeling?'

A woman in white towers over Jimmy, swaying in close and back out again while the room revolves, its features pulsating and changing hue. He attempts to withdraw to the dark, but the insides of his eyelids glow red and he can make out forking electric images. Teeth. He reopens his eyes, semi-aware they're unreliable. The woman seems so disproportionate, like a bowling pin, with her expansive hips and slender face. There's benevolence in her eyes, or is that pity?

'You're going to be fine.'

'Horrible.'

She puts her hand to his forehead, mindful of the swelling on the left, her meaty fingers gentle but too hot. It's not just her; he's too hot. Nothing feels right. It's like his body has been swapped with some other boy's. The woman strokes his hair. 'Don't worry, Jimmy. The worst is over.'

He wants to shout, but he's terrified. A few viscous tears slither down his puffy cheeks. He knows he can't control his voice properly – as if he has multiple voices competing to speak, and all of them are being stifled – but he manages, 'D-Daddy?'

The woman – a nurse? – forces a chuckle. 'He's been with you this entire time. He went to get a coffee. Should be back any minute.'

He tries on a smile, then sleep curls in on him, tugging vigorously, and he's buried in it.

Sitting in a chair at Jimmy's bedside, Eamon looks asleep, but his eyes are only closed because it makes him feel calmer. Jimmy says, 'Dad.'

Eamon opens his eyes and quickly stands up. 'Jim, you're awake. Thank God.'

'My head is thumping.'

'I'll get the nurse. She'll bring something for you.'

'What happened to me?'

Eamon's eyes fill with tears. 'You were attacked by Diarmaid MacGrath's dogs. They got you pretty bad, but Tighe saved you. He made sure those dogs will never harm anyone again. Dogs like that should never be kept. They're a callous breed and, see, they hadn't been fed in a long time. They were very desperate. Jim, you weren't fortunate. By the time you got to the hospital, you'd lost a lot of blood. They didn't know if you'd pull through. They underestimated you, though. You're a tough boy. You're in no danger now. But . . .'

'Dad, why are you crying? You said I'll be fine so there's no reason to be sad. I'm sorry I went into the yard. Don't be angry.'

Eamon wipes his tears away. Smiling shakily, he says, 'You didn't do anything to deserve what happened to you.' Jimmy is worried because he has never seen his father like this. Eamon squeezes his hand. 'They had to amputate . . . to remove your right leg from just above the knee. You'd have died if they hadn't. We're going to get you a new leg, a prosthesis. You'll still be normal, and this setback – it won't stop you from doing whatever you want. There'll be no stopping you.'

'Dad, Dad, it's okay. I think they must've gotten mixed up

and told you about another kid. I can still feel my leg. I can even wiggle my toes.'

Eamon flinches and Jimmy looks down at himself, seeing his whole left leg extending under the snowy blanket as far as it should, next to his right leg, which only extends to a jutting lump where his knee is meant to be. After that, there's a hideous flatness. Eamon tightens his hold on Jimmy's hand, but he pulls free and heaves off the blanket. He sees the stump, swathed in wads of bandage, and tries to grasp what this means. Inevitably, he screams.

A couple of hours after Jimmy first looked under the covers, his second visitor knocks on the open door, interrupting a pep talk from Eamon. Tighe isn't the only one who wants to see him, but because of his heroism, he has been bumped up the queue. He stands in the doorway, a thin book in his hand. Despite the fact that his left hand and arm are bandaged from knuckles to elbow, his posture is relaxed. 'How are you, Jimmy?'

Conscious of his father's scrutiny, and feeling guilty for screaming earlier, Jimmy affects a smile.

Tighe says, 'Dad, why don't you shoot off and give me some time with him?'

On Eamon's way out, he and Tighe exchange words, whispering so Jimmy can't hear. Eamon says, 'How's your mother?'

'I'm not going to lie to you. She's in pieces.'

'Is she coming?'

'Simon's been trying to persuade her, but then he thought it'd be better to get her to calm down first, so he gave her sleeping pills. She's probably asleep now.'

Without much conviction Eamon says, 'She'll be fine once she's had a rest.'

86

'You need it too.'

'Don't worry about me.' He hugs Tighe, says, 'You saved us all yesterday,' and leaves.

Tighe pulls back the window curtains. The sun makes the room fuller and whiter. He takes over Eamon's seat. 'You in pain?'

Jimmy says, 'Not too much. I can still feel my leg. Sometimes it's like one of the dogs is biting me there, even though that's silly. The worst bit is my foot gets itchy, but I can't scratch it. Like, I know this isn't all a nightmare, but it makes me wonder. Weird, huh?'

'I read once that a lot of amputees get that. They call it "phantom limb". It's like the ghost of your leg is always with you. Something to do with nerve endings.'

Being referred to as an amputee makes Jimmy feel like crying. 'Dad said I'd be dead if you hadn't rescued me.'

'That's what I'm here for. You'd do the same for me if you got the chance, right?'

'Definitely, yeah.'

Tighe was going to wait before bringing this up, but he's not one to miss an opening. 'There is a small favour you could do for me that'd help a lot. Remember the deal we made? I let you and Seb go exploring, and you were supposed to keep it quiet that I was having Isabel over. Well, as far as Mam and Dad know, you and Seb sneaked out without my permission. That's what they assumed. All I want is for you to not tell them any different. They don't blame you for leaving the house – you were just being a kid – and all they care about now is your recovery, so it's not like you could get in trouble for it. The thing is, I could. It'd upset them more than they already are, and no one wants that. It would hurt Isabel too – she really liked you, by the way – and so she obviously won't say a word about it to anyone. I already spoke to Seb. He gets that it's for the best. Do you mind?'

'I won't say anything, I promise.'

'Good lad.'

'It was stupid of me to go into the yard. I thought I could outrun them.'

'Don't think about that now. It's over.'

'Did Ripper do that?' Jimmy gestures to Tighe's arm. 'Is it bad?'

'Ripper?'

'The big one.'

'Nah, it was the smaller one.' Tighe raises his forearm to his shoulder and rotates his wrist. 'See? All in working order. They gave me a shot last night so I won't have rabies. Big fucking needle.' He laughs. 'But nothing I couldn't handle.'

'You could handle anything.'

'Maybe. Hey, I brought you something.' Tighe shows Jimmy the book he's carrying. The illustration on the cover is of a yellow-haired boy wearing green. He's standing on a miniature purple moon set against a white sky speckled with yellow stars. 'This was my favourite book when I was your age. Want me to read it to you?'

'Yeah, cool.' Jimmy yawns.

I'm going to listen instead of reading ahead, but before Tighe finishes the first sentence – 'Once when I was six years old I saw a magnificent picture . . .' – Jimmy is asleep. Tighe closes the book, spoiling my chance at a story fix. It'll spend the day on the bedside locker, untouched.

When Jimmy next wakes, in the early afternoon, Maggie is in the chair. Her eyes are pinkish, her fingers interlocked. Art is standing stiffly with his hand on her shoulder. Jimmy wonders if someone forgot to inform them of his survival. 'Granny? Abuelo? It's okay. I . . .'

Maggie winds him with a hug. Art waits a few moments then says, 'Maggie, be careful. He might be tender.'

Alarmed, she releases him and sits back down. Jimmy says, 'I'm all right. Really, Granny.'

'We thought we might have lost you, like poor Paul. Thank God for the doctors, those talented men, and for Tighe, a guardian angel he was. And thank God this wasn't your time. I'm sure He must have great things planned for you.' Maggie shudders and tears come faster than she can wipe them away. 'Great things. You won't have to dwell on this misfortune because your life is going to be so full. You'll have a w-wonderful future, you poor, poor child.' As she speaks, her gaze shunts to and fro from his eyes to his stump. 'The pain isn't too awful, Jimmy, is it?'

'I don't have any pain. None at all, I swear.'

Despite getting the answer she wanted, she places her head in her hands. Art puts his arm around her and helps her stand. She burrows her face between his shoulder and neck and he holds her. Jimmy is taken aback, not only to see his grandmother this upset but also because he has never seen his grandparents display such affection for one another.

Art says to Jimmy, 'Granny has had a small fright. She'll be fine.' He leads her out. 'I'll be right back.'

When he returns a few minutes later, he takes his turn in the worry chair and interlocks his fingers, as Maggie had done, but he doesn't intend to pray. 'Granny has gone for some air. There's no need to concern yourself.'

'She was crying because of me.'

'Because she loves you. Knowing you're getting better has made her very happy.'

'I don't think she's happy.'

Art sees from Jimmy's penitent expression that he's going to have to try again. 'Have you ever watched your mother when she has something boiling in a pot?'

'Like potatoes?'

'Yes. Like potatoes. Good. When the lid is on too long, sometimes it trembles because of the heat, so you lift the lid off and the bubbling of the water settles down, but if the lid is not lifted, the water may spill over on to the cooker and the floor. An avoidable messy accident. Perhaps you see where I'm going?'

This parallel sounded more elegant in Art's mind, but Jimmy stares at him blankly, then shakes his head. It occurs to Jimmy that his grandmother might be upset because she ruined Sunday dinner.

Art says, 'When you were in surgery last night, we didn't know what the outcome would be, so Maggie was holding her breath. We were all keeping the lid on, so to speak. Just seeing you awake and, ah, fighting fit was a huge relief for her. It was like taking the lid off, but when you release pressure there's often a dramatic reaction, like when all the steam from the potatoes rushes out, or in your Granny's case, a big need to cry. But it was good crying and she would be much worse off, all of us would be, if you weren't such a fighter. Understand?'

'Yes, Abuelo.'

Maggie returns, her eyes clear. She apologises to Jimmy excessively and gushes about his bravery. She says to Art, 'Isn't he such a brave boy?'

Art ruffles Jimmy's hair. 'As brave as the bravest men I fought with in Spain.'

Jimmy thanks them, then pretends to fall asleep. Reassuring

his grandparents that they're successfully reassuring him is hard work.

He's visited by a nurse, and shortly afterwards by a doctor. They ask if he's in any pain. He lies that he isn't because Art and Maggie are there, but the nurse gives him painkillers anyway. When the doctor tells him what a special boy he is, Maggie says, 'So special!'

Eamon enters as dinner is being served, supplanting Art and Maggie, who promise to be back tomorrow. Eamon is still looking worn out, but less so after permitting himself an hour's nap. 'How's your meal, Jim? Looks good.'

The chicken is overdone, the potatoes are soggy, and the peas and corn are shrivelled. Jimmy swallows his mouthful with a chug of water. 'Yum.'

'Do you think you'd be able for any more visitors?'

Sounding more eager than he means to, Jimmy says, 'Is Mam going to come?'

'I'm afraid not. She's exhausted today. Maybe tomorrow. It depends.'

'Oh.'

'She was here with you during the night, holding your hand. You don't remember because you were asleep.'

'I think I remember a little bit.' Now they're both lying.

'If you want, and only if you're not too tired, Elizabeth would like to see you, and also Seb's mam said he wants to come in. Would you like that? I could go ring Mrs Quinn now and tell her.'

Jimmy agrees, and within an hour of Eamon's phone call, Seb is standing in the doorway, his mother behind him. They have a seriousness in common, with their pinched lips and dilated nostrils. Seb's mother nudges him forward. 'Hey, Jimmy.'

'Hey, Seb.'

Eamon stands. 'Michelle, maybe we should get some coffee and let the boys catch up.'

'Good idea.' To Jimmy she says, 'I'm pleased to see you're looking so strong.' Her face reddens as she feels a flood of gratitude that this has happened to him and not to Seb. She turns away, not too abruptly she hopes, and leaves with Eamon.

Seb sits, wringing his hands, and he and Jimmy are silent. They seem much older than they did before their misadventure. Finally Jimmy says, 'Thanks for coming.'

Seb pleads, 'If I could, I'd give you my leg instead.'

'I'd rather you have both of yours. It's not so bad for me. I kinda deserve this.'

'No you don't.' Silence weighs between them again before Seb says, 'You're my best friend, Jimmy.'

'You're mine too.'

After Seb and Michelle have departed, it's Elizabeth's turn. Art drives her to St John's. When they pull into the car park, night has fallen. He says, 'I'll be here when you're ready.'

Elizabeth, who, despite having recently turned fourteen, still has her hair in pigtails and is wearing a pink Mickey Mouse T-shirt, says, 'B-but don't you want to see him?'

Art refrains from being curt – she has been so indulged that even the idea of walking alone from the car into the hospital agitates her – and replies, 'I've already said goodbye for the day. He'll like it if you visit him by yourself.'

'Okay, Abuelo. I won't be long.' She fumbles with the lock and he leans over her to pull up the catch. She apologises, then exits the car and goes inside. He sighs and switches on the radio.

Elizabeth meets Eamon in the hallway outside the room. He smiles doggedly and hugs her. She can sense how fearful he is, not just for Jimmy, but for her as well, because if something so terrible could befall her brother, then she's even more vulnerable than he had previously realised.

Before he can ask, she says firmly, 'Don't worry, I'm holding up fine. How's Jimmy?'

'He has been incredibly resilient, but he needs us. He's asleep now. You can pop in, though, and see him if you're quiet.'

Eamon leaves to go tell Art that he'll remain at the hospital tonight, and to check, unnecessarily, that he doesn't mind having Tighe and Elizabeth stay with him and Maggie.

In Jimmy's room, Elizabeth creeps close to him, synchronising her breathing with his. The lights are off, but the full moon is shining through the window. His eyelids are scrunched, and he sucks air noisily through his mouth and pumps it out. She kisses his cheek lightly and whispers, almost inaudibly, 'We love you.' Then she sits on the chair, without a squeak.

She's taken in by his pretence of being asleep. Jimmy believes he can feel her watching him, but doesn't hear her. As the minutes tick by, he's tempted to open his eyes and confirm she's still there. He's about to when he feels his blanket shift and slowly rise away from his chest, then from his lower body. Spiky air probes his bare whole leg and his mummified stump. He cracks open his eyes and, squinting, sees Elizabeth standing there, pulling the blanket up by its hem. Her rapt grimace as she stares at his stump is positively ghoulish.

Chapter Nine

Fantasy

I
June 1960

GRACE, AGED FIFTEEN, LIES IN HER NARROW BED, WITH her blanket on the floor. Her legs are bound by the twist of the bed sheet. She's on her side, one eye pressed into the warm pillow. Her other eye stares into the darkness beyond the open window. She has pulled her nightdress up and her hand is in her underwear, two fingers rubbing. What she's doing doesn't feel wrong; it feels good.

She doesn't have a name for this, but she isn't the only one who does it. Her best friend, Cliona, is a sinner like her. They tell each other their fantasies. They laughed together, in tears, when Cliona told her about imagining it with Father Theodore, and when night fell, Grace imagined her hand was his, commanding repentance. He has been the best so far. At her next confession, she confessed none of it. She sensed her coy smile caused him some confusion.

Tonight, the object of her desire is Cliona's father. Mr Devoy's ears stick out as if they're attached to his head sideways, but she likes those fingers of his, which stretch out long.

She pictures his beard scratching her neck, him gasping into her ear, and their skin burning on contact.

She hears the sudden thumping of boots, and before she can turn, she's punched in the back and cries out as she tumbles off the bed. Her hand slaps the floor. Her forehead crunches her hand. She inhales dust, and coughs, tasting blood. Her foot is tangled in the sheet, but she wrenches it free. She hears heavy breathing. Sliding her good hand underneath her, she tugs her nightdress down over her body. She gets to her knees and stands, using the bed for support. She faces her father.

He has acquired a habit of not looking at her directly, but he's glaring at her now, his eyes swelling and his thin lips seeming to disappear as his teeth clench. She doesn't flinch, not even when, voice rising, he says, 'God help you. How can you look at your father like that?'

Dorothy appears in the doorway wearing her billowy white nightdress. Her confusion evident, she says, 'Peter, what's going on? Are you all right, Grace?'

Peter turns and strides towards her, his boots banging on the floorboards. She back-steps into the hallway. He grabs her wrist and neck and throws her against the wall. He yells, 'No, she's not all right! She's . . .' He slaps her face. 'Just . . .' Slap. 'Like . . .' Slap. 'You!'

After his fourth slap, Dorothy crumples to the floor and curls her knees into her body.

Grace hurls herself at Peter. He grabs her face in one hand, his thumb under her cheekbone, and pushes her all the way to her bed, which she falls on to with a bounce. When she tries to get up, he shoves her down again. 'I am leaving this house! I am washing my hands! Of you!' He marches into the hallway, steps over Dorothy, and goes into their bedroom.

Grace hears him jerk open drawers and rip out clothes. She scurries over to Dorothy.

'Mam, please.'

As Grace helps her to her feet, Dorothy says, 'You're all right, aren't you, dear?'

'Everything's fine.' Grace guides her into her bedroom and gets her to sit on the bed. She closes the door, then wedges a chair against the handle. They climb into bed and hold each other. Grace stares at the handle, but it doesn't budge.

There's more banging, and doors slam.

When it has been quiet for a long time, and daylight is filtering into her room, Grace gets out of bed, careful not to wake Dorothy. She removes the chair and ventures into the hallway. She checks every room. He's gone.

II
June 1960–May 1965

Dorothy's sanity retreats piece by piece and Grace loses her, despite continually being at her side. Some days there are little victories, where there's a hint of improvement, but they are always temporary and time is a cruel enemy. The point of no return, as Grace views it, is the sunny morning her mother walks right out the front door completely naked and with her head held high. Her neighbours watch from their windows – they *gawk*, rather, and some laugh – but none of them intervene. She makes it all the way to the top of her street before Grace catches up, covers her with a blanket, and brings her home, where she tends to the cuts on the soles of her feet. The worst thing is how happy Dorothy had appeared, the oblivion in her eyes and smile. Grace phones Simon for help, and that afternoon they check her into St Augustine's.

One day, when Grace is visiting her and they are sitting in the oval garden – which is surrounded by the hospital buildings, notable for their barred windows – Dorothy has a rare lucid moment. She clutches her daughter's hand and says desperately, 'Promise me one thing.'

'Anything, Mam.'

'Leave me, and this town, and don't come back.'

Grace goes to see Simon in his big new house, where he lives with his new wife Sarah, and tells him what her mother said. Over a brandy each in his drawing room she asks, 'How do I know she meant it?'

He tells her, 'You just do, because you knew her when she wasn't sick. If you can't shake your doubts, take her brother's word for it: she wants you to be free and you don't owe anyone anything. If you'll pardon my French, fuck what the naysayers think.'

Simon – with his blessing, and financial aid, and his promise to ensure that Dorothy will continue to receive the best care available – makes it possible for Grace to leave for America, and so she does.

III
July 1967–May 1969

'This will be good for us. You'll see.'

Stan, lying propped on his forearm, strokes Grace's curls – her fair hair has been bleached golden by her two years under the Californian sun. She's wearing sunglasses and, wishing to look into her eyes, he begins to lift them off. She touches his wrist. 'Don't.'

He spreads his hand on her bare belly and she exhales. He says, 'You want to, right? It's something we can truly share.'

She shifts on the beach mat and tilts her chin so his shadow doesn't block the sun. 'I only say yes to things I want to do. I *like* that it's unconventional. It's probably natural. And it doesn't have to change anything about how we feel about one another.'

'Do you know how much I love you?'

'You love me as much as I let you.'

'Do *you* love *me*?'

She flips over, unclasps her swimsuit top, and lifts her feet in the air. 'Do my back.'

He sits up on his knees and takes the sunscreen tube from their hamper. He squirts some on her spine, making a flatulent noise. They laugh. He rubs, beginning with the exposed sides of her breasts. 'Well? Do you?'

She cocks her head back. 'You're so needy!' He tries to look offended, sticking out his lower lip. 'You're such a sand magnet! There are grains all over your chest and in your stubble.' She doesn't mention the sand in his hair, because he's sensitive to any attention being directed to his receding hairline. 'I don't know what to make of you.' She turns her face to the mat, resting her chin on her hands.

He massages the sunscreen into the small of her back. 'Don't be mean. Tell me you love me.'

'I don't have to. Tonight I'm going to *show* you.'

After hours of lolling around on the beach, they go to his modest one-bedroom apartment – it's all he can afford on the severance package his Midwestern university gave him, minus the alimony he pays to his ex-wife and young children. They eat croissants and shower together, then, running late now, they get into his station wagon and take the freeway to John Wayne Airport.

As he drives, he tongues a toothpick from one side of his

mouth to the other. She watches him while smoking a joint. Her arm is on the rolled-down passenger window, her elbow buffeting air. She hates his toothpick habit – she imagines him swallowing it, the point cutting into his throat. She has never hassled him about it, though. She figures it's more of a hang-up of hers than a real danger to him. In turn, he doesn't like her smoking in the station wagon but wouldn't dare argue about it now and risk spoiling her amenable mood.

She fiddles with the radio dial, stopping when she comes to a station playing 'San Francisco'. Yes, in Grace's opinion it's a great song, or it was the first hundred times she heard it. She could, however, do without listening to it five times a day, and especially without Stan singing along. When he launches into the chorus, she puts her palm to her forehead and says, 'You have your talents, Stan, but for the love of God, stop!'

He makes a zipper-pulling motion across his mouth. She takes a drag of her joint and blows smoke in his face.

Standing at the arrivals gate with her arms folded, she assesses every pretty woman who appears to be between twenty and thirty – Stan's basic criteria for potential 'soulmates'; he's forty-eight. She indicates a woman in flares with straight black hair down past her ass. 'Her?'

'Try again.' His face lighting up, Stan calls out, 'Judy!'

An Asian woman with short boyish hair, her thumb hooked in the strap of her bulky backpack, meets his eye and waves. Spotting Grace, she looks her over. As Judy approaches, Grace whispers to Stan, 'You never told me she was Chinese.'

'Is that a problem? I don't see people as belonging to a race. Besides, she's not Chinese anyway. She's Japanese American.'

He steps forward to meet her. Judy drops her backpack to

the ground. 'Hey!' As he leans down to hug her, she wraps her hand around his neck and kisses him on the mouth. When they separate, her lips are glistening. 'Missed you.' Turning to Grace, she says, 'Is this her?' Stan nods. 'Wow. She *is* beautiful.'

Grace offers her hand. Judy hugs her instead. Grace can feel that she's bra-less underneath her T-shirt. She mumbles, 'Nice to meet you,' and kisses her cheek.

Judy returns the kiss to Grace's lips. Grace blushes. Judy laughs. 'I think I'm going to like you.' She says to Stan, 'Where to? I could kill for a martini.'

He says, 'We could check out the Elephant Room – it's far out, I swear, and it'd be the perfect place for you two to get acquainted.'

'Sounds good, huh, Grace?'

There's a smugness in Judy's expression and Stan is grinning like a dope, but still Grace says, 'Works for me. Sure.'

Stan slings Judy's backpack over his shoulder and they make their way to the exit. The women are hand-in-hand, but Grace is avoiding Judy's gaze. As they step into the sun, Judy says, 'She's real cute, Stan.' To Grace she says, 'You got some of that Irish fire, huh?' Grace hesitates. 'Are you shy around me, sweetie?'

Grace stops walking and looks Judy in the eyes. 'Shy?' Then she puts her hands to Judy's cheeks and kisses her, sliding her tongue in as soon as Judy parts her lips to take a breath.

The next morning Grace wakes with a horrendous headache, a snoring body to either side of her, and the memory of a night she's already regretting. Though she had tried to act as if they were all sharing equally in some collective triumph over archaic societal norms, she didn't appreciate how Stan and Judy had looked at her, as if they'd won something from her and she wasn't included in the joke of it.

She lives in America for nearly two more years, spending four months of that time with Stan before he dumps her for a nineteen-year-old. There are other Stans after him as well, men who are keen to be of service in her quest for empowerment so long as she doesn't put any restrictions on their behaviour either. She realises that saying yes to everything isn't all that freeing – really, it just creates another kind of prison. Disliking how jaded she feels, she decides to return home, where perhaps she can think more clearly about what she wants from her life. It doesn't have to be forever and at least, she assures herself, she did succeed in fulfilling half of what her mother asked of her.

IV
October 1993

'Jimmy?'

'Y-yeah?'

'Breakfast is ready. Can I come in?'

'No. I haven't put my leg on yet.' Grace is silent. Jimmy says, 'I'll be there in a minute.'

'Don't let it get cold. Okay?'

'One minute.'

In his dream, Jimmy had all of his limbs, at first. He was hovering in the air, fixed in place, and then some invisible force tore off his right leg, blood spouting everywhere, followed by his left. I was not that force – I'm as powerless in his dreams as I am in his reality. He still couldn't move as the same thing happened to his arms, with more blood raining, and he could feel the tendons in his neck snapping as his head was pulled from his torso. Somewhere nearby, Tighe and Elizabeth were watching him, in cahoots and roaring with laughter.

His body is pinned to his bed and his mind is slowly cutting
through the nightmare vapour. When he wakes like this, both
roiled and drained, he feels like a substantial part of himself
remains left behind. As he goes about his day, he'll forget every
detail of what he dreamed. I won't, though. I never forget anything.

With great effort, he reaches out and presses play on the tape
recorder on his bedside locker. As Kurt sings about teen spirit,
Jimmy sits up and, with his left leg hanging off the bed, pulls
a silicone liner over his stump, then fits it into the socket valve
at the top of his artificial knee and tightens it with the knob at
the side. This is his third prosthetic. He got it a month ago,
after a summer growth spurt. It's lighter than his previous
ones and doesn't squeak. To someone who doesn't know better,
he appears to just have a very slight limp.

When he enters the kitchen, Eamon is kissing Grace's cheek
as she stands at the sink scrubbing the pot she used to make
porridge. She smiles without looking up. Hands on her waist,
Eamon says, 'Happy anniversary.'

'You've already told me twice.'

'I like saying it, I suppose.'

Jimmy had forgotten what date it is today – if Tighe or
Elizabeth still lived at home, they'd have reminded him – but
he musters some enthusiasm and says, 'Happy anniversary!'

Eamon and Grace turn, looking for a moment like an ideal
couple, comfortable together and mutually affectionate after
twenty-three years of marriage. Then he drops his hands from
her waist and comes to sit at the table, while she turns back
to the sink.

She keeps her hair shorter these days, about an inch above
her shoulders. This afternoon she has an appointment at the
hairdresser's to have it straightened and dyed blonde, but her

roots are currently quite grey. She's wearing her bathrobe and hasn't put her make-up on yet. Once Eamon and Jimmy leave, she'll apply a face.

Eamon doesn't like how much make-up she wears. He prefers her with those wrinkles around her eyes but won't tell her that, or how he misses her curls.

Jimmy is wearing the shorts he slept in, so his prosthetic is exposed. He knows that in the more than five years since he got his first one, his mother still hasn't gotten used to it, but that hasn't made him alter his routine of eating breakfast before changing into his uniform. It's his way of daring her to accept his abnormality.

When there's nothing else to wash or dry, Grace sits at the table. Her stomach is typically uneasy for a few hours after she wakes, so she doesn't eat before lunch. She sips her tepid tea and observes her husband and son. They both sprinkle sugar on their porridge, consume it in about the same number of spoonfuls, then spread butter evenly on their toast, eating the crusts last. Their cups of tea – dash of milk, with sugar – aren't touched until they've finished eating. They seem unaware that they're mirroring each other.

Eamon asks, 'You know we're going out for dinner this evening?'

Jimmy says, 'I remember.'

'Isabel said she can babysit. If that's okay?'

Eamon would be open to letting Jimmy stay home alone, but he answers, 'Yep.'

'Want to invite a friend over?'

'Nope. I should get my homework done and not leave it all till Sunday night.'

'You listen to me then.'

'Yep.'

Grace smiles. She knows Jimmy doesn't really plan on doing homework. To her, his crush on Isabel is obvious.

Jimmy has been in secondary school for less than two months and hates it. The other boys claim to as well, but as he walks into the grey yard, enclosed by grey buildings, he thinks most of them are lying. They stand around laughing in scattered cabalistic groups, or they're playing football. Backpacks are being used as goalposts. School blazers hang from the railings.

He spots his friends by the bike shed. Seb, Brian, and Finbar have been trading football stickers, but as he approaches they shove their albums into their backpacks. To no one specifically he says, 'How're tricks?'

Brian, who looks about three years younger than his age and whose voice is unbroken, says, 'I was telling Seb what a great ride his mother is. There's nothing she won't do.'

Seb says, 'You're just mad at me for having a foursome with your mother and your sisters.'

Finbar laughs, showing off his train-track teeth metal. 'But the fat one's a hippo!'

Brian says, 'Shut up, Finbar! She can't help her glands.'

The bell rings and the boys line up. Seb stands next to Jimmy and they wait to march inside. Seb is about four inches shorter than Jimmy. Six months ago, it was two inches, and in another six months it will be back to two inches again. His hair is asymmetrically long on one side. A few other boys at St Bonaventure's also have this style, violating the rule that hair should be short and of equal length all over. The crackdown has yet to come. Most say they wouldn't cut their hair if ordered – 'I don't give a fuck' is regularly boasted – but most would if threatened with suspension. Seb sweeps the hair from his forehead to behind his ear and whispers to Jimmy, 'Want to go see *The Fugitive* tonight?'

'I can't. Family problems, y'know?'

He doesn't feel guilty about using his reflex excuse to get out of something without further explanation – he has earned it. Besides, it irritates him that the mother jokes his friends slag each other with are never directed towards him, and they never mention his leg. When they arrange to meet to play football, they do it when they think he's out of earshot. Even if it's due to misplaced respect, it's still insulting. In his friends' defence, they'd be less wary about his leg if he ever joked about it himself.

Seb says, 'Another time then, when it's better for you.'

'Sha-la-la-la-la-la-la . . . ooh . . . ah, ha!'

Isabel doesn't just sing along to the song; she performs it. Barefoot, she hops up and down – like the living-room floor is a trampoline – except for the sad part in the middle, then she closes her eyes, raises her face to the ceiling, and sways, gliding her fingers through the air. Whenever she doesn't quite know the words, she hums loudly, and when she does know them, the lyrics burst from her lungs.

Jimmy sits on the black-dotted couch. He watches Isabel's frizzy hair, black with crimson stripes, prance. He absorbs her face's soft-cheeked loveliness. The sight of her belly-button piercing as her buttoned cardigan jolts from her midriff is another confirmation of how sexy cool she is. The lift of her skirt, never more than a couple of inches north of her knees, is simultaneously thrilling and frustrating. But her most eye-drawing facet is, somewhat predictably, the globular wonder of her breasts and their perfect bounce. Yes, Jimmy has discovered women. No, he won't ever recover.

Stationary now, Isabel asks, 'Well, what do you think?'

'Wh-what?'

'Of the song! What do you think of it?'

'It's spectacular.'

She beams. 'I want to listen to it again, and this time you're dancing with me.'

'I can't dance.'

'Don't be silly. Is this because of your leg?'

He sighs. 'It's not made for dancing. It's a prop, really.'

'Maybe you just don't want to dance with me.'

'It's not that! I can't, y'know?'

'Let's make a deal. If you properly try for one song, and it's completely impossible, I'll drop it. But you've got to try, okay? It's rude to tell a girl you won't dance with her. You don't want me to think you don't like me, do you?' Jimmy shakes his head and is about to protest again when she says, 'I promise to catch you if you look like you're going to fall.'

He stands. 'I won't fall.'

She smiles and kisses his cheek. Seared by the imprint of her lips, he looks away. 'That's my man!'

She springs as high as she can, all her limbs thrusting. Initially he tries to get away with nodding his head to the music while pumping his fist, but she fastens her hands on to his waist and entices him to swing his hips. He uses his pros-thetic as a pivot as he mixes a few ungainly air-kicks of his whole leg into his dance repertoire. She says, 'Smile! Sing with me! Shout!' He smiles and sings and shouts. They laugh and she's sublime and he doesn't fall.

He believes that if she would keep rooting him on he could overcome anything, and the idea of them being together feels *right*. But although she tries to talk to him like he's an equal, she's twenty and he's only thirteen, so of course she still sees him as Tighe's little brother. She can intuit he has a crush on her and leads him on slightly because it's ego-boosting in a cute way. It doesn't occur to her that this crush could have a sexual element, or that whenever she compliments him, she's nourishing his hopes.

When she's all danced out, she frowns. He laughs. 'What is it?'

'I should be providing you with a better example, but I wanted to ask you . . .'

'Anything.'

'I'm dying for a fag. It's a filthy habit, don't ever smoke, and I shouldn't be doing it either, but would you mind if I had one outside and could you not say anything to your dad? I was going to hold off until you were in bed, but I don't want to deceive you. We're like mates, right?'

'Right. I'll come with you.'

They sit out on the patio chairs. The outdoor lights keep Isabel illuminated, so Jimmy can make out her endearing features, from the high curve of her eyelashes to the brown mole on her neck. As she savours a drag of her cigarette, he says, 'You make decent wages at Hogan's, don't you?'

'Why, need to borrow money? In trouble with loan sharks?'

'No!'

'Waitressing isn't what you'd call a lucrative profession, but I make a living. Why do you ask?'

'I was wondering why you babysit me if you don't need the money. You could be out tonight, having fun.'

'I *am* having fun. You're a pretty cool guy, y'know? Your parents have been good to me so I like helping out, but mainly I like spending time with you. I hope you don't mind having me around.'

'I love having you here!'

He's chuffed, but what did he expect? She's obliged to say she likes babysitting him. As it happens, she does enjoy his company, but she didn't disclose her real motivation. It's all about the boyfriend who got away: Tighe. When they started going out, her parents forbade the relationship, thinking she was too young. Tighe called over to their house to convince them of his honourable intentions. They admired the modesty with which he recalled saving his brother's life – his bandaged arm on full display – and primarily because of that, they changed their minds.

What had happened to Jimmy brought Isabel and Tighe closer in other ways too. She revered him for his bravery and he helped assuage her guilt when she asked whether he would have allowed Jimmy to go off if she hadn't been coming over. Tighe said, 'Kids will be kids no matter what you tell them to do, and if *I* don't feel guilty, after I was the one who gave him permission, why on earth should *you*?'

When Seb came running, yelling for Tighe, they had been in his bedroom and she had taken off her top for him. Before rushing to Jimmy's aid, Tighe told her to go home and to not tell a soul where she'd been. She obeyed his wishes, but afterwards she questioned if she should have been the one to call emergency services; failing that, she could have gone with Tighe and been of help. He laughed at her. 'It was too late for all of that. And what could you have done? Sewn his leg back on? Besides, it worked out fine for him. I think he likes all the attention he gets for it.'

She accepted he was right, most of the time that is.

She had wanted to wait until she was fifteen before losing her virginity, but didn't quite make it. Tighe had a way of pressuring her, talking a lot about respect and love, that didn't seem coercive. When they were alone, and they began to kiss and touch, he would say, 'I'll stop whenever you tell me to.' He was so patient and understanding that, after three months together, she felt like she owed him something, so one evening she didn't tell him to stop. She didn't regret it, not then. It had been painful, but he made her feel special. There didn't seem to be any reason not to keep doing it. The vigour of his appetite was flattering, and while he could be too rough, she never doubted his feelings.

Until they broke up. He was leaving for college, and although she didn't think the distance – about a hundred miles – between Rathbaile and Dublin posed much of a problem, he claimed it wouldn't be fair to her: 'You deserve more than I can give you right now.' When she became upset, he added, 'This doesn't mean we don't have a future together. It just means that future isn't now.' She believed him when he said this too.

Since then, when he has come home for holidays, she has seen him and they've ended up in bed, but he has remained elusive about getting back together. She volunteered to be Jimmy's babysitter because she thought it would increase the odds of a future with Tighe.

She lights another cigarette. 'Do you hear from your brother much?'

Her offhanded tone is so contrived that Jimmy has a sudden insight into where her affections really lie and, just like that, the hammer drops. Eyes stinging, he says, 'Occasionally. He loves it in London. Calls it a "better life". I don't think he'll ever move back.'

'Oh. Is he seeing anyone?'

'It's hard to keep up with his love life. He's probably seeing a few girls.'

She takes a long drag of her cigarette. Pulling it away, she says, 'Good for him.'

Back inside, when she suggests listening to more music,

Jimmy brusquely claims to need an early night. Any suspicion she has that she has upset him is dismissed by how keenly he returns her goodnight hug. She's unaware he's soaking up her smell, and the feel of her body, because he still wants to fantasise about her.

Lying on his bed, wearing shorts now, with his prosthetic off and leaning against the bedside locker, he stares at the curving lamp-cast shadows on the ceiling and imagines how possessing Isabel would be possible. In his scenario, he's whole and taller, and he exudes a kind of carnal charisma. Her exudations are of a more weak-at-the-knees variety. Tighe has tragically passed away in some vaguely emasculating manner. She's indifferent to his death. No, wait. In fact, she's distraught and the only one who can make her feel better is Jimmy. She's with him, after the funeral, on the bed, weeping and pressing her breasts against his chest. His powerful arm is affixed to her supple shoulder. For some reason, she attended the funeral wearing a cleavage-baring few-sizes-too-small schoolgirl uniform, including an outrageously short skirt. He soothes her with the occasional 'there, there' while she applauds him: 'What would I do without your selfless generosity?' Her tears dry when she notices his mammoth erection.

Reality Jimmy, the one with the less mammoth but equally eager erection, yanks open the top drawer of his locker, knocking over his prosthetic, which clatters on the floor. He takes out a handful of tissues. Fantasy Jimmy passionately kisses Fantasy Isabel, melting any silly reservations she might have had about post-funeral statutory-rape etiquette, and rips open her blouse as she applies similar single-mindedness to pulling down his trousers. He's primed to mightily pleasure her when he opens his eyes and sees Reality Isabel standing in his doorway.

She's mortified, but not as much as he is, with one hand clutching tissues, the other clutching his rapidly wilting penis; his criss-cross-scarred stump, where a knee should be, is exposed too. She manages, 'Should've knocked. Sorry, sorry, sorry.'

Then she's out the door, slamming it as she goes, before he can sputter a response, whether it be a puny denial or a scream at her to leave.

I knew she was there – she put her ear to the door after she heard his leg fall over on her way to the bathroom – but I could only wait for the disaster. She thought she could pop her head in without being noticed and didn't knock because, if the noise signified nothing, he could have already been asleep. There's something to be said for having less consideration.

I'm sympathetic to his humiliation, but she won't think any less of him. That doesn't matter, though. A reasonable perspective is inaccessible to him and he can't imagine talking to her again. Turning his face into his pillow, he sobs.

The next morning, as he eats breakfast with his parents, Jimmy is wearing pyjama bottoms instead of his usual shorts. Eamon is across the table from him and Grace is at their side. Her hair is brightly blonde. Jimmy asks, 'You had a good night then?'

Eamon lies, 'Yeah, we did.'

Over their dinner, he had tried to reminisce with Grace about their courtship and the early days of their marriage, and brought up stories of their children growing up, but she seemed to have become allergic to their past – she mainly listened and didn't contribute much. He probably should have known better, but he mentioned Paul, and as soon as he did, she shut him down with a sharp 'Don't.' After that, they just made small talk and endured silences, with his finely honed smile being met by her dispirited eyes.

Eamon asks, 'You and Isabel got on okay?'

Jimmy's eyes widen, but his father doesn't pick up on it. 'Of course, yeah, why? What did she say?'

Eamon chews on his toast. 'Only that you were a model of good behaviour, that you're more of an adult each time she sees you.'

'Ah, Dad? Isabel's super and everything, but I'm getting too old for babysitters. Do you think next time maybe I could stay in by myself?'

'If your mother doesn't mind.' She's gazing at her hands and rotating her wedding ring around her finger. Eamon puts his hand over hers. 'Grace?'

She looks up and brushes her hair from her eyes. 'Yes?'

'You don't mind, do you, if Jimmy doesn't have a babysitter again?'

She shakes her head and gives Jimmy a concerned look, which he doesn't acknowledge.

Eamon smiles. 'That's settled then. No more Isabel.'

Grace tentatively says, 'Are you cold, Jimmy?'

Puzzled by the apparent randomness of her question, he says, 'No, not at all. Why would you think so?'

'You're not wearing your shorts.'

On the defensive, he says, 'Oh, well I figured I should make more of an effort to spare people the sight of something that's repulsive about me.'

Eamon had been about to sip his tea, but he puts his cup back down on its coaster and says, 'Jimmy, there's nothing repulsive about having a prosthetic and it doesn't reflect who you are. You shouldn't ever think that way.'

'You don't agree, do you, Mam?'

She says, 'I think to some people it *is* repulsive.'

Eamon says, 'Grace!'

Ignoring him, she tells Jimmy, 'But you shouldn't feel you have to hide anything like your leg, anything that's part of who you are, especially from people who are repelled or who can't handle it for whatever reason. That's their problem. Don't make it yours.'

Jimmy nearly asks her, 'If you're so wise about that, why can't *you* handle it?' but there's something too wounded in her expression, so he lets it be.

Chapter Ten

Old Man

I

September 1995

EAMON AND ART STUDY JIMMY'S PIMPLE-DOTTED FACE as he takes a sip of Guinness that becomes a slug. Grimacing, he plants his glass on the beer mat and emits a low 'ahh' sound. Art says, 'Well?'

Jimmy muffles a burp. 'I could get used to it.'

Eamon frowns. 'You're cut off after this one. And don't tell Granny, or dinner will become a sermon.'

Jimmy has another slug, which Art interrupts by pulling his elbow. 'Lad, it's not a race.'

It's after mass on Sunday and they're sitting in the snug of the Long Man. While Jimmy has joined Art and Eamon here before, this is the first time he has drunk something stronger than Coke, having turned fifteen over the summer. The idea to give him a 'real' drink was Art's, but Eamon would have preferred for it to have come from him.

Jimmy takes intermittent sips, gulping quickly once the stout has passed his pursed lips. His Adam's apple flexes, the hop flavour lingering in his mouth. Who ever knew that Abuelo could be quite cool? To Jimmy, he has always been an old man. He knows some facts about his grandfather's life. Art grew up on a ranch in Mendoza. He had siblings, but Jimmy isn't sure how many. He fought a war in Spain and afterwards came to Ireland and married Maggie. He has never returned to Argentina.

Jimmy tries to picture him without silver hair, with a black moustache or, more difficult, without one, and with wrinkle-free skin and the muscular posture of a soldier. He has a musky smell, as if his clothes are washed with chalk, but he must have smelled different in his youth. As they're all drinking as men, Jimmy feels he should show more interest. 'Abuelo? You were a soldier in a war, weren't you?'

Eamon straightens up. This isn't a subject he has openly talked about with Art either. When he and his brothers complained about something when they were kids, it wasn't unusual for Art to go off on a tirade about how clueless they were as to how cruel life could really be. He never elaborated, but Eamon always assumed he was referring to the war. When he asked his mother about his father's experiences, she just mentioned 'sleeping dogs'. That war was a sensitive subject for her too, so he didn't press.

Art sets his pint down and locks his eyes with Jimmy's. 'I was, a lifetime ago, in Spain in the thirties. We fought and lost, and fascism got its dirty foothold, and it all fell to hell.'

'What was the fighting like?'

Within the pub, there's plenty of bustle as orders are commanded at the bar and drinkers pontificate, but in the snug a silence hangs. Jimmy second-guesses asking his questions. Eamon wonders if he's about to know his father better. Art is surprised that there are things he feels like saying. 'There was a lot of waiting. Then the calm would snap and everything would be quick, with no time to think, and the fighting was madness. We did, all of us, try to be good and to fight for the right cause, but it wasn't a war worth having. Don't you ever be fool enough to fight in one, lad. If you ever listen to a thing I say, that's it. Far-flung ideals don't mean much when it comes to killing and dying for them.'

Jimmy nearly responds with 'They wouldn't take me, not with my leg,' but recognises in time that turning the conversation towards himself would make light of what has been said. He sees Art's hand shake when he raises his glass and drinks deep. When Art releases his glass Jimmy says, 'I hear you, Abuelo.'

Eamon says, 'Yeah, Papá, it must've been really—'

Art cuts him off. 'We'd better be drinking up. Maggie and Grace are waiting, and letting a hot meal go cold would be bad manners.'

'Right then. Right you are.'

A short while later, the three of them are walking up Bianconi Street, Rathbaile's main shopping street, with its clothes shops juxtaposed with the five-hundred-year-old St Mary's church on the corner. A wiry black-and-brown-mottled mongrel catapults towards them, perhaps chasing a pesky cat spectre, sounding off with a rat-tat-tat bark. Jimmy lets out a shout and slams back against the nearest shop window. The glass reverberates, and it isn't until the dog is out of sight, having come no closer than a couple of feet to him, that the blood returns to his face.

He sees a group of four girls inside the shop, about his age, laughing at his expense, but the worst part is how Art is staring at him with embarrassment on his behalf.

Putting his hand on Jimmy's arm, Eamon says, 'It's okay. He's gone. Let's get moving. Papá?'

Art hears the reproach in his son's voice and is aware he

could say something to reassure Jimmy that his flash of panic is understandable. Instead, he strides forward without looking at either Jimmy or Eamon, leading them home, where if they must talk, hopefully it'll be about trivial things.

II

To Jimmy and Eamon, Art will always be enigmatic, but not to me. I've surveyed from his mind's eye the memories that moulded him.

August 1937–October 1938

The red-and-black handkerchief ripples sharply, cracking in an odd direction, and disappears from the corner of Art's eye. He turns his head to see his cousin slumped against the sun-baked stone parapet, a cigarette smouldering between his fingers, one hobnail-booted foot pinned underneath the other leg. His posture looks ridiculous, but for once Gustavo isn't kidding. The handkerchief is tied around his neck – Art wears one like this too – and there's a fissure at the jugular. Smoke drifts out and blood gushes over his shirt. He emits a gurgling noise and blinks, twice, three times. Art drops his cigarette, ducks under the sniper's line of fire, and rushes to fill the hole in Gustavo's throat with his hands.

He knows they were wrong. If Gustavo hadn't already ceased blinking, he would yell at him for getting shot over the comical idea that they were going to make a difference.

In the letter Art received back at the beginning of March, Gustavo had asked him if he wanted to be a hero in Spain or stay in Mendoza and let other people decide the fate of the world. His challenge had a mocking tone, but that didn't mean he wasn't serious. As Gustavo put it: *This is a war where conviction will be weighed in blood.* Art finished reading and laughed as he ran to find his father.

Andreas was in the stables, washing one of the stallions. When he noticed his son at the entrance, he stopped whispering in the stallion's ear but continued rubbing his shiny coat with a sponge. After sparing Art just a glance, he said, 'You have something to tell me.'

Art kept his smile in check. 'Gustavo is going to Spain to fight the fascists. I'm going too.'

Giving him his full attention now, and with resignation pulling on his mouth, Andreas said, 'Why would you want to do such a stupid thing?'

'Because when you believe in something, you must be willing to stand up for it.'

'To kill and die for it?'

'Yes.'

'You're talking about making a man's decision.'

'I am.'

'Arturo, you're just a boy. And you know it.'

'We'll see.'

When, before sunrise, he left his parents' house without saying goodbye, Art was certain that on returning he would be mettle-tested and triumphant. His father would have to look at him with awe.

He took the long way to Spain. First he travelled through South and Central America on clanking buses, their seats always too small. He entered America at El Paso and from there took more poky buses through state after state. He hadn't seen his cousin in three years, when he had been sixteen and Gustavo nineteen, so when he stepped off the bus and on to the Chicago pavement, his knees mercifully unlocking, he almost didn't recognise him in his trilby and with his coarse beard, but then Gustavo broke into his infectious grin and shouted, 'Witness the fierce Arturo Diaz, the man who will slay Franco!'

They shared a backslapping hug. Art said, 'Maybe, Gustavo, but I must rest first. I'm exhausted.'

'Rest after the war. This afternoon you take your physical. Tomorrow we leave for New York.'

In New York, Art joined Gustavo by becoming a member of the Comintern at the Ukrainian Workers' Club. They stayed in a seedy hotel on the Lower East Side, waiting for enough volunteers to assemble to form a travelling party. The cousins didn't have much money, so they couldn't live it up, but nonetheless, Art was enthralled by the city. Chicago's once-imposing skyline now seemed undersized. The buildings in New York really earned the term 'skyscraper'. When Art gazed up at the Empire State Building, he knew that no ambition of man could be too daring.

It took six days aboard a steamship to sail to France. Gustavo vomited up everything he ate – his seasickness surprised Art, who had thought him invulnerable. They spent a week in Le Havre waiting for the International Brigades' recruiting office to find rooms for them in Paris. Gustavo swiftly recovered his strength. 'Hopefully this will be a long war,' he joked. 'I don't want to ever set foot on a boat again.'

In Paris, they languished for a month in rooming houses, and steadied themselves for what lay ahead with cheap whiskey and cheap prostitutes. Art had been a virgin, but quickly accumulated experience. He justified his conduct by telling himself that God would judge him by the penances he would perform in Spain.

They took the 'Red Special' train to Perpignan. The French had closed their border with Spain, so there were two options for making it across: a sea or a mountain route. They chose the latter because of Gustavo's woeful sea legs, and were led by smugglers along hidden trails over and through the Pyrenees. To avoid getting caught, the trek had to be completed in one night. On making it to a verdant Spanish valley, they were met by a truck, which brought them to the base at Castillo de San Fernando. Two days later, they were on a southbound train to Albacete, the International Brigades' headquarters.

Art and Gustavo became the only Argentines in the Abraham Lincoln Battalion, composed mostly of Americans and also featuring a column of Irishmen, but they both spoke nearly fluent English – something Art owed to Andreas's strict education. This wasn't the army of his imagination. They lacked a common uniform, but that was okay – they were united by their comradeship. The absence of guns during training did bother him, however, and the news of the Lincolns' defeat at Pingarrón bothered him more. Gustavo said, 'This is why we're here. The republicans aren't supposed to win without you and me turning the tide.'

Their faith seemed affirmed when they heard that a steamer carrying Internationals from France to Barcelona had been torpedoed by the fascists, killing everyone. If it wasn't for Gustavo's divine seasickness, they would have been on board.

They fought their first battle at the village of Brunete. From a distance, Gustavo shot and presumably killed two fascists, while Art shot and presumably killed one. He had expected to feel some residue of remorse but didn't. The pull of the trigger and the spasmodic collapse of his remote stick-figure enemy was empowering. The Lincolns had their numbers cut by over half without establishing much strategic gain. Ugly as it was to see comrades die up close, he found nobility in this suffering. The morale of others may have been easily deflated by the realities of war, but they didn't possess his self-belief.

Later that summer, the Lincolns were moved to the Aragon front. They took Quinto after three days of door-to-door fighting. Their casualties were low, but one of those soldiers could have survived if he had been less arrogant.

It was in the evening of the third day that Art and Gustavo decided to smoke on a café's parapet-lined roof. Standing out in the open, they joked about how they were sitting ducks, but didn't believe it. They had acquitted themselves well, seeing the whites of their enemies' eyes this time, and the fascists were on the run. They chose this roof so they could reflect on a view of the 'free' town. Art lit their cigarettes with his tinder lighter, and a destiny-ignorant bullet tore through Gustavo's jugular.

'Do you know why you're a shit chess player, Art? It's because you keep making the same feckin' mistakes. I find new ways to beat you just for the hell of it, but I could play you the same way as long as I liked and you still wouldn't get it. It's not just dumb; it's verging on insane. You know what Benjamin Franklin said insanity was? Repeating the same behaviour and expecting a different result. You know who Franklin was, you spic fuck?'

'Stewart. You're a blabbering cunt.'

'Hah! You're a quiet one, Art, but when you open your gob you're fucking profound.'

It's Christmas Day and Spain is in the midst of its coldest winter of the twentieth century. The snow is three feet high on the plains and Art is on sentry duty, playing chess with an idiot, a skeletal-legged table between them. They are sitting by the barracks, under the tarpaulin canopy of a sand-bag-rimmed shelter. As the snow mounts, the canopy's centre sags. The chessboard is a portion of soggy cardboard and its pieces are pebbles, charcoal-marked for type, except for the kings, which are represented by bullet shells. There's also a rusted revolver on the table. Between moves, Stewart spins it in circles.

The other Irishmen of the Connolly Column don't like being around Stewart. Not because he talks too much and with little tact – many of them do that. They don't like the wet sheen of his eyes, or how his jaw hangs, his mouth a flycatcher. He's a good soldier, brave and ruthless, but in combat he sniggers, even when he's being shot at. While Art doesn't like Stewart either, he prefers his company to that of the others, most of whom can be divided into those who still believe this war can be won and those who are walking bundles of nerves. The former are grating because they remind him of his old idealism; the latter because fear is contagious so it's better to stay numb. He doesn't find the timing of Stewart's laughter unnerving. On the contrary, it's appropriate to their situation.

He scrutinises the board, then takes Stewart's rook with his knight. Stewart counters by taking Art's knight with his bishop. 'You know why my dear father and mother christened me Stewart? Course you don't. My middle name is Charles, which won't help either. In the shithole you're from, you wouldn't have heard of Charles Stewart Parnell, the "great" Irish statesman. The truth is he got us nowhere because he couldn't keep his dick in his trousers, but you don't need to hear the entire story. To most in Ireland he's a hero. Doesn't matter that he failed. There's nothing more romantic to the Irish than a man who gets close to real achievement but fucks it up as soon as it's within his grasp. My folks revere the fucker so that's why they named me after him. They thought I could be a leader as well, a man of high principles. Hah! I suppose I was thick enough to aim for it as well or I wouldn't be sitting here in this fucking country playing chess with an illiterate. And now, if Franco has his way, I'm likely to get shot. That's one upside of war: it rids the world of some fools. There are far too many of us. We *should* die. That's how to make the world a better place. Problem is, if you kill all the fools you're not left with many people, are you? You agree. You're a misanthrope, like me. It may be a bitter way to be, but it's the stance any man with his wits about him inevitably arrives at. Hah! What am I going on about? Do you even know what a misanthrope is?'

Art takes Stewart's bishop with his queen and glares at his opponent. Stewart says, 'Well? Enlighten me if you don't agree.'

'Checkmate.'

Stewart slaps the table, knocking a pebble from the board to the frigid ground. 'Hah! Never trust a quiet man!'

In the new year, the republicans' odds of winning the war become increasingly low. Proletarian solidarity is a thing of the past and deserters face execution. By the summer, the International Brigades are so depleted that their numbers have to be filled out with Spanish soldiers. In July, when Stewart learns that the Lincolns are going on the offensive again, he decides to desert. He tries to persuade Art to do the same, but Art has to see the war through. He could never face his father as a deserter. Stewart laughs – 'You've no fucking sense' – then asks for a favour: if he's killed trying to escape, he wants Art to send some letters to his parents and sisters. They agree that if Stewart makes it to Paris, he will leave word at an estab-lishment nicknamed 'L'Hôtel de Péché'. If there's no message, Art can assume Stewart is dead and post the letters.

The day after Stewart is driven off, hiding in the back of

a supply lorry, Art crosses the Ebro with the Lincolns in inflatable boats for an attack on a depot. When the fascists strike back, the Lincolns hold their ground as long as they can, but by the end of August they are forced to retreat, having lost five hundred out of seven hundred men. Art prays that the republicans will have no more victories, because only wishful thinking is keeping them from surrendering.

Within a month, the Lincolns are withdrawn and sent to camps near the French border to await repatriation. He hears that there's a plan for a farewell parade in Barcelona and doesn't want any part of it – all of his comrades who had been worth something are dead and he can't even remember when he stopped caring about the plight of the 'common man' – so he chooses to make his own way to France. When his relatives see him again, they will want to hear about Gustavo, and though the prospect of it sickens him, he feels compelled to invent a more heroic end for him, rather than admitting that Gustavo was shot in the throat when they were just standing about, stupidly believing they were untouchable. If Art tells the truth, the immediate thought people will have is how it could just as easily have been him who took the bullet, followed by the thought that maybe it *should* have been him. He doesn't want to return to Mendoza any time soon, but he can't think of anywhere else to go. First, though, he has a promise to fulfil.

He struts into the lobby of L'Hôtel de Péché, noting its peeling wallpaper and ripped carpet. Once he has discovered what has happened to Stewart, he's looking forward to fucking a whore, hard; the uglier the whore, the better.

The man at the reception desk, his liver-spotted skin stretched across his skull, is reading a newspaper through a thick-glassed pince-nez perched low on his nose. Art coughs. '*Anglais? Espagnol?*'

Looking up from an article on the brewing German threat, the clerk sighs as if he had expected to see someone more impressive than this unshaven stranger with his tatty woollen pullover. 'How can I be of service?'

'My name is Diaz. You should have a letter for me from Stewart Charles Callaghan.'

'The loud Irishman is a friend of yours?'

'You've seen him?'

'He's not what you would call an inconspicuous man. Second floor. Room six.'

Art smiles as he trudges up the stairs. He hadn't expected to see Stewart again and is glad he's still loud. His nostalgia lasts until he approaches the room and hears a woman's shriek, then the bang of hard objects colliding and Stewart's voice shouting, '*Putain!*'

Art reaches into his pocket for his folding knife and pulls the blade from the handle. He's about to force the door when it occurs to him to turn the doorknob. It's unlocked.

Knuckles white around his knife, he steps inside.

Stewart stands naked on the bed, his back turned and a revolver in his hand. His meaty body is streaked with sweat and the light slicing through the cracks in the window blinds tints his fair hair grey. Between the inverted V formed by his legs lies a naked woman with tangled black hair and a bloodied mouth. Her feet are pushing against the sheets, her skinny legs quivering and her pale vulva exposed. Her hands are raised to Stewart.

Seeing Art, hope flickers in her swollen eyes. Stewart turns his head. His fat lips are smeared with lipstick, and mascara cakes his eyelids. He stares vacantly at Art, his jaw hanging, but then his eyes spark. 'Hah! Art, welcome!' He points the revolver at him. 'Close the fucking door, will you?'

Art tightens his grip on his knife and considers whether he could cross the fifteen feet to the bed before Stewart gets a shot off.

'The door, Art. Were you born in a barn? Show me some manners or I'll do something terrible with a bullet.' Art closes the door. Stewart says, 'Much obliged, comrade. Why do you look so sad? I'm still me, y'know.'

'You're scaring the girl. You don't need a gun. There's no one left to shoot.'

'Hah! There's always someone.' Stewart lowers the gun to his side. 'Don't you dare move. If you try to stick that knife in me, I'll do worse to you. This isn't a girl, Art. She screams like a fucking devil.'

Stewart gazes down at the woman – she shuts her eyes – and points the gun at her face. From his ears to his ass to his feet he's pink going on crimson, as if his blood is sizzling under his skin. The woman's skin is a bloodless alabaster. She whispers, '*Please*. I have children.'

Art rushes forward. Stewart glances at him, exclaims, 'Hah!' and pulls the trigger. A bullet smashes through the woman's forehead a moment before Art jumps on to the bed and plunges his knife between Stewart's shoulder and spine. The revolver falls, bouncing off the mattress and on to the floor. Wrestling Stewart around, and smelling his stink, Art wrenches the knife from his back. As blood spurts on to the dead woman's feet, he stabs Stewart in the gut.

Stewart groans, but then smiles. Art throws him off the bed. Landing in a heap, Stewart presses his hands to his stomach. Blood streams down his waist, to his clump of pubic hair and his limp penis. He spits blood and tries to curl himself into a ball. Art hops from the bed, sending a tremor through the floor. He pulls Stewart up by his hair, twisting him to his feet. Seizing his throat, he smacks him against the wall. Stewart closes his eyes, but Art puts the blade to his cheek. 'Open your eyes or I'll cut them open.'

Stewart stares into Art's contorted face. 'You're killing me for nothing!'

Art squeezes Stewart's throat harder. 'Did you see what the bullet did to her face? Did you see it!'

Tears spilling from his eyes, Stewart rasps, 'I have a family that loves me.'

'There's no hope for you. Maybe none for either of us.'

Art slashes Stewart's throat.

Art will never experience another day in which he doesn't think about what he did. But so much life will follow from it too: if he hadn't entered that room, he never would have gone on to meet Maggie and so they never would have produced three sons, and Eamon wouldn't have existed to father his children. I would have no story to tell.

III
September 1995

Jimmy rings the doorbell. He has had a bad day: some of his classmates laughed at him when he was yelled at by the teacher for doing a sloppy job on his homework, and he could swear that someone muttered, 'Ahab' – he misheard that, though, and his classmates invariably laugh at everyone who gets yelled at. He isn't in the mood for being a considerate grandson, but Eamon asked him to drop by.

Maggie answers the door, wearing an apron featuring a

cartoon orange-skinned woman holding a ladle and the exclamation *Mamma Mia!* She hugs him. 'Jimmy, I think you've
grown since last Sunday! Come in. Your grandfather wants
to talk to you and I'm making buns. They'll have icing, the
way you like.'

While she returns to her kitchen, Jimmy finds Art in the
living room, sitting in his armchair and reading one of
Eamon's movie reviews in the *Rathbaile Chronicle*, even
though he never goes to the cinema. The paper makes a
cracking noise as he folds it. Jimmy dumps his backpack on
the floor and sits on the couch. Art says, 'I have something
for you.' Jimmy wonders if he's about to receive more alcohol.
'It's a responsibility.'

'Oh.'

'Do you want it?'

Trying to sound appreciative, Jimmy says, 'Sure. Thanks,
Abuelo.'

'Don't thank me yet. See what it is first.'

They go outside and walk down the garden path – passing
the chestnut tree Luis and Manny took turns falling from
when they were kids – to the shed. Art unlocks the padlock,
then looks at Jimmy intently. 'I want to tell you something.
Every man has his fears. If there wasn't anything to be afraid
of, no one could ever be brave, because bravery isn't fearlessness. Fearlessness is a form of stupidity. Bravery is overcoming
fear. Understand?' Jimmy nods. 'When I fought in that war, I
was afraid all the time. Even when I convinced myself I wasn't,
and acted like I wasn't, I still was. There's no shame in that.

'One of the men I fought alongside was your granny's
brother, Stewart. She doesn't talk about him, so don't mention
him to her. Before he was killed, he asked me to send some
letters to his family if he didn't make it. He showed me a

photo of them and they reminded me of my own family. I wasn't in a rush to go home and I decided the best thing to do, the right thing, would be to come to Ireland and deliver my condolences in person. I thought if I could tell Stewart's family that he didn't die in vain, that would provide comfort. Seeing them scared me more than anything else ever has, but it was a matter of honour. You can't give in to your fears because then they multiply. Got it?'

'I understand.'

'Are you afraid of anything?'

Jimmy knows what he's referring to. 'I get scared by dogs. I know I shouldn't.'

Art puts his hand on Jimmy's shoulder. 'Anybody with your misfortune would be the same. But you don't want to spend your life afraid whenever you see some mutt, do you?'

'No.'

'Then there's someone I want you to meet.'

They enter the shed. When he beholds the size of the dog Art has gotten for him, Jimmy breaks into a sweat.

The shaggy grey dog, lying on a pile of rugs, is chewing on the remnants of a rubber duck. Seeing he has company, he grunts and lumbers to his paws, revealing his full length. He steps forward and nuzzles his nose against Art's stomach. His tail wags, gusting air in Jimmy's direction, while Art pats his head.

Art says, 'I picked him up from the pound. He's a big softie. The lady there said he's about eight months old, so he should almost be fully grown. Still a bit of a pup, a handful maybe. Eamon says you can keep him if you're willing to take care of him. I reckon you're up to the challenge. Say hello. He won't bite.'

Jimmy comes closer and, with Art gripping the dog by the

collar, allows his fingers to be licked. 'Wh-what sort of breed is he?'

'An Irish wolfhound, a dog straight from mythology. Cuchulain had one, and in ancient Rome they used to have them fight lions.'

'Did they win?'

'You bet. They're loyal dogs too. You can trust this fellow. They called him Colossus at the pound, but you can name him whatever you want.'

'Colossus is fine.'

Art lets go of the collar. Jimmy, his hand shaking, strokes Colossus's head and behind his ear. Art says, 'You afraid of him?'

'Yeah, but it's okay. Bravery, right?'

Chapter Eleven

Roll With It

July 1998

ELIZABETH ARRIVED IN RATHBAILE A FEW HOURS AGO, her first visit down from Dublin in five months. Now twenty-four, she doesn't bear a close likeness to the ten-year-old who wet herself at the Rathbaile racecourse, or to the fourteen-year-old who peeked at her brother's stump when she thought he was asleep. Her hair is tied in a ponytail, pulled back tight, and she has rings in her left eyebrow and lower lip, as well as four in each ear. She's wearing a grey tank top, and on the exposed small of her back she has a tattoo of a black rose with a thorn on the stem. Her red fingernails dig into the steering wheel of her second-hand car. To Jimmy, sitting in the passenger seat, she says, 'Does Mam seem off to you?'

Jimmy had been gazing out the window, through sliding raindrops, at the passing, slightly warped, houses and trees, but he looks at her now. 'No more than usual. If you're worried, ask Dad.'

'Because he'll give me an honest answer.'

'Then ask Mam herself.'

'Don't you notice anything? You see her every day.'

'Yeah, I do. And tonight I don't want to think about her.

I'm celebrating France beating Brazil. Seb owes me a fiver on every goal France scored.'

Elizabeth bites her lower lip, tucking the silver ring into her mouth. She releases it. 'You've got your priorities straight.'

'It's the next right.'

When they turn into Seb's driveway, she waits for Jimmy to get out without glancing at him. 'Aren't you in a hurry?'

He knows that if he leaves things like this, she'll be cold to him all weekend. 'I don't think she's any worse. Just because I prefer not to talk about it doesn't mean I don't care, okay? There's nothing to worry about, nothing out of the ordinary.'

'I hugged her when I got in today. Her shoulders clenched.'

Jimmy pauses – the rain taps on the roof – then offers her a platitude. 'She loves all of us in her way.'

Elizabeth doesn't really believe that, but she says, 'You're right.' She smiles sadly. 'Say hello to the actor for me and call me when you want a lift home.'

It's been a lousy week for her. She had been working at a club, but a few nights ago, her boss grabbed her ass. She threw a pint of beer in his face and shouted at him, 'I quit!' which she regrets because it was surely implied. She was disappointed that none of the other girls working there followed her cue – the groping treatment hadn't been reserved for her alone – but she was relieved to be shot of the place. She feels she's better suited to the service industry than to an office job, where she would have to sit still more, but she doesn't want to work in another club or pub. Men get creepier and creepier when they're drinking and you're not.

Until she finds something, she needs the means to cover her rent. There's a guy she has kind of been seeing and she could borrow from him, but then she'd be obliged to be his girlfriend for a while and, frankly, she would prefer to end it altogether than to be that. Not everyone, she thinks, meaning her specifically, is suited to being in a relationship. Tighe would give her money if she asked, and he wouldn't expect her to pay him back, but he would lord it over her – not by bringing it up; it would be written on his face. And so she has come home to ask her father. Now that she's here, though, and can see how stressed he is about her distant mother, she's inclined to wait another week. In the meantime, she'll speed up her job search.

As she drives away, Jimmy rings the doorbell. Seb answers the door. 'You're late!'

'I was giving you more time to fix your hair, big shot. Don't bother telling me that's not what you were doing.' Jimmy is right: Seb had just been sculpting his hair with gel and checking himself out from all angles in the mirror.

'I'm not dignifying that with a response. My mother wants to see you. Alice, too.'

Jimmy steps inside. 'You owe me fifteen quid.'

Seb isn't put out at having to pay up. Jimmy profiting at his expense on some inconsequential event lets him feel like the balance between them has received a dose of positive karma. It also doesn't hurt that he presently has cash to spare.

Seb has been a member of the Rathbaile Drama Club since he was ten. He only ever landed supporting roles in their annual plays, but while he claimed to agree that 'there are no small parts', he wanted to be the star. When he heard of an open casting call in Dublin, for a film by the acclaimed director Niall Shanahan, he went for it.

Starting Line is about a young distance runner called Denise – played by Shanahan's saucy daughter, Rachel – who's training for the Olympics to gain the respect of her domineering father while struggling to make time for her bit-of-a-rebel boyfriend, who's domineering too. She eventually asserts herself by ditching the boyfriend and standing up to her father: she'll run on her own terms now! The final shot is of Denise's determined expression as she launches from the starting line of her Olympic race – win or lose, she has completed her journey of self-discovery.

Seb was cast as Jack, who's in three scenes, all in the café where Denise works as a perpetually under-tipped waitress. In the first, he makes eyes at her but they don't talk. In the second, they have a flirtatious exchange where he quotes Emily Dickinson for some reason, bringing an intrigued smile to Denise's face, but she's still with her boyfriend. In the third, he's out of the picture and she asks Jack out. He eagerly accepts and is content to wait for her to return from Atlanta. The part of Jack required some pretty-boy sex appeal and a distinctly non-domineering manner. Seb nailed it.

He attended a red-carpet premiere in London and was named one of Ireland's ten 'stars of the future' in the *Irish Times*. They had nine obvious choices and, luckily, they wanted a round number. In the caption next to a headshot of him looking broody, he's quoted: 'I'm still a small-town guy, but I've tasted success and I'm hungry for more.' *Starting Line* opened in Ireland a week ago, and he hasn't walked around town since without being asked about his stardom. But the best bit, which he confided to Jimmy, was 'Get this: Rachel Shanahan let me shag her.' It was true. Rachel, who at twenty-seven is nine years his senior, had propositioned him, making it clear she wouldn't be interested in him afterwards and that all she wanted was sex. 'She fucking used me, man. She was cold and it was hot.' Jimmy did his utmost to hide his jealousy.

Seb leads Jimmy into the kitchen, where his mother, Michelle, and his sister, Alice, are sitting at the table, drinking tea. Alice greets Jimmy, hiding the acne on her chin behind her cup. Michelle hugs him and offers a range of warm drinks and sugary snacks. She has a tendency to fuss, but more so with him.

Seb says, 'Mam, the lads are waiting.'

She flicks on the kettle. 'Let them. Fifteen minutes won't ruin your night.'

Jimmy consents to tea and sits next to Alice. Seb, leaning against the counter, cracks his fingers. Michelle says, 'Sebastian! You'll give yourself arthritis.'

Alice gulps her tea. 'Your Leaving Cert go okay, Jimmy?'

He wants to do medicine and believes he has done well enough in his exams to get it. 'They'll let me in somewhere. You sat your Junior Cert, didn't you?'

'Yeah. I'm dreading the results. I always write lots, but half the time I don't know what I'm talking about.'

Seb says, 'You always *think* you've done badly.'

'It's different this time. I really don't want to even talk about this.'

Michelle pats Alice's hand and says to Jimmy, 'What are tonight's plans then? Is Brian having a party?'

Seb says, 'Don't answer. She's fishing for something incriminating.'

'You're no fun.' Michelle ignores Seb mimicking her scowl and says, 'Don't worry, Jimmy, I trust you. But watch out for that son of mine.' She jerks her thumb in Seb's direction. 'He's a brazen chancer.'

Before Brian's parents departed for the weekend, his father jangled a pair of keys in front of his nose – one to enter the den, the other for his bar – and said, 'There better be some drink left. Don't even think about smoking the cigars.'

Brian snatched the keys. 'On my honour.'

Jimmy, Seb, Brian, and Finbar sit around the poker table holding two cards apiece. They're playing Texas Hold 'Em while drinking expensive Merlot from Waterford crystal glasses and smoking Montecristo cigars. Jimmy, Seb, and Finbar are wearing T-shirts and jeans, but Brian is wearing his father's best suit, his collar loose. He's a fan of the Rat Pack and would like to look like Dean Martin. With his fair hair and chubby face, he doesn't come close.

The flop is a jack of spades, a queen of hearts, and an eight of diamonds. Brian checked, but Seb has bet twice the blind. Finbar has an eight and a seven of hearts, and the least amount of chips, but he'd like to stay in and see if his hand improves. His decision would be easier if he was better at reading his friends' faces. Seb looks at his cards and grins. He only has a pair of threes, clubs and spades, but likes to bluff. Brian's indifferent expression isn't a pose – they've been playing for two hours and he's bored. Jimmy is distracted by the entertainment in the corner of the room.

Seb says, 'For fuck's sake, Finbar! Call or fold?'

Raising his voice over the moaning emanating from the TV, Finbar says, 'I can't concentrate with *that* going on!' He gestures to the screen, where a blonde woman is masturbating while her large breasts are being massaged from behind by a Hispanic woman with even larger breasts. 'Could we turn off the fecking box?'

Brian takes the cigar from his mouth and blows out a puny smoke ring. 'Not into hot bitches who like to "check their pulse", Finbar?' The moaning increases in pitch. 'Would you prefer two blokes going at it? I'm afraid I don't have any tapes of that sort of thing.'

Jimmy laughs, then inhales too much smoke and starts coughing. A slug of wine cures him. 'So you in, Finbar?'

Finbar ignores him and tells Brian, 'Get lost. There might be a time and place for porn, but this isn't it. I'm seeing tits on my cards where I should be seeing suits!'

Brian says, 'You don't typically find a time and place, do you? It's not really your genre.'

An uneasy glance passes between Jimmy and Seb. Brian has been in a bizarre mood all night – he was already tipsy when he opened the door to them. Despite his smile, he isn't taking the piss in baiting Finbar. Holding his cards closer to his chest, Finbar says, 'I don't judge others, but my dad wouldn't buy sleaze and my mother raised me to respect women.'

Brian says, 'You wouldn't be slagging off my parents in their own home, would you?'

'No, Brian. I just want to play some poker.'

Jimmy says, 'You in, Finbar?'

Finbar pushes the required combination of chips into the pot. 'There, Jimmy. I'm in. Right?'

Jimmy matches the bet – he has a queen of diamonds and an ace of clubs. It's Brian's turn to call or fold his seven and eight of spades, but he's still staring at Finbar. He says, 'Lads, we've a decision to make. Telly on or not? To be a homo or not to be?'

Finbar rises to his feet. 'What are you calling me?'

Brian rises too. He's shorter than Finbar, but much stockier. 'You know.'

Seb stands with his palms up. 'Guys.' The women in the video scream with delight. Seb grabs the remote from the table and switches off the TV. 'We're all *friends* here.' Brian and Finbar sit back down, both looking unconvinced.

Brian folds. A two of hearts is dealt, then a four of clubs. Seb bets big, Finbar folds, and Jimmy calls, winning the pot with his high pair.

Within the next few hands, Finbar's chips are whittled away to nothing; Brian goes all in on a hand in which he doesn't have so much as a pair, and is called by and loses everything to Seb; Jimmy and Seb go all in against each other with Jimmy's full house trumping a flush. His lips blackened from the wine, Seb says, 'Jimmy fuck-ing Diaz. Poker fuck-ing stud.'

Jimmy smiles and pockets four fivers without saying a word.

Brian gets up and goes behind the mahogany bar. He takes out a bottle and four shot glasses, then stamps the glasses in front of the others and pours everyone a shot, spilling some on the table. 'Time to switch to dice, lads. Tequila with every new game.'

Finbar pushes his glass forward on the table so the whiff isn't so strong. 'I don't want to play any game that comes down to luck.'

'Jesus, try something, will you?'

Jimmy puts out his cigar, then lifts his glass to his nose, smells it, and shudders. 'Brian, got some lemon?'

'Lemons are for pussies.'

They all proceed, lemon-less, to knock back the shots.

On each game they bet two pounds apiece and roll two dice against a wall. After a round, the player who has rolled the lowest combined score is eliminated and the others continue on. Brian and Seb win a game each, then Jimmy wins three in a row. Before the sixth game, Seb throws up in the toilet and is unwilling to drink to play another. He sits at the table with his head on his forearms, his hair a mess, while Jimmy, Brian, and Finbar play on.

After Finbar throws a three-two and hangs his head, Brian throws the dice hard against the wall, skinning the amber wallpaper. Four-four. 'You cunts are going down!'

Jimmy rattles the dice in his hands, his fingers interlocked. He lifts his thumbs, blows on the dice, and tells Finbar and Brian, 'Learn from a master.'

Jimmy rolls a six-six. Finbar yells, 'Fuck!' With a bewildered smile, he takes a seat.

Seb, showing signs of life again, raises his head and says, 'Jimmy fuck-ing Diaz. Jimmy fuck-ing Diceman. Brian, you better quit now. Jimmy Dice has voodoo on his side.'

Brian says, 'It's just luck.' He knocks back an extra shot and tears come to his eyes. 'This game's mine.'

Jimmy says, 'Put another tenner on this?'

'You're on.' Brian squeezes the dice in his fist, then flings them in a catapult motion. Six-five. 'You're fucked!'

Jimmy concedes, 'That's almost certainly true. Almost.'

Drumming his hands on the table, Seb chants, 'Jimmy Dice, Jimmy Dice.'

Finbar joins in. Brian tries to silence them with a glare. Their chanting only gets louder.

Jimmy rattles, blows, and rolls. The dice skip across the floor until they collide with the wall. One die comes to a stop. A six. The second ricochets off the wall and dives under the TV stand, where it rests unseen. Brian says. 'There's no way you've thrown the same pair twice in a row.'

Jimmy says, 'It's a one-in-six shot that I have and another one-in-six shot that we roll again. Could be worse odds.'

When Jimmy steps forward, Brian puts his arm out, blocking his way. 'Let someone else get it. Your hands are biased.'

Finbar jumps up, and before Brian can object, he's on his knees with his head sideways on the floor and his arm extended under the stand. 'Got it!'

Brian says, 'Don't knock it on to a different side.'

Finbar retracts his arm, die cupped in hand, and gets to his feet. He looks at it, laughs, and reveals the face-up six. 'Bad luck, Brian. Jimmy Dice, you're a legend.'

Seb, his eyes half open, says, 'Nice one.'

Brian slaps the die out of Finbar's hand. 'You turned it over, didn't you, you prick.'

Finbar turns red. 'What's your damn problem? You keep pecking at me like some bitch.'

'Get the fuck out of my house then!'

'Glad to! For the last time, too!'

Seb stands. Jimmy says to Finbar and Brian, 'Guys, fuck, chill, both of you.'

Finbar strides to the door. Brian picks up an empty shot glass and shouts, 'Fucking faggot!'

Finbar turns and Brian throws the glass. It smashes against the top of the door, showering shards over Finbar, but not cutting him. Finbar says, 'Crazy fuck!' and lunges at Brian. Jimmy manages to restrain Finbar, while Seb, wide-eyed now, restrains Brian, as he and Finbar continue to exchange insults.

When Brian and Finbar have finally calmed down enough so that Seb and Jimmy can let them go, Jimmy pours himself a shot and slugs it. A headache zinging from temple to temple, he says, 'How about we call this one a night?'

A phone call and twenty minutes later, Elizabeth pulls up to Brian's house. Jimmy is already outside, by himself, leaning on the gate as rain pelts down. She shoves the passenger door open. He sits in, dripping everywhere, and closes the door. 'Thanks for coming.'

'Why didn't you wait inside? You know it's pissing out.'

She sounds angry and her eyes are slightly glazed. He can smell what she was doing before she drove here. 'Smoked something?'

'What's it to you?'

'I don't want to get in an accident tonight.'

'I was clear-headed enough to make it here in one piece. I'd wager I'm twice as clear-headed as you.'

'Maybe.'

'If you don't want to take the risk, feel free to walk.' Jimmy puts on his seat belt. Elizabeth says, 'Good.'

Her driving is faster than he's comfortable with, but there aren't many other cars on the road as they pass the old Supreme cinema, vacant five years now, then turn on to Bianconi Street, peopled only by shop-window sentinels with painted eyes. Elizabeth is doing that thing where she chews on her ringed lower lip, spits it out, and chews again. Something specific has probably set her off, but Jimmy doesn't want to know what. All he does want is to press his face into his pillow's cool softness. And soon he wants to leave Rathbaile and never come back.

Elizabeth breaks the silence. 'Tell me about your night.'

'What about it?'

'Something, fuck, anything.'

'I cleaned out the lads, then a lot of bullshit aggro happened. Typical bollix.'

'What do you mean?'

'Just that Brian was being a dick. Something's wrong with him.'

'Did you ask him what it was?'

'Guys don't ask each other what's wrong.'

'Nice attitude, Jimmy. I'm sure all your problems will solve themselves as long as you never speak about them.'

'What are you talking about? Brian's the man with problems. Nothing to do with me.' Jimmy's knee is throbbing, the one that doesn't exist, his non-existent foot too.

'I'm not talking about . . .' Elizabeth is conscious her voice is rising, so she lowers it. 'I'm talking about you and Mam and Dad, and Tighe, whenever he's actually around. I'm talking about our pitiful excuse for a family. I'm so tired of all of us. How we hide our own agendas, storing up secrets, and for what? How can anything change when no one ever *says* anything?'

'You need to stop smoking. It's supposed to relax people, but it just makes you mega-paranoid. No one in the family has a treasure chest of hidden secrets. And slow down, will you?'

She turns her eyes on him – the glaze has been cut through. 'Don't tell me what to do or think.'

'Fine. Just watch the road.'

Elizabeth refocuses on the empty road, but she's still speeding. They're out of town now, a couple of minutes from home, where the bends are sharper and it would be quiet if it wasn't for the rain's frenzied patter on metal and glass, like the hammering of a typewriter. She says, 'Let me ask you something: how many siblings do you think you've had, including the dead?'

'I know about Paul. What's your point?'

'Humour me. How many?'

'Three, okay? Two alive, one not.'

'Try again. The score is two-two. Recall your stay in Mam's womb? You weren't alone. You had a twin. Maybe it was survival of the fittest, but our dear sister didn't make it to the other side. She was stillborn. Ever get the sense that half of you is missing, Jimmy? Well maybe she is.'

'That's . . . ridiculous. If that's true, someone would've told me. That's crazy.'

'Don't you dare call me crazy!'

'The road!'

142

She looks back at the road and brakes, rolling the wheel. He grabs the dashboard, so hard his knuckles hurt, and the car screeches into the other lane then comes to a thudding halt in the waterlogged ditch.

Breathe in, breathe out.

He looks at her. Her arms are rigid against the wheel, as if she's trying to push it away. He releases the dashboard and looks over himself. He's no less intact than before.

She covers her eyes and starts to cry. Her mouth visible below her hands, she says, 'Did you see the cat or whatever it was that cut across the road? I had to swerve to miss it.' He hesitates. She repeats, 'Did you *see* it?'

'Yeah, I did.'

There was no cat. But there was a fox. Jimmy didn't see a thing.

Elizabeth lowers her hands. 'I'm so sorry. I didn't mean to scare you.'

'I'm not scared. We're okay. This didn't matter. But sometimes you *do* scare me.'

Replace 'sometimes' with 'most of the time' and that would be an accurate statement.

Regardless of the agitated tenor of their conversation, being mentioned at all feels rewarding, but I would have liked for Jimmy, in that moment, to have been more open to the news of my existence – that said, I recognise how the fear of potentially dying or being gruesomely scarred in a car crash may have distracted him from fully contemplating the ramifications of me.

It's true that, before I was strangled by the blind python of Jimmy's umbilical cord, I was female. Post-life, it hasn't really stuck. Without receiving the gender-role instruction, and not possessing any of the basic body requirements, I haven't grown up to feel womanly. I feel marginally more male than female, due to having spent more time in Jimmy's head than in anyone else's, but if I was to apply a third-person pronoun to myself, I would select 'she' over 'he' or 'it' because at least it's matter-of-fact in regard to what I would have been. Like the other options, it doesn't quite fit, though.

While Jimmy is confounded by the otherness of women, I'm not. Not having a body of my own helps me to appreciate that simplified generalisations of gender traits can be counter-productive to grasping the psychology of an individual mind, but inevitably his maleness has influenced my perceptions too. While the bias he has instilled in me might be minor, I don't doubt that it's there.

Chapter Twelve

Fast Enough

August 1998

JIMMY TELLS ALICE SHE'S GORGEOUS, BUT WHILE SHE recognises that he's being courteous, she hopes to hear him say something before the end of the night that shows that he *sees* her.

'Put some feeling into it, you two!' Alice and Seb's father, Declan, smiles as if to demonstrate how it's done. He raises the camera to his eye, and shoots Jimmy and Alice for the third time.

Alice is wearing a pink gown and high heels. When she discovered the dress, her friend, Rosie, had to talk her into buying it. Alice thought it showed too much. Rosie asked, 'Do you like him?' Alice admitted it. Rosie said, 'Then be *daring*.' Rosie was more experienced, by virtue of having kissed a few boys while Alice had yet to kiss one, so Alice deferred to her judgement. Now, she's questioning her choice, not because of her overt cleavage – she felt flattered when she caught Jimmy staring – but because she hates having her lumpy shoulders bared, and the slit on the side exposes the width of her thigh.

The collar of his tux is chafing him, but Jimmy has stopped tugging because that only makes it worse. His trousers are too long and they bunch up at his shoes. They also have dog hairs on them, thanks to Colossus bounding up to him earlier. No matter how many he removes, their number is seemingly legion.

At the beginning of the summer, he had been looking forward to this. He wanted to invite a girl called Tracy, but as soon as he mentioned the debs to her, he could see pity creeping into her eyes and he bottled it. Shortly afterwards, she agreed to go with Brian. By mid-August, it looked like every girl was taken, but then Seb asked Jimmy for a favour. 'Alice has a crush on you. God knows why. It's probably been pretty blatant.' Jimmy, who hadn't noticed a thing, nodded. 'It'd give her confidence a boost if you brought her. She's aware you're heading off to college so you wouldn't need to follow it up.' When Jimmy asked Alice, she stuttered her consent.

With Jimmy and Alice captured on camera, Seb and his date, Jasmine, are up. Declan instructs them to stand by the fireplace. Michelle interrupts to fix Seb's tie. He says, 'We haven't got all night.'

Jimmy watches on. Jasmine is such a ride and knows it too. You can tell from the pout of her lips and how her red dress is so tight that even the dimples of her ass can be made out. He wonders if Seb realises his luck, or if he's so used to everything going his way he just expects it.

Different rules, Jimmy feels, apply to his own life. He had believed he would be accepted to study medicine at Trinity. He'd worked hard and was smart, and yet when the results came, although he had one of the best marks in his school, he was sixty points short of the requirement. Eamon suggested trying again next year, but Seb had been accepted to study drama at the Gaiety School and Jimmy wasn't willing to be left behind so he settled for the consolation of arts at UCD.

With his hand around Jasmine's waist, and her breast pressed against his chest, Seb laughs as Declan takes the photo. He doesn't need to be prompted to say 'cheese'.

Jimmy plucks another dog hair from his trousers, the longest yet, and hopes no one notices when he flicks it into the air.

Brian dips his head and raises his eyebrow. 'At the very least you should get a Lewinsky out of this.'

Jimmy says, 'A what?'

'Use your fucking imagination.'

They are standing by the bar in Ashburnham House. Jimmy has a fresh pint in hand. Brian has two. The place hasn't changed much since Eamon and Grace had their first dance here. The bar is shinier and there's a more eclectic mix of drinks on tap. A bandanna-wearing, head-bobbing local DJ is playing 'Brimful of Asha' by Cornershop. Jimmy liked the song when it was released, but is sick of it now.

'She's Seb's sister.'

Brian laughs and drinks. 'So?'

'I should treat her well. Out of respect. Besides, she's young.'

'We're all young. Seb doesn't expect you to be a saint. And just so you know, she wants you to try and get what you can from her.' Brian shakes his head. 'Sometimes I wonder if any of you lads get women. They want what we want. They just prefer making it difficult on themselves.'

'Why's that?'

'Because society oppresses them and they're manipulated into thinking they should be virginal angels when that's completely unnatural. They're also all a bit mental. Some shit anyway. I'm not unsympathetic. In fact I see it as my mission to liberate womankind.'

'You're a regular feminist. God's gift to women.'

'You're catching on. What do you think of my lady for the night?'

'Tracy's a prize.'

'I'll tell you, I'll shag her or I'm not my father's son.'

'Good for you.'

Brian skirts around the dance floor, nudging by ex-classmates and their dates, with his elbows out to protect the pints. Jimmy follows close behind. He has had a glass of wine and this is his third pint, yet he still feels too sober. He hadn't been planning on making a move on Alice, figuring that even if she let him kiss her, it would go no further than that. Now he's reconsidering. Brian has a perplexing reputation for success with women, so he might be on to something. Maybe it would be okay to use Alice if she wants to be used.

At their table, the dishes have been cleared and the white tablecloth bears a few food stains. Jasmine's hand rests on Seb's knee as he recalls a tantrum Niall Shanahan threw on set. Tracy is whispering something to Alice, who nods earnestly. They laugh when they notice Jimmy and Brian, then Alice smiles with what Jimmy takes to be a guilty look.

Finbar is sitting next to his date, Vicky. Her eyes are half closed and, with her elbows on the table, she's mashing her face against her palms. Brian plants a pint in front of Finbar. 'Get that down you! You're supposed to be having the time of your life. For fuck's sake.'

Finbar glances dourly at Vicky. 'Sound. I *am* having fun.'

Jimmy sits between Alice and Finbar. Brian sits next to Tracy and kisses her cheek. 'Miss me?'

She says, 'Terribly,' and laughs. Brian muffles a burp out of deference to the women.

Alice meets Jimmy's eyes then looks away and fidgets with

the stem of her wine glass. He sips his pint and tries to think of a seductive conversation starter. What, he asks himself, would Tighe say? He decides to show her his sensitive side. 'Wasn't what happened in Omagh awful?'

She almost tips over her wine glass, before steadying it with both hands. 'Oh! Absolutely. I don't understand how anyone could intentionally cause so much suffering.'

'All those dead bodies.'

'Right. Nothing justifies such pointless cruelty. I mean, all cruelty is unjustifiable.'

'I couldn't agree more. It was completely tragic, twenty-nine dead I think it was, but, y'know, the story from it that reso-nated with me the most was that one of the victims was a pregnant woman. She would have had twins. And the thing is, I wouldn't really count the unborn babies as real people – I don't think you're fully alive until you're born. Like I'd be pro-choice and all that . . .'

'Oh, me too. I think abortion is definitely not good, but women should have the right to do what they want with their own bodies. Sorry, you were saying?'

'Just that I don't know what stage of the pregnancy it was, but it really struck me that, after all their time next to each other in her womb, those twins deserved to know they existed together. They were robbed of that. Do you get what I mean?'

'I think I do. It's really really sad.'

She holds his gaze for the longest she has managed so far.

Having no more profundities to offer regarding Omagh, he asks, 'What's your opinion of the mess Clinton's gotten himself into?'

Alice sips her wine, then covers her mouth with her hand as she swallows. 'I guess it's kind of stupid, y'know, that there's such an overreaction?'

'Totally. At heart, America will always have that puritan tendency that brought about things like Prohibition and, like, this. They're prone to rushing to judgement, even if it's over things that don't really matter.'

'Yeah, it wasn't wise for Clinton to risk his position and his marriage, but I suppose it's something that men, that *people*, do – affairs, I mean – and what matters is that he's a good president. I'm sure other powerful people do much worse.'

'Definitely. There's lots of corruption out there. Lots. What do you think of Lewinsky's role in it all?'

She frowns. 'I kinda feel sorry for her. She should've thought about what was at stake, but I guess she probably had real feelings for him and ended up being humiliated. It must be awful to have everyone knowing about it and laughing at her.'

'I imagine she got caught up in her fantasy, then acted without thinking. It's human, I've always felt, acting on desire. We shouldn't judge harshly when we all have impulses that can cloud our common sense. It would've been worse, maybe, if they'd had proper sex. Maybe what she did for him isn't quite as big a deal. It's still adultery, and I don't condone it, but it's not as bad as if they'd gone the whole way and, like, consummated their passion.'

She looks at him, a little mystified. 'Right. I guess. Right.'

They both drink, then she excuses herself to go to the bathroom. He closes his eyes and winces.

'Jimmy?' He opens his eyes. Finbar is staring at him. 'You okay?'

'I'm fine. Swallowed my beer too fast.'

'Cool.' Finbar, lowering his voice, says, 'Looks like Alice is eating out of your hand.'

'She might not be my type.'

'Really? I know the feeling.' Finbar looks at Vicky, who has passed out, crushing a napkin on the table with her face. 'She said she could drink me under the table.'

'Maybe she'll get a second wind.'

After Brian and Tracy get up and head for the dance floor, Finbar leans in closer to Jimmy and says, 'Listen, I want your advice. It's about Brian.'

'I thought you two were getting on okay.'

'That's part of the problem. He rang me the day after that fight at his place and apologised. I'm not one to hold a grudge, so I forgave him. When I heard all that stuff about his dad screwing around behind his mother's back, I could understand he hadn't been himself that night anyway. Since then, he keeps buying me drinks. You see, he *was* in the wrong, but not as much as he thinks.

'Remember that six-six you threw when you beat Brian?' Jimmy nods. 'You actually rolled a six-one. I turned the second die over.'

'Why are you telling me this?'

'Because what I did was petty and I'd rather not get away with it.'

'You're going to tell him?'

'That depends on you. You won some money on the bet.'

'Yeah, like fourteen quid.'

'Well, if I tell him, he'd have the right to ask for it back. I doubt he'd be bothered – it'd be me he'd be mad at, and I'd insist on paying him myself anyway. If he refuses to take the money from me and does get it from you, then I'll pay you afterwards. But I figured I should get your go-ahead before I confess, because you'll lose your bragging rights.'

Jimmy laughs. 'You're overcomplicating it. I don't care about bragging or paying the money, but it could stir things up for no reason. It was a dumb night, everyone else has forgotten about it, and you were provoked. There are worse sins than biting your tongue.'

Finbar drinks. 'That's just it, though. It'd be a sin not to confess and I don't want sins on my conscience. The rest of you might not feel the same, but I believe we're all being watched, and judged too.'

'I'll tell you what: if you still want to unburden yourself in the morning, go for it. Just not now. You've had a few drinks. He's had even more.'

'Tomorrow, then.'

Vicky raises her face from the table, her fake-tan-smudged napkin hanging from her cheek. Looking at Finbar, she says, 'Sick. I'm going to be sick.'

Springing to his feet and putting his arm around her waist, he helps her up from her chair. 'Hold it in, okay? I'll get you to the bathroom.'

She lets herself be guided away from the table. 'Uhh. You're my knight.'

Across the table, Seb chuckles. Smiling flirtatiously at him, Jasmine slaps his shoulder. 'Hush.'

Alice returns and says to Jimmy, 'Finbar and Vicky just went by me. Should I try to help?'

He shakes his head. 'They're beyond it.'

The DJ starts playing 'Viva Forever' by the Spice Girls. Alice says, 'Hey! I love this song! Would you be up for dancing?'

Jimmy, who hates the song, abruptly says, 'No.' She looks hurt. 'My leg, y'know? I don't like to dance.'

'I'm sorry, I should've . . .'

He reaches out to touch her hand, hesitates, then does so. 'Please, it's fine.'

'I'm always speaking without thinking.' This is far less true of her than of most people. Nevertheless, she believes it.

He removes his hand from hers. 'I don't want you to see me as impaired.'

'I don't! You make life seem effortless. I wish I had your confidence.'

He's intimidated by the admiration in her eyes, but says, 'Want to take a walk? We could check out the grounds.'

They stand, and as they go around the couples on the dance floor, she slips her hand into his. At the door, he looks back. Brian and Tracy are near the centre of the floor. His hands are on her hips. Her face is against his neck. Brian catches Jimmy's eye and gives him a knowing smile, Tracy's glossy lipstick on his mouth.

Outside, Jimmy and Alice hurry past a few like-minded couples, whose presence, generally concealed behind trees, is given away by the odd laugh or groan. When they come to a set of stone steps leading down to a pond with a fountain, they can no longer distinguish what song is playing in Ashburnham. Only a vague beat is audible. Using his shoulder for balance, Alice takes off her high heels and holds them by the straps. They descend the steps. Mindful of her bare feet, he says, 'Be careful.'

As they proceed along a pathway, he crunches pebbles under his shoes. Tiptoeing, she says, 'Quiet. You'll scare the fish.'

'Fish are clever. They'll realise I mean no harm.'

'How do you know?'

'I'm significantly older than you. I've learned a lot about fish in my extra time.'

'Two years older is nothing.'

'And you're mature for your age, is that it?'

'Very.'

They sit on a bench by the pond. She rubs the sole of her foot. He says, 'Did you hurt yourself?'

She releases her foot and, wiggling her toes, says, 'I'm fine.'

The expanse of still water glistens in places, but is otherwise as black as oil. Jimmy wonders if there really are any fish beneath the surface.

Alice shivers. She allows him to put his jacket around her shoulders. He says, 'Inside, you said you thought I was confident. Well you should be too. You have a lot going for you.'

'That's sweet of you.'

'I'm stating the obvious.' He puts his hand on her knee. 'You're really attractive.' She laughs nervously. His expression remains serious. 'I think you're sexy, y'know?'

'I'm not.'

He kisses her. Their front teeth bump as soon as she opens her mouth. He withdraws. 'Sorry.' She returns his kiss. This time their teeth don't meet, and though it's initially rushed, they settle into some coordination.

He runs his hands along her thighs to her hips and up under his jacket over the light material of her dress to the bare skin of her shoulders, then moves them around to her breasts. He gives her a few moments to pull away. When she doesn't, he starts to squeeze in near rhythm to their kissing, his fingers and thumbs increasingly rough. She sighs – he thinks it's a good sigh. Although his erection is cramped against his trousers, it's uncomfortable in a pleasurable way. He removes his hands and stops kissing her.

They look at each other, dazed. He says, 'Thank you.'

She laughs.

'I want to kiss you again.'

She leans into him. 'Then let's . . .'

He puts his hands on her shoulders. Her smile freezes. He says, 'I feel kind of exposed out here. I want to kiss you, but I don't want anyone to see us.'

'Where else is there to go?'

'How about behind the trees?'

'The trees?'

'I just thought privacy would be good. If you want to.'

'I guess that'd be fine.'

Hand-in-hand, Alice still barefoot, they tread across pebbles, grass, and mud into the dark copse. When Jimmy thinks they're hidden from view, he guides her to an oak. With her back to the bark, they kiss again, pushing against each other. He wants her to be aware of his hardness, and she is. He drops his jacket from her shoulders to the mud, then he's pulling down her shoulder straps and unzipping her dress. As he undoes her bra, almost breaking the clasp, he says, 'Is it okay if I look?' She breathes more heavily and doesn't answer. He doesn't wait, dropping her bra on his jacket. With her dress stripped to the waist, he strokes her back and, bending down, puts his mouth to one of her soft breasts. Her fingers are in his hair, and she's saying his name as he sucks on her stiff nipple.

He straightens up and meets her eyes – something he hasn't done since they were on the bench. 'How far? How far do you want me to go?'

She hugs him and looks in the direction of the pond, which is obscured by trees. 'I don't know. I don't think we should, y'know, make love? I don't want to risk getting pregnant.'

He considers telling her he has a condom – it has been in his wallet for three years – but decides not to, in case she might conclude he had a calculated plan all along.

She says, 'I'm sure it's pretty obvious that I'm not experienced at all, and I don't know what I should be doing, how to make this good for you. I guess I want to do what you want me to do. I just need to know you feel something for me too. Something real.' She kisses him. 'You do, don't you?'

'Of course. You're great.' She smiles with relief. 'Really great.' He takes a half-step back.

She hesitantly places her hand on his belt. 'So, what . . .'

He puts his hand on hers. 'We'd better . . . get back. Someone might be wondering.'

'Wondering what?'

'Nothing. Just where we are.'

He picks up her bra and his jacket. She takes the bra from him, puts it back on, and zips up her dress. He holds out his jacket to her. She waves it away. 'I'm warm now.'

She starts walking and he has to jog a few steps to catch up. At the bench, she collects her shoes and they set off the way they came. He wants to take her hand, but doesn't.

Inside Ashburnham, the music seems to blare louder than before, the lighting seems harsher, and everyone is so drunk, their expressions more moronic. Their motions on the dance floor are exaggerated to the point of self-parody. Tracy rushes up to Jimmy and Alice. 'There you are!' She takes Alice by the wrist. 'You're just in time.'

Alice says, 'For what?'

'To accompany me to the ladies'.' To Jimmy, Tracy says, 'You'll have to amuse yourself for a while, I'm afraid.'

As they move away, he says, 'I'll be at our table.' Alice doesn't give any indication of having heard him. Tracy is already whispering in her ear.

Their table is unoccupied. Brian and Seb's jackets are lying on their chairs. Vicky's orange-brown-stained napkin is propped against a half-drunk pint. Jimmy sits, then removes his bow tie and shoves it into his pocket. He swipes the napkin away, knocks back the pint, and slams the empty glass on the table. He takes fourteen pounds from his wallet and puts it into Brian's jacket. With what money he has left, he goes to the bar to buy another drink.

Alice isn't the only one feeling aggrieved at Jimmy. I'm stuck on their conversation about Omagh, and those unborn twins who were among the casualties – they have genuinely been on his mind, and what irks me is how he chooses to vicariously ponder their origins instead of his own and mine. Elizabeth told him about me a month ago, but he hasn't questioned Eamon or Grace, or anyone, about whether it's true. He doesn't intend to either, mainly because the idea of having a twin is at odds with his concept of individuality; as if being one of two would reduce him as a person, which is an inane way of looking at it. You're either a person or you're not; there's no in-between. He doesn't owe it to me to confront the truth about his past. I'm immaterial in both senses of the word. He owes it to himself. But he wouldn't agree.

Chapter Thirteen

Who You Know

October 1998

JIMMY'S JAW ACHES FROM FALLING ASLEEP WITH HIS face pressed against the wooden armrest of someone's couch. His tongue feels leaden, his throat raw. He has been using his jacket as a blanket and his arms are crossed, his hands tucked into his armpits. There are over a dozen empty beer cans on the glass-topped table a foot from his nose. In the corner of the room there are plastic bags crammed with crushed ones. He breathes in the cigarette-saturated air, and as he sits up, rubbing his arms, his jacket slides off his shoulder to the floor.

He's in Dublin, a UCD student flat in Merville. Last night he was talking to a guy that lives here, a Texan, who said how he appreciated that Irish girls dress provocatively but play hard to get. He liked their 'pirate' accents and was in awe of their drinking abilities. His name was . . . No idea. Good guy, though.

Jimmy puts his hands to his face, for warmth and to check that his eyebrows haven't been shaved off. He stands and manoeuvres around the table without knocking any cans. A lip-smacking sound is produced every time he peels his runners from the sticky linoleum.

In the hallway, there's a 'girls of the week' poster on the wall, featuring seven busty lingerie models. Late in the party he had debated the merits of each of the airbrushed, cosmetically altered models with some other guys for almost an hour. Someone said, 'They'd make a pretty good week.'

Jimmy said, 'Make that a pretty good *life*,' to much laughter.

By the time they switched topics, all the girls who'd been at the party had departed. Jimmy doesn't blame them. How dumb the guys must have sounded, himself in particular.

In the bathroom, he discovers that someone vomited in the shower then covered it with a hand towel. In the mirror he sees that his jaw bears a diagonal indentation from the armrest and his brown hair is coiled in random directions. His eyelids tend to droop over his eyes a fraction more than for the average person, but they look especially heavy now. He drinks from the cold-water tap, soothing his throat. He gargles and spits. Then he splashes his face and dampens down his hair, using his T-shirt as a towel.

When he steps outside, he yawns with his entire body, stretching his fingers to the grey sky. He feels spacey, but he doesn't have a headache and he isn't nauseated. Taking his alcohol intake into account, this is a victory.

Wind nips at his eyes, so he keeps them fixed on the ground ahead. Soon he's second-guessing whether he was fortunate to have been spared retribution for passing out. Someone must have put his jacket over him, the kind of extra consideration afforded to people you laugh along with because you perceive them as having a disability and they might be delicate.

At the row of bus stops, he checks his watch – it's eight a.m. – and the timetable. The first 46a won't be here until after ten. He sits in the shelter and leans back against the glass. Closing his eyes, he senses a tingling in his absent leg, then a spreading itch, and a spasm runs from his imaginary kneecap to the sole of his imaginary foot. The phantom pain, the subtle differences in how people treat him, even this wait – it all feels like part of a mass conspiracy. He wants to smash something but won't, because his suffering is nobler if he exercises restraint.

He falls asleep. When he comes to, his mouth and throat are dry again. He kicks his prosthetic with his real heel, not hard, to confirm what's fake. He checks his watch – it's only 8.20. He hears crying from the adjacent shelter, but then it stops and a female voice says, 'Fuck you . . . *Fuck you!*'

He doesn't know if there are two people in the shelter or if the woman is crazy. He tells himself that it's better to be a Good Samaritan and go and see what's wrong than to play it safe, when really he's just curious.

The woman, sitting alone on the plastic bench, has light-brown skin and looks around his age. She's wearing a black blouse and skirt, and holding a mobile, her arm curled against her lap. Her other hand covers her eyes. Jimmy clears his throat. 'Excuse me? Are you okay?'

Her shoulders steady and she withdraws her hand from her face. Her dark eyes are accentuated by long eyelashes, but it's the sharpness of her stare that makes them so striking. 'What are you looking at? Who are you?'

He blushes. 'Just thought I'd check you're all right. I didn't mean . . . anything.'

She turns her eyes to her shoes, as if the very sight of him is causing her anguish. 'Sorry, okay? Whatever you want, find someone else.'

'Right. My mistake.'

He walks briskly away. In the time it'll take for the bus to arrive, he'll be home. And it's good to get exercise and fresh air. Well, no, not fresh air exactly; this is Dublin. His hands are clenched into fists, but he doesn't say aloud what he's thinking, that he hates this fucking city!

'Is it true what the man himself was telling me about you?'

Sinking into a bloated beanbag, Jimmy smiles drowsily. 'Who?'

Laid out on the couch, Gavin has a drag of the spliff. 'Tipperary's answer to Tom Cruise.'

'Probably not, then. What did he say?'

'That you're a lucky man.'

Jimmy pushes himself up so he's leaning back on his elbows. 'Lucky? Me?'

Gavin stretches out his arm, the spliff between his fingers. 'The word is that when it comes to games of chance, chance smiles upon you.'

Jimmy takes the spliff. 'Seb said that?'

'Less eloquently, but that was the gist. Does he speak the truth?'

'I've had the odd run, but only with friends. I'm not about to drop the education, go professional.'

'Humility and luck. They won't know what hit them.'

'Who won't?'

Gavin grins. 'Tonight, my friend, we're hitting the town. But it's all a bit hush-hush, if y'know what I mean.'

'I rarely do.'

'We're going to a casino.'

'I wasn't aware that Ireland has casinos.'

'You just need to know where to look.'

Jimmy met Gavin when he and Seb first moved to Dublin and they were searching for a place to live. Gavin's flat was on Windmill Lane, a minute's walk south of the Liffey and its rat-piss-steeped aroma. It was drab, but the rent was reasonable and he had two box rooms available. Gavin was twenty-two, and while he'd never been further afield than the UK, Jimmy and Seb thought he possessed a worldly air. After they explained what brought them to Dublin, he smiled as if nothing could be more ridiculous than being an arts student or an aspiring actor. He let them have the rooms anyway.

Despite living together, Jimmy and Seb haven't been seeing a lot of each other. Seb's been keeping busy with his course and its social scene during the week, then on most weekends he's in Rathbaile. Jimmy has yet to return.

He sees much more of Gavin. Originally he had assumed Gavin was renting the flat and subletting it on the sly, but it turned out that he was paying a mortgage. When Jimmy asked how he could afford it, Gavin claimed to be an entrepreneur. He was evasive about the specifics until one drunken night he admitted, 'Between us? I act as a conduit between a certain supply and demand. I'm a dealer. I only sell the non-serious stuff, yer basic hash and weed, pills occasionally. I don't sell nothing to kids. That's for scumbags. I'm not greedy and I won't be doing this forever.' Jimmy tried not to look too impressed.

He told Seb and regretted it. Seb wanted them to move out, because they could be implicated if Gavin ever got busted. Jimmy convinced him that the Gardaí were only interested in the dealers selling harder drugs, and besides, Gavin was too clued in to get caught. The truth was that Jimmy believed it would be cool if some of whatever notoriety Gavin possessed rubbed off.

Jimmy hands back the spliff, barely more than a roach now. 'Man, it's Sunday, and I was out last night.'

Gavin laughs. 'C'mon. Life is there for the living. Experience something!'

Jimmy sits up as straight as he can manage on the beanbag, thinking that his resistance will be aided by a more dignified posture. 'I'm a poor student, y'know. I don't have the funds. If this place is at all upmarket . . .'

'You said you had a job during the summer, that you had something saved.'

'I worked in a newsagent for minimum wage and my earnings are meant to last.'

'Look, if you can muster up twenty quid, I'll spot you another twenty – for the sake of flatmate solidarity. It'll be an investment. You make something, we split it. Lose it all, my loss.'

'I appreciate it, but I don't have it in me tonight.'

'Can't twist your arm?'

'Afraid not.'

An hour later, they are in the docklands, standing outside a warehouse without any lights shining through its windows. The only sign that something is happening within is the large number of cars parked nearby. They go past the padlocked main doors and around to a side door, which is ajar. They enter and proceed down a corridor to another door that has red light emanating from underneath. Gavin says, 'Ever hear about the light at the end of the tunnel being the headlights of an oncoming train?' Jimmy says nothing. Gavin points at a camera peering at them from above the door. 'You're on the telly.'

Jimmy glances up, then hangs his head. Gavin raps his fist on the door. There's a buzzing, a click, and the sound of a bolt being undone. The door opens. A hulk of a man stands before them. His bowling-ball-shaped head is adorned by oiled, and apparently permed, red hair. His eyes, nose, and mouth are small and squashed-looking compared to the broad canvas of his face, and he's wearing a trench coat featuring silver studs on the shoulders and cuffs. Gavin says, 'Sugar! How are you keeping?'

Sugar, his voice soft, says, 'Can't complain.' He motions them inside. 'Gentlemen.'

As they descend a staircase, Gavin whispers, 'What did you think of yer man's hair?'

Jimmy says, 'Vaguely psychotic, but I wouldn't say that to his face.'

'Not above vanity is old Sugar. Nice guy, though.' Gavin puts a finger to his lips as they approach a muffled sound of overlapping conversations.

At the bottom of the stairs, there's another bouncer, guarding another door, his thumbs hooked in his trouser pockets. He has a closely shaven head and a neat moustache, and there's a suggestion of disdain in the churning motion of his jaw – he's chewing gum. Jimmy's eyes are drawn to the handgun holstered against his side. Gavin nods at him, but he doesn't return the acknowledgement. He pushes the door open and Jimmy and Gavin go through into a room that stretches wide and long, with a high curved ceiling. The impression is created of being inside an immense barrel. Jimmy counts two blackjack tables, two roulette tables, a craps table, and four poker tables at the back. There are more than a hundred patrons, and most of them are in a raucous mood.

Gavin says, 'Let's drink!'

Jimmy follows him to one of a cluster of tables and they sit. 'I don't see a bar.'

'That's one of the perks. It's all waited service.'

Gavin waves a folded twenty-pound note in the air. A waitress comes over, balancing a tray on her fingertips that holds some empty shot glasses and loose cash. She tucks one of her blonde curls behind her ear and flashes a smile. 'How can I help you, fellas?'

Gavin looks her up and down, while Jimmy is slightly more discreet. She waits patiently. Like the other waitresses, she's wearing a short skirt and a back-baring waistcoat that pushes up her breasts – being leered at is part of her job description. Gavin says, 'Darling, we'll have two bottles of yer finest lager.'

'We've lots of different—'

'I trust yer good taste.'

She swivels around and doesn't break her strut towards the back room, even when some drunk pinches her ass as she passes. His friends cheer as he shrugs, raising his hands.

Gavin says, 'You see that guy over there?' He's referring to a triangular-chinned man in his late twenties, sitting in a booth set apart from the rest of the tables. Two men, both fiftyish and heavyset, are sitting across from him, and at his side is a pretty brunette, her mouth open and ready to laugh as he tells them all a story. One of his hands is in the air, his fingers making a tapping motion, as if he's striking piano keys. His other hand is on the brunette's thigh, his small and ring fingers snaking under her skirt. Gavin says, 'Now him, he's somebody.'

'A tough guy, huh?'

'Well . . .' They are interrupted by the waitress bringing them their beers. After Gavin has given her a large tip, she moves on and he says, 'That's Vinnie. His father owns the place and he's the real tough guy. Linus Cosgrove, aka Big C, aka the Ballyfermot Reaper. Ring any bells?'

'Didn't he kill someone?'

'You don't get called a reaper if you've only killed *one* someone. He never got caught for any of it, though. Nobody was ever so suicidally inclined as to be a witness. The guards eventually nabbed him on armed robbery. Stupid way to go down, really. The Big C was a boss and a millionaire a couple of times over. He could've just sat back on the bank job and collected earnings. Guess he got too much of a kick out of sticking a gun in people's faces. Now he's on a ten-year stretch in Mountjoy.'

'Is the son more of the same?'

'Vinnie's not quite so hardcore. He's never strangled anyone to death, far as I know. They call him Little C. He sees himself as a people person. But I wouldn't recommend fucking with him.'

'I'll try to remember not to.' Jimmy pokes his temple. 'Note to self.'

'Like to meet him?'

Jimmy laughs, then stops when he sees Gavin means it. 'You know him?'

'He's an acquaintance.'

'I doubt we'd have a whole lot in common.'

'Don't be a pussy. We'll just say hello.'

Jimmy swigs from his bottle and stands. 'Okay. I'll follow your cue.'

'Smart man.'

In the time it takes to cross the room, Jimmy finishes his beer. When they arrive at Vinnie's booth, the two older men are standing and Vinnie's hand is two fingers further up the brunette's skirt. Gavin waits for the men to leave, then steps forward and holds his hand out. 'Vinnie, good to see you.'

His head swaying as he shakes hands, Vinnie says, 'Gav! When'd you get here?'

'When everyone least expected it. This is Jimmy, my flatmate.'

To Jimmy Vinnie says, 'Any friend of Gav's and all that shite.'

Jimmy says, 'Cool place you have.'

'Yeah, I'd say tell all yer friends, but that depends on who yer friends are. Ah, I'm sure they're all sound. Bring whoever the fuck you want. Where are me manners? Sit, sit!'

Gavin and Jimmy slide in opposite Vinnie. He waves over the blonde waitress. As soon as she's near, he yells, 'Champagne!' and makes a circular motion over the table with his free index finger. She turns in her tracks. With his thumb disappearing under his companion's skirt, Vinnie says, 'This sweet lass is Cheryl. Cheryl, these are my good friends.'

Her eyes as bleary as his, she says, 'How do you do?'

Vinnie says, 'Jimmy, would I be correct in suspecting yer not from Dublin?'

Gavin says, 'He's a culchie from Rathbaile. I'm showing him the ropes.'

'I've never been there. Quaint, is it?'

Jimmy says, 'It's getting bigger every year, but it still feels like everyone knows everyone.'

'I like towns like that, I confess, or the idea of them anyway. I hope you're enjoying the hustle and bustle up here. You realise the secret, don't you, to really taking to a place? It's all about who you know. Meet the right people and anywhere can feel like home. You don't, no matter where you are, it's shite.'

The waitress returns with four flutes and a bottle of champagne in a bucket of ice. She sets her tray on the table and lifts out the dripping bottle. 'Want me to pop it, Mr Cosgrove?'

'Give it here.' He snatches it out of her hands. 'You can go.' She does.

With a big grin, Vinnie shakes the bottle. Gavin says, 'Maybe you shouldn't . . .'

'Yer supposed to.' Vinnie pops it and the cork shoots in Gavin's direction, just missing his head. 'Fuck! Sorry, bud!'

The foam overflows from the bottle. Gavin smiles and hopes that no one noticed him flinch. 'No worries.'

As Vinnie pours the champagne into the flutes, he knocks one over. It rolls off the table and smashes on the floor. 'Motherfucker!'

Cheryl strokes his forearm. 'Don't sweat it, Vinnie. We can get another.'

'I reckon we'll manage as we are.' He hands a flute to Jimmy. 'That's for me new friend.' He hands another to Gavin. 'That's for me old friend.' He pulls the third flute closer to himself. 'And this is for yours truly.'

Cheryl protests, 'Vinnie!'

'Don't worry, darling. I wouldn't leave you out.' He grabs the bottle. 'Open yer mouth. Stick out yer tongue.'

She hesitates and glances at Gavin and Jimmy. Gavin is sipping from his flute. Jimmy's face is inexpressive, but his heart is beating rapidly. Cheryl laughs and does as she's been told. Vinnie lifts the bottle above her head and pours it down her throat. She swallows as quickly as she can, but some of the champagne spills from the corners of her mouth and dribbles down her neck. Vinnie smirks. 'Quite a guzzler, eh, lads?'

Cheryl starts coughing and champagne spurts from her mouth. She grasps Vinnie's arm and pushes him away. Putting down the bottle, he stares at her as she grips the table and coughs herself under control. She croaks, 'Sorry . . . just . . . too much. Sorry.'

He rubs her back. 'There, now. My fault. I gave you too much. Yer grand.' She looks at him, her cheeks tear-streaked, her pink lipstick smeared. He wipes her face with his thumb and laughs. 'You really have made a mess. Why don't you go clean yourself up? I'll be nice when you get back.'

She squeezes past him. 'I won't take long.'

Once she's gone, Vinnie says, 'Ah, now I almost feel bad.'

Gavin says, 'There wasn't any harm done. I wouldn't take it to heart.'

'I wasn't planning on it. Don't think I'm in the business of mistreating women, lads. I reckon I'll even let her go on top later. Until I decide not to.'

Gavin laughs, but Jimmy's smile is pained. Vinnie lifts his flute. 'Anyway, James, is it?'

Jimmy says, 'Right. But Jimmy, though.'

Vinnie raises his flute a little higher. The champagne sparkles gold in the light. 'Welcome to our humble city, Jimmy-James. May she treat you well. Now, down in one.'

Gavin says, 'Hear, hear.'

They clink their flutes together and drink.

Jimmy only realises how thirsty he is when the champagne washes over his tongue. He's the first to finish. He watches Vinnie and Gavin race to be second. It strikes him that Vinnie is undoubtedly an asshole, and that most likely Gavin is too. And so then: what does that make him?

As much as Jimmy's discomfort is growing, and he's increasingly looking forward to leaving, if he truly understood what a nest of vipers he's in – if I could warn him about what Vinnie is capable of – he would run a mile, limp be damned.

Chapter Fourteen

Glass

I
December 1979

GRACE FILLS PAUL'S PLASTIC CUP WITH MILK. 'THAT'LL give you strong bones.' Paul, who turned four a fortnight ago, is sitting at the dining-room table, along with Elizabeth, Tighe, and Eamon. His chair has a cushion on it to give him a boost. He takes the cup in his hands and sips. Grace pats his shoulder. 'That's my boy.'

Tighe, who is eight, stuffs a spoonful of mincemeat into his mouth, even though his cheek is already bulging. Elizabeth is five. She chews on a piece of carrot. Her eyes are on the jug in Grace's hands. Eamon affixes a cumbersome corkscrew to a bottle of wine. He rotates the handle at the top and the spiral bores into the cork. Grace pours Elizabeth a glass of milk, repeating, 'Strong bones.'

Tighe holds up his glass. When Grace has poured his milk, he gulps it and swallows his food. To Eamon he says, 'We can see *Star Trek* on Sunday?'

As he retracts the corkscrew, Eamon says, 'Wouldn't miss it.' The cork pops. Elizabeth's hand jerks and a few drops of milk hop from her glass on to the tablecloth. She looks at Eamon. When he laughs, she does too. She dabs at the stain with her napkin.

Grace goes into the kitchen. She washes the jug in the sink and places it upside down on the drying rack. She presses her hands flat on the counter to stop herself from doubling over. Closing her eyes, she breathes deeply. She wishes Eamon would see through her everything-is-fine front – she shouldn't be *that* convincing. Her queasiness passes.

Eamon calls, 'Grace! Come have some wine!'

She opens her eyes. 'Just half a glass for me, okay?'

She re-enters the dining room. Eamon, his back to her, has poured two glasses. She seizes the one with less wine in it as she walks by, and sits at the opposite end of the table. He's looking at her with a crafty smile. Part of her wants to strangle him. How can he not suspect that earlier this week she slapped Elizabeth's face? It was only because she was crying over something trivial and the noise was unbearable. Grace cried then and, holding Elizabeth, asked for forgiveness. Elizabeth gave it and hasn't told anyone, but she has been avoiding eye contact with Grace ever since.

Eamon raises his glass. 'A toast?'

Grace raises her glass too. 'To what?'

'You choose.'

'Well, we could toast the new Taoiseach.'

He looks a little disappointed. 'Sure. To the new man so.'

They sip. Tighe says, 'Will he be any good?'

'It remains to be seen, but we'll give him a chance.' To Grace Eamon says, 'Is the wine okay?'

'It's good.' It's bitter. She drinks more anyway.

There's a clatter. Paul has knocked his cup to the floor. It rolls in an arc on the wood, bleeding a trail of white before it comes to a weary impact with the wainscoting at the nearest wall. Paul cringes, tears in his eyes. 'Sorry, Mammy.'

She stands. 'Not to worry, only milk.'

Eamon says, 'I can clean it up if you—'

'I've got it.'

She leans down and picks up the cup. As she stands, something treacherous flips in her guts and she feels too hot. She drops the cup. With one hand pulled into her stomach and the other covering her mouth, she rushes to the bathroom. There, she collapses to her knees on the woolly mat and, gripping the toilet seat with both hands, vomits repeatedly. After her last heave, she stares at the colourful mess she has emptied into the bowl and feels Eamon's hand on her back. He sweeps her hair from her face and helps her to sit against the tiled wall, then tears off a few toilet-paper squares and wipes her mouth and chin. 'You okay?'

She fights an urge to laugh. 'Never better.'

He smiles cautiously. 'Are you pregnant?'

'Do I have a motherly glow about me?'

'Are you?'

'Yes.'

His smile is now ear to ear. 'You're sure?'

'I am.'

He hugs her. 'What a wonderful early Christmas present. I love you so much.'

She holds on to him, resting her cheek on his shoulder and looking away. A tear slides down her nose. 'I love you.'

She supposes she probably does still mean it. She vows not to tell him she doesn't want another baby, no matter who it might turn out to be. She doesn't want Jimmy. She doesn't want me.

November 1998

'You've got to keep trying.'

'Why?'

'Tighe needs you. Elizabeth needs you. Jimmy needs you.'

'They really don't. They've moved on and I doubt any of them are coming back. I don't blame them. Even when they visit, this town, being around me, it's the last place they want to be.'

'*I* need you, Grace. So much. I can't live without you.'

'You only *think* that, Eamon. You'd be better off without me.'

'How can I persuade you that you're wrong?'

'You can't.'

'Don't give up. Please. Let me help you.'

'Do you have any idea what it's taken to keep trying as long as I have? I've made far too many mistakes. There's so much I'd change, but I can't, because once you make a decision it stands forever and nothing can be erased. Nothing helps either. They've got me on all these pills. Like happiness could come in a pill! But maybe I can't even recognise it any more. It's been so long since I've felt it. Eamon, don't look at me like that . . . I know so much of this is my fault.'

'I don't blame you. I know things have never been easy. Just remember how you're *loved*. Never forget that I love you.'

'You think you do.'

'Grace . . .'

'You think you do, but the truth is you don't know who I am in my heart. I wonder how well you even know yourself.'

'I know you. I know myself. I don't know what you *mean*, though. I don't know what you're trying to *say*.'

'I'm saying that maybe the reason I'm unhappy is because I'm the rare person who knows herself. And that's because I've tried to be other people and failed. I've failed terribly and I settled for all the wrong roles. You don't know yourself because you've only ever tried to be one person.'

'How can I begin to make sense of that?'

'I don't expect you to.'

'Do you doubt I know what I want? That I've always wanted you?'

'I know you believe what you're saying, but you would've been better off without me.'

'Despite all that's gone wrong, despite our lost baby girl, and losing Paul, and everything our children have gone through, despite the fact that I've never made you happy, if I could go back to when we met, I would still choose you and our life together. We've suffered, yes, but it *has* been worth it. Are you listening? I would still choose you.'

'Eamon, don't you see? If I could go back, I wouldn't have any of our children. And *I* wouldn't choose *you*.'

Through the wire-meshed square window in the door to her mother's private room, Elizabeth observes her. On the far side of a neatly made bed, and at one corner of a window that looks out on St Augustine's rain-soaked garden, Grace is sitting on a padded rocking chair, with her legs pulled up on to the seat, the heels of her feet resting on the edge and her knees propped against the armrest. She's wearing a cream woollen cardigan over pyjamas, and has thick socks on. Rubber doorstops are wedged under the rockers. Her expression is inscrutable.

Elizabeth knocks on the glass and Grace looks askance at her. She opens the door and goes inside without waiting for an invitation, then walks directly over to Grace, who remains seated, and kisses her on the cheek while squeezing her shoulder, which feels hard and narrow under the layers of clothes. Grace accepts the kiss but doesn't return it.

When Elizabeth steps back, Grace says, 'This is a surprise. Your father was supposed to hold off on spreading the word about me.'

'I phoned him last night. It was obvious that something was wrong so I got it out of him against his will. I wanted to see for myself how you are. So here I am.'

'And how do I appear to be?'

Elizabeth gives her honest appraisal: 'You look very tired and like you haven't been eating. You've lost weight and you didn't have it to lose.'

'Sounds right. Pull up a chair.'

Elizabeth fetches a chair from the opposite side of the bed and sets it down by the other corner of the window. She unzips her slim black leather jacket, which is wet from the rain, but doesn't take it off.

Grace says, 'I see you've removed your lip ring. Why's that?'

'It's in my pocket. I guess I didn't want to look like the kind of daughter who would terrorise her mother into therapy.'

'You should have kept it in. No one here would have thought that. They know my "difficulties" stem from deep inside me.'

Elizabeth doesn't respond to the odd joking note in Grace's voice. She looks about the room – the walls and the bed sheets are all white, and there's an en suite bathroom. 'I had imagined this place differently. It doesn't seem so bad.'

Grace makes a scoffing noise. 'Try staying here and see how you feel about it then. I mean, didn't you hear the dulcet tones of the music they have playing or see how all the paintings on the walls are warm colours? They all have lakes and rivers in them with hardly a ripple on the surface, as if a hint of stormy weather might set off all the inmates – this is Ireland, for Christ's sake; we only have to look out the window to see torrential rain! And then there's the staff with their clean and ironed uniforms, and their oh-so-reasonable voices. Could there be a more patronising place in the world? On top of all that, there's the dark irony – and I really do see the humour – that this is where my mother lived out her final years; this is where she *died*. No doubt she's still here, in spirit, wandering the halls.' Conscious of Elizabeth's large eyes, Grace says, 'You don't need to look at me like that.'

'Like what?'

Grace laughs. 'Oh, like I'm crazy. Actually, I take that back. The way you're looking at me is spot on.'

Elizabeth doesn't modify how she's looking at Grace. 'If being here is getting to you, I could bring you some books.'

With a minimum of effort, Grace shakes her head. 'Thanks, but I'm just not interested.'

'You should spend some time in the communal area then. You'd be able to watch TV. You could make some friends.'

'You mean with the zombies and the loons?'

'Mam, you shouldn't call them that. They're only people who are having trouble.'

'No, *you* shouldn't call them that. I get to because I'm one of them. It's just not clear whether I'm a zombie or a loon. If you get the chance, you should ask a doctor which one I am. It's more likely that they'll tell you than me.' Quickly catching the exasperation in Elizabeth's eyes and in the jut of her chin, Grace says, 'Something on your mind?'

'I shouldn't say anything that might disturb you.'

'I don't see why not. I'm already disturbed.'

'Okay then. I haven't seen Dad this upset since Jimmy lost his leg, although he won't admit how much pain he's in. He's the sweetest man I know, and you said something to him, didn't you?'

'He *is* the sweetest man. I told him too much of the truth, and there aren't many things that are crueller than that.'

'Can you not – I don't know – fix it with him?'

'When have you known me to be able to fix anything?'

'You used to try.'

'Did I? Maybe I did. But something got broken in me along the way.'

'Was it Paul? Was that the end for you?' Grace looks stung and stops meeting Elizabeth's gaze. 'Do you blame me for his death? Is that why you and I have never—'

'Don't be ridiculous. You were what, seven years old? I blame only myself. I was the one who was responsible for him. You were a victim of what happened, but you can't fixate on it forever. You'll drive yourself mad that way.'

'Like you?'

Grace bats the air with the back of her hand. 'Not like me. You're stronger than I am.'

Elizabeth feels guilty for taking the conversation in this direction – she's aware that her mother is ill – but she still asks, 'Did people say that to you about *your* mother?'

Drawing her knees closer to her, and crossing her arms over her chest for the added warmth, Grace says, 'I don't worry about you becoming like me. I worry more about Jimmy and Tighe than I do about you.'

'Thanks.'

'You know what I mean.'

'I don't think I do.'

'How much you worry about someone and how much you care about them – it's not the same. Jimmy and Tighe both have reckless streaks; different kinds of reckless streaks, but still. You're not reckless. You're vigilant over yourself. They're not. I wasn't either, not enough, not like you.'

Remembering how, only four months ago, she spun her car off the road with Jimmy as a passenger, Elizabeth isn't convinced by Grace's assessment. 'How can you be certain that you know us so well?'

'I may not have done all I could have to earn the title, but I'm your mother. It counts for something.'

They sit facing one another for a while longer, mostly in silence, until Grace says, 'Elizabeth, I'm talked out and I want to sleep before they make me eat something. You should go be with your father.'

'Fine. Is there anything you'd like me to tell him?'

'Tell him you love him and give him a hug. He'd like that.'

'But nothing from you?'

'No, nothing.'

'How about Jimmy or Tighe? Is there any message you'd like me to convey to them?'

'There's nothing'

Trying to keep her voice from cracking, Elizabeth says, 'And what about me? Is there anything you want to say to *me*?'

'Elizabeth . . . I'm lost. Whatever it is you're hoping for, just pretend I've said it if that makes you feel better. And if it doesn't, then don't.'

Grace gets up from the rocking chair – her body appears to ache with every motion – and climbs under the covers of her bed, pulling the blanket up over her shoulder and turning away from her daughter.

Elizabeth stares with fury at her mother's blanket-humped back before striding to the door, shoving it closed behind her.

Grace watches her leave, then closes her eyes.

* * *

Jimmy answers his phone after one ring, but Elizabeth doesn't speak straight away. He hears movement and people talking in the background. He sees it's her from caller ID, but after saying, 'Hello?' twice with no response, he assumes she has called accidentally. He's about to hang up when she says, 'Jimmy. Where are you?'

'In my flat, studying. What's up?'

'I'll be there within half an hour. Don't go anywhere.'

'What? Why?' She has already hung up.

Sitting on the beanbag in front of the TV, he's about to pick up the joypad for Gavin's PlayStation and press play – a game of *Doom* is paused, with a fuming horned monster frozen in mid-extermination – when he changes his mind and calls her back. His call rings out, then goes to voicemail. He calls again, direct to voicemail this time. He texts her: *Answer your phone whats going on?*

He gets up, kicks the joypad out of his way, and goes into the kitchen. He makes a cup of coffee and is blowing on it when she texts him: *Dont call just wait for me want to talk in person ill b there quick as i can please ill explain everything.*

He considers calling home – if something is wrong, it's likely a family matter – but he doesn't want to worry Eamon if she's being ominous about a mess of her own making.

He returns to the beanbag, sets his coffee aside, and presses play on *Doom*, sealing the fate of the horned monster. While he annihilates plenty of other foes by way of rocket launcher, machine gun, and chainsaw, he's too distracted to be efficient, and after one too many hits, it's game over.

Eventually the intercom rings. He buzzes Elizabeth in and opens the front door. Leaning against the door frame, he hears her footsteps as she ascends the stairwell to the third floor.

At the top of the stairs, she halts, steadies her breathing, and rubs her eyes. For Jimmy's sake, she braces herself, then turns the corner and meets his eyes. He says, 'This better be good.'

She steps closer, her expression beseeching him to prepare himself for the worst. 'Jimmy, there's no way to say this gently. Mam . . . She's dead.'

His initial reaction is confusion. He turns and goes into the living room, moving like a sleepwalker. Elizabeth closes the front door and follows, keeping him within arm's reach.

Glancing back at her, he says, 'You're sure?' As they sit on the couch, he half smiles upon realising the inanity of the question. 'How?'

She pauses, her throat painfully dry, then says, 'Dad called me. He said it happened this morning. She had checked back into St Augustine's last week. I don't know if you were aware of that.'

'I wasn't. No one tells me anything, do they? Sorry. I'm sorry. Please just go on.'

'I went down at the weekend, and she was very low, and maybe I talked about things I shouldn't have with her, but I didn't think anything like this would happen, so I came back up to Dublin. I was worried, obviously; it just didn't occur to me – I didn't *let* it occur to me – that she would do what she did. Mam killed herself. I wouldn't be doing you any favours if I didn't tell you that. I'm so sorry.'

'Right, right.' His elbows digging into his knees, he grips his left fist in his right hand.

She puts her hand on his back, but he shies away. She says, 'It's okay to cry, or anything. It's okay.'

Without looking at her, he says, 'You're not crying.'

'I did when I heard about it.' That's true. She wept, and she didn't know if she'd be able to make herself stop, but

Eamon had asked her to go and break the news to Jimmy in person so she pulled herself together.

'There'll be time for tears. How did she kill herself? You must've asked Dad – you would have demanded to know – so what did he say?'

'If you're sure you're ready to hear it, I—'

'Elizabeth.'

She draws her lip ring into her mouth, then releases. 'It looks like she tried to break the mirror in her bathroom – they use safety glass, so that didn't work, but she had a make-up compact and she smashed the glass in that. She used a piece of it to cut her wrists. Then she got into her bed and let herself bleed out.'

'Why the fuck would she do that?'

'She left a note. Just one word: *sorry.*'

'That's it? "Sorry"?'

He imagines Grace smiling, but she doesn't look right. Her smile is fake and her deep-blue eyes mock him. He squeezes his eyes tightly shut. I see Elizabeth turn white as he says, 'I wish I could talk to her one last time, to confide in her that I don't accept her apology. I never will.'

I'm not surprised that Grace committed suicide, but I'm stunned regardless – it's impossible to ever be fully prepared for the loss, no matter how inevitable, of someone you love; and she loved me too, even though she never knew me. Without her, I'm one step closer to being forgotten.

Chapter Fifteen

Bruises

November 1998

WATER SPILLS DOWN JIMMY'S FACE, THE SHOWERHEAD hanging over him like a scythe. His fingers are splayed against the tiles. He runs his tongue over his teeth. A few of them feel loose, but none are about to fall out. The bump on the back of his head aches. There's a foggy thumping behind his forehead. Now and then a memory pierces through from the previous night. He made some mistakes after hearing of Grace's death:

- Refusing Elizabeth's strongly worded offer to drive him home to Rathbaile. He was adamant that he needed a night alone before facing everyone else and would follow on in the morning.
- Before she left, Elizabeth secured a promise from Jimmy to call Eamon to let him know he was okay. He didn't.
- When Gavin arrived home, Jimmy failed to mention Grace's death, but did suggest a casino night. Gavin might have dissuaded him if he'd been aware of what had happened.
- Eight bottles of beer. Five tequila shots. Two lines of cocaine.

- Emptying his bank account of all £400 so he could invest it in his 'gambling venture'.
- Playing at a poker table that had a £200 minimum stake.
- Not laughing at Vinnie's jokes and eyeballing him. When he ran out of money, Vinnie offered him a tab.
- Accepting that offer.
- And then: Jimmy had amassed a sizeable debt and was barely standing when he loudly asked Vinnie if his nickname Little C stood for 'Little Cunt'. He burst out laughing at the stone-faced response. Gavin apologised on his behalf – 'Vinnie, he doesn't have a fucking clue what he's saying' – and managed to haul Jimmy out of the casino without him taking a beating.

But the story doesn't end there. He woke this morning to a man with a shaved head and twitching moustache stomping into his bedroom and ripping away his blanket. The man seized a fistful of his shirt – he was still dressed in his clothes from the night before – and heaved him to his feet. 'You're the twat who goes by the name Jimmy Dice, aren't you?' As he stumbled back, Jimmy vaguely remembered rattling dice at the craps table and shouting, 'Call me Jimmy Dice!' The moustached man interpreted his groan as being in the affirmative. 'Know who I am?'

'You work for Vinnie.'

'I do. The name's Mr Casey. And you're familiar with Mr Gorman.'

Sugar, wearing a trench coat, was standing just inside the door, blocking the hallway from view. He nodded at Jimmy, who, straightening himself up, nodded in return.

Casey shoved him with one hand back against the wall. 'You didn't conduct yerself like a gentleman last night.'

Jimmy, not meeting Casey's eye, said, 'I'm sorry.'

'I'll pass on yer apologies. Vinnie can forgive a young man for having a few too many, and for forgetting himself and all that. But forgiveness in business isn't an option. You know how much you owe, don't you? The small matter of four grand.'

Jimmy nearly laughed. 'I'm not sure I'm awake.'

Casey kicked him in the prosthetic, expecting to deliver a dead leg. When Jimmy barely reacted, Casey punched him in the jaw, his head smacking into the wall. He slid down it, raising his hands to shield himself. Casey said, 'Real enough for you?'

Jimmy lowered his hands. 'Everything is very real to me. How long do I have?'

'Twenty-four hours. Can you get it?'

'I assume I have no choice.'

'You catch on, Jimmy! There'll be some what you might call permanent repercussions if you don't have it in full when we return tomorrow. I'll leave it to yer imagination.' Casey turned to Sugar. 'Anything to add, Mr Gorman?'

'Pay the money. Chalk it up to experience.' Sugar shrugged. 'We'll be seeing you.'

After they left, Gavin came in and pulled Jimmy up. 'They would've kicked in the door if I hadn't opened it.'

Rubbing the back of his head, Jimmy said, 'It's not your fault.'

'What are you going to do?'

'Take a shower. Learn to pray.'

When Jimmy steps out of the shower, he reaches for his towel and, unbalanced with his prosthetic off, slips on the wet floor, but is just quick enough to grab the rack. He rights himself, then burrows his face in the white towel. The throbbing of his jaw is welcome. He feels like he's coming back to life.

Once he has dried off and gotten dressed, he goes to his room and packs some clothes into a duffel bag. He finds Gavin, in his bathrobe, lying on the living-room couch. His eyes are puffy and he smells of alcohol and sweat. When he sees Jimmy, he sits up. He lies, 'Listen, I'd lend you the money if I could, but I don't have that kind of cash handy, y'know? Sorry.'

Jimmy lies too. 'I wasn't going to ask for anything. This is my own fault. I'll deal with it.'

Gavin eyes Jimmy's bag. 'Going somewhere?'

'Rathbaile.'

'Jimmy, if you're not here tomorrow, those guys will fuck you up when they catch you.'

'So be it. Will they do anything to you?'

'Not if I tell them where you are.'

'Then do. I'll have the money in a few days when I'm back. Tell them that too.'

'Don't be a fucking muppet. If you need to go ask yer folks for the money, do it, but get back by morning.'

'I can't.'

'Why the fuck not?'

Smiling weakly, Jimmy says, 'I have to go to my mother's funeral. She killed herself yesterday. Slit her wrists.'

Gavin flinches. 'Jesus, Jimmy.'

Elizabeth opens the door and glares at Jimmy, his duffel bag at his feet. He says, 'I'm sorry. I should've called Dad.'

'You not only didn't call, you turned your phone off. Everyone was worried sick.'

'I've been selfish. I'll do whatever I can to make it up.'

'See that you do.' She steps aside. After shutting the door, her sympathy exceeds her anger and she hugs him. 'I'm glad you're here.' She puts her hand to his jaw and tilts his face so it's at a better angle to the light. 'What happened?'

'Nothing.' He moves back from her. 'A wake-up call. Where's Dad?'

'He's off consoling Simon, or Simon is consoling him. He'll be home soon. Tighe's here though. C'mon.'

Tighe is in the kitchen, on his mobile – he works as a trader for a prestigious investment bank in London, for which he's very well compensated, and he's talking to his boss. His shirt-sleeves are rolled up, and if you look closely, you can see a few old white teeth-marks on his left forearm. He holds up a finger to Jimmy and says, 'It'll have to wait until . . . I realise that. Look, I have to go. I'm needed. I will. Appreciate it. Bye.'

He pockets his mobile and stressfully exhales. 'My boss is a fuckwit. He sends his condolences, though.' He hugs Jimmy, who instantly feels a little shorter and skinnier. 'Finally made it, eh? What happened to your face?'

'A fight.'

Elizabeth touches Jimmy's elbow. 'A fight?'

Tighe says, 'You win it?'

Jimmy says, 'No.'

'Don't fight fights you can't win, Jimmy. That's rule number one of fighting. Do I have to be concerned about you?'

'I'm fine. Getting through the week. How are you?'

Tighe smiles grimly and puts his hand through his gelled hair. 'I'm about the same as you, I reckon, minus the bruising.'

Elizabeth sits at the table, slumping forward and resting her chin on her palms, her fingers framing her face. 'I'm waiting until after the next few days before I let it sink in. Dad needs us to be strong for him.'

Tighe and Jimmy sit with her. Jimmy says, 'I know it's a dumb question, but how is he?'

Tighe says, 'He's worried about everyone else and he's keeping from standing still any longer than he can help. Obviously he's suffering a great deal, but eventually I think he'll be okay.'

Elizabeth snorts, lifting her head from her hands. 'That's bullshit. Don't listen to him, Jimmy. Dad's fucked. Mam shredded him. And he's not even pissed at her. He should be. I am. The more I think about it, the more livid I get.'

In a calm tone, which is guaranteed to get under Elizabeth's skin, Tighe says, 'There's no point in blaming her. It's not like she can be held to account, and besides, she was very ill. She wasn't responsible.'

'Oh come off it!'

'Your attitude isn't helpful. We should think well of her. We owe her that much.'

'You remember her your way; I'll remember her mine.' To Jimmy Elizabeth says, '*You* don't have all nice thoughts and fond memories.'

Jimmy looks from her to Tighe, who is a picture of forbearance, then back at her. 'She was who she was. I don't want to blame her for what's happened.'

Elizabeth throws her hands up. 'Of course you don't *want* to blame her. That doesn't mean she doesn't have a lot to answer for. And Jimmy, if you *don't* blame her, that's news to me.' She stands. 'I'm going outside for a fag. Fuck it, I'm going for five. You boys can stay and reminisce.' She walks to the door, where she stops. 'It isn't either of you I'm mad at. When Dad's back, I'll be sweetness and light.'

Tighe waits until she's gone, then says, 'You weren't in a fight, by the way.'

Jimmy says, 'What?'

Tighe gestures to his jaw. 'They're already fretting about

187

you. Abuelo would probably approve, but Dad, and Granny especially, would freak out if they think you're coping by getting into scraps.'

'Fine.'

'Is there a decent story behind it?'

'Well, there's a story. I need your . . . advice on something, but not now. For the moment, I want to deal with what's right in front of me. See Dad first. Later, maybe we could talk?'

'I'll be waiting.'

The amputated Diaz family are eating dinner.

Eamon sits at the head of the dining table. Tighe is at the other end. He thought it would be grotesque to leave Grace's chair unoccupied, so without being asked, he assumed her position. Jimmy and Elizabeth sit on either side of Eamon. Art sits next to Jimmy, Elizabeth next to Maggie.

It had been a family joke that Eamon would ask Grace to say grace when they sat down to eat. Despite being an atheist, and having tired of all the puns about her name, she went along with it, because the children used to laugh. Eamon didn't ask anyone to say grace this time. He believes in God but didn't feel like thanking Him. He thanked Maggie and Elizabeth for preparing dinner, and they all waited for Maggie to finish her silent prayer – she bowed her head and fastened her knuckles tight – before they dug in.

She demanded that everyone have a full dinner, but she has been the slowest eater. When she looks at Jimmy's bruised jaw, she winces. She believes his story about slipping in the shower, only that's alarming too – he needs to be more careful! She swallows down the sharp-cornered lump in her throat with water and stares at her son. He has been quietly keeping his eyes on his food. Although he could have done much better,

Maggie doesn't wish that he hadn't married Grace – together they brought her grandchildren into the world – but she was a terrible wife and mother. Apart from the damage she has done to Eamon and their remaining children in this life, she has also abandoned them in the next, for surely they'll all join Paul while her final act has thrust her in the opposite direction. Maggie had always prayed for Grace, but now she'll save her prayers for those who aren't beyond redemption.

Art reaches across the table and squeezes her hand. His eyes are difficult to read even when he's being tender. Maggie scoops up some potato and peas with her spoon. A tremor runs through her hand as she lifts the spoon to her mouth. She puts it down and hides her hand under the table until the shaking has stopped.

Normally Art is happy to sit without talking – the Irish inclination for filling good silences with prattle is a pet peeve – but on this occasion he's searching for something to say that wouldn't be upsetting. While he's curious about what really happened to Jimmy's face, he doesn't think it's his business to ask and doubts it's a cause for concern. He cleaves a chicken fillet in two until his knife hits the plate. Gesticulating towards Tighe with his chicken-skewered fork, he says, 'How long can you stay before you go back?'

Tighe sips red wine. 'I leave on Wednesday morning. I'd like to be here longer, but there's a deal being held up because of my absence. I'll return for Christmas, though.' To Elizabeth and Jimmy he says, 'How about you guys? Staying long?'

Elizabeth is annoyed once again by Tighe and the casual way in which he poses his question – like he's asking if they're going to extend their holiday – although she recognises that the problem is more hers than his. 'My boss told me to take as much time as I need, so I'll see. That's the benefit of not having a high-powered job: they can survive without me for a while.'

Maggie says, 'It's nice they treat you well, dear.'

Elizabeth suspects her grandmother thinks that all the jobs she has ever had have been given to her on some sort of charity basis. She lacks the energy to insist that the people at the restaurant where she works have complete respect for her competence. With a forceful look she prompts Jimmy to state his intentions.

His hangover has eased, but his stomach is still jittery. 'Next week is the last of the term before we break until January. I've an essay due that I can't imagine tackling any time soon. I'm sure they'll give me an extension.'

Maggie says, 'Of course they will! I can phone your professors for you if you'd like.'

'Thanks, Granny, I can manage. I'll go up on Tuesday, sort a few things out, then come back here until next term. Or I might take a few more weeks than that. My degree won't fall apart if I wait until February.'

Eamon says, 'That's not a good idea, Jim.' Everyone turns to him. He hasn't slept in thirty-six hours, and looks it, but with resolve he says, 'You shouldn't take too long. You don't want to lag behind and you have to make the most of things. You see? For the three of you, life must go on.'

'Okay, Dad.'

'Good lad.' Eamon's eyes return to the food he has been moving around his plate.

As I watch them all, I wonder if I'm the lone ghost in the room. I've never seen one, but maybe the dead are all invisible to each other to save us from the horror of seeing centuries upon centuries of ghastly faces. If so, Grace could be floating around, looking over the shoulders of her loved ones, unable to touch them.

Unlike Maggie and Elizabeth and Jimmy – when he's being honest – I don't blame her for ending her life. I wish she hadn't, but she really believed that everyone would be better off without her. I hope she isn't a ghost, though – I don't want her to be like me. She deserves to be at peace.

Late in the evening, Jimmy knocks on Tighe's door holding two beers. He hears, 'Enter.'

Tighe is at his desk, his shadow cast large against the wall by his bedside lamp. His laptop is on and multiple spreadsheets are open. He presses save and closes the cover. Jimmy gestures to the laptop. 'Watching porn?'

'Sure. Mathematical porn. One of those mine?'

Jimmy opens a beer, gives it to him, and sits on the bed. Tighe takes a gulp. 'You've a story to tell me.'

Jimmy opens his beer, drinks, rubs the side of his neck, and has another drink. 'I'm sorry to be laying this on you, especially now.'

'Just fucking say it.'

Jimmy explains how he was 'too wasted to think' after hearing about Grace, before progressing to his hazy memory of being coaxed into gambling and accepting a loan. He leaves out select details – the coke, calling Vinnie a cunt – but he does describe Casey and Sugar in sinister detail and he demonstrates the force of Casey's punch by throwing back his head.

Tighe drinks and listens without interrupting. When Jimmy has finished, he asks the most pertinent question: 'How much money?'

'Four grand.'

Tighe pinches the top of the bridge of his nose. 'When do you need it?'

'As soon as possible.'

'With the funeral and everything on Monday there won't be a chance to get to the bank, not discreetly, but I can sort it out on Tuesday morning. Is that soon enough?'

'I think so, yes. I don't know how to—'

Tighe waves his hand. 'Don't. All I need to hear is that you'll never be this stupid again.'

'I promise.'

'Okay. Let's just get through the next few days.' Tighe downs the rest of his can and holds it out. 'Get rid of this, will you?'

Jimmy takes it and stands. 'I won't forget this.'

'You'd better not.' Tighe smiles wryly. 'That's twice now I've saved your ass.'

Chapter Sixteen

Cost of Living

November–December 1998

Jimmy, in a black suit, stares at Grace's coffin, set on wooden planks above her grave, and imagines her wrists. They say the way to do it right is to make vertical cuts, but he doesn't know if she realised that, or how many it took. Were they quick, neat incisions or were they more berserk? Did she dig in with the glass and rip crookedly? He imagines black-red scars like overlapping bursts of forked lightning, her flesh held together by fat maggoty stitches.

At the viewing last night, wedged within her open coffin, she was wearing a silver blouse and her sleeves were buttoned tight over her wrists. Her face was too yellow, her neck too white. With her eyes protuberant under her eyelids, her expression was far too still.

I picked the undertaker's brain so I know what her wrists look like. She did make vertical cuts, two, an inch apiece, and the incisions were fairly neat considering how her implement was jagged glass. She now has four thin stitches on each wrist. I doubt it would make much difference if I could share this information with Jimmy. Maybe the tidiness of the scars would

*become his new obsession, replacing the more mangled
wounds of his imagination.*

*I don't have access to Grace's final moments. I don't know
how long she took to die. Jimmy imagines she bled a lot. He
sees her curled beneath increasingly bloodstained white sheets,
her lips turning blue, but I've no light to shed. And I don't
know if, sometime after too late, she wished she could take it
all back.*

A LARGE WREATH LIES TO THE SIDE OF THE COFFIN. THE
flowers are bright with their variety of pinks, whites, and reds.
The grave next to Grace's is her son's. A week has never gone
by without fresh flowers being placed at Paul's black marble
gravestone. Beside him lies Grace's mother. Dorothy died after
a series of strokes within a month of Jimmy's leg amputation.
The grief at her passing was outweighed by relief.

Jimmy is near the bespectacled young priest conducting the
service, Father Ivor, but isn't quite following his words. They
evaporate too quickly in the blustery wind and Jimmy's
thoughts are loud as well. Only an occasional phrase or word
hammers home, such as the references to dust and ash, which
jar with the solidity of a human body, dead or not.

He feels likes he's plummeting through a trapdoor in his
mind, yet he's also aware of the throbbing coldness of his
nose, ears, and knuckles, the heaviness of his eyes, and the
beads of icy sweat slinking down his back. He feels isolated
and numb, but with nearly a hundred other mourners here,
enmeshed in the collective grief too. Death has never felt more
vibrant, life never more morbid.

Standing next to Jimmy are Tighe, Elizabeth, and Eamon.
Tighe's hands are in the pockets of the hefty coat he's wearing
over his suit. He's listening to Father Ivor's every word.

Elizabeth has taken out all her rings – her lip ring for good. Her auburn hair is loose around her shoulders and her features appear softened. She's holding Eamon's hand, her head on his shoulder. He's crying. She's not.

At the grave's toe-end are Art, Maggie, Simon, and Simon's second wife, Joan. Art has his arm around Maggie. His eyes are watery – it's the wind, he thinks – and he keeps having to blow his nose into his handkerchief. Maggie is looking in Eamon's direction, but her vision is too blurry to see him properly. Her sobbing is fitful.

Simon's arm is linked with Joan's and he's pressing his hands on a gilt-handled walking stick, which he has had since breaking his hip on a flight of stairs five years ago. He calls the accident his 'lucky break' because it was during his rehabilitation that he met Joan, a nurse. He wasn't criticised around town for poaching a woman twenty years his junior because with her doughty, pockmarked complexion she wasn't considered attractive enough to be the object of lascivious attention. There were some whispers that she was a gold-digger, but he knows better. She's kind and has made him feel years younger. Not today, though. Today the pain in his hip is fierce and he feels decrepit. An oily tear burns his cheek. Joan puts her hand under his elbow, pushing him up so his bad side bears less of his weight.

Jimmy's friends are here too. Finbar is holding hands with his now-girlfriend, Vicky. The last time you saw them, he was rushing her to the bathroom at Ashburnham. He held her hair back while she threw up. It was something of a bonding experience. Brian is holding hands with Tracy, his Ashburnham date. To the lads, he claims to be only seeing her on and off – 'getting what I can, y'know?' To her, he has pledged his commitment. Seb is at the outer edge of the gathering, beside his parents. He's frowning in the same way as his mother, Michelle, with his nostrils flared. She's grateful, yet again, that her family has always been more fortunate than the Diazes.

Alice is closer to the grave than her family, watching Jimmy. She had been upset with him because he hadn't contacted her after the debs, but now she has put his inconsiderate behaviour down to the burden of his mother's condition. She wishes she could put her hand in his without seeming desperate about it, as he stands there, so lost within himself.

Jimmy turns his head, surprised to find Tighe's hand on his shoulder. Tighe isn't crying now, but his cheeks are damp from the mass. While Jimmy had cried then too, avoiding all eye contact and quickly wiping away his tears, Tighe wept freely, a peculiar smile at the corner of his mouth and his eyes seeking out others.

Jimmy sees Father Ivor pocket his bible and his glasses. Two gravediggers rest their gloved hands on their shovels, waiting for the mourners to disperse. Jimmy says, 'It's done, huh?'

Tighe says, 'C'mon. It's too cold for standing around.'

'I might be in trouble when I return to Dublin.'

Jimmy is sitting on the lino with his back to the washing machine and the soles of his shoes against the freezer. Colossus lies on his blanket, his chin on Jimmy's knee, his paws across Jimmy's shins. Jimmy rubs the soft spot behind the dog's ear. 'Don't worry. Even a gangster can't fuck up a guy too much if his mother just died. What do you think? Will I live to fight another day?' Colossus snorts and his paws spasm. Then he's still. 'That's what I thought.' Jimmy bangs the back of his head a few times against the washing machine.

On arriving home, he came to the laundry room to feed

Colossus a bowl of dog food. That was twenty minutes ago. It's time to deal with other people. He nudges the dog with his knee and Colossus groggily sits up so he can stand. 'Bet you know, don't you? Mam didn't love us enough to stick around.' Jimmy rubs and shakes his trousers, trying to rid himself of canine hair. 'Fecking shedder.'

He goes into the kitchen, where some family and friends are standing around or sitting at the table. Most of them have a drink in hand and their voices are quiet. Jimmy nods whenever someone catches his eye. He takes a beer from the fridge, rolls the cool aluminium across his forehead, then opens it and drinks.

Across the room, Eamon has been cornered by his brothers, who look distinguished with their grey hair, in the L-shape formed by the counters. Luis's hands are on Eamon's shoulders. Jimmy hears him say, 'That's how you get through this, you hear me? One day at a time.'

Manny nods, as if he thinks Luis's trite advice might be astute. He's about to swig from his hip flask when he pauses and holds it out to Eamon instead. Eamon looks at it like it's an alien object. Manny says, 'Can't hurt. Might help.'

Eamon shakes his head. Manny sighs, then drinks and hands the flask to Luis.

Out the window, Jimmy sees Seb and Finbar sitting in chairs at the patio table, with Brian perched behind them on the three-foot-high red-brick wall partitioning the patio from the garden. Ties off, they're drinking beer. Finbar and Brian are smoking. Jimmy goes outside and his friends watch him approach, their brows knitted. He says, 'You lot look like you've been to a funeral.' They smile, but none of them dares to laugh. Finbar is staring quizzically at him. Jimmy says, 'A penny, Finbar?'

Finbar jerks the cigarette from his mouth. 'What's that, Jimmy?'

'A penny for your thoughts?' Finbar still appears confused. Jimmy, trying to keep the edge from his voice, says, 'What are you looking at?'

Finbar takes a swift drag and blows out smoke. 'There's a smudge on your face. The colour's not quite right.' Brian kicks Finbar's chair. Finbar shrugs. 'I could be seeing things.'

Jimmy rubs the side of his mouth with his thumb. 'Can't get anything past you. It's make-up.'

The lads share concerned glances. Finbar says, 'Oh, right. Why's that?'

Jimmy withdraws his concealer-smeared thumb from his face. 'I have a colourful bruise. Tighe thought people might conclude that it's a physical manifestation of a damaged psyche, so Elizabeth worked her magic.'

'How'd you get the bruise, then?'

'Slipped in the shower.' Seb rises and Jimmy says, 'For fuck's sake, you don't need to give up your chair. I'm not about to fall down again any time soon.'

Seb's eyes widen. 'I wasn't offering. I was just wondering: could I have a word? It's a private matter – of no concern to these eejits.' He grins.

Jimmy thinks Seb should ask for a refund on his acting lessons if this is what passes for a subtle intervention. As he turns to go with Seb, the relief on Brian and Finbar's faces doesn't escape his attention.

They step off the patio and squelch through the dewy grass to a line of trees just inside the garden fence. Jimmy says, 'Let's have it.'

Seb says, 'I'm not going to bullshit you.'

'Thank God for small mercies.'

'Gavin called me yesterday.'

Jimmy holds out his beer. 'Take this?' Seb does, and Jimmy gives his tie a diagonal tug, undoes the knot, and pockets it. Seb hands back his beer. Jimmy drinks. 'What did he say?'

'He told me about Thursday night, and about the money, and how it was due on Saturday.'

'Yet I'm still standing.'

'You realise this is serious?'

'I haven't gone soft in the head, if that's what you're asking.'

'Listen, I understand if you don't want to go to your dad or Simon for help, and I don't have much cash flow, but I could give you a few hundred and ask my parents for the rest. They'd understand and it could be kept under wraps.'

Jimmy finishes his can and rubs his eyes. 'Thanks, really. I'm on top of this. Tighe already promised to sort me out with the money. And I talked to Gavin. He said that when Vinnie's guys came to collect, he told them about Mam. They weren't happy, but it looks like they'll wait. I'll get the money in the morning, be in Dublin by late afternoon, and I'll go hand it over then. I've fucked up, clearly, but the lesson is well and truly learned.'

Seb scrutinises him. 'Is there anything else I can do? Not the money, then, but with what's happened here?'

'No one can raise the dead. And I don't mean to sound callous, but I'm not sure I'd want her back. What I need is, a day at a time, to forget her a little more. That's the closest thing I can think of to a solution.'

'I doubt that's healthy.'

'Fuck healthy, and don't ever tell anyone I said this, but fuck her.'

Seb offers, 'You can say whatever you want to me. I understand you need to vent.'

Jimmy tightens his grip on the can, denting the sides. 'I'm *not* venting. I've never felt greater clarity. Seb, you've got to stop looking at me like I'm about to lose it at any moment. All I need is some space, and some sleep, and another beer.'

'Okay. Let's get that beer.'

By seven p.m., the last of the guests have left. After insisting that Eamon isn't to lift a finger, Tighe, Elizabeth, and Jimmy clean up.

Tighe leaves to meet a friend, who Jimmy correctly guesses is Isabel. He saw her at the funeral. She hadn't changed much since her babysitting days, although her black hair was no longer frizzy but straight, and without those crimson stripes. While Jimmy didn't speak to her, he watched her flirt with Tighe from afar, the touch of her fingers on his wrist.

Elizabeth makes Eamon a cup of tea and he sits in his armchair, forgetting to drink it. Before taking Colossus out for a walk, she tells Jimmy, 'Don't leave Dad alone while I'm gone.'

'Give me *some* credit, would you?'

Jimmy isn't thirsty, but he makes a mug of black coffee anyway so he has something to do with his hands as he joins Eamon in the living room. He keeps sipping even though it scalds his tongue. He has no desire to turn on the TV – any dramas featuring death would be too close to the bone, the news would be absurdly trivial, and a comedy, especially one with a laugh track, would be offensive. Eamon stares into the grey TV screen. Hating his own question, Jimmy says, 'What are you thinking about?'

Eamon blinks, turns to Jimmy, and says, 'All of the things about her. I wonder if she knew that I could see more than what she showed.'

'She knew that you loved her.'

'Yeah, she did, but there are other things, gone now. She was really two people. She was the person who lived in this house and couldn't figure out how to be happy. You must always believe that she really tried. But she was someone very different too. It was the real her, who was wonderful, that I married. She changed and I don't understand how. If I'd known I was losing her . . . You must believe me; if I'd seen it in time, properly seen it, I would have found a way to never let go.'

'You did everything you could, Dad.'

'It wasn't enough.'

A hitch in his voice, Jimmy says, 'It came down to *her*. Some people, there's no way to save them.'

Tighe hands Jimmy a stuffed envelope. 'There's an extra grand in that.'

They're parked in Eamon's car, Tighe in the driver's seat, Jimmy next to him. Jimmy puts the envelope in the inside pocket of his coat. 'Why?'

'Because you're late with what you owe, and if they don't take that well, it gives you the means to placate them. If they don't want more, use the rest to live on. Eat some healthy meals. Girls like guys to be lean, but not too much. You're too bony. Bulk up.'

'Thank—'

'Don't. Just get smarter, quicker. No more loser mistakes. It's a matter of discipline.' Tighe drums his fingers on the steering wheel. 'I must be off. I'd wait with you if I could.'

Tighe drives away. Jimmy, sitting in the empty bus shelter, buttons his coat, conscious of the bulge of the envelope. He closes his eyes. A cough is percolating in his lungs. He's sure that by tomorrow he'll be spitting gobs of mucus, and in two days tops he'll have a can't-think-straight head cold.

A car snarls in the distance, then zooms closer and comes to a tyre-mark halt. He opens his eyes. Across the road there's a gleaming metallic-grey Lexus, its engine purring. Casey gets out, rubbing his closely shaved head. He slaps a hand on the roof and shouts, 'Jimmy Dice, fancy meeting you here!'

Casey beckons him with a wag of his fingers. Jimmy reluctantly slings his bag over his shoulder and crosses the road. Casey holds his hand out. When Jimmy takes it, Casey grips hard and doesn't let go. 'Yer a difficult man to find.'

'I was about to get the bus to come meet you guys.'

'We happen to be going in yer direction. Get in the car.'

'I can give you the money now.'

'Can you?' His thumb bores into the back of Jimmy's hand, sending a sharp pain to his elbow. Jimmy flinches. Casey laughs and releases his hand. 'That's excellent. I repeat: get in the car.'

Jimmy sits behind the driver's seat. The passenger seat is pushed all the way back to accommodate Sugar. His knees are squashed against the dashboard. He turns awkwardly, his trench coat rippling, to look at Jimmy with his small blue eyes. He sighs. 'Are we going to have any problems with you?'

'No, Mr Gorman.'

'Put your seat belt on.' Jimmy does as instructed. Sugar sighs again. 'Sorry to hear about your mother.'

Casey says, 'Yeah, a real fucking shame. Bad luck.' He revs the engine and speeds out of Rathbaile.

Looking into the rear-view mirror to see Casey's face, Jimmy says, 'I can give you the money and this can be done. You could leave me off at the side of the road.'

Casey's eyes flit from the rear-view to the road. 'It's good that you have it, but it's not that simple. It was a few days ago. Then you did a runner, not the smartest move. Reckless, in fact.'

'There were extenuating circumstances.'

'Yeah, well, life's a bitch and Vinnie's a man of principle.'

'I'm only three days late. My mother *died*.'

'Calm the fuck down. You don't want to rain on my sunny mood.'

'Look, I can pay interest. I have the four grand plus one more. Will that make us even?'

Casey whistles. 'Big money, huh, pal? Yer a resourceful kid. It's not my call, though. I'll need to check with the boss. But I've fuck-all reception in this shithole end of Ireland. Sit tight. We'll sort this out before you know it. You have the Casey guarantee that you'll walk away from this in one piece. I couldn't be any fairer than that, could I?'

Jimmy stares out the tinted window at the countryside rushing by. He's aware that mobile reception is fine in this area.

After driving north for nearly an hour, they turn on to a bumpy country road, then down a muddy driveway. They stop outside an old house with broken windows and a front door rattling in its frame. Casey claps his hands. 'Leg-stretching time. Out you get.' He stares at Jimmy through the rear-view. 'Well?'

Jimmy says, 'Should I bring my bag?'

'Why not?' Casey and Sugar put on gloves. Seeing Jimmy's frightened look, Casey says, 'It's cold out!'

They all exit the car. Standing close to Jimmy, Casey says, 'The money?'

Jimmy drops his bag, unbuttons his coat, and takes out the envelope. He hands it over. Casey slides it across the bonnet to Sugar, who puts it inside his trench coat. Jimmy says, 'You can count it.'

'We trust you. Even you wouldn't be stupid enough to lie to us now.' Casey chucks Jimmy's bag into a ditch. 'Actually, don't think you'll be needing that.'

Keeping his voice even, Jimmy says, 'What are you going to do?'

'You'll see. Sugar, why don't you take the lad for his walk? I must make that all-important call.'

Sugar trudges around the car and lightly pushes Jimmy towards the garage at the side of the house. As they walk past Casey, Sugar says, 'Make sure to tell him about the extra grand.'

Casey laughs. 'What sort of thieving bastard do you take me for?'

At the garage, Sugar pushes the keyhole button in the door's pronged handle, popping the button out. He twists the handle, then bends on to his haunches, grips the door two-handed at its base, and heaves. With a rumble the door shifts up and back, relocating in the metal frame attached to the ceiling.

Inside, the cement floor is strewn with tools, foxed newspapers, and lots of dust bunnies and sawdust. At the far end there's a large table, covered by a tarp with many uneven protrusions – Jimmy imagines there being a miniature mountain-range model underneath. Sugar gestures to a wooden chair next to the table. 'Sit.'

Jimmy does. Looking up at Sugar, he says, 'Don't let him kill me. My family have been through enough.'

Sugar breathes loudly through his nose. 'No one's killing anyone. Apart from that, I can't make you any promises.'

Casey enters the garage carrying a cooler, which he sets down on the floor. He says to Jimmy, 'You look like you've the weight of the bleeding world on yer shoulders.' He takes off his jacket, exhibiting his gun in an underarm holster, then pivots a chair around and straddles it, resting his forearms on the back. Jimmy, facing him, can smell the rot of his breath. Casey says, 'I've good news and bad. Which do you want served first?'

Jimmy looks over at the cooler. 'The bad.'

'Think positive, Jimmy! We'll start with the good. Vinnie accepts the interest on yer debt, so I've the pleasure of informing you that it's officially paid in full and you're one hundred per cent debt-free. Does that not warrant a smile?'

'I'm waiting for the bad news.'

'All right so. Here's the thing: you were very loud when you got yerself in trouble and you disrespected Vinnie in front of friends of his father. Sometimes it's necessary to make an example so the next fucker will think twice before showing bad manners. You were three days late.' Casey holds up three fingers. 'The penalty is a finger per day.'

Jimmy was already pale, but now he's going on grey. 'I don't understand.'

'Yes you do. Like I said, you'll be walking away in one piece. It's just, well, you'll be leaving three small pieces behind. Call it the cost of living. You're young and this'll provide a bit of focus by narrowing down those pesky career options for you. It doesn't look like you'll be playing the piano. To make things fair, I'll let you pick which fingers you want sacrificed. I recommend holding on to yer thumbs, but it's your call.'

Sugar drags the tarp off the table, revealing a selection of power tools: a nail gun, a drill, a jigsaw. The jigsaw is the one for the job. On noting the sharpness of the blade, Jimmy has to swallow rapidly to prevent himself from vomiting. 'What if I refuse?'

Casey scratches his head. 'This isn't a take-it-or-leave-it choice. But, for argument's sake, just say myself and Mr Gorman are flat-footed cunts, and say I didn't have a gun. Even if you got away, we'd find you and kill you. If you went to ground, we'd go after yer family and cut off three fingers of every one of them we could get our hands on, until you surfaced. Does that answer yer question? Now, it'll be a quick, humane procedure. We've brought along some ice for you to apply to the wounds, and we'll leave you here, but once we're on the go, we'll call you an ambulance. We will, however, be taking yer fingers with us. Not as twisted mementoes, but just because, with the marvels of modern medicine, we don't want to take the chance that you could get them reattached. One last thing, and I can't stress this enough, if you rat us out, we'll kill you slowly, then we'll go after yer family. Do we have an understanding?'

'Yes.'

'Excellent. Shall we begin?'

Looking Casey in the eyes, Jimmy says, 'If it has to be done, I want to be the one who does the cutting.'

Casey's eyes light up. 'Now that . . . is something I'd like to see.'

Jimmy stands. 'Let's get it over with. I need something to bite on.'

Casey stands, turns his chair sideways on the floor, and with two kicks of his heel breaks off half a leg. He plucks a few loose splinters from it. 'This mightn't be the cleanest thing to chomp on, but that's probably the least of yer worries, eh?'

Jimmy takes it, his hand shaking, and places it on the table. Sugar lifts the jigsaw by its handle and presses the on button so Jimmy can see how it works. The blade, extending from the base, shimmers as it vibrates. Sugar turns it off and adjusts the setting to its maximum speed. 'It's heavy, but it has a good grip. When you start cutting, do it as quick as you can, before your brain knows what it is you're doing to yerself.'

There's a wooden board on the table, and Jimmy presses the little, ring, and middle fingers of his left hand on it, keeping them straight. He tucks his index finger into his palm and restrains it with his thumb. He asks Sugar, 'Could you hold my hand down?'

Sugar nods, pushing down on the back of Jimmy's hand and wrist with one hand and squeezing his forearm with the other. Jimmy puts the piece of chair leg into his mouth and bites. He picks up the jigsaw and turns it on. The blade whirs alive. He looks at Sugar, who's averting his eyes. Over his other shoulder Casey says, 'I've got to tell you, Jimmy, if you've the balls to go through with this, you'll have my undying respect. If you can't quite pull it off, don't worry, I'll be standing by.'

Jimmy aligns the blade with his hand. He thinks of Grace, of her wrists and the glass. His teeth crunch on wood. He shoves the blade hard against his little finger. It slices off with startling ease. Raging pain comes a moment later, as the blade sticks in the bone of his ring finger. The teeth-indented leg drops from his mouth, hitting the floor and rolling. His hand, the board, and the blade are covered with blood. He pulls on the jigsaw with all his might, slicing off the remainder of the bone and propelling through his middle finger as well. He smashes the jigsaw on the table. He screams and screams. Sugar releases his hand and arm and backs away. Jimmy's little and ring fingers are lying in a pool on the board. His middle finger is hanging from his knuckle by a thread of flesh. Casey is staring at it. Jimmy grabs the finger, rips it off, and shoves it against Casey's chest, splattering his shirt with blood.

Casey reaches for the finger but misses it, and it falls to the floor.

Jimmy staggers towards the cooler, head spinning, the pain intense and surreal. With his intact hand he wrenches open the lid and throws it away. Falling to his knees, he punches his mutilated fist into a plastic bag bulging with ice.

PART TWO

What Matters

Chapter Seventeen

The Testimony of Jimmy Dice

I
December 1998

Even I was surprised that Jimmy volunteered to saw off his own fingers. It was a spur-of-the moment decision, but I could appreciate the motivation: something terrible was going to happen to him no matter what, so he wanted whatever control he could have over it and to retain some dignity.

Jimmy can only bear the burn of the ice against his fresh finger stumps, and the convulsion surging through his arm, for a few seconds before he pulls his hand free from the cooler. When he turns and locks eyes with Casey, he doesn't just want to kill him; he wants to dig his teeth into his throat. He rises from his knees, blood and ice water seeping from his hand, and manages to lumber two steps forward. His undoing is the sight of his severed middle finger on the floor. His vision blurs. He feels like he's shrinking, and it's as if an invisible hand reaches up and drags him down, not just on to the floor, but into the compact darkness beneath.

I'm reminded of how he lost his leg. He was unconscious and at the mercy of a pair of predators then too – this time, however, Tighe is nowhere to be found. Standing on either side of him, Casey and Sugar stare down at his defenceless body, but they mean him no further harm. They glance at one another – they're both impressed by Jimmy Dice's willpower – then go about finishing up their work. While Sugar wraps Jimmy's ruin of a hand in a dirty rag, Casey picks up his severed little and ring fingers from the wooden board on the table and his middle finger from the floor, collecting them all in a plastic bag, which he zips shut and drops into the cooler – he'll present the fingers to Vinnie as a souvenir later on. The two men leave and Casey phones for an ambulance from their car.

Unlike in the instance with the dogs, I'm not worried that Jimmy will die, but I am worried about his mind and heart, and how he'll deal with this, especially on the heels of losing Grace.

The sound of a siren whips him awake. He's lying on his chest with his eyes turned to the open garage door. He rolls on to his back and looks at his hands on his stomach. His right hand is squeezing his left hand hard, the rag sopping with blood, and they appear almost fused together. The knuckles of his right hand crack when he releases his left and tears away the rag. When he roars, it's due less to the ferocity of the pain than to the body horror inherent in processing a reduction of parts.

From his skewed and shaking perspective, the paramedics pound towards him like giants.

IF HIS FAMILY WEREN'T UNDER THREAT TOO, JIMMY would be forthcoming with the guards. He only confesses the truth to Tighe and Seb – who vow to take it to their graves – because they were aware of his situation before it caught up with him.

As good as he is at lying to everyone else, the account he offers is at best suspicious.

He claims to have been kidnapped at the bus stop by masked men who cut off his fingers for the hell of it. He can't provide many details because they attacked from behind and blindfolded him before he was shoved into their car, which he never saw either. He says there were two of them, but can't be sure. Whenever he gets fuzzy on his facts, he blames his traumatised psyche. He doesn't have to fake *that*. He's grateful for it. Even the guards are careful about grilling him.

He's ashamed of the publicity – the newspaper articles and the *Crimeline* segment – but there's no clean way to stop any of it. From the guards' point of view, there are multiple psychopaths on the loose and who can predict what unlucky person will be abducted next? His identity is withheld. Everyone in Rathbaile hears that he's the victim anyway. They only have to see his hand to confirm it.

Not for the first time, he resolves to exercise better judgement in the future and he hopes that his worst experiences are behind him.

II

This doesn't come easily for me – I don't like surrendering what meagre power I have – but for the sake of the story, I'm ceding the narrative reins to Jimmy for a while.

He wrote the ensuing journal entries nearly thirteen years after he became a seven-fingered man, in an attempt to make sense of the events that occurred in the years following that incident. Everything he put to paper was for his own eyes, but as always, he never suspected that he had my full attention.

You'll still, from time to time, be hearing from me too.

12/11/2011

Whenever she looked at me, she cut right through my insincerity.

That's not how I should start this. It is Nicole I want to write about, but I don't have to jump right in. I can build up to her.

I'll try something more obvious: my name. I'm James Arturo Diaz. James because my mother liked it, but most people call me Jimmy. Arturo is after my grandfather. While his health has been a little dicey lately, he's a tough man and I think he has some years left. Not that I've ever been good at predicting the longevity of others. Despite my name, I'm very much Irish. In my thirty-one years I've only once set foot in another country.

It's a family tradition that our middle names are passed on from relatives. So my brother is Tighe Eamon after our father. My sister is Elizabeth Grace after our mother. My other brother died when I was a baby and he was five. That changed everything in my family, apparently. I don't know what things were like before. His name was Paul Andreas. He'd have been Paul Arturo, but Abuelo asked Dad to use my great-grandfather's name. Naming me after my other grandfather was never a possibility. He walked out on my grandmother when Mam was a teenager. Never heard from since. Most likely dead. I've heard I had a twin. She was stillborn. Sometimes I imagine what she would have been like. I've never come close to an idea of her that seems real. I wonder if it was either her or me and I murdered her. Maybe all that has transpired since is punishment. Bad karma because she was the one who should have lived. I think I could imagine her if she had been named. Her middle name would have been Margaret after my other grandmother, Dad's mother. They wouldn't have passed on Mam's mother's name because Dorothy was crazy. They wouldn't have wanted my twin to be cursed.

I'm writing this from a hospital bed, propped up by pillows. I hate hospitals. I suppose everyone does, and funerals too, but there are degrees of negative connotation. Being here is my own fault. I learn lessons slowly. They have to be blunt. Something usually has to give. This time it was my nose, some teeth, my jaw.

No one knows I'm here. My phone keeps trembling on the bedside locker. That's Seb. He's worried. I disappeared last night. And I've been known to be accident-prone. If I picked up, hearing my heavy breathing wouldn't ease his anxiety. I might be able to drool out a few words, but it would sound nothing like me. These are just excuses. I could text him or ask a nurse to phone. The young red-headed and red-cheeked one gave me this notepad and pen. I wrote, Rest. She told me to press the buzzer if I needed anything, putting a lot of effort into not looking at my left hand. My gun hand. My L-for-Loser hand. I keep it visible. My index finger and thumb are tapping a jig on the blanket. The other nurses have an attitude of business-as-usual around me. The redhead seems to genuinely care. She might not be cut out for the job.

Christ. My face feels like it's been ripped off and nailed back on. But I'm disinclined to ask for more painkillers for my corkscrew headache, the rhythmic sting encircling my eye, the beat of my swollen cheek. My nose feels huge under the bandages and cotton wool. My brittle jaw is wired tight. I drag my chewed-on tongue against my loose teeth. They're hypersensitive and chock-full of newly sharp edges. It's a relief to feel something tangible and extreme.

The absurdity, and stupidity, of damaging myself *again* is funny. I mean, this inglorious incident ranks a mere third among my experiences of physical self-destruction. My jaw and nose will heal. I only lost three teeth. That's less than ten per cent. They're to the side. Not even notice-able unless I open my mouth wide and someone practically sticks their head in. I've already lost plenty of skin, flesh, and bone. A little bit of my mind. And my heart isn't looking too whole either. I'm not qualified to answer for the whereabouts of my soul.

    I'm supposed to go to Rathbaile today. I told Dad and promised Elizabeth. It's three o'clock now. By six they'll be wondering where I am. If I cancel by text, Elizabeth will phone and my ability-to-talk problem might compro-mise my ability to lie. I've been trying to show my family I'm not a danger to myself. Not too crazy or too doomed. Now I'm back to square one.

So could last night have been avoided? Obviously. But I was defending a woman's honour. Sounds impressive. It's not. She didn't even know her honour had been offended. Still, there was the principle involved. And behind everything that I damage and/or destroy are impeccable principles.

    I'll backtrack. I went out last night to appease Seb.

I'm lucky to count him as a friend. That doesn't work both ways. Although we live in the same city, we hadn't seen each other in two months. That's on me. He's been inviting me to something every week. I've always had excuses, piss-poor ones. I don't really have much of a social life. I live alone. I get office work through a temp agency and lately I've been doing a lot of data entry. I'm a surprisingly adept typist and I get a kick out of how my co-workers indiscreetly watch my seven digits play frenetic twister on my keyboard. Apart from that, the work is dull as shit and I only need to be half awake to do it. I spend my evenings consuming novels and movies, and playing online poker. Seb thinks my being a hermit is a bad thing.

I met him in the Stag's Head for a few beers, just us, so we could catch up before rendezvousing with his cool new friends. By 'new', I mean any friends he has made since leaving Rathbaile when we were eighteen. They're mostly struggling actors and struggling writers. I hadn't given them much of a chance when I met them previously. I'm a little wary of people with long-term goals. My chief ambition is to not lose more body parts. Anyway, Seb wanted to talk about what I was doing with my life, my state of mind, etc. I answered what I wanted to, shrugged a lot, and steered the conversation towards him. Beneath his cheery demeanour, he was stressed. For the last year he has had a small role in that soap *Dirty Old Town* and his contract is up for renewal. If they keep him on, his character might be developed, but he doesn't want to get stuck doing bad TV forever. If they fire him, he'll probably have to return to theatre work, which he prefers, but it's another step removed from the big time and it's been years since he even auditioned for a movie role. *Starting Line*, his only movie to date, remains his heyday. He told me, 'I just want a chance to prove what I can do.' While a competent actor could easily flounder in *Town*, I've watched all of his episodes and he doesn't stand out. And yet I've encouraged him to pursue his dream, no matter how unattainable it might be.

We went to a club called The Good Knight and headed directly to the VIP room, where there was a party for the cast and crew of the show. Seb shook hands and traded backslaps as he passed through the room. I followed at a step behind, lame hanger-on that I am, to a table where half a dozen acquaintances applauded his arrival. He introduced me as 'a man who always tells it as it is. A friend of mine through thick and thin.'

I sat between a guy with wavy brown hair who looked like a young Richard Gere and a somewhat emaciated girl who kept glancing doe-eyed at a nearby table where a few of the show's bigger names were sitting. She plucked her cigarette from her lips and sighed smoke. Gere was drinking a blue-green cocktail as he studied an A4-sized photo. It took me a moment to realise that it was a black-and-white headshot of himself, his hand immersed in his hair, his grin that of a man secure in his own charisma. When he noticed me staring, he said, 'I can't decide if it's quite serious enough.'

'Well you probably don't want to be *too* serious either, right? For the sake of . . .' I racked my brain for actor terminology. 'Range?'

His eyes squinted and his chin muscle twitched: his concentration face. Matching his grin from the photo, he said, 'He's right!' On the other side of the table, Seb was whispering something to the pretty girl next to him. She was laughing. Gere shouted, 'Sebastian, your friend does tell it how it is!' The club was loud and I doubt Seb heard, but he smiled as if he did. Gere said, 'Where are my manners?' He karate-chopped the air in front of me. 'Laurence Heffernan. Heffer.'

I shook his hand and checked, 'Heffer?'

He nodded approvingly, then monologued to me about his rise to the middle from the bowels of obscurity and his elaborate plan to leapfrog to the top. I performed well in the part of an attentive listener. It helped that I was drinking. He excused himself when he saw someone important-looking to talk to. He took his photo.

The doe-eyed girl leaned in and breathed smoke in my face. 'You're amazing.'

I pocketed my left hand and took a right-handed drink of my pint. 'Why's that?'

She batted her long, possibly fake eyelashes and laughed. 'Your patience with that poser's babble. Amazing.'

'He wasn't too bad.'

'Wanker! Not you. Him.' Her eyes focused on me, unfocused, focused again. 'You seem to be, like, the opposite of a wanker.'

It struck me that if she was less undernourished and perhaps more sober, and if I was more drunk, she could be cute. I said, 'I'll be right back.'

I went to the bar and had a shot of whiskey, then I went to the jacks and took a piss. Ever since Nicole, I get anxious being around women if I'm even slightly attracted. It's dumb, but I always think about all the bad things that could happen.

At the sink, I splashed water on my face and wiped it off with a paper towel. When I looked in the mirror, I saw Heffer standing behind me. He frowned. 'You okay, my friend?'

'Certainly.'

I threw the paper towel in the bin. Despite him talking my ear off earlier, he noticed my pincer hand for the first time. It was probably just to defuse the silence, but he patted his jacket pocket and asked, 'Coke?'

On the previous occasion I'd tried it, I didn't have a fun night. I believe in second chances.

We went into a stall and locked it. Heffer extracted a small mirror, a black straw, and a vial of white powder from his pockets. He held out the mirror and vial. 'Can you hold these?'

With my finger shortage on his mind, it may have been a genuine enquiry. I said, 'Sure,' taking the mirror with my good hand and the vial with my pincer.

He produced a credit card and a penknife. When he flicked out the blade, it occurred to me that I might have made yet another terrible mistake, but he only needed it to cut the straw in half. I held the mirror steady while he poured the coke and cut four parallel lines with his card. He snorted two lines using one of the half-straws. I gave him the mirror and he gave me the other half-straw. I took my turn, shooting two miniature cyclones from my nostrils to my brain.

Between sniffles and blinks, I thanked Heffer and said something about having a hunch that he was destined for stardom. I wasn't even being insincere. I suddenly felt like Seb was going to make it big too.

Once we rejoined the packed VIP room, I offered to buy

Heffer a drink. He asked for a rain check, as he'd left his headshot with someone 'for safe keeping' and wanted to retrieve it.

Seb was at the bar paying for a pair of cocktails. I went and asked him who the other drink was for. He said, 'The Italian girl I've been talking to, Giulia. I'll introduce you. I've fancied her for ages and she's just dumped her boyfriend.'

'I presume you're in there?'

He smiled. It's petty to feel jealous of your friends, especially when they deserve their success. My jealousy gave way to guilt. I compensated by getting us each a Jägerbomb. He then insisted on buying me a pint so we'd be square. He said I should make a move on the doe-eyed girl, Joanna. 'Even if she's a bit barking, I hear she's worth it. In the short term, anyway.'

My altered state may have been a factor, but I resolved myself to go for it. And, as odd as this girl might be, she had referred to me as 'amazing'. That was a start.

A few minutes after I'd sat down beside her, Joanna hadn't so much as glanced at me and I was feeling foolish. Over the noise of the club, Seb introduced me to Giulia and we shouted over the table for a bit. That grew tiring and I didn't want to get in Seb's way, so I phased myself out of the conversation. I tried to not look antsy while I drank. I was thinking of excuses to leave when Joanna made contact with me. Only she didn't mean to. She absent-mindedly reached for her phone on the table and put her hand on mine instead, my bad one. She was squeezing my index finger and thumb when she realised her error. She screamed. Everyone at the table stopped talking and looked at her, then at me, then at my pincer.

I hid it under the table. She blubbered apologies. I laughed and told her, 'Happens all the time.' She apologised once more and turned away.

Seb and Giulia started talking to me again. I was all smiles. I finished my pint and told Seb I was going to the bar, but headed for the exit. Walking out without telling him was rude. I was pissed off with myself because of it and also because I don't really have much of a hang-up about my hand. Or at least I thought I'd gotten over it, thanks to Nicole, a long time ago.

I should've sent Seb an apology text then gone home and slept it off. But no. As I was stumbling by another club, I overheard an exchange between two bouncers about a petite young blonde wearing a short red jacket, a mini-skirt, and fishnets who was at the kerb trying to hail a taxi. She looked like the wind was piercing her and she just wanted, more than anything else, for her night to be over. The bouncers were large men, even by bouncer standards, and they had swollen ears, noses, and lips. One of them made a loud remark about slipping the girl Rohypnol and the other doubled over with laughter. The girl didn't hear it and maybe it was just a joke, but, fuck it, I took offence, and while I don't mean to blame everything on what I'd been drinking and snorting, my hard-earned awareness of the limits of my invincibility was compromised.

I launched my best punch at Mr Rohypnol's face. It hurt. Me. He didn't budge. I should have run away, even if my leg might have prevented me from getting very far, but I held my ground. I guess I was curious about how he was going to respond. It crossed my mind, a moment too late, that the bouncers' swollen features were probably the products of a battle-hardened history in boxing or rugby rather than unfortunate birth defects.

What happened next wasn't a fight. That would imply some element of resistance. Mr Rohypnol dragged me into an alley, where he delivered blow upon blow to my face. I remember collapsing then being lifted up by Mr Laughter, his hands under my arms. He wasn't helping me. He was making my face more fist-accessible. I would've made out better if only I hadn't kept smiling between punches. I felt so alive.

Until I blacked out.

Then a paramedic was flashing a torch in the eye I could still open. I tried to tell her I was fine, but the blood in my mouth was drowning out my tongue. I passed out again, then woke up in a vibrating ambulance, driving along a bumpy road. I thought of hunchbacks buried face-down. I vomited, passed out, and came to some time later in the hospital.

I did what I had to do. I gave a note to the nurse with Elizabeth's phone number and: *Tell her I was mugged but that I'm okay.* The mugging nonsense is preferable to the truth. People will worry less if they believe it wasn't completely my fault. I don't want to press charges against the dickhead bouncers, because that would blow my cover and it *was* my fault.

To stop hating my life, I need to get a grip on why everything went so wrong. I can't pretend what happened with Nicole didn't matter and I want to preserve my memories of our time together before they become too muddled. So I'm going to write a testimony. Then I'll be able to perform a grand trick of self-preservation. I'll change who I am.

It's been almost ten years since I lost Nicole. I have to understand why.

Chapter Eighteen

Captain Claw and the Princess of Lost Souls

14/11/2011

Yesterday, when Elizabeth arrived at the hospital, she was distressed at the sight of me, but she tried to hide it. She had questions. I nodded when she asked if I was okay and shook my head when she asked if I needed anything. When she wanted to know what happened, I scribbled in my notepad about how a couple of guys had mugged me. She told me I had to go to the guards. I wrote: No point. Didn't get a good enough look to ID them. She said, 'You didn't see their faces, huh?' Pretending not to register her tone, I shook my head. Exercising restraint, she didn't press.

I was discharged this morning, against my doctor's wishes. He recommended that I stay for another twenty-four hours to give myself time to heal. I wrote: I've a proven track record of healing fast and I can do it just as well at home. He frowned as he read it – he may have been more apprehensive about my talent for accumulating new injuries than about my ability to cope with the ones I already had.

Elizabeth was there too, having supplied me with

non-blood-spattered clothes, and she resolutely said to him, 'I'll keep a close eye on the patient.'

Her intervention was patronising, but the doctor seemed convinced by her air of reliability so I let it go. Once he had left, I conveyed my gratitude to Elizabeth with a thumbs-up. I took her sigh to mean 'you're welcome'. She drove me back to my flat and she'll stay over tonight. While I'm grateful for her consideration and the cream-of-mushroom soup she made me – which I ingested with difficulty through a straw – I'd rather be alone. But I don't have much fight in me right now, so I'm being agreeable.

I know I have a tendency to take her for granted. It's unfair of me, and I don't think I do that with Dad or Tighe.

I'm sitting up in my bed and tonguing the craters in my gum as I write this. I'm in some pain – I should really quit with the tonguing. And on some painkillers. Clarity and focus feel elusive, but I hope to improve on both.

It's time for me to get going with my testimony about Nicole. I could ease into it by writing something first about who I was before we knew each other, maybe jour-neying back to my childhood. My family tragedies. My physical traumas. The formative influences of my adoles-cence. But all those memories feel like they belong to someone else. I didn't really become the person I am until she was in my life, and that's why I'm beginning with how we met, properly, twelve years ago.

The end of October 1999
Her visible skin was chalk-white, except for the coal-black-ness around her eyes and lips. Blood tears streaked her

cheeks, or maybe they were meant to be claw marks. Her throat was cut too, an extravagant crimson slash. Her hair stood starched on its ends, reaching out dementedly. She was wearing a battered black ball gown with a plummeting neckline. There was a large spider on her chest just below the hollow at the base of her neck. I could have sworn the spider was scurrying south, but I stared until I realised I was mistaken. Then I looked up and she smiled that undead smile. I was standing in the doorway of the dim room, which was crowded with people, and she was twenty feet away, so I hoped she couldn't tell I was blushing.

Seb pushed me. 'C'mon, kitchen.'

I staggered into the room with a plastic bag containing a bottle of wine swinging from my hook. I didn't meet her eyes as I passed her. I think I feared even then that she could humiliate me with a look. My paranoia was understandable. Bad experiences were raw in my mind. I'd only moved back to Dublin in September, restarting the first year of my degree after having spent nine months at home in Rathbaile, where I had been rehabilitating and lying low.

In the kitchen, I took the bottle from the bag and found an opener. I pressed the bottle between my left forearm and my chest for grip and fastened the opener to the top. Screwing the corkscrew in was easy. Retracting it was more challenging. Seb's pronounced concern undermined the effect of his unimaginative costume: cape, frilly shirt, fangs. Other than my hook, I was wearing a bandanna, an eye patch, an open white shirt, and pirate boots. My costume might not have been much more creative than his, but considering what I was concealing, it possessed some ironic value. He said, 'Need a hand? I mean, can I help?'

I growled, 'I've got it,' and pulled harder.

From over my other shoulder I heard a woman's voice, her accent Australian. 'Why don't you remove your hook while you do that?'

'Because I'm a real pirate.' The cork popped and I turned to the undead girl. 'Are you supposed to be a ghoul? Maybe a wraith?'

She fluttered her eyelashes. 'I'm the Princess of Lost Souls.'

'Not the Queen?'

'Some day. You're Captain Hook?'

'Captain Claw.'

'Why's that?'

'Beneath my hook is my claw.'

'You're odd, aren't you? I like your moustache.'

'It's a homage to one of the men responsible for my claw.'

'Is he your ticking crocodile? And you're on a revenge mission?'

'You're not too far off.'

She stepped closer. 'You'll have to tell me more. You can't just tease me with suspense.'

Trying to smile casually, I said something like, 'If I disclose the full story, I might erode my mystique, or maybe I'm talking rubbish. The point is, you shouldn't trust a word I have to say, so for your sake, I should be careful about saying anything at all.'

Her smile was fading. She must have been wondering why I sounded nervous and maybe even a little angry. I attempted to make amends. 'Where are my manners? Some wine?'

She hesitated, then said, 'Sure.'

Seb had been standing back, but I gestured to him. 'The Prince of Darkness, meet the Princess of Lost Souls, soon to be the Queen.'

He took out his fangs, shook her hand, and kissed her on the cheek. 'Seb, actually. What's your real name?'

'The Princess of Lost Souls is my real name. My parents are very eccentric.'

'The King and Queen are known for that.'

They chatted as I ferreted for drinking receptacles among the flotsam and jetsam on the counters. I assumed he had already won her over.

In a fruit bowl, I found a fallen tower of plastic cups. I poured the three of us a cup each and asked Seb to guard mine with his life as I needed to use the jacks. Then I walked past the Princess, with unintentional brusqueness.

In the bathroom, I felt like I was going to vomit. Despite the rancid sensation in my stomach and a scratching along my throat, I only managed a few dry retches as I gripped the sides of the sink. I saw sparks on the insides of my eyelids and concentrated on slowing my heartbeat.

I lifted my eye patch to my forehead. When I reflected on my reflection in the mirror, I appeared to have a half-circle hole in my head. There was a coyness in my copy's eyes, like he knew something I didn't. Maybe not something that would cataclysmically change my life, but an insight that could shift my perspective enough to feel like I had more control.

I thought about my mother. Her one-year anniversary was approaching. She felt dead, yet not gone. I had assumed that if anyone was at risk of being infected by whatever got her it would be Elizabeth, but she seemed more confident somehow after Mam's death. I had also

229

worried that Dad's will to live might disintegrate, but though he was tormented, he was still doing better than I'd expected. In the wake of my 'incident', it was me everyone was looking at cross-eyed. I got why.

Added to all that, in August, Simon had died of a heart attack. He was my great-uncle but he felt like more of a grandfather to me, and he was a very dear and generous man. As much as I loved him – and largely because I loved him – I elected not to attend his viewing or his funeral, where I would have been a pallbearer, because I didn't want to be in the vicinity of his body. I wanted to remember him as he was when he was alive and I had regretted not making the same decision with Mam. For the most part, people respected my decision, to my face anyway. The exception was Elizabeth, who – not unusually for her – was angry with me. She thought that I should have gotten over my issues and paid the appropriate tribute. She didn't buy my argument that I was paying tribute in my mind, and that even if I had gone to the funeral, it's not like Simon would have known about it. She also wasn't placated by how I'd made a point of privately expressing my deep condolences to his widow, or by how I did attend the post-funeral reception – she suggested I only went to that because of the drinking involved, a comment she later apologised for.

By the time I was at the Halloween party, Elizabeth and I had made peace – mainly by agreeing not to talk about the matter – but it was just one more thing contributing to my general anxiety.

As I stared into the bathroom mirror, trying to pull myself together, there was a knock on the door. When I was slow to reply, it was followed by 'Come on!'

I muzzled an impulse to yell something like 'Do you have any idea how hard it is to separate out the symptoms of delayed grief from those of post-traumatic stress, which are really quite similar, while also trying to find the courage to go hit on an attractive undead girl? I'm going through a lot here!' Instead I called out affably, 'One second!' and shifted my eye patch back into place.

I opened the door and sidestepped around a guy in a gorilla suit, unzipped and peeled to his waist, the furry arms dangling. In the hall, I passed Superman, Batman, a werewolf, and a few zombies, including one of the original zombies, Jesus. When I entered the living room, Seb and the Princess were over by the steamed window. Despite her spooky costume, she looked like a damsel in distress. Seb was, after all, Dracula, and as he talked into her ear, her ashen neck was deliciously exposed to his fangs. Seeing me, they beckoned.

I manoeuvred my way over to them. Seb retrieved my wine cup from the sill and handed it to me. 'You fall in?' I shrugged. He shook his empty cup. 'I need to top up. Princess, I'll bring you back some.'

She said, 'I have half a cup left.'

'That's still half empty. I'll bring the bottle. Talk to this girl, Captain. She's been telling me how brilliant it is in Oz, and she told me the story of how you two first met as well.'

He walked away before I could ask him what he was talking about. The Princess laughed, staring at me with secrets in her eyes as she sipped her wine. I said, 'We've already met?'

'Yeah, Jimmy, but I mustn't have made much of an impression.'

'Sorry, you are familiar.' I tapped my forehead with my hook. 'My mind is a sieve. Could you give me a clue? Maybe your real name?'

'Only because you shared your wine. I'm Nicole. Ring any bells?'

I shook my head. 'Wait, have we slept together?'

It was a dumb line, and my voice faltered as I uttered it, but I drew a smile from her before she adopted a mock-offended expression. 'Believe me, you'd remember that. Regardless of whatever gigolo life you may have led on the high seas.'

'It'll come to me.' I couldn't think of anything witty to say, and after looking about me for something worthy of comment but finding nothing, I meekly asked, 'So, you and Seb had a good chat?'

'He talked a lot about you, actually. He holds you in high esteem. He said you're his best friend.'

'He's mine. I don't have a bad word to say about him.'

'Why would you?'

'Exactly.'

'And he asked me about Australia. He didn't seem to notice that I was glad to leave. He said you and him and a couple of mates are going next summer, to travel around for a year and get the full backpacker experience.'

'We've talked about it. I guess you noticed that he's practically on the plane, and on the beach.'

'You're not up for it?'

'It should be a blast, but I'm not sure about the timing. I have obligations here. Why were you glad to leave?' She sighed, so I said, 'You don't have to answer.'

She smiled. 'There were heaps of reasons, none of them mind-blowing. I had just lived there all my life. Dad moved us around every few years, so we weren't always in the same spot, but by the time I finished school, as vast as Australia is, I felt walled in. My parents wanted me to go direct to uni, and in Sydney so I'd be close to them, but I wanted space. I got a flat in Melbourne with this guy I thought I was in love with, who turned out to be a major dickhead. After I worked shit jobs for a while, I figured maybe a degree might be a good idea, but it had to be somewhere new. Ireland was about as far away as it gets, and I liked what I'd heard about the place, so I thought fuck it and came here to study science. Don't let me put you off about Australia. It would be new and exciting and warm, and plenty of Aussie girls like the Irish accent, so I reckon you guys would do all right. You really should go.'

'We've only just met and you're already trying to get me to leave the country? Most people wait until they've known me a day or two.'

'First of all, we *haven't* just met. And second, it'd be pretty forward of me to ask you to *stay*. But maybe you have everything you need here. Is your life complete?'

Seb returned with the bottle and gave me a sly grin. I think he wanted me to score Nicole as much as I did. He topped us up, then excused himself to go say hello to a girl on the other side of the room.

Nicole and I kept talking, in that corner, for the next hour. I shared a few anecdotes about my family and friends, suavely dodging any involving madness, maiming, or death. She told me about arguing a lot with her parents and repeated her dislike of her ex-boyfriend without elaborating in much detail on either subject. It's hard to explain why I felt close to her so quickly. It wasn't the alcohol. Even though I continued to drink, she had a sobering effect on me. I suppose we had an instinct about each other. Despite what I've learned since, I don't think I was wrong. I wish I could say the same for her. One thing I became certain of was that this was our first encounter and she was having a joke at my expense. Regardless of her disguised face, if I'd met this girl before, I would surely have known.

We'd been out of wine for a while when I suggested scouring the kitchen for strays. She said she didn't feel like another drink. I was disheartened, because I figured it meant she was fixing to leave. She was, but that was good. The party was in a Merville flat and she was living on campus too, in a block five minutes away. She asked if I wanted to go have tea with her in her living room. I blurted out that I was absolutely up for it if she had coffee.

She had coffee.

I took Seb aside to tell him not to wait around for me whenever he decided to head off. He barely allowed me to explain before he was shoving me away. 'What are you worried about me for? Go!'

Nicole and I retrieved our jackets from a bedroom and, one-handed, I buttoned my shirt to fortify myself for the cold. Then we stepped into the night, a pirate and his corpse bride.

Outside her block she said, 'Don't get any ideas about spending the night. I've a reputation to uphold.' She said it breezily so I could take it seriously but also treat it as a joke. I told her I had no expectations.

Her flat was a duplicate of the one we'd come from: the

front door opening into a hallway, with bedrooms on the left, and the living room and kitchen behind a glass-panelled wall and door on the right. Her flat was quiet, though, and the lights were off. She whispered that her flatmates were probably asleep and showed me into the living room, where she switched on a lamp. She asked me to boil the kettle, then excused herself to go get changed.

I went into her kitchen and flicked the kettle on. I would have made her a cup of tea, but there were a bunch of different brands in the cupboard and I didn't know which was hers or how she preferred to take it. My phone vibrated in my pocket. It was a text from Seb: *Dont fuck it up.* I deleted it. I sat on the couch in the living room, took off my jacket and my eye patch, and tapped the coffee table with my hook.

She returned wearing a T-shirt and sweatpants. Her hair was wet and tied back. Her forearms and hands were make-up-free. The crimson slash was miraculously erased from her neck, but her face was still in character. She had a wet cloth and a towel. She sat beside me, set the towel on the table and gave me the cloth. I was slow to get what she wanted me to do. She said, 'I thought you could help me with my face. Maybe it would be easier if you removed your hook?'

'I just need my right hand.' It was only as I saw her forearms and neck in the glow of the lamp that I realised something I had missed earlier. I stated my great revelation. 'You're black.'

She laughed. 'Nothing gets by you.'

It hit me where I knew her from. I waited to confirm I was right. Avoiding her stare, I used the cloth to wipe the blood tears and chalk-white make-up from her cheeks, then

235

moved on to her forehead, nose, and mouth. She let me turn her face to various angles with the light. I was fascinated by her. I didn't comprehend then that not everyone thought she was beautiful. I suppose I could only ever see her from my perspective. Her prominent round cheeks combined with the flatness of her nose may have given her face a vaguely plump appearance. Her smile was conspicuously askew – she always smiled out of the left side of her mouth. Her upper lip was thin and her lower lip full, with a belligerence in the curve. She had a sickle-shaped scar above her right eyebrow that she hated, but I liked.

I paused with only the black blotting around her eyes left to clear. 'Your face looks like a Rorschach test.'

'Shut up. Fix it.'

I refolded the cloth and used an unstained section to rub the make-up from her eyelids. When I was finished, I put the cloth on the table. If she had looked at me just then, I'd probably have bottled it, but her eyes were still closed when I leaned in and kissed her. I was half expecting her to slap me. Instead, she smiled, put her hand on my chest, and kissed me back.

I was the one who pulled away. 'That morning, a year ago, at the bus stop, why were you crying?'

She laughed. 'Congratulations, Sherlock. I was foolish. There was a guy. I thought he'd broken my heart. A day later, I ceased to remember he existed. I'm sorry I shouted at you. I haven't always been good at telling when some-one's trying to help.'

'I haven't always been good at knowing when to leave well enough alone.'

'We should get along famously then. Anyway, you've unmasked me. It's my turn.'

236

Without further warning, she ripped off my moustache. It smarted, but I didn't flinch. She reached around my head, undoing my bandanna and dropping it on the table. She took my hook in her hand. I put my hand on hers. She said, 'What are you afraid of? Your claw won't shock me.'

'You don't understand. I wasn't joking when I said I had a claw.'

'I know. Seb told me you had an accident where you injured your hand.'

I was frustrated with myself for not realising I'd been exposed all along. 'What did he say? "Injured" might be understating it.'

She placed her hand on my knee. 'Just that you've been through a lot. Some accidents. He said you have a prosthetic leg. And that your mother passed away.'

'Is there anything he didn't tell you?'

'He only said all of that because he was praising your resilience.'

She squeezed my knee and I laughed with some bitterness. 'That's the fake knee. My leg starts a little higher up.' She switched her hand to my good knee and squeezed that one. I said, 'I'm not a cripple. I won't tolerate any pity from you.'

'Good. I have none to give. And I still want to see.'

I let her untie the elastic band around my wrist and slide off the plastic hook covering the remains of my hand. She raised it to her mouth and kissed my inflamed knuckle stumps.

Jimmy remembers this as the night he fell in love, but if he was honest with himself, he could admit that he was still searching for the guts to truly fall for her. One thing he got right was that he could only see her from his own limited perspective. That's where he and I differ. I ventured into her mind and knew her as well as she knew herself. Jimmy was hopeless at telling when she was lying, but she couldn't hide it from me. While he idealised her, I saw her for who she was, flaws and all, and I wasn't cautious. I was aware of my love for Nicole from the very start.

Chapter Nineteen

In the Distance

31/12/2011

In the distance, I still see her. Usually I'm on some busy street when a familiar figure catches my eye. As I move nearer, more details register until I'm overwhelmed by my mistake. Up close, none of the women look anything like her. I know that I can't expect to ever see her again. But I still can't stop searching for her in crowds.

I'm feeling better, physically. I had lost some weight during my soup-diet days, but I put most of it back on at home over Christmas. My face is no longer swollen. The scars on my nose aren't so bad. I have three new, fake, teeth. My jaw is no longer wired and I've never been more appreciative of being able to yawn.

In an hour it will be a new year. I bought a bottle of Prosecco to mark the occasion, but I've started early. I've lit five candles that are scattered about my living room. I like the shimmer they cast on my glass. The bubbles rush to the surface with an extra voltage. To an observer, it might appear like I've created a cosy or even romantic ambience. That wasn't my intent. No one will be knocking on my door. The presence of the candles speaks to my obsession. Nicole liked candles. They remind me of her.

I haven't written anything for six weeks. But I'm in the mood again and I've readied myself for exorcism.

The end of October to early November 1999
After I showed Nicole what was beneath my hook, we were kissing and I wanted to keep going, but I stopped. 'I should really leave.'

She released my pincer. 'Don't you want to . . . have that coffee?'

I muttered something about how I'd never sleep if I did and she made no further attempt to persuade me to stay. We exchanged numbers and I suggested we should go for a drink sometime soon. She agreed, somewhat stiffly. She walked me to the door. I kissed her goodnight. She returned it with her lips sealed.

As I walked home, the magnitude of how I had mishandled the situation sank in. There had been some indications that she liked me, so I'd rationalised to myself that if I could leave without revealing my inexperience or exposing any more wounds, it would be reasonable to expect other chances. I was young enough to not realise how finite great chances in life are and I'd been scared off by the possibility of getting something I wanted so much, a fear that's even dumber than it sounds. I'd thought that, because of the easy connection between us, I could excuse myself smoothly and she would be impressed by my self-control. Instead, I put questions in her mind about whether I was really interested and whether I was spineless.

It was four when I returned to the flat Seb and I shared

in Rathmines. I went straight to bed, where I tossed about and occasionally tried to punch my pillow into submission.

In the morning, Seb barged into my room and shook me until I opened my eyes. 'I'm guessing you didn't get laid, but you'd still better tell me everything.'

We went to a dreary café on the corner of our street, where we ordered pancakes and coffee from a waitress who was far too chirpy. She recognised Seb from *Starting Line* and said she didn't care about a tip as long as he left her an autograph.

When our order was on the table, Seb said, 'Out with it.'

I told him the gist: that Nicole and I had kissed and then for some inexplicable reason I left; that I fancied her big-time, though I expressed this as more of a lust dilemma rather than admitting that she held my heart in her hands; that now I didn't know what to do. I neglected to mention how I'd washed away her mask and how she'd kissed my mutilation · because, well, Seb didn't need to know anything that would make me look soft or unduly weird. I refrained from calling him out for sharing the bullet points of my tragic life with her because I'd admitted to myself that she probably wouldn't have invited me to her flat if he hadn't.

He laughed at me, stuffed his face with pancake, and, chewing and talking simultaneously, said, 'What are you worried about? You're well in there. I'd recommend calling her, but just to bypass getting a case of the stutters, it might be smarter to text her. Ask her out today. Even if she acts aloof at first, she'll meet up with you. You're overthinking it.'

'I don't want to look like a fool.'

He pointed at me with his pancake-coiled fork, a syrupy morsel dangling. 'Any guy with balls should be willing to make a fool of himself for the right girl. If you get burnt, so be it.'

I texted her that afternoon, inviting her for a drink the following night. Then I passed the time playing shoot-'em-up video games, committing sloppy errors and getting killed repeatedly. After two hours of countless game-overs, she texted me that she was swamped for the next few days, but if I was free on Thursday, five days away, she was 'almost definitely' sure she could go for a drink then. I texted that I was 'pretty confident' it'd be doable and she responded that she'd confirm one way or the other on Wednesday. I pitifully took solace in her text ending with: *Ill b in touch! :-)* See: an exclamation mark and a smiley face. Surely she couldn't be planning on blowing me off.

By Wednesday, I was devoid of hope. So I fancied this girl and had chatted her up and kissed her. So fucking what? For all I knew, I'd only gotten that far because she was on some pity trip. I was a survivor of real problems and I was allowing myself to get bent out of shape over a girl who probably hadn't lost a moment's sleep thinking about me. I decided I'd be better off if she did cancel. Fuck her. Fuck everything. Then she texted to confirm she was free for a drink and: *Really looking forward to it!!* Two exclamation marks. It would have taken a crowbar to prise the smile from my face.

I was in the pub on time. I bought a pint and sat on a two-seater bench at a table in an alcove. There was a pair of chairs at the table, but I moved them away to encourage Nicole to sit beside instead of across from me. I tensed myself into what I hoped appeared to be a relaxed pose. I played with my phone and didn't take more than a few sips of my pint.

Twenty minutes later, she walked in. She flashed a smile and cut a path. Her hair was down around her shoulders and she was wearing a denim jacket, a Pearl Jam T-shirt, with *Vitalogy* splashed across her chest, and tight-fitting blue jeans. I was straining not to ogle her every curve.

I stood as she neared, unsure of how to greet her. I leaned in for a pat of her upper arm and a kiss that barely grazed her cheek. She smacked her lips to my cheek and gave me a firm body-to-body embrace.

We decoupled. She laughed. 'I'm so sorry for being late. Have you been here long?'

I gestured to my almost-full pint. 'Just arrived. What do you want to drink?'

'Whatever you're having. Next one's on me.'

Upon my return from the bar I found she had pulled up a chair. I consoled myself that this would facilitate talking eye to eye and she probably wanted to avoid being presumptuous.

I said, 'Wow, you look so normal tonight.' Her eyebrow perked up. I clarified. 'You look *great*, in a normal way, or normal in a great way. What I mean is you look completely different from Saturday night.'

'What was wrong with how I looked on Saturday?'

I took a drink. 'Nothing. Don't fuck with me. You look gorgeous.'

'Thanks. You're less like a pirate.'

We chatted, but unlike previously, our small talk felt small. I was more self-conscious of everything I said, and being sober to start with didn't help, but it wasn't just me. She was acting strangely, not so much stand-offish as cautious and preoccupied. I wasn't being paranoid. As we were finishing our first pints she said, 'I've something to tell you, and please don't take it the wrong way.'

I naively said, 'Whatever it is, I'll be fine.'

She ran her hand through her hair, making a fist and pulling on it. Then she let go and her hair fell back into place. 'You're this cool, super-interesting guy and I want us to spend lots of time together because I want to know you and be your friend. Okay?'

'I'd like that too.'

'I've given you the wrong impression. I'm sorry. You see, I'm not really available.'

Smiling, smiling, always smiling. 'You have a boyfriend.'

'Kind of.' She pressed her forehead into her palm. 'I've been involved with this guy and I thought it was over. On Saturday night I was resigned to it, and I was trying to get some distance from him, and you came along and you were sweet. Then I discovered that me and him . . . Maybe it's not done with. And I shouldn't be with someone else until I've sorted out what I feel. I'm a messy girl, Jimmy. Always have been. But I genuinely want to spend time together. I'd understand if you were mad.'

'I'm not.' I swallowed the dregs of my pint and the gluey froth wormed down my throat. 'I want to be friends too. I think it's for the best this way.'

'You do?'

I shrugged, gaining some satisfaction from her look of surprise. 'It's not meant to be. Better to know that now.'

'Want another drink?'

I wanted ten. 'Sure.'

I was determined to show her how happy-go-lucky I was. If I needed to pursue a close friendship to prove to her that she hadn't hurt me, then so be it.

She didn't bring up her boyfriend again and I didn't enquire further about him. I didn't ask if I had done something to scare her off me or if, after considering it, she decided I had one too many wounds. While we talked, I displayed my pincer, holding my beer with it.

We were on our third pints when she said, 'Can I ask what happened to your hand?'

'Which version of the story do you want? Fact or fiction?'

'I don't plan on checking sources.'

'It all started a year ago, with my mother. She couldn't find a reason to live so she slit her wrists.'

She flinched. 'You don't have to . . .'

'It's fine.'

I told her about my self-destructive behaviour in the aftermath of Mam's death and the consequences that came of it, sparing Nicole nothing because I wanted to shock her. She seemed more fascinated than shocked, though.

When I was lingering on the graphic details of chopping off my own fingers, she interrupted me to suggest that maybe I had picked the wrong ones. 'I think if it had been me, I would've kept both my middle fingers and opted to lose the pinkie of my other hand instead.' She became embarrassed. 'Sorry, you really don't need to hear me questioning your selection.'

I laughed. 'My mindset was that it was better to have just one severely maimed hand rather than dividing the maiming between the two. The small finger of your writing hand is more important than you might think – it's an underrated part of your overall hand equilibrium, so, for instance, there'd be a strain involved in using a pen without it and my handwriting is bad enough as it is. Besides, if I'd gone down the fingers-on-both-hands route, I couldn't have done all the work myself and it would've been a shame to delegate away that once-in-a-lifetime experience. Ultimately though, while I respect your point, maybe it's one of those situations where you kind of had to be there.'

She nodded, smiling just a little. 'I'm glad to hear you thought it through. Did they catch the gangsters who made you do it?'

'I never fingered them. Sorry, I'm inviting further calamities whenever I make terrible puns. I heard that one of them, Casey, has ended up in jail on a murder charge. Maybe festering in a cell is worse than losing a few non-essential body parts.'

'I don't think it's a fair trade, for you.'

'It is what it is. My "friend" Gavin – who told them where to find me – is in jail as well, for selling crack to kids.'

'Sounds you know a lot of people who've gone to jail.'

'Just two. But I've become pickier about who I associate with. So if you're engaged in any criminal enterprises, please tell me and I'll go sit at a different table.'

'How about we work from the assumption that I'm innocent until proven guilty?'

'I can give you that much. But I've got my eye on you.'

She leaned forward. 'What about your leg? That was something else?'

'Yeah, starving dogs.'

I told her that story too, and she listened, rapt.

When I finished, she said, 'I've never known anyone who . . . You've been through the wars, but you don't need me to tell you that.'

'Not the wars. Bad luck and worse decisions. How about you?' I gestured to the scar above her eyebrow. 'How did you get that?'

She touched her fingers to it. 'It's a boring story in comparison. Remember the ex in Melbourne I told you about? He was nice to look at, if you didn't look too long. Charming and popular, conceited and mean. He'd gotten aggressive with me a few times, but it was when I told him I was leaving that he really lost it. He punched me in the stomach and that dropped me to my knees. When I looked up at him, he brought his fist down. His ring cracked me right here and gave me my memento. He broke a finger and howled like a little bitch.'

'Did you tell anyone about it? Anyone sort him out?'

'Nah. Was his snapped finger not enough comeuppance?'

'No, not nearly.'

She talked about it like it wasn't a big deal, but I'm sure she wanted me to know it was, and I admired how she was simultaneously tough and vulnerable.

I realised I didn't have a choice. She could get to me with any flicker of kindness or hint of sadness. I could, I thought, accept not being with her. What I couldn't accept was being unable to protect her, and I understood then that my ability to do so was the measure of me.

We didn't tell any more war stories that night. And I made no declarations of affection or promises to save her, although I was already carving them into my mind. We talked about the oncoming millennium and the menace of millennium bugs. It's funny now how that future already feels like ancient history. I expressed outrage when she divulged that she hadn't seen a single episode of *Father Ted*, despite having lived in Ireland for over a year. I extolled its virtues, even attempting a rendition of 'My Lovely Horse'. She patted my hand. 'I guess you have to be Irish.'

The bartender kicked us out at one. We stumbled across the road to the line of stops beside Trinity College. We needed different Nitelinks, but our stops were next to one another so we stood between them. She asked me to hug her while we waited. Because she was drunk and it was so very cold. She didn't have to ask twice. I could feel her breath teasing my neck, her hair against my jaw, and I knew she was looking up at me. I didn't look down because I didn't want to kiss her when I feared that she would wake up the following day and call it a mistake. Some idiot walking by shouted at us, 'Get a room!' We laughed it off. I still didn't meet her eyes. I fixed mine on a point in the distance and held her close. Mercifully, the buses came and I was able to let her go.

Chapter Twenty

A Taste of Blood

1/1/2012

Last night, I poured the remainder of the Prosecco into my glass, but I wasn't thirsty enough to cap off my New Year's celebration. I stopped writing because I couldn't bear it. Sitting out on my balcony, I listened to the noises of the city, all that machinery and blinkered chaos, and watched the revellers sway and totter along the street. Only a few people looked up to my fourth-storey perch. They seemed unable to see me. Maybe alcohol had obliterated their vision, or the night had made me invisible. The cold got the better of me and I retreated to my bedroom. I took off my clothes, detached my prosthetic, and hid under the quilt.

I've been awake for half an hour. The aroma of my first mug of coffee is more powerful than the whiff of flat Prosecco in the glass at the far side of the table. I'm starting on a new memory.

November 1999

During the weeks following rejection night, Nicole and I spent a lot of time together, mostly just us, going for coffee in college and for beers in pubs around town. We went to the cinema to see a horror movie, *Stir of Echoes*. She rested her head on my shoulder and grappled her hands around my arm. My hands were locked to the armrests. Being around her was invigorating and torturous. I'd have tried to get some space if only being away from her wasn't worse.

Then there was this boyfriend. It was such a tired story. Alistair was the older-man figure, twenty years her senior and going through a trial separation from his wife. He had two kids, who Nicole wasn't allowed to meet. She said their mother was responsible for that. I suspected it was really because Alistair was planning on discarding her as soon as he'd had his fill. I didn't need to meet the guy to hate him. Obviously I was biased, but fuck that smug mid-life-crisis bastard.

Nicole announced she was turning twenty-one. While she claimed to hate birthdays, a celebration was called for, so she rented the basement room of a pub called Pugg's. She warned me that Alistair had promised to drop by and checked whether that was okay. My chosen words were 'The more the merrier.'

'You sure?'

I insisted.

She asked me not to be late because she didn't want to be there drinking by herself, 'like the loneliest birthday girl in the world'. I obliged, getting there a few minutes before she did. I bought us cocktails and we sat at a table facing the door. The stone-walled room was darkly lit, but the lacquer on the wooden tables gleamed. I gave her a present: a silver-and-gold bracelet with a weaving Celtic design. She said she loved it, but was worried it was too pricey. I carefully clasped it to her wrist and reassured her of its cheapness. She didn't believe me.

Within an hour, fifteen people had arrived; within two, there were forty. They were mainly science classmates and other foreign students. With so many well-wishers clamouring for attention, she was switching tables with every drink. That was fine with me. I didn't want to be sitting with her when Alistair turned up, and to have nowhere else to look while he leered and she encouraged it.

I found myself sitting side by side at a table with Marilyn, a New Yorker who was one of Nicole's flatmates. Nicole occasionally referred to her as 'the nun', due to her promiscuity, which she claimed was a way of affirming her feminist principles. Nicole had said to me, 'I'm all for sexual liberation, but couldn't she have some standards?' and I defended Marilyn. My fear was that if women were ethically required to have a minimum-standards rule, a ten-toes-and-ten-fingers clause might be included.

An hour into our conversation, Marilyn had yet to mention sex. As she spoke, she had a habit of touching my arm, and sometimes her shapely leg pressed against my misshapen half-artificial one, but I didn't get the sense that she was intentionally flirting with me. I was with her, though, laughing loudly at anything she said if there was even a chance of it being a joke. I wanted Nicole to notice how much fun I was having, and if I could make her jealous too, all the better.

Laughing at Marilyn's wit wasn't helped by her lack of it. She thought Pauly Shore was the funniest man alive and referred to Friends as 'high satire'. My head may have been nodding, my laughter whorishly at the ready, but my mind was elsewhere. Even without knowing what Alistair looked like, I kept picturing some muscular version of him with Nicole: one of his sweaty hands crushing the bracelet I'd given her against her wrist as they fucked, and her screaming for him and forgetting my existence.

Despite inhabiting my thoughts, he was absent from the party and it had gone midnight. If Nicole was on tenterhooks, she was hiding it well, but he might have cancelled earlier on and she just hadn't told me. I could see her chatting to a burly Canadian called Greg, who, in his glasses and tight white T-shirt, looked like a second-rate Clark Kent. He whispered something in her ear and she erupted into laughter. He put his hand on the small of her back. I waited for her to move away so he wouldn't get the wrong idea. She didn't budge.

'Are you listening to me?'

Marilyn's question registered a few moments too late for me to argue with any plausibility that I was. Still, out of panicked politeness I said, 'Of course, and I totally agree.'

She stared at me and I worried she was going to make a scene. Instead, lowering her voice, she said, 'If you like her, why don't you do something about it?'

I was too proud to be honest. 'We're just friends. It's nothing else.'

'If you change your mind about that, maybe you should tell her. Although . . .'

'What?'

'She's cool and all, but on closer inspection, you might find she's not everything you think she is.'

'She's my friend.'

She looked at me like I was the most transparent guy in the world. 'Yeah, you said.'

'I need another drink. Can I get you anything?'

She shook her vodka and Coke, jostling the ice cubes against the glass. 'Thanks, but I'm a few sips from heading off.'

I went to the bar and ordered a whiskey. I was about to sit down again when I felt a draught.

Nicole and Greg were at the door leading up to the street and he was holding it open. While he was wearing a duffel coat, she didn't have her jacket, so it looked like he was leaving and she was staying, but then she went up the stairwell with him. My hope was that she was just walking him out to say goodnight, only why couldn't she do that inside?

I drained my whiskey, opened the door, and clomped up the stairs, steadying myself with my hand on the railing. I could hear giggling and it was fake and flirty, demeaning to her. The silence that followed, however, was far worse.

I was drunk, but I can't blame my actions on that. I just wanted her so much and it brought out everything that was ugly in me. I stepped on to the street and there they were. She was in his arms, his tongue in her mouth.

Before I could articulate a clear thought in my head, I was shoving him. I realised I'd clenched my hand into a fist when it was colliding with his face and breaking his glasses, obscuring one of his eyes behind a web of cracks.

He took a single step backwards, and then he was shoving me and I was stumbling. Nicole yelled, 'Greg, don't!'

Anger only gets you so far in a fight, and alcohol is no friend to reflexes and balance. These are lessons I learned.

I took two quick blows to the jaw and tripped over my

feet, crashing to the pavement. When I tried to get up, I discovered that, like my dignity, my prosthetic had come undone.

Greg loomed over me, his nostrils flexed and his upper lip quivering. He leaned down with his hand out, and for a second I thought he was going to help me up. The joke was on me when he seized a handful of my shirt and delivered another punch to my face, which was doubly effective because it sent the back of my skull smacking against the pavement. Every star in the sky was suddenly a shooting star.

In a violent rather than a romantic sense this time, Nicole threw herself at him and slapped his face. He backed up on to the road and a car narrowly avoided hitting him. The driver pounded on his horn but kept on going. Greg grabbed Nicole's wrists, pushed her to the wall of the pub, and shouted, 'What the fuck is wrong with you? He attacked me!'

She kicked his shin hard. He let go of her wrists and she screamed, 'Just fuck off! Don't you see he has a handicap? Don't you see what's happened to his leg?'

He looked over at me. I had gathered myself into a sitting position, with my palms on the ground, but I didn't pose a danger unless he came within biting distance. On noticing the bulge and absence under my jeans where my prosthetic had become displaced, he jumped, his banjaxed glasses bobbing on his nose. 'Jesus!'

One of his punches had caused me to bite my tongue, and I spat blood, which propelled no further than my chin. Greg was on the verge of fainting. I pulled up the leg of my jeans and revealed my prosthetic. 'Relax. I'm a fucking cyborg.'

Tearful, he said, 'I'm getting away from this freak show. You're welcome to this crazy bitch.'

He ran across the road before I could shout an empty threat.

Then it was just me and Nicole. She approached slowly, like I was a wounded animal. I suppose that's exactly what I was. She got to her knees and put her hand on my shoulder. 'Let me help.'

I knocked away her hand. She quietly watched me as I hiked up the leg of my jeans, pushed my liner-covered stump into the socket, strapped it tight, and jerked my jeans to the ankle joint. She tried again to help, putting a hand on my back and the other on my elbow, but again I brushed her off and raised myself ungracefully to my feet. She stood too. It was clearly a false statement, but I said, 'I'm not handicapped.'

She had a right to be angry, and I wanted her that way, but when she spoke, she just sounded sad. 'I didn't mean—'

'Don't ever call me that again.'

'Okay.'

'I told you I don't tolerate pity and I don't need excuses made for me.'

'Okay, Jimmy. Why did you do that?'

'Because I'm a selfish prick who can't bear for you to be happy, so if you have any sense, you won't put up with it. You'll cut me off like . . .' I laughed. 'Like a diseased limb.'

She lifted her hand to my face and wiped my spit and blood from my chin with her thumb. 'You know you can't just attack someone.'

'But I did and I'd probably do it again. You should give up on me.'

'Not tonight.' She hugged me. Part of me wanted to push her off, but I returned it, one-armed because I didn't want to contaminate her by touching her with my pincer. I didn't understand her reaction. I still don't.

She pulled away. 'We have some talking to do. Wait here for me. I'll only be a minute.'

I nodded. She descended the stairwell to the celebration below.

My shirt was thin, and feeling the chill, I leaned against the wall and rubbed my arms. My tongue was still bleeding so I hacked up more saliva and spat on the pavement. A pair of fake-tanned girls in high heels gave me disgusted looks as they walked by.

I only brought my shaking under control when Nicole re-emerged. Her presence didn't calm me, but I'd already betrayed too many weaknesses, so I was bracing myself. She was wearing her jacket and she gave me my coat. I put it on, punching my arms through the sleeves. 'You can't leave your party because of me.'

'It's my birthday. I can do whatever I want. I've already said my goodbyes.'

'What was your excuse?'

'I said you were out-of-your-mind drunk and I had to make sure you got home in one piece. It was an easy lie.'

'That I'm out of my mind?'

'You might well be that. I lied about you going home. We're going to mine. The taxi's on you.'

I hailed one. We sat in the back and didn't speak to each other during the journey. I stared out the window and thought I could feel her watching me, but I don't know if she really was. When we were almost there, she put her head on my shoulder. I didn't look at her.

In her flat, she led me into her room and I shut the door after us. She drew the curtains over the windows. I could hear her breathing. From behind, I put my arms around her, and kissed her cheek and neck as she leaned back against me. I dug my pincer into her hip, grasping her breast with my whole hand. She turned around and, her hand on my neck, she pulled my mouth to hers.

I clumsily undressed her, sputtering, 'Tell me to stop and I will.'

She laughed and slid my belt from its buckle.

For the life of me, I've no words to describe the look in her eyes.

The next morning, I woke with the taste of blood in my mouth and a buzzing behind my eyes. My prosthetic was off. I was pinned to a strange bed, not by my hangover but by Nicole. She was naked, her back to me. My left arm was under her side. I could feel her stomach against my palm, my thumb and index finger enclosed in her hand.

I didn't mean to wake her, but I was cold and her body was warm. When I put my right arm around her, she turned and looked blankly at me. I whispered, 'It'll come to you.'

She closed her eyes and touched her forehead to mine. 'Whatever you do, don't kiss me. My mouth is the flavour of five types of alcohol, every one of them sour and poisonous.'

I kissed her. 'You don't need to keep coming on to me.'

She laughed, groped for my stump leg, and wedged it between her knees. 'There's something I want you to do for me.'

'What?'

'Fuck me like you really mean it.'

I waited until she opened her eyes, then I gave her my honest best.

As we lingered in her bed, I became fearful.

I said, 'I'd prefer for last night not to have happened rather than for this to be a one-night stand.'

'We're already well into the next day.'

'You know, I think, what I'm saying.'

'Don't worry. We're at the beginning of something, not the end.'

'You understand that there can't be any more Alistair? You're with me or I can't—'

She covered my mouth with her hand. 'I'm with you. You're with me. There's no one else.'

I wanted to say 'I love you' right then, but I decided it would be too soon. It's funny how I still thought being prudent was possible.

While I love my twin, I resent him too, a bit, because he got to touch her and I never could. He touched her body and her heart, and it sent shockwaves through him, but he didn't comprehend the full extent of his good fortune. I'd give anything – all I have is my consciousness, but I'd give that – for her to have seen me, for just a short while, when I looked at her. That's if there was something of me to see.

I know my envy is futile and even creepy. Sometimes I succeed in rising above it, and in those moments I'm truly happy for them that they got to share what they did. Sometimes I fail miserably.

Chapter Twenty-One

Acrotomophiliac Love

8/1/2012
I don't remember it being this freezing, but if the weather had been the most memorable thing about that night, I wouldn't be here now. Here is Whiterock Beach, site of a former glory, and later a place where mistakes were made.

I came prepared. I'm wearing a long coat, buttoned to the neck, a woolly hat, and gloves, one not quite filled out. I'm sitting on a rug with my back to the craggy rock face and a notepad on my lap. In my rucksack I've brought a torch in case I'm still here when it gets dark and two bottles of red wine, the second in case of emergency. I should have brought white wine instead, which would be nicely chilled. The red is cold to my tongue. No one is around to observe my eccentric behaviour. Whiterock is forsaken this time of year, except for the occasional masochistic fishing enthusiast, perhaps the odd psychotic skinny-dipper. And me.

Anyway, the glory.

December 1999 to January 2000
Nicole and I had been a couple for a month, but we hadn't seen as much of each other as I'd have liked, because of

her exams, the essays I had due, and then my trip home for ten days around Christmas. Before I left, we spent a few nights at my place and affirmed our lust. I didn't feel like I was on steady ground, though. She was my first girlfriend and I had no idea how a relationship was supposed to work. I suspected that it was only a matter of time before she realised I wasn't whoever she thought I was.

My time in Rathbaile didn't soothe my misgivings. Being around Tighe was a reminder that there were better men than me and that while I was away Nicole had every opportunity to meet them. Around Elizabeth I was reminded of my deficient understanding of women. And Dad's drifts into glass-eyed reverie reminded me that women can cut men to the core.

I hated talking to Nicole on the phone. I couldn't communicate anything of value without looking her in the eyes, as disarming as hers were, and without being able to touch her. She might as well have been a voice in my head.

I got back to Dublin on the evening of New Year's Eve. She met me at Busáras, looking as effortlessly gorgeous as usual. My heart was pounding – my excitement at seeing her was exceeded only by my nervousness – and she was excited too, not about spending the night alone with me, but about spending it with scores of people. She'd been invited to some rich guy's party in Dalkey and wanted us to go together. I feigned enthusiasm.

We dropped off my bag at my place, staying for less than five minutes. I was conscious of how we actively didn't have sex. She said we shouldn't be any later than we already were when time was so central to the purpose of the party. I was worried that she'd decided to break up with me and was waiting for the right moment to do it, such as after a few remorse-deadening drinks.

If I'd been there without her, I might have enjoyed the party. It was in a mansion with a deck overlooking the turbulent Irish Sea. There was an abundance of communal alcohol and, not unrelated, everyone other than myself was having great craic. I mingled to demonstrate to Nicole how socially independent I was. I didn't warn off any of the guys she talked to. That shouldn't have been such an accomplishment, but whenever she laughed at another guy's joke, it killed me.

When the countdown began, I lured her into a corner and mauled her for all I was worth. She mauled me too. We didn't stop for the cheers as the twentieth century expired.

Soon after, despite our mutual ardour, I had the idea that maybe she'd seen Alistair when I was away. I managed, just about, to restrain myself from demanding to know.

At two a.m., with the party still going strong, she came up to me and, sounding anxious, said, 'We have to get out of here.'

I didn't question her until we were on the road. Then I said, 'What happened? Is there something I need to—'

'You didn't look like you were having fun, so I thought we should split.'

'I was having a ball.'

She laughed. 'Yeah? I guess it was just me then. Too many people were keeping us apart. And there's a place I want to show you.'

'I didn't know you knew this area.'

'There are lots of things you don't know about what I know. You trust me, right?'

She led me along winding roads. There were no lamp posts and we were dressed in dark colours. Whenever a car was about to speed by, we had to step into the ditch.

Whiterock came into view below us, isolated at the bottom of a cliff. We passed through a gap in the low wall flanking Vico Road and strolled down a muddy path. We descended about one hundred and fifty stone steps, pausing on the final one so she could remove her shoes; then her tights too, slowly and acting like she was unaware of my eyes never leaving her legs as she did so. With a roguish smile, she held her tights out to me, draped over both her palms, as if she was presenting me with a rare and precious gift. I sighed and took them from her. Stowing them in my coat pocket, I said, 'You might as well have let them get ruined. I'm only going to ladder them for you later anyway.'

She just turned and hopped across the threshold, her feet sinking into the sand. I followed, my shoes on.

Nicole ran to meet the tide. She shrieked as her bared legs were submerged to her knees and froth sprayed all over her dress, even though she was lifting it up to the tops of her thighs. The tide was sucked back out to sea and she retreated to where I was standing, at a comfortable distance from the wet sand. 'I'm soaking!'

I rubbed my hands over her dress, front and back, groping her dry. 'What did you expect?'

She wrapped her arms around me, pressed her face against my chest, and closed her eyes. 'Shush. All I want from you is warmth.'

I brushed her hair from her forehead with my pincer. I looked out to where the sea and the sky appeared to make contact. She synchronised her breathing to mine and I let it slip out: 'You know I'm in love with you.'

She was silent for long enough that I wondered if she had heard. Then, without raising her face, she said, 'No, I don't. So you are?'

There may have been a trace of anger in my voice when I answered, 'I am.'

She wasn't smiling when she met my eyes and put her hand to my cheek.

The sun didn't emerge blazing into the sky. There were no trumpets. But yes, my soul took flight when she said it too.

It was hard to believe she felt what I felt, even if she thought she did. For her, love might have been any point on the infatuation spectrum and not the all-or-nothing emotion it was for me. I heard her claim to love ice cream, the *MacGyver* theme tune, and the idea of extraterrestrial life. It could have been a convenient word she used to denote a minuscule degree of preference, or there was the possibility that she knew exactly what it meant and was lying – not to be cruel, I didn't think that, but to be kind, because it would be awkward not to say it and she pitied me. I waited before speaking the three key words again.

I told myself it was the relationship I distrusted, as if that was a separate entity from us, which we had some participation in and little conscious control of. But really I didn't trust her, mostly because I couldn't read her. While I realised I was a strange guy, in my own way I added up. From what I knew of her, she didn't.

She told me stories about her life in Australia, and the more personal they were, the more removed from her I felt.

Not because I couldn't handle sad stories. I could. I wanted her to confide everything; nothing would've been too ugly or shocking. I wouldn't have judged her. What threw me was that the more difficult her stories should have been to tell, the calmer she became.

She told me with a shrug that neither of her parents loved her. Her mother, Natasha, was a failure at everything. She'd gotten married for the first time when she was nineteen and was divorced before turning twenty-two. After that, she went to law school, but flunked out. Her second marriage was to Nicole's father, Darrell, a self-made businessman with a chip on his shoulder. They married for reasons of race. He was black and she was white, and she wanted to stick it to her bigoted parents. It helped that he was rich. If he hadn't been, it would have been difficult to live without her parents' bailouts.

Darrell was a member of the 'stolen generation' of Aborigines. When he was seven, he was taken from his grandparents' care and placed in an institution because the Australian government believed that Aboriginal children would receive a better education if they were robbed of their culture and assimilated into the mainstream. At thirteen, he was adopted by a well-to-do white couple and raised with white siblings. As an adult, he directed his resentment towards his own skin. He wasn't interested in rediscovering his heritage and only had white girlfriends. Natasha was blonde and paler than pale.

They didn't live up to one another's expectations. He didn't stay rich enough. She didn't stay beautiful. To her mind, it was when she had her daughter that her looks started to go. Nicole grew up used to her mother's bitterness, and to her father's disappointment in her. She laughed. 'Did he think I was going to come out white?' She insisted that being unwanted didn't bother her.

These are all things she told me.

She didn't have any photos in her room of her parents or of any friends from back home. When I asked if she missed her old life, she said she didn't give it much thought. When I frowned, she added, 'You know who I am here and now. Understanding who I used to be isn't important. If you met my mother and father, you would see that we're nothing alike. It's possible for someone's parents to have had a minimal influence on who they are.'

'Is it?'

'Yes. Maybe I'm funny that way. And no one who knew me in Australia understood me there, so they definitely wouldn't understand me here. If you don't get hung up on the facts, if you trust what you feel when it's just us, you'll understand me better than anyone, in the ways that matter.'

Perhaps out of a compulsion to be consistently erratic, she didn't extend her philosophy of 'experiences and family relationships don't make the person' beyond herself. Without having set foot in Rathbaile, and knowing I only returned when obliged, she declared that I had yet to really leave there. She was also convinced that I hadn't dealt with my mother's death and it had left me with major issues in how I perceived women. I didn't agree with her verdict, but if I'd shown how much it frustrated me, she would have taken that as evidence that she was right. And, of course, she thought my physical losses were deeply permeated in my sense of self. No points for being astute there. Anyone could've put that together.

Elizabeth insisted that I bring Nicole to meet her – offering us the incentive of free food – and Nicole was keen for that too. I had mixed feelings about it. I was proud that Nicole was with me of all people and I wanted Elizabeth to see that I was sorting myself out. But I was also wary of them getting on too well and forming an alliance, where they would unite in psychologising me and telling me how I could be living my life better. Yes, I was thinking too hard about this..

Nicole and I arrived at Santé, the small restaurant Elizabeth was managing, after it had closed for the night. She'd drawn the blinds so passers-by wouldn't see us dining and think the place was still open for just anybody.

I fumbled the introduction. 'Elizabeth, this is Nicole, my close, ah, special friend.'

Nicole elbowed me. 'His *girlfriend*, and we won't be close for long if he continues to introduce me as his special-needs pal.'

Elizabeth gave me a facetiously critical look. 'I'm his sister, in case he hasn't clarified that either.'

Elizabeth directed us to the only table not mounted by inverted chairs. Blue glass plates and blue wine goblets had been laid out. She disappeared into the kitchen, then emerged with a knife-impaled blackberry pie on a dish, and a bottle of wine. She set them down, sliced and served the pie, and opened the bottle with a corkscrew she produced from the pouch in the apron slung around her waist. She poured us each a glass and sat.

She asked Nicole to elaborate on how we'd gotten together, seeing as how I was hopeless at telling her anything. According to Nicole, she'd done all the chasing: 'I was crazy about him for ages, but he didn't give any signs of wanting to be more than friends. I'd almost given up.'

I didn't try to set the record straight.

Nicole asked Elizabeth about what I'd been like as a kid. Elizabeth said, 'He was more than a little oblivious. Spent lots of time in his own imagination. But he was adorable too.'

I said, 'Fuck off.'

'Be quiet, Jimmy. The women are talking. So, yeah, he had a huge head of hair on him and his head itself was disproportionally large. His body eventually caught up and his hair is neater now. Other than that, I don't know if he's changed much.'

I topped up the glasses. 'I don't recognise who you're describing.'

Nicole said, 'Sounds believable to me.'

Elizabeth raised her glass and Nicole met it with hers. Elizabeth said, 'Sometimes the people watching us see us more clearly than we see ourselves.'

Suspecting I'd be outnumbered, I didn't argue. We polished off the pie and opened another bottle of wine. Nicole and Elizabeth each tried to make me look good. Nicole laughed at all my jokes, no matter how witless. Elizabeth didn't criticise me – she probably wouldn't have acknowledged, even privately, how often she used to. Regardless, slagging me off in front of Nicole wasn't the same thing. She gave the impression that we had always gotten along seamlessly.

A few days later, I returned to Santé. Elizabeth took a break and we talked over coffee. Rather than properly framing my question, I only had to say, 'So?'

She said, 'Nicole's lovely, really lovely. I'd guess that I'm not imparting anything you haven't figured out for yourself.'

'I'm aware of my luck. Am I being paranoid? I feel like there's a "but" coming.'

She bit her lower lip, then released it. That confirmed I was right. 'It's just you should be careful. If you can.'

'What do you mean?'

'You're nineteen.'

'So what? And I'll be twenty in three months.'

'Nevertheless. Don't let her break your heart.'

'Why would she? And what makes you think I'd let her?'

Her expression said it all: if you don't know, I'm not going to tell you.

I was nonchalant with Elizabeth, but I added her implied prediction of doom to my own tally of evidence against Nicole and me surviving much longer.

May to September 2000

After Nicole and I sat our exams, I wondered if concluding the college year might encourage her to end other things that had run their course. We'd been going out for over six months, and while she appeared to be enjoying my company, maybe she believed I had nothing else to offer. I couldn't broach my concerns without planting my fear in her mind and allowing it to grow.

She decided to leave the country for seven weeks to Interrail around Europe with a couple of friends – both of whom I deemed to be bad influences, a judgement that made me feel prematurely old. The timing was perfect, she felt, because her lease was up and she didn't have a new place yet. She mentioned how the other girls weren't bringing their boyfriends so I would understand that she couldn't invite me. I told her the trip was a great idea and suggested she use my flat for storage while she was away. She couldn't break up with me if I had all her stuff, could she?

At the airport, I saw her off with a sustained embrace. She kissed me and whispered a farewell, with tears in her eyes. Then Marilyn and Theresa hooked her arms and took her from me. Their conspiratorial laughter was swallowed up among a crowd of people, all of them rushing around with adventures to commence. It's embarrassing how long I waited there on the off-chance that Nicole might come running back.

I was a drag to live with during that stretch. I wasn't, in my opinion, moping around, but I was certainly on the quiet side. Seb was already annoyed that I'd backed out of going to Australia. Now it was just him, Brian, and Finbar, and he was likely to get stuck in the middle whenever they bickered. Seb being Seb, he was more both-ered that, by not being willing to journey into the unknown, I was letting *myself* down. He didn't think I should be staying behind for a relationship he viewed as temporary, something he never admitted outright.

My reticence didn't extend to when Seb and I went to the pub. I was happy to talk then. Alcohol didn't turn me into a conversationalist. A conversationalist can switch from topic to topic. Everything I had to say converged on Nicole. I didn't even have to say her name. If I was talking about women generally, I was really talking about her specifically. If we were pondering some aspect of happiness, or unhappiness, or something in between, whatever I said was within the context of her effect on me. When I was pretending to listen to Seb, I was holding imaginary conversations with her in my cramped mind. In these, I was incredibly articulate and held nothing back. And she understood everything.

A week before she was due to return, I decided to ask her to move in with me. With Seb moving out, I had to either get a new flatmate or a new flat by the beginning of September, and she needed a flat too. I didn't expect her to say yes, but she couldn't turn me down without providing a clue about whether she thought we had a future together, however limited. Logic dictated that I should wait to ask her in person, in a mature and sober fashion.

Seb and I discussed it in the pub and he agreed that the proposition made sense, maybe in the hope that I'd shut up about it. After an indeterminate number of pints, I lurched to the jacks. I was at the urinal, dick in hand, when my phone rang. I finished my immediate task and answered. Nicole was calling from Dubrovnik, where she was standing on a promenade and looking out at the Adriatic Sea. 'I wanted to share with you how stunning it is.' Judging by her fluctuating volume control, she sounded not a little drunk herself.

Pressing my hand to my free ear to block out the din of the pub, I shouted, 'I have to ask you something! But don't make up your mind now. Think it over until you see me. Can you promise that?'

I heard her suppress a hiccup. 'Ask me anything.'

'I want you to move in with me! It might be sudden, but I think it could work, and if it doesn't, you could move out whenever—'

'Okay!'

'You'll think about it?'

'No.'

'Oh. I understand. It's—'

'I won't think about it because the answer is yes. I want to move in.'

She was even drunker than I realised. I hung up before she could change her mind.

The day she was due back, I bought her a bouquet of flowers, then at the last minute chose not to bring them to the airport. Her friends would be there and I didn't want to look like a sap. But more than that, if Nicole was fostering second thoughts, I wanted to know, and she might have put it off if I was carrying flowers.

I waited in the arrivals hall with my fists in my pockets and my toes writhing within my shoe.

As soon as I saw her, she ran into my arms and kissed me. True to form, I didn't take much reassurance from that. She could have been putting it on for Marilyn and Theresa. When I opened my eyes, I caught their impatient looks. We all took the same bus into the city centre. Before they got off, Nicole hugged them both. After they were gone, she said, 'I'm so sick of all their bitching!'

At our stop, I strapped the larger of her bags to my back and, hand-in-pincer, we walked to my place. I listened to her tell me about her adventures and barely spoke a word.

Seb was in, and he and Nicole kissed one another's cheeks. She playfully shoved him away, but the spark of jealousy I felt was stamped out, or significantly diminished, when she said, 'When are you moving out, you fucker? Jimmy promised me your room!'

I didn't give him time to answer. I grabbed her wrist

and led her down the hall and into my room. She had told me before that, not being very girlie, flowers didn't do much for her, but when she saw the red roses on my bed, she exclaimed, 'Jimmy! Since when did you become a character out of a Richard Curtis movie?'

'They're for Seb. There's something I've been meaning to tell you.'

'Don't even joke about it.' She pushed me on to the bed and I pulled her down on top of me.

We crushed the roses.

Seb moved out three weeks later. I waited until Nicole signed the lease, watching her for any hesitation, and then, nine months into our relationship, I told her, for the second time, that I was in love with her.

When she asked if I had jungle fever, I didn't deny it. We were lying in bed at some late hour, her legs sticking to mine. 'Do you know how cool having a black girlfriend makes me look? And even the people who don't think I'm cool can't deny I'm resourceful.'

When I asked her if she was an acrotomophiliac, she smiled and nodded. She said she was only with me because of my many scarlet scars. She praised how my 'grotesque' leg stump displaced my weight just enough that I was able to pound her sweetest spot from the most perfectly intimate of angles. As for my hands, she pointed out how she'd always taken more pleasure from my 'bad' hand than my good one. She whispered, 'Everyone needs a fetish, babe. You're mine. I can ignore the failings of your substandard personality so long as you have stumps.'

'I'm thinking of having another accident. My nose has

always gotten in the way of my face. And who needs two arms anyway? Or all these teeth.'

'You're getting me wet.'

'Show me.'

I miss the taste of her beautiful cunt, what a tender and vivacious fuck she was. There's nothing remotely ugly about these thoughts.

Chapter Twenty-Two

With Open Arms

19/1/2012

Today is the ten-year anniversary of when I lost Nicole for good, but the day was softened by some unexpected news.

I'm working a stupefying office job, for a car magazine this time. At the beginning of the week I was handed a box of slips featuring names of people who have entered a competition for a year's supply of premium unleaded petrol. I've input the info for thousands of potential winners into a spreadsheet for the raffle. You'd think if someone was going to bother entering, they'd make sure their writing was legible, but people can be self-defeating. I was giving every slip one glance, one chance, before entering an approximation of their details. Someone will win, but a few wrong numbers may be dialled first. Tomorrow's my last day.

At lunchtime, I picked up a newspaper and dropped into a pub for a sandwich and a beer. I'd stuffed half the sandwich into my mouth when my eyes alighted on the headline: 'Son of Ballyfermot Reaper slain in brutal gangland murder'. I washed my mouthful down with an inch of pint, then read the article. Vinnie Cosgrove was discovered in the boot of a car. His hands and feet were bound with cable ties and he'd been shot, once in the head and once in the heart. I wasn't smiling about it, but I didn't doubt that the world was a rosier place without him.

In the afternoon, I gave each slip a second glance. Everyone deserves a chance to be a winner.

Now I'm in my flat and wired on coffee. I'm going to write about another death, one worth being upset about.

Late June 2001

The third member of my immediate family to go – or fourth if I count my twin, and maybe I should – was my dog.

Nicole and I had been living together for about ten months, and we were standing in the kitchen having an argument, a recurring one. She had a habit of disappearing for hours on end, often late at night. She didn't like my tone when I questioned her whereabouts. She tended to be evasive, I tended to press, and we would arrive at her stock explanation: that she'd gone for a walk, due to her perpetual need to clear her head. Then, in keeping with our tango routine, she would demand to know if I thought she was lying. As incensed as I might be, I knew better than to be honest about that. This particular fight was on the morning after she'd arrived home hours after finishing a shift at a pub where she was bartending. She'd turned her mobile off, and I'd stayed awake worrying and leaving her voicemail messages. When she brought up the trust issue, I countered with the safety issue. Dublin is a dangerous city to be walking around alone at night, but she didn't concede anything. I believe she put it, 'And yet I'm remarkably unscathed.' I could hear the words forming in my head – 'I wish something bad *had* happened to you, at least then you'd fucking learn' – when my mobile rang, saving me from spewing a taunt that I would have regretted forever.

I saw it was Dad so I turned my back on Nicole and went to my room, leaving her to fume. I answered and he said, 'Are you sitting down?'

He'd found Colossus curled up in the laundry room, his chin on his paws. 'I reckon his heart gave out as he was dreaming about chasing fat cats with short legs.'

I sat on my bed. 'You okay, Dad? You don't sound surprised.'

'No? Well I am, but I may have seen it coming too. He'd been slowing down and sleeping much longer than usual. It was his time, as they say.'

'Where is he now?'

'What do you mean?'

I stifled an urge to be flippant. I wasn't enquiring about his soul. 'His body?'

'He's where I found him. I'll bury him this afternoon. I need to tell Elizabeth too. She was fond of the old fella. Tighe's never been a dog man, so he shouldn't be very upset.'

I saw Nicole watching me from the hallway. She came and sat beside me, putting her hand on my back. I told Dad that I'd call Elizabeth and I'd be down in Rathbaile later that day. I asked him not to bury Colossus until I arrived. He said he'd wait.

I hung up and said to Nicole, 'My dog's dead.'

'I gathered. I'm sorry.'

She did what she could to help me feel better, in her

compassionate way, and I remained angry with her, cloaking it with exaggerated heartache.

I called Elizabeth. She quickly took charge of the situation, even though Colossus was *my* dog, but I didn't challenge her on it when she volunteered to drive and said she'd come pick me up straight away. 'I don't want us to leave Dad by himself any longer than we have to. I've a horrible image of him sitting in the laundry room with Colossus's head on his lap.'

When I began packing a bag, Nicole said, 'I'm coming with you,' and went to her room to pack before I could dissuade her. Our earlier argument, combined with my loss, must have left me unusually passive, because I would've preferred to take a bus and go alone. I called Dad back to tell him to expect a guest.

For the journey, in Elizabeth's messy old car, Nicole sat in the passenger seat and, after clearing it of rubbish, I stretched out in the back. I wanted to sleep but couldn't, so I faked it and listened to their conversation instead. Elizabeth voiced her concerns about Dad. After Mam died, he had retired. Having Colossus to feed and walk twice a day gave him a routine. She wondered if she should encourage him to get a new dog, but Nicole suggested holding off. 'You never know, he might make that choice on his own.' Elizabeth agreed, although beneath the goodwill she may have felt a thorn of resentment at having an outsider to the family offer advice.

It was after seven when we pulled into the driveway. We went inside, and from the hallway I shouted out for Dad. There wasn't any response. Elizabeth went to look in his room and Nicole followed me through the living room into the kitchen, with no sign of him. I asked her to stay there while I checked the laundry room.

I thought Elizabeth was going to be proved prophetic and I would discover him cradling Colossus, but all I found was Colossus's red blanket, crumpled next to the washing machine. Nicole called my name, so I hurried back into the kitchen.

She was leaning over the sink and staring out the window. 'Got him.'

Dad was at the far end of the garden, his back to us. He was shirtless and had a shovel in his hands. Colossus was slumped on the grass. I asked Nicole to let Elizabeth know where Dad was and said I'd appreciate it if they waited inside.

I went into the dining room, slid open the patio door, stepped out, and shut it behind me. His shirt was folded over a patio chair, so I grabbed it on my way. I called out to him. For a moment, he looked at me like I was a stranger. By the time I reached him, though, standing next to a shallow hole, he was smiling. 'Jim, you're early.'

He rammed the shovel into the ground, but it was only upright for a few seconds before it toppled with a thump and a cloud of dirt was coughed into the air. I said, 'I think we're right on time.'

'I lost track.'

I handed him his shirt and he put it on. As he buttoned it, I got to my knees and stroked Colossus's ear with my pincer, lightly, as if I might disturb him. I placed my good hand on his motionless chest, something I used to do when he was asleep to feel the rhythmic swelling out and sucking in of his ribcage. Dad, watching me, said, 'I know I was supposed to wait, but

I thought seeing him like this might make it harder to remember him full of life.'

He was probably being mindful of how that had been my rationale for not viewing Simon's body when he died, but this time I felt differently. I stood. 'Seeing him makes it more real. Do you have another shovel?'

'I'll root one out of the garage. First I want to see my daughter, and I take it that you have someone new for me to meet. Someone special?'

'They're inside. Should we just leave him here?'

He patted my elbow. 'Yeah. C'mon.' As we walked, he asked, 'Will I like her?'

'Everyone does.'

On the other side of the glass patio door, Elizabeth and Nicole were sitting at the dining-room table. Elizabeth was making a strangling gesture with her hand and speaking vehemently about something. With a deliberate movement of her eyes, Nicole alerted her to our presence. Elizabeth relaxed her hand in mid-air. They stood as we entered.

Elizabeth hugged Dad. 'Are you okay?'

'Fine, dear, I'm fine.'

She looked him up and down, the fault lines on her brow stressing her scepticism.

Nicole appeared bashful, which was strange for her, especially so considering how Dad is the world's least intimidating man. I made the introduction, my palms out priest-like, and, grinning at one another, they shook hands. Nicole said, 'I'm so sorry about your dog.'

Dad repeated that trite remark about it being his time, as if the most serene thing about life is that it ends.

Elizabeth made us all tea or coffee, waving me down

279

when I offered to do it, and brought us a plate of chocolate biscuits too. We sat around the table and Dad lobbed Nicole some questions about the Australian climate and landscape, her impressions of Ireland, and what she was planning on doing with the rest of her life once she had finished her studies. The last question she sidestepped: 'After I've climbed the mountain of my final year, I'll inspect the view then.'

It was good to see Dad engaged by someone. I hadn't been very forthcoming about her, so there was plenty for him to be curious about. Unless Elizabeth had told him, he hadn't even been aware she was black. Taking that in his stride, he asked jovially, 'Would both your parents be coloured then, Nicole?' Elizabeth nearly spat out the biscuit she was eating. Dad rephrased: 'I mean, would they be of colour or black like proper Aborigines?'

I avoided Nicole's eye because I didn't want to make her laugh. She sipped her tea. 'My father is. My mother's white.'

'Ah. You look somewhere in between. With your hue, that is.'

'My mother's as white as they come, my father as black.' She motioned to her face. 'Everything's somewhere in between. My father's eyes are brown. My mother's eyes are green. Mine are more of a hazel shade. And so on. I don't think I've any of their individual features.'

'I imagine they're able to spot quite a few similarities. Parents like to look for themselves in their children, the best of themselves anyway.'

When I suggested to Dad that we should go bury Colossus while we still had the light, Elizabeth said, 'I'll help.'

I said, 'We only have two shovels. I mean, you must be tired after driving us here.'

'I'm not.'

'Look, Abuelo got him for me, so he's my responsibility, and Dad's been the one taking care of him the last couple of years. I know you loved him too, but I think it should be just me and Dad who do it.'

Perhaps only out of deference to Nicole being there, Elizabeth curtly said, 'Fine.'

Dad wasn't shirking, but I did most of the digging, mainly to demonstrate that my missing fingers didn't hinder me. Once the hole was deep enough, Dad lifted Colossus up by his hind legs and I took his forelegs. We lowered him into his grave and covered him.

When we were done, Dad wiped his hand on his forehead, speckling his sweat with dirt. 'Where were you planning on putting Nicole tonight?'

'Tighe won't mind if I give her his bed.'

He shook his head. 'I don't have a problem with her sleeping in your room.'

'It's your house. If it would be uncomfortable for you . . .'

'Life's too short for me to have any hang-ups about something that makes you happy. You're an adult now.'

I didn't feel like one, but I thanked him as if he'd acknowledged something obvious.

The next day, Dad suggested that Nicole should meet Abuelo and Granny – they'd be offended otherwise – and so he booked a table for dinner in Hogan's Hotel.

Getting ready in my room, I put on the same suit I'd worn to Mam's funeral, but with a brighter tie. Nicole inspected its straightness. 'Look at you.'

'No one will be looking at me. It's *you* everyone's interested in. My grandparents will be assessing whether or not you're a hussy giving me the runaround.'

Her smile vanished and I felt bad. She asked, 'What conclusion do you think they'll come to?'

I rested my good hand on her hip and grazed her face with my pincer. 'I don't care.' She didn't look reassured. 'You've already won over Elizabeth and Dad. If my grandparents don't fall in line, I'll disown them.'

The restaurant was quiet, with less than half of the tables occupied. Ours was in the middle of the room, with Dad and Abuelo anchoring either end, and Nicole and I sitting across from Elizabeth and Granny. After we were brought a round of drinks, Abuelo stood and raised his glass. I thought he was about to propose a toast to Mam, which on occasion he tended to do, but instead he made it to 'the most loyal and honourable of companions': Colossus. We all raised our glasses high in response, even Granny, who had never warmed to my 'beast of a dog' – he was docile, but after what had happened to me, she distrusted all dogs, as if they bore some species-level guilt. If Nicole thought the toast was a bit much, she hid it behind an imperviously solemn expression. When Abuelo sat back down, he recounted to her how, after my injury, I'd marched right out and insisted on becoming master to the biggest dog of them all, disregarding how there had been an interval of seven years, or that the idea to get Colossus was hardly mine. He said, 'My grandson is a fighter. He's never been one to let the odd misfortune get in the way of being his best self.'

Nicole gave me a look of affection – for all to see – and said, 'That's one of the attributes that drew me to him.'

The flattery was nice, but Abuelo may have been talking me up in part because I'd lucked into being in a relationship with someone who most people – not least myself – would've considered to be the far greater catch and it was important for me to appear to be more than what I was if I hoped to hold on to her. I still appreciated his efforts and I was glad that he took to her. I think he could see the respect between us – we did hang on each other's words – and also the respect that she paid to him, and Dad and Elizabeth and Granny too. She made steady eye contact when speaking with them, something Abuelo valued.

Granny was a harder sell. Despite who she'd married, she was suspicious of foreigners, but the greater knock against Nicole was her gender. I'd never known Granny to think highly of another woman. She loved Elizabeth, but had no space for her on the pedestal where she placed Tighe and me, and while she might have loved Mam too, in some way, her disdain for her had shown no signs of abating in the two and a half years since her death. Not only was Granny sceptical of Nicole being good enough for me, she was wary of her having designs on stealing me away from the family. This was made evident when we all had our main courses before us and, out of the blue, Granny put down her knife and fork and said to Nicole, 'When are you thinking of moving back to Australia?'

Nicole and I hadn't discussed her plans at all, or our future generally – presuming we had one – but if she was thrown by the question, she didn't act like it. She said, 'To be honest, I'm not sure if I'll ever move back. I can't predict everything that might happen, but right now, I don't know of a single reason for why I'd want to leave Dublin.'

Granny nodded, apparently satisfied, and started to cut up her slice of lamb. 'That's good. Jimmy would burn down there.'

Putting my hand on Nicole's, I said, 'You haven't ascended from some kind of hell, have you?'

Before she could deny anything, Dad laughed and said, 'I think what my mother means is that Jimmy hasn't inherited my father's complexion, and in the warmer climate he'd be in danger of a bad sunburn if he didn't apply the appropriate sunscreen. Am I right, Mam?'

Granny said, 'I just don't think it'd be the right weather for him, and they have snakes and sharks there, but that doesn't matter if no one's going anywhere. And there's only one hell, Jimmy, and no one ascends from it.' I provided a chastened look, and she turned her attention to Elizabeth. 'When are we going to meet your boyfriend, dear?'

Elizabeth drank a healthy sip of wine and said, 'It would be difficult for me to introduce you to someone who doesn't exist.' Receiving a baffled look in response, she added, 'I'm single, Granny. Happily so.'

'I understand. It's all very well for you to be as free as can be while you're young – it's even admirable – but a woman's options become limited over time. I'm only saying you wouldn't want to leave it too late, that's all. It's just a little something for you to think about.'

Elizabeth looked like she was struggling to hold her tongue. Failing, she said, 'I'll see how I go. Spinsterhood is becoming quite the fashion these days and remaining childless is good for the environment. I wouldn't want to jump the gun by ruling out those options too early either.'

With an absence of amusement in her voice, Granny said, 'That's very amusing, Elizabeth.'

Elizabeth passed me a glance that let me know she was blaming me for this subject being brought up, and she had some grounds for it: by bringing Nicole to meet Dad, Abuelo, and Granny, I was implicitly declaring to them that my relationship was a serious one, and if her younger brother could manage it, that put more pressure on Elizabeth to produce a partner of her own. She was still only twenty-seven, but Granny had been a teenage bride, so to her mind, her granddaughter was getting on in years.

Once dessert was eaten, Abuelo took out his wallet and laid some notes on the table. He said that he and Granny should be heading home because he was tired, but that no one else should rush themselves. The real reason for his urgency was that he'd noticed Granny's hands shaking – we all had – and she didn't like to take her Parkinson's medication in public. Everybody else was about ready to go anyway. There was some obligatory fussing over the bill, and I was proud of Dad when, after arguing heroically, he secured the right to pay for everything and Abuelo took back his money.

Outside Hogan's, Nicole and I said goodnight to the others, then we went to meet Finbar and Vicky for a drink. Finbar was supposed to still be in Australia with Seb and Brian, but he'd returned early, although he hadn't divulged an explanation when he'd emailed me.

In Sterne's, we found him and Vicky at a table in the back. He was finishing off a Guinness and she was sipping a 7 Up. She'd been a teetotaller ever since our debs. By contrast, he'd become a harder drinker while developing a reputation for having a roving eye whenever he was under the influence – a regular at confession, he was a firm believer in the clean slate it promised – so I was perpetually surprised that they were still a couple.

I introduced them to Nicole, and Finbar wasted no time before slagging me off for wearing a suit to a dingy alternative-rock pub. I took off my tie. He insisted on buying us both pints. After returning from the bar, he set them in front of us and told me, 'You'll want that.'

'I don't need convincing, but any particular reason? And why did you abandon Seb and Brian? I'm presuming they're still over in Nicole's hellishly warm homeland.'

She half-heartedly elbowed me in the ribs. Finbar drew a breath. 'They are. Seb is the same as ever, but Brian isn't the man you remember. Brian is . . .' He drank some Guinness. 'He's gay now.'

'You're kidding. Brian's the straightest guy I know. If he's gay, then it's just as likely that we all are.' Finbar, alarmed, put his hand on Vicky's knee. I turned to Nicole. 'I'm not, am I?'

She affirmed, 'Jimmy's not, Finbar. We've checked.'

Finbar said, 'I'm not speculating. A month ago, he sat down with me and Seb and told us, glaring at us like he was ready to say "fuck you" if we weren't okay with it. Seb thanked him for being open with us, said it changed nothing, and hugged him.'

'What did you do?'

'Firm handshake. Then we all went to the pub and got wasted, which did help with the awkwardness between me and Brian. Seb was annoyingly unfazed by it all. He said it's what he has long suspected, and he's well used to that kind of thing in his arty circles. He even made fun of me for being a bit weirded out.'

I glanced apologetically at Nicole and asked Finbar,

'So you came all the way back because you were "weirded out"? Do you have any clue how badly his parents will react when they find out? Especially his father. He'll need his friends.'

'What do you take me for? I would never have left just because Brian's gay.' He jabs his thumb in Vicky's direction. 'I missed yer one, didn't I?'

Vicky drily says, 'Thanks.'

I said to Finbar, 'You are okay with it then?'

'I'll get there, but what bugs me is that I don't know if he'd be as magnum with me as I'm being magnum with him.'

'Magnum? Like PI?'

Helpfully, Vicky says, 'Magnanimous.'

Finbar laughs at himself. 'You see why I came back? Not all that long ago, it was Brian who used to throw those accusations at me, and that was when he was secretly gay and I was as clearly straight as I am today. If, in some alternative universe, our positions had been reversed, can you imagine how much worse he would've been to me?'

Nicole said, 'I don't know your friend, but it sounds like he was only mean to you out of his own defensiveness, to strike at you before you could strike at him. You can't really know that, in your alternative universe, he wouldn't have had empathy for you.'

With grudging good humour, Finbar said, 'I get your point.'

I asked, 'Does anything else bother you about it?'

'Listen, I don't believe there's anything wrong with leaning in that direction. Brian's my friend no matter what. I just wish things didn't have to change. I don't want to be an asshole about it, but I don't know what I'll talk to him about now.'

Vicky gave him a look of mild reproach. 'Why can't you talk about the same stuff?'

'Ninety per cent of everything he's ever said has been about women. And he didn't, y'know, keep it in the most respectful manner. I get now that he was massively over-compensating, but he had what you might call a bawdy sense of humour. I don't know what his next great subject matter is supposed to be.'

Finbar looked to me for corroboration. I smiled and said, 'You're worried he'll apply similar conversational enthusiasm to cock?' He laughed, and so did Nicole, while Vicky appeared unimpressed. Finbar didn't deny it, though. I said, 'You've nothing to worry about. He's bound to be self-conscious around us. We'll just show him we're okay with it, then we'll move on.'

'I never thought he was self-conscious before. I guess he's been hiding it, and I get why, but now it's like he's a new person. We *will* move on, although I reckon there'll be a longer adjustment period than you think. I expected you to be more taken aback. It seems like I'm the only one, or at least I'm the only one being honest about it.'

I shrugged. 'No one is really who they present themselves to be and no one can be relied on to stay the way we see them. So, yeah, I'm prepared to adapt to whatever needs adapting to.'

For the next couple of hours, we chatted about other things. Nicole wasn't quite herself, but I put it down to her being a little shy around new people in an unfamiliar environment, and Finbar hadn't exactly made the best of first impressions.

It wasn't until later, when we were in bed, in the dark, that she said, 'No one is who they pretend to be. No one can be relied on.'

I said that I didn't use the word 'pretend', and that I hadn't been making a subtle dig at her, then I claimed to be wrecked. She wasn't looking for a fight. I kissed her, and when we fell asleep, it was in each other's arms. But I'd heard the sadness in her voice when she paraphrased me; I just didn't want to address it, and what was left unsaid remained loud between us.

Early October 2001
A few months later, I introduced Nicole to Tighe. She and I walked through the arrivals gate at Heathrow, and I spotted him standing behind the barrier. He clapped his hands once, as if to say 'finally'. I pressed my pincer to the small of Nicole's back and pointed him out. She waved and we came around to him, trundling our luggage behind us. He hugged me, then made a show of hugging her too. Actually, it's an exaggeration to say he made a show of it; he did it like it was the most natural greeting in the world.

He offered to take her suitcase. She declined. He insisted. She allowed him, not wanting to cause offence. He led us out to the car park, where his silver BMW awaited, iridescent under the glow of a lamp post.

This was my first trip abroad, and as we drove, he said, 'Tell me if we stray too far from the airport and the fear sets in. I can U-turn this car and have you on a plane home before the sky crashes down.'

Nicole laughed with him. She didn't make any cracks of her own, having exhausted her repertoire while we were airborne.

At his luxury apartment, Tighe held open the door and motioned us inside. In the hallway, we were assailed by the aroma of meat being cooked. We followed it into the kitchen, where we discovered Tighe's posh girlfriend, Veronica, bending over and staring through the oven window at a plump chicken simmering in a Pyrex bowl. Noticing us, she straightened up and exclaimed, 'Oh!' She pulled off her oven mitts and stuck out her hand to shake with me, then with Nicole. Blushing at the sight of my pincer, she blew a curl from her face. 'What perfect timing!'

We ate dinner and shared three bottles of wine. Veronica talked the most. She seemed to want to butter me up. She must have had designs on becoming Mrs Tighe and figured it would be to her benefit to get his brother on her side. She had a striking pout and the long-leggedness of a model, but Tighe's eyes would occasionally glaze over as she was telling stories, and so, rightly as it happens, I doubted their relationship would last.

I did the second-most talking, listing the names of books I was studying and going on about deconstructionism, of all things. For some reason, I launched into a speech about how pleased I was that Dad was unretiring and returning to work for the *Chronicle*. I made it sound like my opinion had something to do with it, as if he needed my advice on how to live a fulfilling life.

Nicole spoke about herself only when she had to and deflected more than a few questions in my direction. She acted like she was fascinated by my literary ruminations, and at one point, probably when I was at my most tedious, she assured Tighe and Veronica, 'He really knows what he's talking about.'

Tighe laughed whenever a joke was made and was a

courteous host, but he spent most of the night reclining in his chair, sipping his wine and observing everyone.

The next night, Veronica had other plans and, after a day of sightseeing by ourselves, Nicole and I met Tighe in a trendy Soho bar he suggested called the Electric Churchill. We sat in a booth under a red-and-white Warholesque painting of Margaret Thatcher arm-wrestling Johnny Rotten. Tighe put his credit card behind the bar and paid for everything, beginning with a round of sambuca and a bottle of champagne. After we downed the shots, I asked him if we were celebrating anything. He poured the champagne. 'Extracting you from the home-land.' He motioned to Nicole. 'Meeting your beautiful girlfriend. And . . .' he rubbed his index finger and thumb together, 'I made a nice profit this week.'

'Why weren't we celebrating that last night?'

'I didn't want to make the night about me. Besides, I haven't mentioned it to Veronica yet.'

'Why not?'

He laughed. 'She asks too many questions.'

Tighe was some sort of trader for Worth & Walcott, and also claimed to dabble in a few entrepreneurial dealings of his own, but I didn't really understand how he earned his money. I knew that he'd been making six figures for years, so if he was feeling celebratory, he must have made a killing this time.

We clinked flutes, and when I saw he was downing his, I did the same. I finished just after him. Nicole sipped hers. 'Boys, pace yourselves.'

Tighe topped us up. We drank these ones slower, although I was faster than him. I wish I could say I had nothing to prove, but of course, I wanted Nicole to see I could do something better than Tighe, even if that was only outdrinking him. He was all the things I wasn't: successful and rarely, if ever, anxious; two-footed and with a complete set of fingers. He never seemed to fuck up. He was just better. The one thing I had that he didn't was Nicole, but he didn't have it in him to begrudge me her. He was happy for me.

We hadn't really gone drinking together before and I was curious to see if he'd let his guard drop. He drank almost as much as me, so he must have been feeling the effects, but apart from an off-colour joke or two, he didn't say anything foolish. There was no slurring of words. He eyed up various women, and they eyed him up too, but he didn't talk to them. He was faithful to Veronica.

The three of us went to some club to dance. The fact that I was up for it is proof that I wasn't sober. None of us performed well on the dance floor. We were zestful; I'll give us that. I couldn't totally unwind though when I was aware of every guy even glancing in Nicole's direction. I shouldn't have worried. She didn't have eyes for anyone else. Tighe was dancing next to us, but was careful not to invade her body space.

When we returned to his apartment, he mixed us each one of his 'secret recipe' cocktails. What they lacked in taste, they made up for in potency. When Nicole finished hers, she was also finished for the night. I was determined to keep drinking, saying, 'Let's make it till sunrise!' Tighe said he could cope with another. Nicole said good-night and headed for the guest room, which was double the size of the bedrooms in our Dublin flat. Somewhere between her going to bed and Tighe making me a second cocktail, my alcohol consumption caught up with me.

When I opened my eyes, I was lying face down on Tighe's couch, my hand in a fist under my stomach. Sunlight flared across my vision and a drum solo started up in my friable brain.

My hangover took the better part of two days to dissipate, and Nicole's was worse if her moroseness on the flight home was anything to go by.

In our trips to Rathbaile and London, I saw the effort Nicole made with the people who mattered to me and how nervous she was to come across the right way. It finally kicked in that, despite my many flaws, she really wanted to be with me. That made me uneasy, because if she loved me nearly as much as I loved her, then I had power over her. I'd realised early on that she had the power to hurt me and, correctly, I thought that was inevitable. But it was the other way around that was truly scary. I didn't know how I'd be able to live with myself if I ever broke her heart.

Chapter Twenty-Three

The Reinvention of Nicole Winters

I

There's more of Jimmy's testimony to come, but I'm interrupting him to share a few of Nicole's memories with you – there are important things that he can't see, because he doesn't have the access to her point of view that I do and because she has misled him at times; she has lied.

I also want to take a moment to confess that I've been feeling insecure. It's not for a lack of self-belief. If I don't believe in myself, I cease to exist.

My second-guessing is due to my – your – oblivious protagonist. This is his story, not mine. Placing myself front and centre was never an option – I would need life to have a life story. But by putting Jimmy in charge of the narrative, I've relinquished a significant portion of the one thing in my control. I feel a petty urge to compete with him. In his writing, he can brandish all his revealing actions, his clumsy cause and effect, whereas I'm like a mime in an invisible, soundproof box. Even if I could yell, it wouldn't make a difference.

And, let's be honest, when he writes about his emotions and I write about mine, whose seem more real? If he says he loves Nicole and I say it too, he's more convincing because he can point to examples of the influence she had on him, whereas with me, you have to take my word for it. It's a cliché of unrequited love that the object of affection doesn't know her admirer exists. In my case, Nicole really can't be blamed for that.

I've enough ego to believe I have insights to offer on the lives of the people I watch, but my personality is still an impotent one. My ability to enter minds is the nearest thing I can get to a bona fide sensation of my own, and it's like falling and soaring simultaneously. There are so many feelings and stories to absorb and I have a skeleton key for such a wealth of knowledge – every mind is a virtual library. What I can do is a gift, but it's poor compensation for all that I can't.

I try to keep my bitterness from becoming overly self-indulgent.

Sometimes I think about whether there's a God. I wonder if She or He or It is up above, or down below, and enjoying this game. I've been granted no glimpse of divinity. I'm not quite an atheist, though. I'm more of an irritable agnostic. Maybe I'm closer to God than all of these living people, and a curtain has been lifted for me that hasn't for them, but there's still a barrier between a Creator and me. Maybe the final curtain will never be lifted, and limbo, purgatory, oblivion – whatever this is – is eternal.

While I'm hardly a miracle, I am evidence for there being more to the world than what can be observed or comprehended by scientific means. My capacity for seeing without eyes, hearing without ears, thinking without a brain: these are, at least, neat tricks. My nature poses a challenge to theories of consciousness, of the soul, and of the afterlife, but I may only be an exception to the typical rules of being. My uniqueness doesn't console me. I haven't earned it, or anything else. I just flaccidly am, regardless of wish or will.

I've considered the possibility that I'm not what I think I am. I believe I'm real, that the people around me are too, and that the memories I've steeped myself in have happened. But if I was delusional about what I perceive, how would I know? Some of the insane are knowingly so; others couldn't be more unaware. I've no friends who can reassure me of my mental stability or that I don't need to have matter to matter.

If I'm crazy, who or what would I be then and where would I be telling this from? The likeliest explanation is obvious. If I'm not me, then I'm probably Jimmy or a particularly deluded side of his subconscious. It would make a kind of weird sense. There are people who suffer from multiple-personality disorders, which can be born of traumatic experiences, something Jimmy is no stranger to. There could be an infestation of splintered disembodied narrators lurking in his brain. I hate to think there are a lot of us, all bursting to tell his story. Maybe they're better at it than me.

If I was him – or an aspect of him – then answers would be needed for how I know the things about the people he's close to that he doesn't. It's simple really. I would have to be a self-deceiving inventor of tall tales.

For the record, I think I have, or am, a lucid mind. Despite being invisible and untouchable, my identity isn't truly isolated. I believe I'm me and Jimmy is Jimmy, but when I read his words and compose mine, I recognise that we have a similar voice. I'm more like him though than he's like me. It's an inevitable carryover from how I've been forced to survive. I'm a parasite on the back of his experiences, and so as his identity develops, mine derives.

I'm in persistent danger of letting his thoughts dominate

mine. He's the default setting among all my options from which to vicariously experience the world. On days when I feel uninspired, I can slip into only seeing things the way he does. I fear the acceptance of those limitations and so, even if I didn't enjoy being immersed in other minds, I would feel a personal responsibility to get out there and be as sociable as I can.

I always come back to him, though, and as undernourished as I am, I feed on his emotions. That doesn't mean I can't feel something unless he feels it first. I don't think, for instance, that I fell in love with Nicole because he did, out of imitation or rivalry. I must believe I'm more than an echo. I refuse to be merely that.

August 1998

A FEW DAYS BEFORE JIMMY'S DEBS, NICOLE IS ON THE other side of the world, soon to depart. She's twenty-two.

Her flatmates, Bree and Reggie, prepare the food and set the living-room table, and the three of them sit down to their last meal together: steaming pasta, grated Parmesan cheese, and garlic bread.

Reggie twists off the cap of his beer and tosses it at the opening of the Carlton Cold box just inside the kitchen. It hits the middle of the box and wobbles back into the living room, resting under the flabby couch. Reggie shrugs and raises his bottle. 'To Nicky's fortunes. A final farewell.'

Bree kicks his leg, puts her hand to her mouth while she swallows a bite of bread, then says, 'Shut the fuck up. She'll be back before we've had time to miss her.'

Nicole clinks her beer with theirs. 'I'll visit to check you two haven't forgotten about me.'

Reggie says, 'No you won't, and you'll forget about *us* within a week.' He's smiling, but when she meets his eyes, he looks away.

She moved in three years ago, shortly after first arriving in Melbourne. Bree and Reggie have been a couple for five years, since they were in high school.

Reggie says, 'How long is your degree, Nicky?'

Wrapping pasta around her fork, she says, 'A brief four years.'

'Then you'll move home?'

Bree says, 'In four years, you'll be living with some sexy Irishman. He'll be begging you not to go, and when he asks you to marry him, do you know what you'll say?'

Nicole, chewing pasta on one side of her mouth, grins. 'That marriage is an archaic institution and I'd rather not vow to obey anyone?'

'You'll say *yes*.'

'Bree, babe, it sounds like you're writing my entire future.'

'It's already written. I'm a conduit between you and what's in the stars.'

'You'll have to come over for my wedding then, and be my bridesmaid. The same goes for you, Reggie. I'll need all the bridesmaids I can get.'

Reggie gulps from his bottle. 'I'd be man enough to do that.'

Bree says, 'Hey, I'm confident your wedding will happen like I said, but we'd better see you heaps before that. We'll be expecting you during your summer breaks.'

Nicole says, 'I might not be able to afford to return *every* year.' Bree looks a little forlorn, so she adds, 'Maybe the Irishman is loaded too. He can pay for me to jet over every other weekend. And I'll tell you what, I promise to return for *your* wedding.'

Reggie laughs, his hand on his stomach. 'I wouldn't hold your breath.' Bree slaps his arm with the back of her hand. He exclaims, 'Ow!' but he's only pretending that she hit him hard.

She says, 'It could be sooner than you think. Just not to him.'

He takes her hand and kisses her knuckles. 'Don't give up on me just yet.'

She smiles at him and says, 'Watch yourself.'

Nicole laughs, but it's a little forced. Reggie stands to get more beer from the fridge.

Hours later, Nicole is in bed, staring at the ceiling. Her walls are bare, having been stripped of posters. She has thrown out everything except for what's in her two suitcases and one rucksack at the base of her bed.

She hears the door of the neighbouring room open, then the treading of familiar footsteps. There's a light knock on her door. Bree whispers, 'Nicky? You awake?'

Nicole considers staying silent, but after seconds pass and the shadow under the door doesn't waver, she says, 'Only for you.'

Bree comes in and scurries to the bed.

Nicole has already shifted over. Bree gets in. She rests her temple on Nicole's shoulder and flops a forearm on her stomach. 'Reggie was snoring.'

'I know.'

Not a lot has gone on between Bree and Reggie in their room that Nicole hasn't heard. But even if it wasn't for thin walls and average hearing, she'd still be up to speed on the ins and outs of their arguments, and their sex life, because Bree is a sharer. She has concluded many of her admissions to Nicole by saying something like, 'I feel so much better for having told you. Best friends shouldn't keep secrets and I know you won't tell a soul.'

Bree says, 'It's not going to be the same when you're gone.'

'Sometimes different is better.'

'Don't say that. Who will I talk to? You *get* me.'

'Talk to Reggie. *He* gets you.'

'Not the same.'

As dear as Bree is to Nicole, she knows they don't actually understand each other.

Most of what Nicole will tell Jimmy about her background will be lies, but to Bree she has confided much of the truth: that she has no idea, and no intention of ever finding out, who her biological parents were; that she was raised in a string of foster homes; in the best of them she was neglected; in the very worst, when she was eight, she was frequently molested by a man who was known in their community for his charity work and his devout religious beliefs; that when she was seventeen, her last foster mother banished her after discovering her in bed with a man twice her age.

Bree cried when Nicole told her these things and hugged her hard. Nicole numbly returned the hugs and didn't shed a tear. Talking about her experiences wasn't cathartic; if anything, she felt more disconnected from her past after doing so. She decided that intimacy isn't the result of what someone knows about you. A person could document every fact of your life, they could even have been beside you throughout your most painful moments, and you could still be a stranger to them.

Bree rolls on to her back. 'Can I ask you something?'

'Speak now or forever hold your peace.'

'Do you really think me and Reggie will last?'

Nicole doesn't hesitate. 'Absolutely. You've made it this far and you love him as much as ever, don't you?'

'Yeah. It's just . . . I think too much when I'm tired.'

'Then stop thinking. Have faith in him and you, and sleep.'

Bree is right to have concerns. She has been betrayed. A month ago, while she was away, Reggie and Nicole got drunk together and had sex. It was only that one time and they made a pact to keep it a secret to protect Bree. The more Nicole goes over that stupid night in her mind, the more she feels that she was the one who initiated what happened, and she did it because, on some self-loathing level, she didn't think she deserved either Bree's or Reggie's friendship – now she has no doubt at all.

Her sadness to be leaving is outweighed by relief.

Bree returns her head to Nicole's shoulder and says, 'Promise me you won't allow us to drift apart.'

'I promise.'

'And that you'll come back.'

'I promise.'

Nicole ascends into the sky, her hands locked to the armrests. Her eyes are scrunched shut and her tongue presses well-chewed chewing gum against her palate. This is her first-ever flight. It hasn't been enjoyable so far.

She hears a laugh and opens her eyes. She turns her head to the girl in the aisle seat beside her, expecting to be the source of amusement, but the girl, who looks about thirteen, isn't paying her any attention. She's engrossed in the agony-aunt column of some frivolous beauty magazine and laughing either at someone's problem or at the advice on how to solve it. She scratches her nose without taking her eyes off the print.

Nicole smiles. She considers herself to be tough, and yet she's freaked out while this kid is barely aware they're airborne. Nicole loosens her grip on the armrests, takes the paper bag from the pouch in front of her, and spits her gum into it.

During this journey, she decides to change who she is. From embarking in Melbourne to disembarking in Dublin, twenty-seven hours pass, and though her flights aren't turbulent, she never sleeps. At both Changi and Heathrow she buys coffee then sits near the departure gates. She takes a paperback from her rucksack, but doesn't read more than a few pages. She glances about her with little inquisitiveness. The choice to cut her losses isn't a light one, but after it's made, it's made for good: she won't keep in contact with anyone – Bree and Reggie will certainly be better off for that – or return if she can help it.

She's tired of the weight of her past and of her identity being based on the sum of her misguided actions and the things that have happened to her without permission. She hasn't had a life that has allowed her to feel very youthful, so in Dublin, when people ask her what age she is, why not dial it back and recapture some of her lost time? She'll be in classes with fellow first years and she could pass for nineteen. And if she's going to alter one detail about herself, there's nothing to prevent her from altering others. Her intention to lie about her personal history isn't because she hopes to impress anyone or because she wishes to test if she has what it takes to live a con.

She just wants a fresh start; to be free.

II
October 2001

The changes Nicole made to her identity felt liberating at the time. In hindsight, the whole idea seems fucked up, a childish trap.

During the night before they go to London, she puts her hand on Jimmy's chest, flattening coils of hair, and whispers, 'Could we forget everything I've told you and start over? Just some details. Not what I've said about how I feel.'

He shudders and turns towards her. His heart pounds against her palm, his eyes remaining closed. He's somewhere in a dream.

Except in her most insecure moments, she trusts that he's committed to her. It might be rare for him to tell her, 'I love you,' but she knows he means it. He isn't, however, sincere in his every word. He often says, 'I trust you,' but with that note in his voice, like he's challenging her to prove him wrong. She knows he doesn't trust her.

She can't blame him for that. The mother and father she told him about, Natasha and Darrell, were amalgamations of different foster parents. She presented the pair of them as being unloving, making them defective, but if Jimmy knew she had five pairs of guardians and none of them had loved her, wouldn't that indicate that *she* was the defective one? Then there was Alistair, who she fabricated to give her some time to figure out what she was willing to risk for Jimmy – she didn't know if she had it in her to be in a healthy relationship.

She has spent many nights awake in bed, or off on long walks, trying to think of a way to confess all of this, while also convincing him that she has always been faithful and would never do anything to hurt him. What if he concludes that her credibility is so shot through that he feels he has no choice but to leave her?

He takes deeper intakes of breath, and when he breathes out, his chest and arms tremble. She raises her hand to his face. When he whimpers, she says loudly, 'Jimmy.'

He grunts and opens his eyes. He stares at her like he hasn't a clue who she is. Then he wipes his eyes with his pincer. 'I had a nightmare?'

'I don't think it was too bad. It's gone.'

He sits up and grasps his left wrist. He isn't wearing his watch. 'What time is it?'

'About four. It's fine if we sleep in. We don't have to leave till after lunch.'

'Are you okay? Did you have a nightmare too?'

'No, why do you ask?'

'Your eyes are . . .'

'I've just been rubbing them too much, or it's a touch of late-night blues. I'm all right.'

He accepts this. He drapes an arm around her and pulls her to him. 'Don't expect Tighe to be like me.'

'I don't have expectations, other than that I'll probably like him. Because you do and I like *you*. Now, get some sleep, yeah?'

She covers his eyes with her hand and kisses him. Soon they are both asleep.

The following evening, they are drinking wine in Tighe's living room, Nicole and Jimmy on one couch, Tighe and Veronica on the other. Between the couches, which are positioned at a right angle to one another, there's a coffee table, centred by a tray with three orange pillar candles bunched amidst a cluster of smooth pebbles. Veronica lit the candles when they moved over from the dinner table. Below a dormant plasma-screen TV, the gilded electric fireplace is also glowing.

Nicole looks about her. 'Tighe, this is a really nice place.'

Jimmy squeezes her knee with his pincer. 'It's quite something.'

Tighe turns to Veronica, who is rubbing her stockinged foot. 'You should have seen what a sty it was before I met Veronica.'

She releases her foot. 'He's a liar. There's never been anything amiss here. He's even a conscientious duster.'

He puts his hand around her waist and she leans into him. 'You make me sound like an obsessive metrosexual.'

'There's nothing wrong with being house-trained.' Tighe smiles to himself and sips his wine. Disappointed not to get a bigger reaction, Veronica declares, 'I know a funny story.'

'Have I heard it?'

'It's the one about Hector and Alicia, and the horse.'

'Ah.'

'What? It's funny!'

'Tell it then.'

Addressing Jimmy and Nicole, Veronica begins, 'Alicia's an old school friend of mine and she bought this horse . . .'

The story is long and not very funny. Between laughing during Veronica's pauses, Nicole's gaze meanders to Tighe's face. He and Jimmy have the same chin, and there's something similar in the set of their mouths, but that disappears when they smile.

Aware of Jimmy's observance of her line of sight, she returns her attention to Veronica, noticing how much rouge she's wearing on her cheeks. It's enough to conceal a bruise. She feels a prickle of guilt for even entertaining the implication. When Veronica delivers her punchline – 'and *that* is the last time Hector will ever try to saddle an animal of any kind!' – Nicole laughs the loudest.

Late in the night, while Jimmy is asleep, Nicole hears a muffled moan coming from the other end of the apartment, where Tighe and Veronica are sleeping or rather not. At least someone is having fun. Nicole had wanted to christen this never-before-used guest room, but Jimmy said, 'I wouldn't feel comfortable in my brother's place.'

When all has gone quiet, other than Jimmy's breathing, Nicole falls asleep and stays that way for a few hours.

When she wakes, she's immediately alert. There's an alarm clock on the dressing table. It's 6.15. She stares at the clock until it hits seven. She gets up, puts on her jeans and Jimmy's T-shirt, and ventures into the hall.

She follows the smell of smoke into the living room, where Veronica is sitting on a couch, watching the tip of her cigarette burn. She's dressed in the same outfit she was wearing last night. Her handbag is beside her and her coat is cast over the armrest. When she sees Nicole, she stubs out the cigarette in a red-stained wine glass. She says, 'Morning,' and motions to the other couch. Nicole sits.

Without make-up on, Veronica looks older and a little worn out, but maybe that's due to the hour or a hangover. There's no bruise on either cheek. Nicole says, 'You're not much of a sleeper either?'

Veronica pulls a box of cigarettes from her handbag. 'Fag?'

'Don't smoke.'

Veronica taps out a cigarette, pops it in her mouth, lights up with a pink lighter, and takes a drag. 'Usually I'm a slob when it comes to sleep, actually. I should probably keep it to myself, but, well, you won't say anything, will you? Tighe and I had a terrible fight last night. I *hate* it when we fight. I can't hope to sleep after. He can, like a baby, with that bulletproof conscience of his, even though it was all him being an asshole.'

'What did he do?'

Veronica opens her mouth to say something, then takes a drag instead, her eyes never leaving Nicole's face. 'You're on holiday and it's too early for melodrama. All I'll say is this: I see who he is and who he could be, and I want it to work, but honestly, I don't see it happening. Still, I'm silly enough that *I* can't leave *him*. He's going to have to do it, which he will once I've ceased to entertain him. That's the Diaz clan for you, eh?'

Nicole's expression tightens. 'Jimmy and I are doing okay.'

Veronica gives her a sympathetic look. 'Sorry. Of course you are. He seems like a keeper. Tighe has his moments too, for all my talk.' She laughs. 'Don't share my voicing of discontent with either brother.'

'It's forgotten.'

Veronica stubs out her cigarette and stands. 'Filthy habit. I must be off before my captor wakes.'

Nicole is nestling her second cup of coffee in her hands, with her feet on the coffee table, when Jimmy enters the room. He's fully dressed, but his eyes are drowsy. She'd been watching a documentary on the History Channel about Franco, with the volume low. She turns it off, and puts the remote and her cup on the table. He bends down to kiss her on the forehead and she hugs him, her cheek against his stomach. She shifts to create space on the couch. He remains standing. 'Let's go get breakfast. Then we can do some tourist stuff.'

'Don't you want to wait for your brother?'

'Let him sleep. He'd pretend otherwise, but he wouldn't be into the whole sightseeing thing, and I want to gawk, like a proper out-of-towner.'

They find a greasy spoon, where they feast on sausages, eggs, and toast, and drink excessively pulpy orange juice and lukewarm coffee.

Shortly afterwards, they're on the tube, hurtling towards

Piccadilly Circus. He whispers to her, 'Isn't it strange how determined everyone is to avoid eye contact?'

'No. It's what I expected.'

Above ground again, as they wander to Trafalgar Square, Buckingham Palace, and Big Ben, Jimmy consults his *Lonely Planet* every time a question occurs to him about what they're seeing or where to go next.

They decide to view the city from the London Eye. At its apex, Nicole stands on the tips of her toes and presses her forehead against the glass. Jimmy says, 'Doesn't that give you vertigo?'

'That's the idea. I'm getting my money's worth.'

He presses his forehead to the glass too and imagines falling. His heart starts beating faster so he steps away. He stands behind her, putting his hands on her shoulders, and she allows him to pull her back from the glass.

As the sun sets, they go for pizza in a restaurant in Soho then meet Tighe in the Electric Churchill, a bar that Nicole thinks is wanky and garish.

Later on, when they return to the apartment, all of them drunk, Tighe takes out his keys and the lock deflects a few of his stabs before he gets it right and opens the door. He flicks on the hallway light with an upwards slap. Nicole and Jimmy follow him in, an arm across each other's back, his pincer on her waist, her hand on his hip. The hallway seems narrower and the carpet seems to be on a slight incline, whereas it was flat before. Nicole thinks she's walking straight until she bangs, twice, against the wall. Maybe that's due less to her impaired coordination and more to Jimmy pushing against her.

In the living room, they collapse together on a couch. She feels much better sitting down, more in control.

Tighe says something about mixing cocktails. Jimmy agrees

enthusiastically and Nicole assents too. She regrets it straight away, but doesn't backtrack, not wanting to dampen the mood. Tighe rubs his hands on his shirt and ducks into the kitchen.

Soon he's standing before them holding two cocktails in martini glasses. They take one each. He goes and retrieves his own, which is in a tall cylindrical glass. The cocktails are a murky red. Jimmy and Nicole don't ask what they're made of. He sips his through a straw. She pushes her straw away and drinks from the rim. Disliking the taste, she drinks it fast.

Tighe, watching them from the other couch, says, 'Well?'

Jimmy says, 'Superb!'

Nicole smiles and keeps drinking.

Although she has been doing her best to give him a chance, she hasn't taken to Tighe, finding him cold, shallow, and a little tedious. The way he looks at her isn't inappropriate exactly – it's friendly – but she doesn't like it.

Her concentration keeps breaking as she tries to follow the conversation between Jimmy and Tighe, which is pretty one-sided anyway – Jimmy is animatedly expounding on his impressions of London and Tighe is mostly just listening. She takes one last gulp of her drink, plants a kiss on Jimmy's cheek that he wasn't expecting, and uses his shoulder to push herself up. She says goodnight to them and ignores Jimmy's protests.

She makes it into the guest room without tripping and closes the door. The curtains are drawn, and it's dark, but she quickly gives up on locating the light switch. She walks forward with her hands out and her legs bump against the bed. She kicks off her shoes and climbs on to the quilt, mashing her face into the pillow. She's out.

She comes to with Tighe on top of her, his hand over her mouth.

Chapter Twenty-Four

Dissolution

29/1/2012

Seb came by yesterday, with a six-pack. We opened a can each and sat in my living room. I asked, 'Good news or bad?'

'How do you know I have news?'

'Psychic powers. Did the bastards fire you from the show?'

He smiled. 'The phrase was "going in a different direction".'

'Sorry to hear it.'

'Don't be. I needed a kick up the ass.'

It was obvious from his expression that he thought I'd benefit from similar therapy. I said, 'Do you have a plan?'

'I'm moving to London in two weeks. Bought my ticket today.'

'Wow, good for you. That's where the big time is. More opportunities than in Dublin anyway.'

'Right. It's just, well, this really has to work.'

'I have faith you'll get where you're going, and hopefully soon, but it's not the end of the line yet, is it? Even if London turns out not to be the answer, you can keep persisting. You could come back if you need to.'

Slumped on the couch, Seb twisted and then snapped the pull-tab off his can. 'I think I'll either break through in the next year or two, or it won't happen.'

'It's not life or death . . .'

'I wouldn't suggest it is. It's just life by itself.'

I don't know why I was needling him. I resolved to stop. 'You'll make it.'

He nodded and, without sounding optimistic, said, 'You should move to London too.'

I was amused. 'What would I do there?'

'You wouldn't need to have much of a plan. Just go, find some work, meet new people. Remember when you used to be known for rolling the dice?'

'That was an aberration. At heart, I'm quite cautious.'

'I doubt the "at heart" bit. I think you've learned caution, and learned it too well.'

I downed my beer and stood up. 'You're lagging.'

I went to the kitchen and took two cans from the fridge. I was hoping his mind would wander, but when I returned and handed him a beer, he said, 'We could get a flat together, like in the good old days. And, hey, you could look into doing a masters. You've talked about getting back into academia.'

'It was just talk.'

'Still. What's keeping you here?'

I limply said, 'I have this flat. I have my temping. I'm, y'know, settled here.'

He had more to say, but was probably worried that, if he pushed too hard, I'd dig my heel in. 'At least give it some thought.'

We finished his beers, but I had reserves so we started on those. While I didn't feel drunk, I must have been, because I wouldn't have brought up what I did if I was sober. 'Remember when you returned from Australia? Did Nicole seem different to you?'

Resting his can against his knee, he studied my face for a sign of what I wanted to hear. 'I only saw her a few more times, and so far as I could tell, she was the same. And she was crazy about you. That was unmistakable whenever I saw you together, even on those nights out when you didn't appear to be getting along.'

'We didn't?'

'It was just that, before my year away, if there was a group out, the pair of you would spend most of the night whispering and laughing at whatever private jokes you shared. After I returned, there was less of that. I could be wrong, but there seemed to be a distance. I figured it was a temporary bump in the road.' When it became apparent that I wasn't going to break the silence between us, he bravely asked, 'Did *you* notice any differences in her?'

'I did. But . . .' I shook my head. 'I'm sorry, I don't want to talk about what I noticed.'

'You don't have to. If you ever change your mind, though, I won't be too far off. London's only a stone's throw away.'

I got one more pointless statement out there. 'She was my life, y'know.'

Speaking about her makes me feel empty and toxic. It's better to stick to the page, where I can work out what I think without contaminating others, and whatever I distort, I can amend later.

Seb strained to think of something comforting. He tried, 'She was lucky you—'

'Don't.' I shrugged and smiled. Maybe I laughed. 'It's all right. Don't worry.'

October 2001 to January 2002

I didn't intentionally fuck it up. I was afraid, all the time, about how strong my feelings for Nicole were, but I didn't turn away. I just failed to communicate when it was most essential and I couldn't hold on. It was like my ability to focus on her deteriorated, and no matter how wide I opened my eyes or how much I squinted, I couldn't see her with any clarity.

She once called me her 'insomnia cure', but from what I observed, she was a terrible sleeper. I usually nodded off before her and woke after. She had a habit of disrupting my sleep. More frequently because she wanted to have sex. She didn't always wake me before starting, although I'd be surprised if I ever slept through it. The other reason was to rescue me. I've always been disposed to nightmares, but they didn't haunt me in the light of day then, not like they have since losing her. I was probably ignorant of the majority of them when they were over, and I told her that, but she couldn't watch me without intervening. 'You scream, do you know that? You scream.'

So considering I was a poor sleeper and she was worse, the 'insomnia cure' tag struck me as funny. Thinking it was a throwaway compliment, I teased her. She was having none of it. She claimed to be used to lying in bed all night without a wink of sleep, and on mornings after she had achieved a few hours, she felt like she'd been in a fight. Before me, that is. It's still a funny compliment: 'No one puts me asleep quite like you do.'

I was sceptical that her insomnia was as awful as she

said, until it returned, around the time we got back from London. I slept through a lot of her not-sleeping, but for evidence of its effects, I just had to look at the darkness tugging at her eyes. Instead of waking up to find her already awake, I woke up to find her gone.

Sometimes I discovered her lying on the couch in the living room, watching TV, with her head on the armrest. She would seem entranced, but when I asked what was happening in whatever crappy programme was on, she could never tell me much.

And sometimes she left the flat, disappearing into the city, so I'd argue with her about it, or rather I'd argue at her. Her eyes were too dulled for her to offer resistance.

When she did sleep, she was the one now enduring violent nightmares. Maybe, late some night, the wraith who'd been plaguing me all those years emerged from my throat and spidered across the pillow to where its new victim laid her head, with her mouth open, and clawed its way inside her. I didn't become aware that she was having nightmares because she confided in me or because I was guarding her at the expense of my own sleep. It was because of her shoves and kicks. She even head-butted me once. I ripped the blanket off her as I tumbled out of bed.

We always slept in my room. She only used hers to study or to get away from me. When sleeping next to her became a hazardous lifestyle choice, she suggested that she could sleep in her bed. I wouldn't hear of it: 'When I wake in the middle of the night, I want to be able to touch you.'

While she'd become averse to confrontation, she was hiding a growing anger towards me. I would see it in her eyes when I caught her staring at me, but then her face would soften and she would smile shyly. She didn't want to feel that way, which was why she was disguising it. My theory is that her anger was born of disappointment with me and that was exacerbated when she met Tighe. I don't think she liked him. Not because he wasn't a good-enough guy, or interesting and successful. It was because he was all of these things. I suffered in comparison. Her feelings for me were still there, but she realised she'd fallen for someone who didn't fully deserve her.

I asked her to come with me to Rathbaile for Christmas. She said she couldn't because she needed to study and didn't want to intrude on my family time. Besides, she hated Christmas. I tried to convince her that she would have plenty of space to study, that my family wanted her there, and none of us liked Christmas either so we could all not celebrate it together. When I saw that nothing I could say would make a difference, I backed off. If she wanted a break from me, she could have it.

That was our fourth Christmas without Mam and it was one of my most miserable ones, which is saying something. It was made worse because Dad, Tighe, and Elizabeth were unusually buoyant, and that obliged me to fake happiness properly. We weren't faking as a team this time. I bore some blame for their good cheer. I'd made it to my final year, having earned back-to-back two-ones. Barring an eleventh-hour implosion, I was on my way to securing my arts degree. But, more than that, they'd all met Nicole and seen that I had something good in my life.

I don't know what the worst part of my phone call with her that day was: when one of us was talking shite or when we were both stumped and the silence stretched out like a chasm.

I returned to Dublin on New Year's Day and had barely stepped inside our flat when she flung her arms around my shoulders like she hadn't expected to see me again. I asked, 'Why are you crying?'

She didn't answer. With a stroke of her hand, she wiped her tears away.

Before I could repeat the question, she was unbuckling my belt and unzipping my fly. We fucked on the hallway carpet, then again, less frantically, in bed. Lying there afterwards, with my arm around her, I allowed myself to believe that things might turn out okay.

My confidence came and went. Sometimes, even the prospect of being apart from me made her anxious; other times, I felt like I was the last person on the planet she wanted to be around.

On the first Sunday of the year, we had a lazy lunch in a Dalkey café, then strolled in the direction of Whiterock. Although the cold caused our breath to precede us, it was also cloudless and bright. Nicole was quiet, but seemed more adrift than pensive. I don't think she was planning on saying the things she said, not that day.

We came on to Vico Road, then to the cliff overlooking Whiterock. We descended the steps. When we set foot on the sand, I turned to kiss her, but the wind blew her hair between our lips. She laughed as she swept it from her face.

She jogged a few paces ahead before settling into a listless walk. Her attention was on the waves hissing further up along the beach. She stopped and, folding her arms, faced the sea. She swayed with the push and pull of the wind.

I took my time catching up. When I did, I touched her elbow gently. She recoiled as if I'd transmitted an electric shock. She smiled apologetically and kept her arms folded.

I led her away and we sat against an outcropping of rock, our asses on the wet sand. She accepted my arm around her and pressed her head uncomfortably against my collarbone. She gazed out to sea, but, as idyllic a moment as she may have lost herself in, I couldn't share it. I said, 'Remember when we were here the first time? It really terrified me to tell you I was in love with you.'

Her voice taut, she said, 'I was only ever going to respond one way.'

'But I didn't know that.'

'I gave you signs.'

'I've never been able to read them. I meant it when I said it then, but I think my feelings for you are even stronger now. I probably don't say it enough, that I love you, but I do. I guess saying it still scares me. I'm always preparing for the day you won't say it back.'

A strangled sound escaped her, then she was pushing me away and scrambling to her feet.

She ran, but only for a few strides. She looked back at me, her fingers over her mouth. As I trudged towards her, my prosthetic dragged a little, with some sand cemented to the sole of my runner. I clasped her wrist and lowered her hand. 'What's wrong? I don't understand why you've been so sad lately, or why you're so sad now.'

She jerked her hand away, and I felt like I was staring into the eyes of someone I didn't know.

No, wait. Maybe I'm only imagining she wasn't herself to make what she had to say easier to take. Maybe she was never more herself than in those moments.

She said, 'I'm sorry for hurting you. There's no nice way to put this, but it's over. You have to believe me that it's for the best.'

I managed, 'So you're not in love with me?'

She didn't even hesitate. 'No. I'm not.'

'Did you ever love me?'

She flinched. 'You know I did.'

I shook my head. 'I don't *know* anything. You're going to have to spell things out. If there's someone else, you need to tell me.'

'Fuck you, Jimmy. There's only ever been you. You were everything I wanted.'

'I'm still here! What's changed?'

'I have. It's beyond your control.'

'That's it then? We're done, for good? Or is there a chance this is a whim, a bad fucking mood, and by tomorrow you'll have changed your mind?'

'I know what I'm doing and there isn't any chance for us.'

'You've known this for a long time, haven't you?'

'I wanted to believe there was hope, even though I knew there wasn't. I'm sorrier than you'll ever know.'

'Fuck you. A hundred times over, fuck you.'

She absorbed my punchless words like the martyr she was, and stared at me with such *pity* that I wanted to scream at her. Instead, I retreated. She didn't try to stop me as I lumbered back the way we'd come. I climbed the steps, as ungainly as Quasimodo, and it was only when I was at the top that I looked back. My Esmeralda was where I'd left her, but sitting now, her arms wrapped around her knees and her head bowed to them. I felt nothing but contempt, for her and for me, and for all I thought had existed between us.

After more than two years together, we were through, just like that. I'd like to say the sting has eased over time, but if I'm not honest, there's no point in writing any of this. That I'm still angry with her, my forgiveness withheld, speaks badly of me. No one should be obliged to maintain a relationship that makes them unhappy. She didn't owe me anything. Yet here I am, coddling my ego.

There were postscripts, regrettable ones, but valuable too because contact is contact and I've been starved of her for so long now that my memories, the good and the bad, are my only sustenance.

The day after we broke up, she returned to the flat when I wasn't in to collect a suitcase of her stuff. I was out for about an hour all day, so I suspect she was stalking the flat from the pub across the street and waiting for my exit, whether due to cowardice or kindness I don't know.

She left a note. I read it, balled it up, and threw it in the rubbish, then retrieved it and flattened it out. I still have it:

Jimmy,

I'll be in touch about picking up my things. I'll keep paying rent until you find someone to take the room. I don't expect you to hurry. I am, and will continue to be, _sorry_. You were the best thing that ever happened to me and no matter how mad you are, or what you think of me, that will always be true. Don't worry about me. Better yet, forget about me entirely. Please, please take care.

Everything about it pissed me off, from the trivialities of the first lines to praising me when she didn't think I was good enough for her, to presuming I was worried about her, which I was, and then telling me to 'take care' when she was responsible for my distress. I was even irritated that she didn't sign the note.

For nearly a week, I didn't see or hear from her. College started back, but I stayed away. I didn't want to bump into anyone who might even say her name to me. My main motivation, however, to get out of bed in the mornings, to shower every day, and to keep the flat tidy, was that I wanted her to be aware of how together I was if she happened to come by without notice.

And she did.

I was lying on my bed, in the middle of the night, listening to a mix of love songs, some dark and bitter, others downright sappy. My light was off, but the curtains were parted and the street lamp outside my window bathed my walls dirty-yellow. There was an empty glass next to the CD player, on my locker, and an empty wine bottle on the floor. I was maudlin and tipsy, but not as drunk as I would've liked. I was debating whether to get another bottle from the kitchen. My prosthetic was discarded at the foot of the bed so I would've had to reattach it.

I heard a key in the front door, followed by it whining open and shut, and the approach of footsteps in the hallway. Then there was a pressure against my bedroom door, like she was pressing her hand to it, or her forehead. I sat up and turned off the CD player, terminating Elvis Costello's 'I Want You' mid-song. I said, 'What are you waiting for?' The door opened and Nicole tipped forward into the room.

She stumbled to me. I reached for my prosthetic. Her hand intercepted mine and, tentatively, held it. She leaned down to kiss me and I said, 'Stop.' She didn't and I

320

didn't. She fell on top of me and we continued to kiss, and our hands sought out all the familiar treasured places. We were half undressed when I said, 'Does this mean you've changed your mind?'

She kissed me again, brushing my face with her teary eyelashes, and whispered, 'Don't talk. Just love me one more time. One last fuck. Okay?'

It wouldn't have mattered if I'd been sober or if she'd caught me at a stronger time. She used me and maybe I used her. In the moment, it was great, but it was heart-breaking too.

Afterwards, she passed out with her back to me. I persuaded myself that there was a chance we could talk it out in the morning and begin to set right all that was fractured. I must have persuaded myself, because I can't imagine how else I could've fallen asleep when I had her right there.

I've never felt more foolish than when I woke and she was gone.

I waited until that evening to ring her, giving her time to call me or come back first. She did neither. When I called, it rang out. My second attempt went to voicemail, and I growled into the receiver, 'Answer your phone. Give me that much.'

After I called her every ten minutes for about an hour, she finally picked up. She said, 'Jimmy,' like my name was a plea.

I barked, 'Do I mean *anything* to you?'

'You always have. You always will.'

She sounded close to tears, but I had no sympathy. 'What did last night mean?'

'It was a mistake. I was weak.'

'So it meant nothing?'

She started choking up and it was hard to make out many words, but somewhere in there, she said, 'Yes.'

I shouted, 'If you can't respect me, if all you can do is fuck with me, I don't want to ever see you again! Have you got that? Stay the fuck away!'

She sobbed. 'I promise to leave you alone.'

I hung up.

Over the next few days, I pulled myself together, or tried to anyway. I went to all of my classes and clocked a lot of hours studying in the library. On a few occasions, I went for coffee with acquaintances, and increasingly when I laughed it was for real. As long as I didn't have to face Nicole, I was okay. I didn't regret the call.

It was Saturday and I was channel-surfing while eating a bowl of corn flakes. Nothing felt strange or off. Until the buzzer sounded. My stomach constricted. I thought it was her, not here for reconciliation, but probably wanting to get her stuff and return her keys. When I lifted the receiver, it was a man at the other end. I couldn't hear who he said he was over the electric garbling. I buzzed him in anyway.

Then came a firm double knock. I opened the door without hesitation. There were two of them: a man with a trim greying beard and a pale younger woman, both in uniform, both with sombre expressions. The man asked, 'Is this the residence of Nicole Winters?'

I was aware that something was wrong, but I still didn't get it. 'She moved out a fortnight ago.'

'And you were her flatmate?'

'I was her boyfriend. Ex now.'

He took off his hat and shared a look with his partner. Really, it was little more than a glance, but I was struck by what it meant. He turned his eyes to me and I . . .

There are no words to express what I felt when he confirmed that she was dead.

I don't want to write about her any more. I don't want to contemplate how she died or how much I was to blame. I'm done.

The moment of impact on hearing the news was ineffable for me too, which was a shortcoming and a relief. Not everything that can be felt can be told, not accurately.

In recounting his version of events, Jimmy hasn't intentionally gotten anything wrong, but he has added a layer or two of false colour.

When he wrote that, as he left Nicole behind at Whiterock, he felt 'nothing but contempt' for her, that isn't true. What he really felt was immense sadness and confusion, which manifested as the anger he called contempt. While he could hate himself, he never felt genuine hate for her. He wasn't capable of it.

And in his final conversation with her, he said the things he reported saying, or near enough, but according to him, he lost his temper, a misconception that causes him considerable guilt. As much as he must have hurt her, his tone was despondent, more of a whisper than a shout – I can't know the precise depth to which his words cut her because I can't read thoughts across a phone call, and I wasn't in her proximity again before her death. When he asked if their last night together meant nothing, she did, as he wrote, say, 'Yes,' but she followed that with 'It has to mean nothing.' He heard it *without understanding and forgot about it. He was unaware that, as heartbreaking as that night was for him, it was shattering for her.*

I wish he could have found a way to save her, for both their sakes. He didn't deserve to lose her, and it's obscene that she didn't get to have a longer and happier life.

Chapter Twenty-Five

Don't Get Carried Away

I

As harrowing as writing about Nicole was for Jimmy, it felt crucial too and he's glad to have a record of his memories of her, so that she doesn't seem so wholly erased. And yet a year and nine months after suspending his project – falling short of describing the manner of her death and its immediate aftermath – he hasn't read over anything he has written or said her name aloud to anyone, even though she remains rooted in his thoughts. He's a captive to his grief and an understanding of why he lost her is beyond his reach, just as helping him to understand is beyond mine.

October 2013

WHEN ART PASSES AWAY OF A STROKE, JIMMY FEELS guilty that he's not more distraught. He's certainly sad, but he doesn't view it as a tragic loss. Art was ninety-five, and while his arthritis was bad, he'd maintained his independence till the end. That he went as suddenly as he did was better, Jimmy thinks, than if his mind had started to go and he had to spend his last years in a retirement home. His had been a life well-lived and it wasn't the same as someone dying too soon.

Jimmy comes down to Rathbaile for the funeral, but he has an invitation to Finbar and Vicky's engagement party four days later, so he sticks around for that and doesn't give in to his temptation to bail on it with a 'need to grieve' excuse. He's the only other member of the old gang present. Seb is doing a play in London, for which he has been getting good reviews, and Brian is off teaching English in South Korea. However, Finbar and Vicky have no shortage of other friends, and their flat becomes crowded.

Securing a spot in the kitchen between the sink and the Formica counter, Jimmy initiates few conversations, but Finbar appears to be on a mission to introduce him to single women. Jimmy tests how quickly he can scare them off by flaunting his pincer. He also encounters a number of old school acquaintances. One guy, whose name he can't recall, sets eyes on him and exclaims, 'Jimmy Dice! Someone said you were dead!'

'That wasn't me. I'm indestructible.'

Jimmy tells himself that he would prefer to be left alone, but he could have departed by now without disappointing Finbar, who is surprised he has stuck around for as long as he has, and he doesn't have to stand at the party's busiest intersection.

A girl with short blonde hair is mixing a drink at the end of the counter. It takes him a moment to recognise her. 'Alice!'

She smiles, picks up her drink, and approaches him. He hugs her, one-armed. Stepping back, she says, 'Yeah, I haven't seen you since . . .' She remembers that it was his mother's funeral. 'It's been forever.'

'You look great. You've aged well. Sorry, you're not supposed to say that to someone in their twenties. Or really to anyone, of any age.'

While his phrasing was clumsy, he meant what he said. She's slimmer, and her skin has cleared up, but it isn't just that. When she was a teenager, she gave off the impression that she was frightened of being noticed. Now, her posture is looser and there's a self-assurance in her stare.

She raises her hand to put it through her hair, before stopping herself so as not to mess it up. 'No, it's a compliment. And I'm thirty-one, but thanks for forgetting that I'm only two years younger than you.' She looks him up and down. 'You've aged well too.'

He puts her appraisal down to kindness, suspecting that he's notably haggard for his age.

They catch up, pausing now and again to pour themselves drinks, all the while ignoring the other people coming in and out of the kitchen, which is enveloped by a mist of cigarette smoke – to keep from disturbing the neighbours, the windows are closed and Finbar has asked his guests to smoke inside rather than out.

After leaving school, Alice studied economics and accounting at Queen's, and lived in Belfast for another six years afterwards. Jimmy, who has never ventured north of the border, asks about her life there and whether, with her accent, she ever felt unsafe. She says, 'Any city can be chancy if you hang out in bad areas and say the wrong things to the wrong people. I kept out of conversations concerning religion and politics, and never had any problems. Belfast does have it dangers, though; it's not like it used to be, but "kneecap" is a common enough verb there. On the other hand, it has the best knee surgeons in the world. Practice makes perfect.'

She left Belfast to travel for eighteen months before moving back to Rathbaile. Jimmy asks, 'How was it to go from the jungles of South America to the humdrum here?'

'I wouldn't trade my experiences for anything, but being away made me realise how much I missed home. As for the charge of humdrum, bumping into you tonight is evidence for it not being that predictable.'

When she asks him delicately worded questions about what he's been up to, he briefly complains about his most recent monotonous office job, clarifying, 'but I knew what I was signing up for', then switches topics to Seb, who they both praise for pursuing his dream career.

Tilting his glass of whiskey, he gives the remaining drop a disappointed look. 'It's late and I've no reserves. Might be a sign to make a move.'

'That's loser talk. I'm practically all out too, but my flat is the next street over. Want to have another drink there?'

'If you're aiming to head home anyway, I'll escort you – I've heard kneecapping is on the rise in Rathbaile – but then I'm probably done for the night.'

'I'll change your mind as we walk.'

At her place, he agrees to have one for the road. Her living room is adjacent to her sleeping flatmate's room, so after taking a bottle of Southern Comfort and another of red lemonade from her kitchen, they go to her bedroom, where they can be louder. She makes them a suddy and red each, then leaves the bottles on her nightstand. She sits on her bed. Instead of sitting beside her, he pulls her swivel chair over from her desk and sits facing her.

He says, 'I've been gearing myself up to tell you I'm sorry. I know it was last century, but at my debs, I was a really bad date who didn't know how to conduct himself around attractive girls. It's a poor excuse for being a tongue-tied asshole.'

'That's sweet of you to say.'

'I'm not saying it to be sweet.'

She drinks and says, 'You weren't the only one who didn't know how to be. I never thought you were anything other than a nice guy, maybe a bit troubled. I probably made up the troubled part in my head, but I wanted to communicate with you and couldn't figure out how.'

'I considered myself troubled too. It may have been a pose, though, to make me seem deep somehow.' He laughs at himself. 'In reality, I was as shallow as the next guy.'

'How about now?'

'All I know now is how little I knew then. Everything else mystifies me.'

'Maybe making sense of everything is overrated.' She shifts forward on her bed, and puts her hand on his knee, the real one. 'I don't doubt that you have sufficient depth. After all you've been through, I can't imagine you've nothing going on beneath the surface.'

He drinks and suppresses an impulse to pull his knee away. 'Bad experiences don't equal depth. Sometimes things wash over you, leaving you with less rather than more.' He shakes his head. 'I might be lapsing into mawkish pretensions.'

'There's nothing wrong with just talking.'

'I appreciate it, but I don't really want to get into who I think I am these days.' She squeezes his knee. When he tenses, she withdraws her hand. 'Sorry, I'm tired and I've had too much to drink.' He raises his glass. 'Thanks for this.' He stands and deposits it unfinished on the nightstand. 'I should go.'

She stands too, and brushes the blanket flat where she'd been sitting. 'You don't have to walk all the way home. You could spend the night.'

Trying, and failing, to sound casual, he says, 'I can't. See, with Dad, and Granny staying with us now as well, I should be there when they wake in the morning.'

He's about to step out of her room when she says, 'You understand that I meant I have a spare couch on offer?' She smiles, and it's painful for them both.

As soon as he's on the street, he starts walking briskly towards his old home, half an hour away.

It isn't until he's on a country road, and nearing his neglected bed, that he unclenches his hands, leaving four crescent indentations on one palm, one on the other. He takes a bend, and the house comes into view at the bottom of the hill. He thinks about Eamon and Maggie inside, then about Art, and that puts his frustration into perspective. In the future, he can be stricter with himself.

As he's walking up the driveway, the curtains of Tighe's room, which is where Maggie is staying, appear to flutter. Jimmy stops and squints against the darkness. The curtains are motionless – and surely if his grandmother was awake she would have a light on – so he discounts the notion that he's being watched. Quietly he lets himself in the front door.

Maggie is awake. When she saw Jimmy approach the house, she drew the curtains closer because she didn't want to be caught indulging a fantasy. She opens the curtains again and sits in her wicker chair. It's Art she's waiting for. She knows her love won't return for her in this life, but at this late hour, it's easier to pretend.

II
January 1939–May 1942

When Maggie is seventeen, she dreams Art into existence. In the bedroom she shares with her two older sisters, she likes to stare out the window at the path weaving from the gate through the garden and imagine a man with soul-piercing eyes coming for her. He will understand life and know what to do with it, and will share his secrets so she can be fearless too.

The idea of this man has enabled her to endure the winter. It's still difficult to accept that her brother is dead, especially when they've only had a letter from a 'comrade' with a Spanish name who claimed to have seen him die. Her father tried to get some other confirmation, but the International Brigades had been disbanded and there was no obvious authority to contact. The house has been joyless for months, silence having settled in every room, interrupted at times by her parents arguing over who is more to blame for letting Stewart go.

Then, one day, while wrapping her rosary beads around her hands, Maggie sees a stranger – in a grey waistcoat and white shirt, his collar unbuttoned – standing with his hand resting on the gate, looking like he's confused about how to get to the other side. He casts his eyes to the sky and she deduces that this is a God-fearing man. As he opens the gate and walks up the path, she observes his dark, distinctly non-Irish complexion.

When she hears his knock on the front door, she moves away from the window and puts her ear to the bedroom door, holding the beads to her mouth. There's another knock, louder, but she doesn't dare go and answer it. Her father does, and she hears his voice and the stranger's, then two sets of footsteps receding into the house.

After a few minutes, curiosity trumps her shyness. Going down the hallway, she hears her mother crying. She enters the dining room.

Her parents, George and Niamh, are sitting at the dinner table with the stranger. His forearms are on the table, his visible hand fisted. Across from him, Niamh's eyes stream tears and George holds her hand, his expression somehow both haunted and relieved. There are two opened letters on the table, with three unopened ones stacked to the side.

His jaw tightening, George says, 'Thank you.' He notices Maggie. 'My dear.'

The stranger twists in his chair and their eyes meet. He stands, arrested by the blaze of her red hair. George says, 'This is my daughter, Maggie. And this is . . . I'm awfully sorry. It's Ar-toro?'

The stranger clasps Maggie's hand in his. 'Art is fine. A pleasure to meet you. Your brother was a hero.'

The following evening, he returns. Maggie is humiliated because he hardly looks at her during dinner, and although he asks her sisters questions, she's asked nothing. That night, she cries into her pillow while her sisters laugh about whether his moustache would tickle when he kisses. She doesn't realise that he was afraid that if anyone caught him looking at her, his eyes would betray his desire.

The next day, he arrives to talk privately with George. In the living room, he asks for permission to marry his daughter. George takes three guesses to figure out which one. He pours two tumblers of whiskey and they discuss his conditions. One: Art won't take Maggie to live in Argentina or 'anywhere outside the boundary lines of County Tipperary. Make that *South* Tipperary.' Two: George will be the one to ask her if this is what she wants. He cautions Art not to get his hopes up.

When her father relays the proposal, Maggie bursts into tears. 'Oh, yes!'

They are soon married in St Mary's church by Father Theodore. While Art doesn't show her the world, occasionally he opens her eyes. Sex is one eye-opener. At first, it's frightening and embarrassing, but this gives way to exhilaration. She thinks there's something wrong with her. In the dark, she asks him if it's immoral or unnatural that she likes it so much. He gently reassures her that it is moral and natural because they have vowed their commitment before God. She's still uncertain, but not enough to abstain.

Then she starts bleeding when she shouldn't be and it stings when she urinates. She goes to her doctor, who, after an examination, asks, 'How well do you know your husband?'

Bewildered, she says, 'He's my husband.'

The doctor shakes his head. 'I'm afraid he's going to have to come see me too.'

Art had given her gonorrhoea – being asymptomatic, he'd been unaware he had it. The couple are treated with colloidal silver, and are clear of infection in a week, but there are repercussions. When the doctor informed Maggie that she had contracted her illness during sex, he neglected to offer speculation about her husband's activities, and Art was unforthcoming about his encounters with Parisian prostitutes. She concludes that the gonorrhoea was God's way of telling her that sex for recreation could have dire consequences for their immortal souls. After Art can't convince her otherwise, he admits how he has always wanted a large family.

A youthful enthusiasm for brothels isn't his only secret. Stewart's ghost feels ever-present. While neither Maggie's parents nor her sisters have asked Art to elaborate beyond his pandering assertions that Stewart's bravery had saved others and his death had been quick, she wants to know more about his time in her brother's company. Art does his best to describe him in purely positive terms, keeping his answers short and changing the subject when given the flimsiest opportunity to do so.

Maggie maintains romantic ideas about war, accepting that it turns boys into men and that the sacrifices made by the soldiers – those on the 'good' side – are worth it. She's as sure that Stewart is safe in heaven as she is of her love for Art.

He has sworn to protect her illusions, not only because he believes he owes it to her, but also because he's trying to forget what he has seen and done, and if she ever grasps how it had been for him, that task would be all the more impossible.

This isn't a time conducive to ignoring the shadow of war. Six months after their wedding, the world descends into the deadliest conflict in history. Ireland has declared its neutrality, but there's a constant danger of being forced from that position, and even in conversations where it isn't mentioned, war is never much further away than the tip of the tongue. Art and Maggie pray for an Allied victory but support Irish neutrality too. She thinks Ireland mustn't fight against Germany unless England surrenders its tyranny over the imprisoned counties. He just wants to prolong his reprieve, knowing that he'll enter the war if Ireland does. He feels that he can't live among the Irish if he isn't willing to die alongside them.

Maggie spends much of the first three years of the Emergency pregnant. Art wants his sons' names to reflect their Argentine heritage, so he suggests both Luis and Emanuel. Liking the sound of them, she has no objections. But during her third pregnancy, she demands that this time she'll pick the name, and he consents.

On a Sunday afternoon, when she's eight months pregnant, Maggie is sitting with Art in their kitchen. His hand is on her round belly. The baby kicks, and seeing the excitement in Art's expression, she lets him know her secret: 'I think I'm having a boy, and I've chosen his name. Stewart!'

Art's jaw drops. She laughs, assuming she has delivered a good surprise. 'What do you think?'

'You can't. I mean no. I don't think so. No.'

'What better name could we give him?'

'We could be having a girl.'

'It's a boy.'

He puts his hand on hers, holding it against her knee. 'He should have his own legacy.'

She pulls her hand away. 'There's nothing wrong with giving him a name that's a tribute, and when he asks about it, we can tell him all about his uncle. It would be a name that could inspire him to have the courage of his convictions. An honour!'

'Please trust me on this. I can't allow it.'

She pushes herself to her feet using the table for support, lifts the washing hamper from a chair, and goes out, closing the back door with a theatrical slam.

Art fixates on the door, his hands clutching his kneecaps. She's as angry as he has ever seen her, but if he agrees, and it's a boy, he won't be able to look him in the eye, and every time he speaks his name, he might hate him a little. Maggie is retrieving the washing from the clothes lines and it would be prudent to let her cool down, then figure out some subtle means of persuasion later on; instead, furious with himself, he follows her.

She's at the further of the two lines. The closer one is stripped. The hamper is at her feet, shirts and trousers piled within. Her hands are on her hips, her head dipped. White bed sheets billow towards her, before gusting away. Her red locks are ripping through the air. He calls her name. She reaches for one of the pegs holding up a sheet.

A wish to be unburdened overcomes his self-control long

enough for it to escape: 'I did it! I killed him because someone had to stop him. I killed him.'

She pinches the peg and half the sheet droops. The peg falls and is lost in the grass. She brings a hand to her face, the other to her belly. He can't see her expression, but from behind, she appears to be in pain, with her shoulders hunching and her legs threatening to buckle. He waits for her to condemn him.

As the wind moans out and wheezes in, she raises her hands to the line. She pinches the remaining two pegs on the first sheet and drops it into the hamper. With the side of her shoe, she kicks the hamper over to the other sheet. She unpegs it and drops it in. Lowering herself to her haunches, she picks up the hamper. She walks steadily towards Art, without looking at him.

She comes to a halt. Her voice drained but determined, she says, 'I didn't . . . I can't hear you out here with this racket.'

He nods, gritting his teeth, and takes the hamper from her. They go inside.

They no longer talk about Stewart.

When their third son is born, Maggie tells Art that he will be named after the Taoiseach. He brushes a strand of hair from her cheek, kisses her there, and says he can think of no finer name.

III
October 2013

Eamon and Jimmy are silent while eating their porridge. When they're both chewing toast, Eamon asks, 'Good night?'

'Finbar and Vicky are going to be very happy together.'

Eamon smiles. 'The first of the old gang to take the plunge, eh? But not the last.'

'It might not be for all of us.'

'Everyone says that when they're young.'

'Some are right.'

Eamon shrugs with one shoulder, dismissing the line of conversation. 'Could you do me a favour?'

Jimmy bites off half the crust he's holding in his pincer. 'Name it.'

'Come to mass this morning. I told your granny yesterday that the three of us will go together. She still believes you're a regular.'

'It's easy to believe something if you want to.'

'She cares about the state of your soul, that's all. She thinks that if we want to get into heaven, we have to keep worshipping.'

Jimmy swallows his last piece of crust, then fishes the tea bag out of his cup and flips it over the edge. It lands on the saucer, where it lies like a sodden body bag. He scoops sugar into the tea. Stirring it, he says, 'I assume you don't believe that?'

'Why do you assume?'

'Because you've never seemed bothered by my lack of churchgoing, and I like to think that if *you* think my soul is doomed, it's not a matter of complete indifference.'

Eamon lifts his cup and blows on the surface of his tea, creating ripples. 'If heaven exists, I imagine getting in is about whether you've lived your life as a good person. So I don't worry about your soul.'

Jimmy bristles at the compliment, but doesn't argue. His father needs to believe in his children's goodness as much as his grandmother needs to believe they all attend mass. 'But how confident are you that heaven exists?'

'The idea of life after death resonates in my gut. That could be something like heaven. I trust in there being a greater good beyond what we can see, and for me, that's God. I like to believe that when people suffer, it's not randomly cruel or meaningless, and when we die, the smoke clears from our eyes and everything makes sense.'

Eamon smiles the wry smile of a man who can't take himself seriously once he has been caught waxing philosophical.

Jimmy says, 'That faith must help you deal with Abuelo's death.'

'What helps is not having regrets. Papá and I weren't big talkers, but not everything needs to be said to be understood. I was very proud of him and he had pride in me. For Mam, though, her faith is essential. It allows her to think of him as not being gone.'

'She told me she'll be dead soon as well, that it shouldn't bother me. She made it sound like she's looking forward to it.'

Jimmy fears that he has spoken too bluntly, but Eamon says, 'I'm sure she is. As different as Mam and Papá were, they were a team. When I was growing up, I never doubted that they were in love. It surprised me when I was an adult and saw that other marriages are often battles of attrition. I think she feels he was half of who she was, so until they're reunited, she's incomplete.'

'That's sad.'

'It's made less so for her because she sees it as a temporary situation.'

When Jimmy finishes his tea, he says, 'I'll put on the kettle again. Then maybe we could talk about something other than the inevitability of death.'

'You're on.' Eamon looks at his watch – it's nearly nine.

'I'll check with Mam which mass we're going to. I don't know why we haven't seen her yet. Unless you'd rather I make the tea and you want to knock on her door?'

'That's okay. I'll do the tea. You go.'

Chapter Twenty-Six

Trajectory

October 2013

IN A LONDON PUB THAT'S TOO BRIGHTLY LIT, MALCOLM Booth folds a damp beer mat, tearing it, then folds the halves, tearing it again. He squeezes the four parts in his fist and wearily focuses on the inquisitive eyes of the man opposite him. 'Diaz, I don't see why you're so calm.'

Tighe swallows the last bite of his sandwich and wipes the corner of his mouth with a napkin. 'We may not have behaved ethically, but that doesn't mean we did anything very wrong. Your sweating guilt only attracts negative attention.' He drinks his pint. 'Take a couple of days off. Get some sleep. Shag someone. Whatever floats your boat. This is a concerned friend talking. And you should really try to eat.'

Malcolm looks at the ham-and-cheese sandwich on his plate, which he'd pushed aside to make room for a pint and a glass of neat vodka, both now drunk. Although the bulge of his belly indicates a weakness for food, and the sandwich appears perfectly fine, his lip curls at the sight of it. 'I can't do serious time.'

'It won't come to that. Even if it did, we'll still be rich when we get out.'

Malcolm opens his hand and the pieces of beer mat fall to the table. 'They won't let us keep the money!'

'I don't know about you, but I haven't been keeping much of mine where they can find it. Look, this whole thing was a calculated risk, one calculated in our favour. Our SPV was legally valid. It's just how we benefited from it that inches into the grey. Grey areas can be argued out of. It's what a good lawyer is for.'

Malcolm pulls his hand through his thinning hair, like he's searching for an odious object buried in his scalp. 'If you were the tiniest bit worried, I'd be less so.'

His tone a mixture of vexation and amusement, Tighe says, 'Worrying won't help us. Bad things will either happen or they won't.'

Malcolm chuckles despairingly. 'You know, I've no idea where you get your balls from.'

'Here, let me show you something.' Tighe unclips the cufflink of his left shirtsleeve, tugs the sleeve to his elbow, and points at the small white scars on his forearm. 'These are from when I was sixteen.' He mimics a set of jaws with his right hand and grips his forearm with it. 'A dog did this, a big fucker. My little brother was attacked by two of them. Can you guess what happened when I arrived at the scene?'

'If they ate your brother, your story won't reassure me.'

'He survived, only slightly the worse for wear, because I killed the dogs. That was what the situation called for. I was bitten, but that was the chance I took. Do you know what I learned from the experience?'

'That fear is for pussies?'

'I was going to say I learned I could do anything when I acted without wasting time dwelling on the worst possible outcome. I prefer how you put it.'

Malcolm flicks his fingers derisively in the air. 'Sorry, Diaz, I don't believe you.'

Tighe rolls down his sleeve and, genuinely curious, asks, 'Which part? My skin bears the evidence.'

'I can imagine even the most submissive dog itching to take a bite out of your Paddy arse, and you murdering puppies too. It's the concept of you having a brother that I'm struggling with. Especially one who views you as his saviour.'

Tighe grins. 'You've got me.' From inside his jacket, hanging on the back of his chair, his smartphone rings. He takes it out and looks at the screen. 'Speak of the devil.' He stands and goes outside to take the call.

When he returns a few minutes later, Malcolm, drinking a fresh pint, asks, 'Bad news?'

Tighe nods. 'I need to go home again. I've another funeral.'

'So you're telling me that over morning tea, you and Dad conspired to do away with Granny, like cold-blooded killers.'

Jimmy sits against the windowsill, his palms flat on it, his fingers over the edge. He withholds a smile. 'That's not what I said. It's just odd how we were talking about her wish to die when it had already happened. It's a coincidence that's hard to ignore because it's disconcerting, not because it means anything.'

Tighe is sitting up on his bed, his interlocked fingers cushioning his skull from the headboard, his elbows pointed at Jimmy. They're both wearing black shirts and black trousers. Tighe says, 'If she didn't want to live, it's for the best.'

'People keep saying shit like that. As if the symmetry of Granny and Abuelo dying within such a short span is a sign of a harmonic order to the world. Doesn't it bother you that she took her last breath in the bed you're lounging on?'

'These are new sheets.'

There's an impatient knocking. Tighe gives Jimmy a look and so he opens the door. Elizabeth comes in, also dressed in black. On reflex, she assesses her brothers' expressions for any hint that they were discussing her. 'Ready?'

The three of them go to the living room. Eamon is standing by the fireplace, looking at the photos on the mantelpiece. Of the nine people featured – Paul, Grace, Simon, Art, Maggie, Eamon, Tighe, Elizabeth, and Jimmy – the dead outnumber the living. His shoulders stooped, Eamon wears a smile for his children. 'Anyone feel like driving?'

Jimmy, who has never learned to drive, ignores the question. Elizabeth looks to Tighe – she thinks he hasn't been pulling his weight since arriving yesterday and it's time he made himself useful. He says, 'I'd be glad to.'

Eamon takes his keys from his pocket and lobs them to Tighe instead of just handing them over. Tighe isn't expecting it, but, no matter, he catches them with one swift grab.

When the doorbell rings, Isabel puts her hand to her throat. On the second ring, she pulls her hand away as if her skin is too hot to touch. She has a hunch about who's there and knows she should pretend to be out; yet by the third ring, she's standing at her door. She doesn't look through the peephole for fear of giving herself away. She can sense him listening.

Tighe says, 'Come on, Izzy! It's been a hell of a day. Let me see you.' He drums his fingers on the door, lightly then harder.

'Please go, Tighe. You *know* I don't want you here. If you've ever cared, leave me alone.'

After a pause, he says, 'Don't make me talk to you through a door. We buried my grandmother today. It's been tough. I can leave, but tell me you don't want to see me to my face. Give me that much.'

'Tighe . . .'

'Obviously I've done something to upset you, so whatever it is, I'm sorry. I would never intentionally hurt you.'

She slides the chain into the slot on the door frame, unlocks the door, opens it a couple of inches, and steps back. Moving close to the opening, he meets her eyes. 'Why are you afraid?'

Her hand returns to her throat. 'You say you'd never hurt me, but whenever I see you, you hurt me a bit more than the time before. I'm a fool because I've been letting you get away with it since I was a teenager.'

He rests his forehead against the door frame. 'I'm a jerk. My feelings for you have never faded, and when I've had the chance to be with you, I've expressed myself clumsily. Last time I was here . . . My grandfather was dead and I went too far.'

She lowers her hand from her throat and lifts her chin, revealing the yellowed bruises around her windpipe. 'When I've gone out, I've worn scarves so no one will figure out you did this and write you off as some sort of fucking psychopath!'

He offers her his best remorseful stare. 'I knew I got a little rough. I didn't realise—'

Crying, she exclaims, 'Yes you did! I couldn't breathe and you kept choking me!'

'I'm ashamed. I was grief-stricken that day and, in the moment, I lost control. I'll never do anything like that again. Please, you can trust me.'

'How? Aren't you grief-stricken today as well?'

'Yes, but I've learned my lesson. Let me in, Isabel. I'll make it up to you.' He slips his fingers into the opening between the door and the jamb. 'If you want to slam the door and break my fingers, I'm at your mercy and I won't tell anyone. But if you're not going to do that, open the door. Whatever decision you make, you'll be in the right.'

She wipes her tears away and touches her hand to his. He retracts his hand from the opening. She closes the door, slides the chain out, and opens the door fully.

He smiles tentatively. 'With your permission.'

She nods. He enters and shuts the door.

She steps back against the wall. He raises his hand to her face. 'My being here with you isn't so bad, is it?'

Hopelessly, she says, 'No.'

His thumb under her chin, he angles her face upwards as he bends his knees. Ever so gently, he kisses her bruised throat.

It's nearly midnight when they set off in a rental car, Tighe driving and Jimmy in the passenger seat. As Rathbaile recedes, Tighe says, 'I won't be offended if you want to nap. I have the radio.'

Jimmy fidgets with the knob on the side of his seat until he manages to push it back to create more legroom. 'If I do that, you'll fall asleep and drive the car into a ditch. I'll wake up mangled by car parts, spitting out windshield fragments.'

'You know that I've never had an accident behind the wheel?'

'Then you should be concerned about the law of averages. I'm not the luckiest person to have next to you. Besides, you've had a long day, between the funeral, the reception, and your "errands". I'm sure it all adds up.'

'I'm not too tired, but I'll accept your offer of vigilance. Is there anything in particular you'd like to talk about?'

'Why don't you tell me something about your life that I don't know?'

Tighe gives Jimmy a probing look. 'How's this for a secret? I'm thinking of getting engaged soon.'

'Fuck off. Really? I didn't realise you were seeing anyone.'

'Technically, I'm not, but do you remember Veronica? I'm planning on getting back with her, and if things go well, I'll take it a step further.'

'What are her feelings on this?'

'She doesn't know yet. We haven't talked in a while.'

Jimmy laughs. 'So why? I presume you could have married her all those years ago.'

'I wasn't ready before. Abuelo and Granny's funerals have got me thinking. I want the support they had for each other. If it doesn't work out, I can always pull the plug.'

'You don't sound like you're in love.'

Tighe smirks at Jimmy. 'I doubt we quantify that the same way. I could love her enough to make it work, and she used to love me. She called her feelings an addiction. Any addict is prone to a relapse if nudged properly.'

'Your wedding vows will be sobering to all the romantics in the room.'

They're silent for a while. Jimmy presses the back of his hand to his window and feels the vibrations. He observes the fields, lined by stark trees, and the lonely roadside buildings, all darkly shrouded by a cloud-swollen sky. Everything they pass appears sluggish and eerie. As they drive along the N76, he's aware of their proximity to the property where he severed three fingers. Feeling his knuckle stumps tingle, he puts his pincer between his leg and the leather seat, and doesn't remove it until they reach the lights of Kilkenny town.

When they're driving out of Kilkenny, he says, 'You know that mutual support Abuelo and Granny had? Dad and Mam didn't have that. Or rather, it was only one-way.'

Disinterestedly, Tighe says, 'That's very perceptive of you.'

'Do you think he should have left her?'

'Yes. It's not how he ever saw it, and it wasn't totally her fault, but she was a millstone to him.'

Jimmy sighs. 'He loved her and he had all of us to think about.'

'If Dad could have viewed her objectively, he would have grasped that she didn't have it in her to be a mother and he'd have walked away before any of us came along. Love should always be conditional on things like respect and loyalty. If certain lines are crossed, the contract should be terminated by the aggrieved party, but it's all over with now anyway. It would be good for him to try again.'

'His feelings for her haven't changed.'

'Yeah, but what's the point of being in love with a ghost?'

'There isn't a point. It's how he feels.'

'I'm not saying he should lose his head over any woman who looks his way, but he's not the only widower or divorcee in Rathbaile. Why not take a measured risk and see what's out there? That goes double for you. I don't only mean your love life. I'm referring to the bigger picture too.'

'I don't know what you're talking about.'

'You've most of your life ahead of you, but you're on autopilot.'

'I'm in the process of deciding what I want. For now, I'm fine.'

'If I remember right, you used to have a reputation with your friends as a formidable gambler. They had a nickname for you.'

Jimmy stares at Tighe to gauge whether he's being mocked. There's no suggestion of a smile on Tighe's impassive face so he gives him the benefit of the doubt. 'It was "Jimmy Dice", but the name was wasted on me. All the risks I've taken have cost me something. I grew up and quit taking them.'

When they come to a red light, Tighe turns to Jimmy. 'It's interesting that you equate playing it safe with growing up.'

'You don't think that's the case, obviously.'

'I think playing it safe amounts to a feeble acceptance of only getting what life gift-wraps for you. There's more to be had.'

'This from Mr Conditional Love. How often have you gone out on a limb and put yourself in a vulnerable position with a woman?'

The light goes green. Tighe returns his eyes to the road ahead. 'That's almost a fair point, but the reason I haven't made myself vulnerable isn't due to a lack of guts; it's my nature. I don't have the capacity to rise to such highs or fall to such lows.'

'Everyone's capable of it.'

'You're mistaken. Don't stop believing it on my account, though. I'd hate to dispel your illusions.'

'Dickhead.'

Tighe laughs. 'I might be that. What I'm not is someone who's afraid to take chances. In the right situation, I tend to stick my neck out.'

'Bullshit. You've always been on the straight and narrow. If every risk you've taken is dependent on the situation being right, if they're all so well measured, your risks aren't that risky, are they?'

'If it seems like I haven't taken chances, it's only because when things go well, it can seem like the outcome was always a sure thing. But bad judgement often delivers roses and good judgement often delivers shit. You must know this. Life is a game. It exists to be played.'

'It isn't a game to me.'

'Well it is and it isn't. You know, we're not all that different, you and me.'

Jimmy raises an eyebrow. 'No?'

'Okay, maybe we are, but we *could* have been similar. Trade some of the key experiences of our lives and we might have ended up being more like each other instead of who we actually are.'

'I think I would always have been someone who hesitates, regardless of what was thrown my way. I suspect that you would've taken the setbacks I've had in your stride. In your approach to things you possess an inner trajectory that I don't have.'

Tighe muffles a yawn with his hand. 'You have too lofty an opinion of me.'

'I've always been stupid that way.'

Before long, Jimmy nods off, his head slumping to his shoulder. His awkward posture will leave him with a neck ache after they arrive in Dublin and Tighe wakes him. I'm not in the mood to venture inside Jimmy's frantic dreams, and my other mind-exploring option is even less appealing. So I watch them both from the outside.

Jimmy's mouth is open. His eyelids occasionally quiver. His pincer is clasped loosely within his whole hand.

Tighe holds the steering wheel with one hand and taps on it with the other. With his confident gaze, he has a trustworthy face, assuming you didn't know any better. I've always failed to understand him. Maybe I've refused to let myself. It's not that I can't cope with the bad memories of bad people. A lifetime of mind-reading has trained me in the art of detachment. He's an exception.

His rape of Nicole is just one more thing he has done that doesn't disturb him. He doesn't think about it a lot, but when I've been inside his mind, that memory has torn at me until I'm in his body, behind his eyes.

I see him dropping pills into Nicole and Jimmy's drinks; waiting for Jimmy to pass out; following Nicole into the guest room; closing and locking the door. He watches her for a few minutes, breathing her in and savouring his anticipation. And then his hands reach down to her and . . .

I've brutalised myself with each replay. I'll never see him as anything other than a monster. This man who sleeps easy every night; this man who has no regrets.

Afterwards, Nicole had a choice, to tell or not, but there was no solution. What if Jimmy had thought she was lying? What if he blamed her somehow? And if he did believe her, what if, when he looked at her, there was even a glimmer of disgust in his eyes?

No matter how much I wished for it, I couldn't tell her: it would have cut him up like nothing else could have – and no, he would never have gotten over it – but he would have believed her, and directed all his blame, and disgust, and rage at Tighe. If she had told him, she might have lived. Jimmy might have seen to it that Tighe wouldn't.

Chapter Twenty-Seven

Breather

December 2013

IF JIMMY COULD TURN BACK TIME, HE WOULD DO IT differently. He'd have told someone he was coming to Rathbaile and arranged a lift. Barring that, he'd have arranged a taxi. He definitely wouldn't have chosen to walk from the bus station to the house in this downpour, rolling a suitcase on the rutted tarmac with his pincer while lugging a hefty sports bag in his good hand and with his seam-straining rucksack strapped to his back.

His hair has been flattened by the rain, his eyebrows are waterlogged, and he has to squint to see the road ahead. He bares his teeth to the clouds and laughs. He'd been feeling dour throughout the bus journey, but that has given way to a good mood.

He makes it home and presses the doorbell. No answer. It's nine p.m. and he'd expected his father to be in, but he has his old keys so he lets himself in. Once he extricates his arms from his rucksack, it thumps to the carpet like an overturned turtle.

He goes into the kitchen and hangs his soaking jacket on a chair. In the fridge, he finds six bottles of beer, snugly bunched together and glistening.

As he's guzzling one, he hears: 'You're not the most discreet of intruders.' Eamon is standing inside the door, his jacket folded over his arm. 'To what do I owe the surprise?'

Jimmy sets his beer on the counter. 'I wanted a break from Dublin. Is it cool if I stay for a bit?'

'You never have to ask.'

'I'll throw my stuff in my room. Then do you want to have a beer with me? One of *your* beers?'

Eamon pats Jimmy's arm on his way to the fridge. 'You're generous.'

A few minutes later, Jimmy, having changed into a dry T-shirt and shorts, retrieves his beer from the kitchen and enters the living room. Eamon is in his armchair, holding a beer against his stomach, his feet on the footrest. Jimmy sits on the couch. Eamon says, 'What's the story?'

Jimmy sips his beer. 'My landlord informed me a month ago that he wanted his flat back. I didn't sort out somewhere new as promptly as I should have.'

'Couldn't Elizabeth have put you up? Or a friend?'

'I didn't want to bother anyone. It struck me that if I came home, I could save on rent for a few weeks. Unless you'd like me to contribute something, which I can do.'

Eamon dismisses the suggestion with a wave of his hand. 'Does this mean you've been out of work?'

'No. I've started a job editing business transcripts over the internet. I can do it from here.'

'Is it challenging?'

Jimmy laughs. 'It keeps the wolf from the door, nothing else. Where were you tonight?'

'Having dinner with friends. I've a more active social life than you might think.'

'I haven't claimed otherwise.'

Eamon sips his beer and smiles at him. Jimmy says, 'Do I have something on my face?'

'It's just good to see you.'

'You too, Dad.'

Two nights later, Jimmy is in a sparsely populated, shadowy pub called Henley's. He has never been here before, so there's less chance of bumping into acquaintances than in the average Rathbaile pub. He has yet to drink any of his pint. He wills his mobile to ring, for it to be Alice and for her to cancel.

Then she walks through the door, skimming her fringe away from her eyes with two fingers. From across the room, they smile at one another, but they don't make eye contact again until she's at the table. He greets her warmly and asks her what she wants to drink.

At the bar, he gathers himself. He already feels like he's misleading her into believing he's someone he's not. When he phoned her, he'd made going for a drink sound casual, but it couldn't be, not when she's the first girl he has asked out since Nicole. He hopes that doesn't somehow become apparent to her and then she feels a need to humour him.

He orders a gin and tonic. The bartender, who is bald and has the beginnings of a double chin, passes an impressed glance in Alice's direction. 'That for yer one?'

Jimmy nods, thinking of how he could do with a shot. When the bartender places the drink on the bar, he's grinning as if he possesses great insight into Jimmy's evident nerves. He appears on the verge of volunteering advice, but Jimmy gives him a look of warning. The bartender says, 'Good luck.'

Jimmy sits opposite Alice and swigs his pint. 'I'm glad you could make it.'

She prods the ice cubes in her drink with the straw. 'It's not every evening that I have the opportunity to meet up with so elusive a figure as Jimmy Diaz. If nothing else, I'll get to update Seb on how you're doing. We Skyped earlier. He said to tell you he'll be home in a couple of weekends, in case you're sticking around for a bit.'

'I'm pretty sure I will be.'

'Really? He'll be pleased. He said you're not the best at keeping in touch.'

'I hope he doesn't think I'm avoiding him.'

'He might.'

'Of all the people I'm avoiding, I'm avoiding him the least.'

She laughs. 'He'll feel comforted by that. Why do you expect to be around? Don't you have commitments in Dublin?'

'Not really. I guess I'm at a point where I don't quite know what to do with myself so I decided to come home, give myself a breather. Maybe even turn over a new leaf. What that would entail, your guess is as good as mine.'

She sips through her straw. 'Jimmy, are you having an existential crisis?'

With a self-deprecating smile he says, 'I shouldn't admit that on my first drink, should I? It's more of a third- or fourth-drink confession. Let's talk about you.'

'What would you like to know?'

'Everything. How's work? Are you doing what you want to be doing?'

'Yeah. Most people might find accountancy boring, but I like working with numbers. They've a reliable logic. It does feel odd sometimes, though, having a career, being a professional. I'm in danger of being mistaken for an adult. I've a fucking retirement plan. Within the next couple of years, I'll be looking to buy instead of rent. I'll have mortgage payments.'

'Jesus. I suppose marriage is up next. Then what? Two and a half kids? Two thirds of a dog?'

She leans forward, feigning concern. 'Is that a proposition? I'd have thought that's more of a fifth- or sixth-drink conversation filler.'

'Guys like me shouldn't get married. You could do much better.'

'That remains to be seen. And what do you mean, guys like you?'

'Oh, y'know, rebels who live outside society's rules, outlaws.'

'Right. Well, I don't see myself as the marrying type. For me, the situation would have to be close to perfect. I'd hate to settle. It's kind of the same with kids. They're fine, but I wouldn't intentionally bring one into the world unless I had an extremely solid marriage, so I don't rate my chances of becoming a member of the motherhood cult. It's not like I need any of these things. I'm happy alone.'

He raises his pint. 'To being alone.'

They drink to that. 'I do want a dog. The full three thirds.'

He's getting on with her more easily than he'd expected, but instead of that being a relief, it causes him guilt. He doesn't, however, seriously consider bringing the night to an early end.

There are some awkward moments.

On returning from the bar with their third drinks, he sets his pint down too hard, spilling foam on the table and on his pincer. He says, 'I'm such a klutz! All left foot, all thumbs.' He laughs, but stops on recognising how hesitant Alice's laughter is. He excuses himself to grab some napkins from the bar and thinks of how Nicole wouldn't have had the same reservation, a comparison he chastises himself for making. He doesn't mention his deficits of hand and leg again.

When they're on their fourth drinks, Alice tells him about a funeral she went to recently for an old classmate who had been killed in a car crash. They weren't close, but it was her first funeral of a peer and it was unnerving: 'There were people there, especially her parents, who you could just see will never really get over it.' The subject doesn't make Jimmy uncomfortable until she says, 'Sorry. I don't want to bring the mood down and, well, funerals might be the last thing you want to hear about.'

'I came to terms with my grandparents' deaths when they happened. I'd like you to feel you can speak your mind.'

He's aware that she was referring to more than them, and she's aware he knows that, but she doesn't clarify what she meant.

After last orders, he offers to walk her home, and as they step outside, she takes his hand. When they arrive at her door, she defuses his angst over whether to kiss her goodnight by inviting him in for a nightcap. He says yes.

He opens his eyes to see her beside him, facing away, wearing only black knickers. His heart starts pounding so he closes his eyes. His heart rate slows. He opens his eyes again. She's still there.

He's wearing only his boxers and his liner over his stump. Cold, he crosses his arms and grips his shoulders. His mouth tastes of beer, but he can't produce enough saliva to swallow it down. His eyes are light-sensitive and he has a mild head-ache, which hasn't blunted his alertness.

He uncrosses his arms and, lifting his elbows into the air, presses his palms to his eyes. Alice rolls on to her back, then on to her other side, pushing her face under his elbow and against his collarbone. He lowers his arm around her shoulder because there's nowhere else to rest it.

Shifting against him, she says, 'Bet you've been thinking about sneaking off.'

Jimmy lies, 'It hadn't occurred to me.'

He hugs her, trying to steal a few moments without looking her in the eye. 'I'd kiss you if my mouth didn't taste like the inside of a coffin.'

'We don't need to test whose mouth tastes worse. Let's wait until our breath isn't lethal.'

'Okay.'

'There are other things we can do. To wake up . . .'

Their hands are active. He gets excited, too fast.

He says, 'Would it be a terrible cliché if I apologised and told you that normally I have more self-control?'

'Spare us both that. Play your cards right and you might get another chance.' She leans over the side of the bed and picks up her bra. As she's putting it on, she says, 'Hungry?'

While she prepares brunch, he showers, turning the dial as far to the red as he can bear. When he steps on to the plastic mat, steam is rising from his skin. He dries off and gets dressed. Staring at his reflection in the mirror, he silently tells himself that this could all be okay.

In the hallway, he's met by the slightly burnt smell of a fry-up. Alice calls out, 'Jimmy? You'd better come see this.'

He discovers her in the living room adjoining the kitchen, standing in front of the TV, which is turned to the news. She's holding a spatula and is seemingly oblivious to the trickle of grease that's threatening to drop to the carpet.

He says, 'What's wrong?'

Sounding like she doesn't quite believe herself, she looks at him, then back at the TV. 'They're talking about your brother. He's done something.'

If I had a face, I would be smiling.

Chapter Twenty-Eight

What Was Said and Left Unsaid at the Wedding

I
December 2013

AT FIRST, IT'S UNCLEAR TO JIMMY HOW MUCH TROUBLE Tighe is in, but that's undeniably a photo of him filling the TV screen. Wearing a smartly tailored suit, he looks debonair, if perhaps a little too sure of himself; borderline cocky actually. The caption at the bottom of the screen states *Massive fraud at venerable investment bank*, which isn't too encouraging, but in voice-over, the newsreader is describing Tighe's accomplishments: his 'meteoric' ascent through the ranks at Worth & Walcott, culminating in his promotion to chief financial officer; the reputation he has earned for having a nose for lucrative business deals, and his uncanny aptitude for devising 'creative solutions' in order to meet quarterly financial targets.

Then the newsreader's tone veers from neutral to tart as she says, 'But Diaz's ambition, it seems, and his *greed*, knew no bounds.'

Without looking away from the TV, Jimmy takes a step towards Alice's couch. Reaching his hand out behind his back, he grasps air until he locates the cushioned armrest and sits

358

on the edge of it, arching forward. Alice quickly goes into the smoky kitchen, where she tosses her grease-dripping spatula on the counter, turns off the cooker, and moves the frying pan off the hob, calming the sizzling of the sausages she'd been preparing. Re-entering the living room, she stands at Jimmy's side.

A clip is shown of Malcolm Booth, tears leaking down his cheeks and his chin tucked into his chest, as he's escorted from his house by two police officers, gruffly tugging him by his elbows. Another clip follows, of the CEO of Worth & Walcott, a white-haired and harried-looking man, addressing a press conference: 'I take full responsibility for trusting someone who did not deserve my trust. I condemn Tighe Diaz's actions. I condemn *him* without reservation.'

The news report returns to the photo of Tighe, in close-up now, with a focus on his eyes, which appear shiftier as the newsreader details his misdeeds.

After the global recession hit, Worth & Walcott's share price was in danger of plummeting, so Tighe set up a special-purpose vehicle titled 'Ripper', a limited company that debt could be sold to without control of the assets standing behind that debt being relinquished. Malcolm Booth was the director in charge of overseeing Ripper, in partnership with a charitable trust for underprivileged children, Leg-Up. Tighe was obligated to protect the bank's interests and Malcolm was obligated to protect the trust's, but in practice, Tighe was overpaying Ripper by huge amounts, and he and Malcolm were embezzling the proceeds. Despite the financial drain, the bank's debt was being repeatedly postponed, keeping its books, in the short term, better balanced and the share price meeting its targets.

This went on for years, but the same rot of incompetence that had allowed Tighe's actions to go overlooked wasn't isolated, and eventually numerous departments within Worth & Walcott were haemorrhaging money. With bankruptcy looming, auditors were brought in and they uncovered the deception. While Tighe was resolutely evasive when questioned about the irregularities in his dealings, Malcolm confessed to being a willing stooge in the scheme and agreed to testify against Tighe in exchange for leniency on his sentencing. Only days ago, with his arrest imminent, Tighe fled, and authorities believe that he's no longer in the UK.

The report concludes with the newsreader calling Tighe 'the most brazen culprit behind why so many of Worth & Walcott's shareholders have lost their life savings, and a man callous enough to steal millions from children'. Then, cheerfully, she says, 'And now for the weather.'

Jimmy stands, his back cracking as he straightens his spine. Looking sidelong at Alice, he says, 'What the fuck have I just watched?'

The next day, two detectives from the Met's Economic and Specialist Crime Command come to Rathbaile to question Eamon, Jimmy, and Elizabeth about Tighe's whereabouts. They also examine their bank accounts in search of stashed funds – there's nothing to find.

Eamon, especially, is humiliated by it all. He believes he can see the judgement in the detectives' eyes of what a poor father he must have been, and he agrees with that. Maybe his pride in Tighe's independent streak led him to be too hands-off when he was a boy. Eamon had assumed he didn't need to spell out the difference between right and wrong, that Tighe, as bright as he was, could learn for himself. He wasn't mistaken there: Tighe didn't struggle to understand the difference; he just didn't much care.

So why did Tighe do it? He was already a millionaire through his legal earnings, but you see, he wanted to find out how much he could get away with. It's what made him feel alive.

Maybe it's still how he feels alive. He's no longer within my reach and it's unlikely that he'll be back unless it's in handcuffs. While I'd love to be wrong, if I could bet, I'd wager against his capture. I think he has slipped into another identity in a faraway country, and aided by money and guile, he's living an unjustly comfortable life – and in my view, any domicile better than a cramped cage would be unjustly comfortable. He'll always have to look over his shoulder, though. I hope with every passing day he grows more fearful of being found out and hunted down.

II
March 2014

Jimmy and Alice are short on time when they pull into St Mary's car park, but they still take a few moments before exiting her car. She switches off the engine and slips her feet into her high heels, matching her green dress with a sash around the waist. She looks at him. He's wearing a navy waistcoat, white shirt, and black bow tie. He's staring out the passenger window, his elbow propped against the door, pincer pressed to his chin. She puts her hand on his thigh. 'You okay? You barely slept.'

'Who needs sleep? C'mon. The festivities await.'

They get out. He opens the back door, retrieves his suit jacket, and puts it on. He takes her hand. She clasps her other hand to his arm, her handbag hanging from her forearm. As they walk towards the crowd milling outside the church, she says, 'You know that, regardless of everything I said last night, my opinion of you hasn't suffered.'

'It's okay. You were right. Let's take our minds off it, though. If there's another conversation we need to have, we can wait till tomorrow.'

She halts, so he does too. '*Is* there something else to be said?'

'We shouldn't be trying to figure that out now.'

She squeezes his hand and they start walking again, picking up their pace.

Most of the people are heading inside, but Finbar is standing by the entrance, in no apparent rush, with his two other groomsmen, Seb and Brian. Brian is the first to see Jimmy. 'What fucking time do you call this?'

Jimmy says, 'Sorry, Finbar. It was all Alice's fault. Hair and make-up, y'know?'

Alice says, 'Don't believe his lies.' She hugs Finbar. 'You look very handsome. In fact you all do. Even my brother.'

Seb says, 'My day is made.'

She nods at Finbar. 'Lads, keep his feet warm.'

After she has gone in, Jimmy shakes Finbar's hand. 'How's the ice in your veins, dead man?'

Finbar smiles uneasily. 'So long as Vicky doesn't come to her senses before I jam that ring on her finger, I'll be grand.'

Jimmy asks Seb, 'Remember the ring?'

Seb says, 'I'll check that I haven't forgotten when the priest prompts me to hand it over. What's a wedding without a bit of dramatic tension?'

Brian says to Finbar, 'It's not too late. Seb could distract everyone with his acting skills and you could do a legger.'

Seb says, 'You only have to ask.'

Finbar says, 'For the laugh, I'm going through with it. What's the worst that could happen? It's only a life sentence.'

Jimmy had thought standing in plain sight of a full congregation would be nerve-racking, but it's not so bad. Sometimes being tired helps. He can't make out Vicky's expression behind her ghostly veil, but he can see how tightly she's clutching her bouquet. While Finbar stares besottedly at her, a line of sweat, shining under the church lights, curves from his temple to his cheek.

As Father Ivor reads aloud from his open bible, pausing intermittently to cough, Jimmy looks away from the happy couple to Brian and Seb.

Brian appears as anxious as Finbar, but for different reasons. Finbar is from a religious and conservative family, and Brian knows that he has been the subject of snide commentary among a significant proportion of those assembled. After living abroad for years, he has moved to Dublin, for now anyway, where he shares a flat with his Korean boyfriend. Finbar made a point of extending a wedding invitation to Ji-hoon too, telling Brian, 'I'd be offended if you felt like you couldn't bring him.' Brian was going to, but as the date drew closer, he changed his mind – he didn't want Ji-hoon to have to put up with any small-mindedness, and more so, he was dreading the added scrutiny. Now, though, he wishes he'd been braver.

Seb, meanwhile, looks calm and collected. Jimmy assumes that the only thing on his mind is how pleased he is for Finbar and Vicky. A few weeks ago, Finbar explained to Jimmy, unnecessarily, that he'd made Seb his best man because 'He's the only one of the three of you who's been around much the last few years.'

Jimmy responded, 'Even if he'd been around the least, you couldn't have done better.'

That was on Finbar's stag, in Cork. Initially, Jimmy hadn't been very up for it – he was stressed about Tighe and by his burgeoning relationship with Alice. Helpfully, there was a copious amount of drinking throughout the weekend.

His most poignant memory from it was a conversation he had with Finbar in one of the many pubs on their crawl. In the early years of their relationship, Finbar had been serially unfaithful to Vicky, but he told Jimmy that while he understood he'd hurt her badly, and that knowledge had hurt *him*, he still didn't regret it. Leaning in to Jimmy's ear, he said, 'As fucked up as it might sound, I would never have realised how much I love her if I hadn't been with other women. Do you get it? I just, y'know, really love her. So much, Jimmy, so much. I'd do anything for her, do y'know what I'm saying? Do you get it?'

Jimmy replied, 'You're saying you love her.'

'Yes! More than anyone, you *know* what I'm talking about!'

Despite an odd urge to punch Finbar, Jimmy gripped his arm and said, 'You'll do Vicky proud. You *deserve* this.'

And now Finbar lifts Vicky's veil and kisses her. There are cheers, and they laugh with relief. Jimmy looks at Alice, standing a few rows back. Her smile has a certain melancholy to it. He averts his eyes.

His elbow on the bar, and with a pint in hand, Jimmy surveys the function room. The caterers are clearing tables and the DJ is setting up. The guests, and there are over a hundred, project a particularly optimistic brand of merriness. Jimmy says, 'It's strange being here again.'

Brian is next to him, leaning with his back against the bar. He's halfway through his pint, while Jimmy has only drunk a sixth of his. Brian says, 'In Ashburnham or the fecking town in general?'

'Ashburnham, though I suppose this is just a part of the greater whole. This place hasn't changed.'

'Places don't change in a hurry unless the people who own them do. There has to be a concerted effort.'

'Are you talking about Ashburnham or the town?'

Brian shrugs. 'Both. The town more maybe. I'm just talking.'

'Sometimes change can happen fast and without much effort. Accidents play a part.'

'What I said might not be true, but it sounds like it could be. That's close enough. Pretending to be wise is useful. Considering yourself wise isn't.'

'Another truism?'

'Sure. My gift to you.'

'Maybe it's more different than I think. The lighting is less severe. The wallpaper used to be a creamy colour. But I feel so drastically removed from who I was as a teenager that it makes this place seem like it's still in the nineties.'

'I don't feel like I've changed much.'

'You don't?'

Brian drinks and says, 'I'm more honest. I'm older. That's all. I've a lot of the same chips on my shoulder. I was always queer, Jimmy, and I'm glad about it. Just because I've changed in other people's eyes, it doesn't mean I'm not fundamentally the same.'

'Fair enough. Look, back when I heard you'd come out, I was surprised, but I hope you feel that I've always been in your corner. You desire who you desire, right? If I've ever been at all weird around you, it's only because I've been over-concentrating on not acting that way.'

Brian's smile becomes more amused. 'You're just afraid to judge me, or anybody you know, because we might all turn around and judge you back.'

'Do you really believe that?'

Brian ponders it, then says, 'Yeah, but it's true about most people, possibly even me.' Seeing Jimmy's frown, he says, 'I haven't noticed you acting weird, other than your usual weirdness. The only thing you've done that's surprised me is moving back here. I was under the impression that you were even more at odds with Rathbaile than I was.' He drinks, nearly finishing his pint. 'I guess your family shit isn't so wonderful right now.'

'I haven't really moved back, and as noble as it would be if I was staying for Dad's sake, it's more like I came for a visit and I've been slow to devise an exit strategy.'

'What about Alice? Is it serious?'

'She's a great girl. I think very highly of her.'

'I'll take that as a no.'

'Let's file it under "a conversation for another day", okay?'

Brian catches the eye of the bored-looking bartender and raises his glass to indicate he wants the same again. He points questioningly at Jimmy's pint, but Jimmy shakes his head. Brian says, 'My only advice is don't get trapped in the wrong relationship.'

'Neither of us would allow that to happen. Especially not her.'

The DJ plays his first song: 'If You Leave Me Now' by Chicago. Finbar leads Vicky on to the dance floor, the perimeter of which is swiftly enclosed by gushing guests. The newlyweds dance, holding each other close. As he and Jimmy cross the room, Brian laughs into his hand and receives a dirty look from one of Finbar's aunts. Jimmy kicks his heel. Brian says, 'What? They've picked a song about breaking up as their fucking wedding song.'

Jimmy whispers, 'Finbar told me they were listening to it when they "consummated" their feelings.'

Brian almost spills his pint as the lyric plays: 'When tomorrow comes we'll both regret the things we said today.'

When the song ends, there's a scattering of applause. 'Every Breath You Take' by the Police is next, and as misty-eyed couples take to the floor, Brian's eyes light up. Jimmy says, 'Don't start.'

Noticing Seb and Alice breaking away from the edge of the dance floor and walking to a table, Jimmy says to Brian, 'Let's go sit.'

'I'll be over soon. I want to talk to Finbar, find out how many of these songs he's masterminded.'

Jimmy moves around people and stray chairs. He's nearly at the table when he hears, 'Jimmy!'

Turning, he finds himself face to face with a woman who once saw him naked. She's wearing a loose-fitting navy dress and a silver jacket. Her hair, dark brown now, is tied back and her mascara is heavy around her eyes. 'Isabel!'

She laughs. 'It had occurred to me that I might bump into you.'

'I didn't see you earlier.'

'I've only just arrived. I don't know the couple very well. I mean, I used to work with Vicky at Hogan's, but the friends I'm with know her much better.' Her smile fades when she sees his pincer. 'I heard about your hand. I'm sorry.'

'Don't be. I had more fingers than I strictly needed.'

'I heard that you've had a cruel time generally. Your girl-friend . . . I was sorry to hear about her too.'

Not quite meeting her eyes, he says, 'She wasn't really my girlfriend. We ended things before she passed away, and it was all a long time ago.'

'Still, it's awful.' Touching her fingertips to her neck, she says, 'Sorry, I haven't seen you in yonks, and on an occasion like this, here I go blackening the mood.'

Smiling, he says, 'By all means, blacken away.'

'Listen, I'd better go, but I have to ask, have you heard from Tighe?'

'No, have you?'

'No.' She looks left and right, then steps closer. 'I'd like to talk to you about him. Not tonight, though. Could we meet sometime during the week? Maybe Monday?'

She takes out her phone and he gives her his number. As she's walking away, he realises that there was something off in the final look she gave him. She was scared.

He goes and sits with Alice and Seb, aware that they've been watching him. As casually as she can, Alice says, 'Who was that?'

Jimmy sips his pint. 'My old babysitter, and an ex of Tighe's, back in the day.'

Seb says, 'Didn't you used to have a crush on her?'

'I wouldn't call it that. I don't know if my voice had even broken.'

Alice says, 'A crush is a crush at any age. It looked like you were exchanging numbers.'

Her expression doesn't betray any jealousy, but Jimmy is mindful to tread lightly. 'She wants to talk to me about Tighe. I couldn't say no. I owe him that much.'

Seb says, 'Think she knows something?'

'My guess is that she only wants to know what I do, which isn't a lot. It'll be a short conversation.'

Alice drinks her gin and tonic, then stands. Jimmy says, 'Where are you going?'

She shakes her glass. 'Top-up.'

'I'll buy you a drink.'

He's about to rise, but she says, 'That's okay. I see Rosie at the bar and we have some gossiping to do. She'll be less forthcoming if you're present. Besides, someone has to keep Seb company.'

Seb sighs. 'That's true. Who knows what I might do if I've no one to talk to for five minutes?'

Alice says to Jimmy, 'Buy me a drink later. And remember, you promised me a dance.'

Jimmy waits until she's gone, then says, 'Alone at last. How come you don't have a date for this anyway?'

Seb says, 'I am seeing someone, but it's at a very early stage so I didn't want to bring her to a wedding. The whole thing might crack if placed under too much pressure from external forces.'

'Sounds promising.'

'I don't know what it is.' Before Jimmy can ask another question, Seb stands and says, 'I want to smoke. Bring your pint.'

They go outside, where they sit on a wall bordering the car park, with their backs to Ashburnham. Seb produces a packet of cigarettes from his jacket, lights one, and takes a drag. As he puffs out a cone of smoke, he observes Jimmy's amusement. 'What?'

'I thought you were only a social smoker.'

'This is social. You're here.'

'I'm not smoking.'

'It's still technically social.'

'I've seen you drunkenly bum cigarettes from people before, but I didn't know you'd started buying.'

Seb laughs. 'Are you my mother?'

'No, I'm a mere groupie, attempting to grasp what makes you tick. It's odd to be taking it up at your age.'

'Way to piss on my parade. Would you feel better if I told you it was for a role?'

'It would.'

'Then let's pretend.'

In silence, Jimmy sips his pint and Seb finishes his cigarette. As Seb is lighting another, Jimmy says, 'Brian was wondering why I'm spending so much time here. There's not much love lost between himself and Rathbaile.'

'I can relate.'

'Really? I understand how he feels, but I would've thought that whenever you're home, you get some nice ego boosts. I'm almost jealous of your popularity.'

'Don't be. It'd be different if my career was taking off, but I'm floundering. When I'm doing that in London, though, people don't pay attention. Nothing makes me feel like more of a failure than being home and everyone asking, "When am I going to see you in something?"'

'No one thinks of you as a failure. Everyone admires your drive.'

'It hasn't amounted to much.'

'It's amounted to you being you. That's something.'

Seb smiles mockingly at Jimmy. 'Are you getting soft on me?'

'Fuck off. Look, most people talk about going for what they really want to do, but they're full of shit. You're the least full-of-shit person I know.'

'Mind if I steal that one for my tombstone? I'm not sure how much longer I'll pursue it. The last play I was in, I did it for free. A man's gotta eat.'

'What would you do instead?'

'No idea.' Seb takes a drag, then puts out his cigarette on the wall and flicks the butt to the ground. 'How about you? What are your plans?'

'Everyone keeps asking me that. Right now, my goal is to get through this pint.' Jimmy drinks. 'After that, I'll work on the next one. I'll think about the future in the future.'

'Good luck with that. And how are things with my sister?' In response to Jimmy's wary expression, Seb says, 'I ask because she's in a strange mood. Maybe it's nothing.'

'We weren't going to say anything – we didn't want to draw attention away from Finbar and Vicky – but we broke up last night.'

Without much conviction, Seb says, 'Sorry to hear it.'

'You don't sound surprised.'

'Should I act it for you?'

Jimmy laughs. 'Not for my sake, no.'

'Who broke up with who?'

'She did the breaking. It was my fault, though. Let's be honest, I don't deserve her, do I?'

Seb chooses his words carefully. 'If you felt about her the way I suspect she feels about you, you would, but you don't, so no.'

'I wanted to.'

'That's never enough.' Seb jerks his head towards Ashburnham. 'I'll buy you that pint you said is standing between you and thinking about the future.'

The night before the wedding, as they lay in bed, a foot of space between them, Alice said to Jimmy, 'There's a third person in our relationship.'

'Who?'

'You know who I mean.'

He sat up. She did too. 'I've never even talked to you about Nicole. I've kept her away from us.'

'No you haven't. I can see you've tried. I don't think you can help it.'

'She's in my past. You're my present, Alice.'

'What about your future?'

'I can't go any faster than a day at a time. I've been derailed too often. I can't promise you something when I don't know. I do care about you.'

'I believe you, but there's a level above caring and you'll never get there with me. If I'm being honest with myself, that's what I think.'

'Alice.' He kissed her. She returned it at first, then stopped.

Her hands on his shoulders, she said, 'When we're having sex, you're so far away it's like you're not with me at all. It's in your eyes. You're always with her.'

'That's not true.'

'I get that you don't want it to be, but it is.'

'You make it sound like I'm being unfaithful to you somehow. How can you count a ghost against me?'

'Because she's more real to you than I am. It's just that you can't communicate with her any more. If you could reach beyond the grave and talk to her, even once, I think you'd choose that over a lifetime of talking to me as often as you like.' When he said nothing, she said, 'Tell me I'm wrong, Jimmy. Even just tell me it would be a hard decision.'

He put his arms around her. She rested her head on his shoulder, her face turned away from him. He whispered, 'I'm so sorry.'

They talked through the night. When she broke up with him, he didn't object.

He didn't tell her that, ever since losing Nicole, he has been drowning, and while there were moments with Alice when she made him feel like he was coming up for air, he still feels doomed. He's upset it's over, but also relieved, because she's no longer in danger of being dragged to the depths with him.

Chapter Twenty-Nine

Remember Me As I Lived

Alice was right, of course, that Jimmy would have given her up, or done anything, to communicate with Nicole. He thinks about it all the time: seeing her again in some kind of afterlife, although the dimension itself is poorly imagined because all that matters to him is that she would be there and that they could speak freely. She would forgive his mistakes and she would let him love her again. This fantasy has never brought him any pleasure, or even solace. It has tortured him, because he has never been able to convince himself that an afterlife could be possible.

This is partly why he has had such minimal curiosity about me – to his mind, there was nowhere that I could have conceivably retreated to once my flicker of a life was snuffed out, and considering that I hadn't lived long enough to possess an individuality, what was there for him to contemplate?

The only life after death he believes in is the one he's been living since losing Nicole.

His relationship with Alice was a sign of progress for him, at least until his struggles with his past undermined it. His desire to make sure he doesn't commit a similar mistake in the future spurs him to write another, final, journal entry about Nicole.

It's late, the night after Finbar's wedding, and Jimmy has countered his grogginess from that with three cups of coffee. In his old bedroom, he's ready to begin.

9/3/2014

I want to complete my testimony so that I'll be done, done, done. Afterwards, everything will be okay, right? Right. Here I go.

January 2002

At nine a.m. on Saturday the 19th, a twelve-year-old girl was exploring Whiterock with her eight-year-old brother. At the end of the beach closest to the steps there was a stone shelter, opened out to the sea. To its left was a cluster of large rocks that extended around a corner and took the brunt of the lashing of the waves.

The girl was in the shelter reading the graffiti on the walls but didn't find anything worthy of her attention. When she surveyed the beach and located her brother, his knees in the sand as he constructed a sandcastle, she was annoyed – he was clearly fascinated by his task, and if she was bored, he should be too.

She palmed a pebble, cocked her hand, and fired. The pebble rifled through the air, then punched through the crowning tower of his castle and the entirety of the endeavour toppled forward like a suddenly beheaded man.

Her brother spun around and she smirked at him, or perhaps it was a condescending wave. He charged towards her and she ran to the rocks, where she jumped from one to another to avoid dipping her feet into any of the seawater puddles. She turned the corner, her eyes still on her feet as she hopped forward. With their seaweed sheen, these rocks were slippery. When she landed on a rock and almost lost her footing, she stopped. She looked back to see if her brother was visible yet. He wasn't. She looked forward and saw Nicole, her body wedged between two rocks.

I don't know how horrific a sight it was. I see her wrenched at crude angles, always bloody and broken, but the image changes in my mind, if only by degree. The one constant is that her eyes are always open. Although they're fixed, they're not lifeless. Somehow she's alive and imprisoned within her corpse, and it's me she's fixed on.

The girl, Officer Finane told me, kept her cool. We were sitting in my living room while Officer Carr clattered about in the kitchen, searching for tea bags in my cupboards. She had asked if I wanted a cup. I didn't, but, my wits not about me, I said I did. Finane, his expression grim but admiring, said, 'The poor thing put on a brave face – she claimed she didn't scream – but she must have been shaken up underneath it all.'

She bounded back the way she came, from rock to rock, and stopped her brother from turning the corner. She led him to the safety of the sand before telling him what she'd found. He was excited, but she wouldn't let him go see. She phoned 999 on her mobile, then her parents. While the adults rushed to the scene, the girl sat with her brother in the shelter, and when he pleaded again, she shut him up with threats. The boy didn't realise she was doing him a favour.

Over the years, I've added plenty of visual flourishes to Finane's account. I tend to imagine the girl looking a little like Elizabeth at that age and the boy looking like me, a wholly two-legged version. I'm pretty sure the toppling sandcastle is mine, although it's possible that

Finane could have mentioned it. I kept asking questions because the sound of someone talking was better than shrill silence, and he kept feeding me information, making it real and perhaps testing if he could make me flinch.

I never want to meet that girl, but I've wondered about her nightmares. Can you grow out of what you see when you're a kid?

Carr set a cup of tea before me and sat. I stared at the tea and the two of them stared at me. I only sipped it to ease the tension.

They hadn't come ferrying the news to me so they could offer consolation. They were hoping for some enlightenment about who Nicole was. The contents of her wallet included her student ID, and someone at UCD had given them her last-known address. They asked me if I had her parents' number. I explained that, to the best of my knowledge, she was estranged from them; but while I didn't have the number handy, I might be able to find it. I suggested, though, that they could always check with the university, who should have it as an emergency contact. Finane said, 'We tried that. The number they had on record for her mother – Elisa Day? – was incorrect.'

'Someone's mistaken. Her mother's name is Natasha Winters.'

Carr wrote the name down in her notepad.

They were both looking at me expectantly. I said, 'I'll go see if I can find that number.'

Finane said, 'If you wouldn't mind.'

I went into Nicole's room and closed the door. I went through her desk drawers carefully, not wanting to leave things out of place. I found her passport and put it in my pocket. When I was done with her desk, I became frustrated,

and after I started searching her wardrobe, it only intensified. Soon I was tossing clothes from hangers, yanking
out shoes and books and boxes of notes on the floor. I got
it in my head that I wasn't feeling enough, so I pulled
her passport from my pocket because I wanted to see her
picture and possibly rip it apart.

I flipped to the photo. While she looked different, with a
stoned look in her eyes and her hair braided, it was plainly
her. But then I saw something that shocked me. It was the
simple fact of her birth date: 3 March 1976. The first time
we'd ever slept together was on the night of 27 November
1999, when she'd supposedly turned twenty-one. According
to her passport, she'd already been twenty-three then, and
she was approaching twenty-six when she died. The lie
didn't make sense. It's not like she was middle-aged and
had some desperate reason to turn back the clock. Why
would someone in their early twenties try to get away
with that?

I went back to the living room. I handed her passport
over to the guards and told them I'd be in touch if her
address book turned up.

They stood. Finane thanked me and said that they
would contact the Australian Embassy about her. He looked
at his shoes before meeting my eyes again. 'There is something else we'd appreciate your help with.'

My last gasp of hope was extinguished when the pathologist peeled the white sheet from her face. There had been
no mistake, or rather none of identification. Finane and
Carr were nearby, their backs turned to grant me some
privacy. The pathologist was standing across the stain-
less-steel table, pinching the corner of the sheet between

his latex-gloved fingers, just above Nicole's naked shoulders. I don't think he was looking at me either, but it was hard to tell as his thick glasses were reflecting the glare of the overhead lamp.

Nicole's hair was wet and knotted. Her face was scratched and bruised, and she had a perfectly round bump on her temple. Her lips were puffy and distorted at one side. Her left eye was swollen shut, her right eye closed peacefully. Her gorgeous brown skin appeared almost purple. Death had made her ugly, but I still wanted to kiss her.

I suppressed a gut-painful laugh. She had reminded me of my mother. Not when Mam was alive; when she was dead – their faces shared a similar slouch and a brutal vacancy. Mam's corpse had been made up to have a nasty jaundice colour, but I'd bet that under that layer, her skin was shaded purple too.

I took a final look at Nicole and tried to breathe in her lavender scent, instead absorbing a sterile tang that stung my eyes. I nodded at the pathologist. He covered her face with an efficient tug of his wrist.

Without choking, I told Finane and Carr, 'It's her, definitely her.'

After driving me back to my flat, the guards offered to phone someone on my behalf so I wouldn't have to be alone. I declined. In the realm of possibility, there was nothing I wished for more than solitude. They also gave me an errand: to find out who Nicole had been staying with so that person could help them re-create her final hours.

I only found her address book, in a shoebox under her bed, because tidying up the mess I'd made in her room appealed to me as an act of penitence. I leafed through the pages for her parents' details, but there were no Australian numbers. To my relief, there was no number for anyone named Alistair either.

I debated holding off before making calls, both for my sake and to give the people on my impromptu list more time without knowing. I decided to get it over with.

As popular as she was, if Nicole had close friends their identities remain a mystery to me. I expected that some people would shed tears on receiving the news, if just to avoid appearing callous, but there were loose acquaintances who could barely speak because they were so overcome. I must have made in excess of twenty calls in four hours. I thought less of people the more feeling they showed. *They didn't really know her.*

I discovered that she'd been staying with Marilyn, someone who she had more bad things to say about than good and who she didn't want to see again after travelling with her. I didn't think that Marilyn had too high an opinion of me, but over the phone she was considerate. While she cried like the others, she put a lid on it to ask how I was holding up.

She filled in some blanks about Nicole's last night. Along with a gang of Marilyn's friends, they'd been having a girls' night out. 'She was laughing as much as the rest of us, more, but I could tell she was unhappy. At about two, she said she was going back to my place because she was tired, although she didn't seem it.'

Cruelly, I asked, 'Weren't you worried when you got home? Or this morning, when there was no sign of her?'

'I thought . . . I was *sure* that she'd gone to be with *you*.'

Marilyn should have been angry with me for insinuating that she'd let Nicole down – when the only person I really felt had done that was me – but she kept asking if there was anything she could do. Did I want company? Should she bring over Nicole's suitcase? I batted away her overtures. I said that as soon as I could get in contact with them, I'd ask Nicole's family if they wanted her things, and then I'd collect the case. I gave her Finane's number and hung up.

The last two calls on my list were to Elizabeth and Seb. I dreaded those the most, but not because of the distress I would be inflicting. It was because I knew it would be hard to persuade them to leave me alone. I was right. Within the hour, Elizabeth was leaning on the intercom. Seb turned up twenty minutes later.

I told them the paltry facts of what I knew and they refrained from asking me the essential question, one I didn't have an answer to.

Elizabeth left the living room to phone Dad. After she'd prepared him for how I was taking it, she called me into my own room and handed me her phone. Dad said he loved me and was there for me. I was, and still am, exceptionally lucky to have such support in my life, but on that day, the love and kindness of others meant nothing.

I spent the evening sitting with Elizabeth and Seb in the living room. We stared at the clock, at our dark reflections on the blank TV screen, and at the bleak sky out through the sheet of dust covering the glass balcony doors. And they watched me while pretending not to. Occasionally my phone would ring, and that brought a reprieve from the silence. The callers were always emotional. I was always tersely polite. About every forty-five minutes, Elizabeth or Seb would offer to make tea or coffee. I only said yes as often as I did because of how relieved they were to have something to do, and the subsequent bladder pressure lent legitimacy to the frequency of my bathroom breaks. Whenever I returned, they always had a look about them like I'd interrupted the most intimate of conversations. I tried to hide how much the sympathy in their smiles irritated me.

From the time Finane and Carr first arrived on my doorstep, they'd been assessing my character and gauging whether my grief was genuine. I must have passed their test. They were tactful in their questioning, both on the Saturday and when they interviewed me again on the Sunday. They never said they were investigating the possibility of foul play, but they must have been. Finane asked, 'Can you think of any reason why she would ever have harmed herself?'

I said, 'It couldn't have been deliberate. She had everything to live for.'

Carr scribbled in her notepad.

I mentioned that I'd found her address book, but not her parents' number. Finane said, 'I'm afraid she may not have been upfront with you about everything.'

He took a breath, his shoulders tightening, and informed me what they'd learned about her through the Australian Embassy: that the parents she told me about were figments of her imagination and she'd actually been raised in foster homes. I don't know how many. Her last foster parent – a woman named Angela Baxter – had been tracked down, but she hadn't heard from Nicole in eight years, not since she'd moved out and severed contact, right after finishing high school. Nevertheless, Ms Baxter had volunteered to arrange a funeral in Sydney.

Before that could happen, a few legal requirements had to be met. After receiving the pathologist's report, the coroner issued a certificate to approve the release of Nicole's body. Then a mortuary passport was promptly processed by the Australian Embassy so her body could be shipped home. It was all sorted out by the end of the week. She was flown out of Ireland on the Thursday and her funeral was on Sunday.

Everyone had assumed I would want to go. Dad and Tighe both offered to pay for my plane ticket, and Tighe even said he would go with me. But I never had any intention of attending and I wasn't about to change my mind. Only Elizabeth dared to push the matter. She said, 'You know it's the right thing to do.'

'I respectfully disagree. I wasn't even her boyfriend when she died. By her choice, I was out of her life.'

'That doesn't mean she didn't love you or that you weren't important to her.'

'That's exactly what it means.'

She chewed her lip. 'You owe it to—'

'I don't owe it to her! I don't know if I even really knew her!'

'You owe it to *yourself*.' She gave me this incredibly sad look. 'I don't want you to have to live with the regret of not going.'

'I want to remember her as she lived, not for how it ended.'

She still disapproved, and I could see that it was difficult for her not to say anything else, but she left it alone after that.

Even today, I don't regret not going, maybe because I've so many other regrets to dwarf that one. If I'd been at her graveside, standing above a hole containing her body in a box, I can't imagine it would have made me feel close to her. And if I'd met this Ms Baxter and she asked about what type of person Nicole had turned out to be, what could I have said that I was sure of? But I was more afraid that Ms Baxter would tell me about Nicole's old life, the one she never trusted me with. I hated the idea of not recognising the person she described.

Maybe I've exaggerated the significance of her lies about her age and her background. I go back and forth about whether I've been overreacting. I mean, are they just minor details? I can imagine how she would have defended herself, making some big argument about how emotional sincerity far outweighs factual accuracy. The thing is, though, if she was willing to tell those lies, what else could she have been lying about? And the other way of looking at it is equally jarring: when was she ever telling me the truth?

The end of March 2002

The inquest was on an uncommonly glorious spring day. I walked right past the courthouse before deciding that I had to hear what was said, and so I doubled back and made myself go inside. Whatever pronouncement was delivered on her cause of death, I knew I'd be unconvinced, but I was hoping to be wrong.

Marilyn was there. As the last known person to have seen the deceased alive, she testified about Nicole's demeanour before she left the club. She said she wouldn't have characterised Nicole as being depressed and that, while she had been drinking, she didn't seem drunk.

383

Finane testified about the discovery of the body. The pathologist read from his report, blowing his nose between statements. Nicole had water in her lungs and drowned. She had a high blood-alcohol level. Her wounds were consistent with the force of waves combined with collisions against rocks. The coroner's verdict was 'accidental death', although she could have chosen 'death by misadventure' or, the most poisonous of conclusions, 'suicide'.

Death by misadventure would have suggested that she'd gone swimming but drowned instead. If she'd walked into the sea with the intention of drowning herself, that was, no shit, suicide. The scenario endorsed by the verdict was that she went to Whiterock to be alone; she lay down on the sand and passed out; when the tide came in and dragged her away, her stupor was too deep for her to be aware she was dying. It was an unfortunate, accidental death and, considering the uncertainty involved, the most humane verdict available to the coroner.

When the inquest was over, I hurried out of the court, but Marilyn caught up to me on the street before I could make a clean getaway. 'Jimmy, it's good to see . . .' I think she blushed, but it was hard to tell with the amount of make-up she was wearing. 'Well no, it's not, is it? Could I buy you a coffee? We could chat.'

Behind her, I saw Finane exit the courthouse. I wanted to talk to him even less than her so I said, 'Let's make it something stronger than a coffee,' and started walking away. Her heels clicked on the pavement as she tried to match my pace, but she didn't ask me to slow down.

I took her to a dive called the Last Stop. The old drunks there shamelessly eyed Marilyn's legs. I ordered myself a beer, and a vodka and Coke for her, and we huddled over a secluded table. She said, 'I phoned you a few times and I texted.'

I drank two fingers of my pint. 'Sorry. It's nothing personal. I've been rude to everyone.'

'It's understandable.' She reached her hand across the table, presumably with the intention of holding mine, but when I didn't return her smile, she withdrew it. 'I wanted to invite you to nights out when a group of us who knew Nicole have been meeting up. To remember her, you know?'

'I appreciate the thought, but I'm not up for that.'

'Maybe you're better off. There are some people who've elevated themselves to having been,' she crossed her index and middle fingers together, 'like that with her. It can't be true of all of them.'

'People can remember her however they want to. I'm not bothered by it.'

'That's generous of you.'

'No, it's not. I just don't care.'

She talked at length about Nicole, emphasising how committed to me she'd been and what a positive influence I'd had on her. The more she flattered me, the more I felt like doing violence to myself. She told stories about their 'wild, but not too wild' travels around Europe, how Nicole had been a wonderful confidante to her whenever she was having 'guy problems', and in return, Marilyn had provided Nicole with a shoulder to cry on whenever she was missing me. 'And she *always* was, Jimmy.'

I interrupted her to ask, 'Do you still have that case of her stuff?'

'It's in my flat. Do you want it?'

'Yes. Can we go now?'

In her flat, she showed me into her spare room, where

Nicole's suitcase lay on the bed, as well as her shampoo, her toothbrush, and a tube of toothpaste, rolled up halfway. I said, 'She wouldn't mind you using her toothpaste.'

Marilyn looked vaguely embarrassed. 'I didn't want to take what was hers. Should I give you a few moments?'

'Please.'

She obliged.

I opened the case. Nicole had left behind four or five changes of clothes and a couple of college notebooks. I flicked through the pages. There were no revealing asides on her frame of mind, no hidden codes that could exonerate me, just facts and figures, scientific formulas, and notes about various theories. I realised then that I'd tricked myself into believing it was possible to find answers, as if she would have felt like I deserved them.

I shoved her things back into the case, including the bathroom leftovers, and aggressively zipped it and clasped it shut. I lugged it into the hall, where Marilyn was leaning against the radiator, her legs crossed at the ankle. I said, 'Thanks for this. I should go.'

It came out abruptly, like pretty much everything I'd said to her, but she didn't seem offended. She touched my good hand. 'You could stay longer. We could talk if you'd like to, or not if that would be better. I think it could be of some comfort to you; that I could be.' She grazed her thumb along the inside of my wrist and stared at me, unflinching.

I felt turned on and repulsed simultaneously. I'm not sure which sensation was greater. I didn't say another word and I left her flat without a backward glance.

The repulsion was mostly for me. I had wanted to fuck Marilyn because Nicole would have hated me for it and that might have freed me of her. I just couldn't go through with it.

At the time, I was angry with Marilyn too. I thought she was hitting on me because she was playing a game and its purpose was to settle some score with Nicole. But now I wonder if I utterly misread the situation. Maybe the only thing she was offering me was some friendship. And even if she did want to have sex, it could have been because she was distraught and wanted to be close to someone who had loved Nicole and was in pain for that reason. I don't know if she was devious or kind or damaged, or some combination of the three. The only thing I'm reasonably sure about is that I behaved like a dick.

Nicole died twelve years ago. In that time, I've tried not to become someone she would have disliked – I know she's not watching me, but I find myself acting as if she is. I like to think that I've been careful in how I've treated other people, because I can't stand the idea of hurting someone and that leading to a consequence like what befell her. That mentality hasn't been working all that well for me, though. Good intentions aside, I worry my family and friends, and I hurt Alice. I don't doubt, however, that the break-up was for the best. In the three months we were together, there probably wasn't a single day in which I thought about her more than I did about Nicole.

Nicole drowned, but I still don't know how it happened or why, and I never will. Whether the odds of it being a suicide or an accident are fifty per cent one way, or ninety-nine per cent, I'm fixed in place, not knowing how to grieve, because grieving for a suicide and grieving for an accident are two very different things, and I can't choose which one I should be doing. Maybe she could never have killed herself because she understood what it would do to me, and so if I allow myself to believe otherwise that would be a betrayal of her. But to rule it out on the grounds of her love might make me a sucker, and I'm unwilling to forfeit my pride.

She wasn't perfect, but she was everything I wanted and, I suspect, everything I ever will want. In the end, what matters is not how much I loved her. What matters is that I lost her. Suicide or accident, I let her die.

Chapter Thirty

How to Solve Problems

Jimmy feels like he has allowed himself to become very unimpressive since losing Nicole; that others in his position wouldn't be as crippled after so much time has passed.

But he's not unimpressive to me. When she died, despair set in at his core, and that's not something that can be purged in a series of simple steps.

I was laid low as well. Like Jimmy, I don't know if Nicole's death was a suicide or an accident. I'm very aware that she had been thinking about killing herself, and I believe she possessed the capacity to do so, but many people think about it who could go through with it. I've no proof that it was suicide – I would have had to be there – so I've no certainty.

For years afterwards, I struggled with my motivation to enter people's minds. Their stories weren't nearly so compelling. In fact, more often than not they felt meaningless. Jimmy's mind was the worst of all for me – his thoughts were repetitive and bludgeoning – but I made myself keep revisiting him and others, and while it would be going too far to say that existing in Nicole's wake became easy, it did become less excruciatingly hard.

I re-engaged with the world, to the best of my abilities, because I would've suffered more if I'd chosen to fully embrace

*my isolation. Jimmy and I differ in this regard: my instinct is
to seek relief from suffering, but he has an attachment to his,
and so weaning himself off it is a more arduous task for him.*

March 2014

ISABEL LOOKS THROUGH THE PEEPHOLE, STEADIES
herself, and opens the door. 'Thanks for coming!'

Jimmy is on her doorstep, his hands in his jacket pockets.
He smiles, and as he enters, she hugs him. With one arm
pinned by her, he can't quite return it, and so he just rubs her
shoulder with his free hand. She takes his jacket and hangs it
on the coat stand, then leads him through her living room,
where there are CDs scattered around a considerable sound
system. She waves her hand at the carpet and states, 'A mess.'

In the kitchen, there's a counter sticking out from the wall,
with stools on either side. He accepts her offer of coffee and
sits facing her. She says, 'One moment, then I want to hear
everything about your life.'

'There's not a lot to tell.'

'I doubt that.'

He watches her fill the coffee machine with water, scoop
ground coffee into the filter, and flick the switch. As she takes
two mugs from a cabinet, the machine is already hissing and
coffee is dripping into the carafe, fizzling as it hits the base.
She looks about for anything else to do, before sitting across
from Jimmy. 'It'll be a minute.'

'There's no hurry.'

He absent-mindedly taps his pincer thumb on the counter.
She holds one arm around her stomach like she's cold and
fiddles with the zipper of her tracksuit top. 'So, what are you
doing with yourself these days?'

'I'm a financial content editor.'

'Sounds important.'

'If you know of a more pointless job, I'd like to hear about it. I work in the evenings, listening to audio over the internet of meetings between financial analysts and higher-ups of big companies, mostly American, while reading the India-sourced transcripts and fixing any mistakes I find. I don't have to meet, or talk to, anyone I work with. I'm quite fond of it.'

She regards him with a puzzled expression and is about to say something when the coffee machine buzzes, startling her. She hops off the chair, pours the coffees carefully, then sits back down, sliding one to him. She has forgotten to ask if he wants milk or sugar, but he prefers it black anyway. He blows at the curls of steam rising from his mug. They dissipate and are quickly replaced by more. He says, 'How do you make ends meet?'

She wraps her hands around her mug. 'Oh, I'm a hostess at the Westbrook Inn, over in Clonmel, which really only means I'm the head waitress. If you come by, I can treat you to an employee discount. Do it soon, though. I'll be taking a leave of absence.'

'Why's that?'

'There's something I need to tell you, involving Tighe.'

'Have you heard from him?'

She shakes her head. 'Not since he was around for your grandmother's funeral. I'm probably the last person he'd contact now. I need to know if *you* have had any communication with him. I swear I'd keep it a secret.'

'None of us have heard a thing, and I don't expect that to change. You might be better off if he keeps his distance.'

'You don't realise how right you are. I had to check.'

'What do you have to tell me?'

391

With a fragile smile, she says, 'I'm pregnant. It's his.'

It takes Jimmy a few seconds to process the news, then he has to remind himself that she's waiting for a response. He gives three in succession: 'Fuck. I'm sorry. It's going to be okay.'

She wrings her hands on the counter. 'I don't know if I want it to happen or if it's the worst thing that could. Before you ask, I'm positive it's his. There was no one else.'

'Isabel, even if I doubted your honesty, which I don't, it wouldn't make much sense, considering his infamy, to pretend he's the father.' She lets him hold her hand. 'Are you planning on keeping it?'

'Why? Would you recommend an alternative?'

'No, I wouldn't. You'll be a good mother.'

'You don't know what I'm like. I may have done some babysitting way back when without completely fucking it up – correct me if I'm wrong – but that's a far cry from being really responsible for another life. I usually only think of myself, and I can be weak, really weak.'

'Everyone can be. And even when I was a kid, I could see you had a good heart. That's the main thing you need.'

'I appreciate that. I do.' She takes her hand back and sips her coffee. 'I'll get my head around it. I just have to keep reminding myself that women have been doing this for as long as there have been women. The world hasn't stopped turning.'

'It never does. We all have to catch our breath on the move. For what it's worth, by the way, you were a great babysitter.'

Her eyebrows perk up. 'Was I?'

He sips his coffee and clears his throat. 'You weren't the best at knocking before entering. Apart from that, you were tops.'

She laughs. 'You'd be amazed at how mindful I've been at that ever since. You wouldn't be blushing, would you?'

'God, no.'

'Because there's nothing to be embarrassed about.'

'Course not.' He gulps more coffee. 'This is a premium blend.'

'I would never give a guest anything less than Tesco's finest.' She assumes a more serious air. 'You've a big decision ahead.'

He puts his coffee down. 'What's that?'

'When I launch my precious bastard out into the world, do you want to be called Uncle Jimmy, Uncle Jim, or Uncle James?'

It's three a.m. when Jimmy logs out of his employer's instant-messaging system, deletes various transcript files littering his desktop, and takes off his headset. He extends his arms behind his back and yawns, then shuts down his laptop and stands. The shift lasted seven hours without a break, and he's stiff from sitting. He rips his Sellotaped 'man at work' sign from his door, discards it on his desk, and plods down the hall.

In the kitchen, he makes two slices of toast. He goes into the living room and finds his father lying in his armchair. Eamon's wearing his pyjamas and bathrobe, and his slippered feet are on the footrest. His head is lolled to one side, but as Jimmy immediately observes, his chest is gently astir. On his lap is a copy of the *Rathbaile Chronicle*.

Jimmy sits on the couch right next to the armchair and prods Eamon's knee. His eyes open with a jolt. As he sits up, the newspaper tumbles slothfully from his lap to the footrest to the carpet, where it lies, its creased pages fanned out from the spine. His hand to his forehead, Eamon says, 'What? Jim, are you all right?'

'Everything's fine. I thought you'd be better off sleeping in your bed.'

Eamon rubs his eyes and reclines into his armchair. 'I tried that. One of those nights, y'know?'

'Should I have let you sleep?'

'No. You're right. I should be in bed. What's your excuse?'

Jimmy takes a bite of toast. 'Want the other slice?'

'I couldn't deprive my son of nutrition.'

'I've only just finished work, and I can never go straight to sleep after. The hamster in my head needs to wind down to a jog before he can collapse off the wheel. I'm glad I bumped into you, actually. I have some news. Although maybe I should wait until the morning.'

'Too late. My curiosity is aroused.'

'Okay, then. Take a deep, deep breath, Dad. You're going to be a grandfather.'

When the wait for a punchline proves fruitless, Eamon says, 'Who's pregnant?'

'Isabel Flynn.'

'Isabel? Yours?'

Jimmy holds his hands up. 'Fuck no. Sorry. It's Tighe's. She told me today and asked me to tell you.'

'You haven't done my chances of getting back to sleep any favours.'

'I should have waited.'

'Never apologise for sharing good news.'

Jimmy considers pointing out that even if he somehow found out about this, Tighe wouldn't come back. He decides to leave it alone.

Eamon interlocks his fingers against his stomach. 'Could you invite her to dinner on Sunday? I want to welcome her to the family.' Noticing Jimmy's amusement, he says, 'That sounds ominous, doesn't it?'

In the living room of her small house in Dublin, Elizabeth sits in the middle of her couch with her feet pressed together on the coffee table, where the cup of tea she made herself is going cold. Her arms are folded and she's biting on her lower lip. Sunlight is pouring through the windows, but despite the beautiful weather, she's annoyed and getting more so. She heard the shower being switched off at least ten minutes ago, and now she's waiting for the man inside her bathroom to come out – usually, she likes that he takes time to make an effort with his appearance, just not when she has something to say to him that she should have said before.

Finally she hears the bathroom door opening and the padding of his feet as he descends the stairs. The living-room door is pushed open and Seb enters the room. His fair hair is damp and neatly combed to the side, and his shirt is tucked into his trousers. He's buttoning the second-to-the-top button, his chin slightly raised, as he catches Elizabeth's glare. His hands dropping from his shirt, he smiles a little nervously. 'What is it?'

'I've decided it *does* bother me. You should've told him, like you promised.'

The first time Elizabeth and Seb ever hooked up was right after Nicole died. They met for a drink to talk about how Jimmy was coping, because he certainly wasn't being forth-coming with either of them, and they bonded over their mutual concern. One drink led to more, and those led to drunken sex back at Elizabeth's place, proceeding to less-drunken sex the following night and to some relatively sober sex on multiple occasions over the following weeks. They fancied each other and had chemistry, but it was tainted by the tragedy that had brought them together and by how it was going on behind Jimmy's back when he was so broken up. Plus, Elizabeth was generally opposed to being in a relationship with anyone. With no hard feelings between them, they stopped it.

Two months ago, without letting Eamon or Jimmy know, Elizabeth went to London with a mission in mind. She wanted to try to make contact with Tighe, not because she hoped to aid him in any way or because she missed him – she didn't. She wanted an explanation for his crimes, for him to apologise to their father, and then, ideally, he would turn himself in. But it was a fool's errand. She met with three of Tighe's ex-girlfriends, and they all told her the same things: that they had a poor opinion of her brother, they didn't have a clue as to how to get in touch with him, and they were surprised she had entertained such a notion. The most she got from them was the numbers of a few friends of his, but 'friends' turned out to be too strong a term – everyone she phoned claimed to be no more than a passing acquaintance. One ex-colleague told her, 'If I were you, I'd say good riddance and forget all about him.' Choosing to follow that advice, she gave up the chase. She still had a night left before her flight back to Dublin, so, feeling like she could do with seeing a friendly face, she sent Seb a Facebook message asking him if he happened to be free. He replied straight away: 'For you I am.'

They went for dinner and drinks at a wine bar. When she explained what had brought her to London, he listened sympathetically – even as she poked fun at the naivety of her 'big plan', he took her seriously. They talked about Jimmy, and Seb confessed that he still blamed himself for his lost leg. Elizabeth confessed that she still blamed herself for the death of Paul. They assured each other of their respective innocence in those traumas, of how they'd only been children, and it was a comfort to both of them to hear that from someone with a similar guilt complex. Elizabeth went home with Seb at the end of the night, and she missed her flight the next day.

Since then, they've been visiting each other whenever their work schedules have allowed it – Seb hasn't been acting during this stretch, but he has been bartending. When he came to stay for a couple of nights before going down to Rathbaile for Finbar's wedding, he told her that he thought he was falling in love with her and she said the same to him – an exchange that was a first for her, with anyone. As she thought about it over the weekend, however, the difference between falling in love and *being* in love seemed greater and greater. The former doesn't really count for much if you don't stick the landing.

Seb returned to Dublin last night, and she didn't ask him then if he'd told Jimmy about them, because if he had, she was hoping he would volunteer it, and if he hadn't, she didn't want to ruin the mood. This morning, over breakfast, he admitted that he hadn't told him, 'not yet', and she tried to appear to be okay with that – she didn't want them to have their first real argument on a day when he was flying back to London – but soon it was bugging her too much to let it go.

Seb sits on the coffee table, next to Elizabeth's feet, and puts his hand on her knee. 'I didn't exactly promise.'

She shrugs away his hand, takes her feet off the table, and sits forward. 'You said you were planning on telling him, so what would you call that?'

As diplomatically as he can, he says, 'It was an honest intention, not a vow. The timing was off. There was a wedding celebration going on around us and my sister had just ended it with him.'

'If you're waiting for a time when everything in his life is smooth sailing, you might be in for a long wait. How could he have a problem with you and me being together anyway, when you've only ever cheered him on with *your* sister? If he's as good a friend to you as you are to him, he'll be happy for you, but even if it upset him somehow, he'd have no right to say anything. What is it that you think you owe him that he doesn't owe you?'

'You know what I owe him: a leg.'

'Don't make this about that. I don't think that way and Jimmy doesn't either. The only person who does is you.'

Seb stands, nods contritely at her, and glances about the room. Spotting his shoes by the door, he goes and picks them up with one hand, then sits on the chair by the table on the other side of the room. As he puts his shoes on, he says, 'You're right. Telling him will be fine. I just don't see the harm in waiting a little longer, and seeing how things go. You matter to me, a lot, and I don't want to add anything to the mix that might complicate things for *us*. It's not about him.'

Wondering how she went from being someone he was falling in love with to merely mattering a lot, she says, 'What it's really about is getting clearer. You're thinking: what's the point of telling him when you don't know if we'll last much longer. You're getting tired of me.'

'Elizabeth, nothing could be further from the truth. What I'm worried about is that you'll figure out that I'm wrong for you.'

She snorts. 'Don't give me some "it's not you, it's me" bullshit.'

'That's not what I'm doing. Listen, I have to leave for my

flight in half an hour. This might not be the best time for us to be having this conversation.'

'So you'd prefer to discuss it over Skype?'

'I'd prefer to discuss it when you visit me at the end of the month. You're still coming, aren't you?'

'I don't know, Seb. I haven't bought my tickets yet. Depending on how the next half-hour goes, maybe I won't.' Her phone starts ringing. She takes it out of her pocket and looks at it. 'Oh, for fuck's sake. Guess who?' Standing, she says, 'I'd answer this in front of you but I'd be too tempted to put you on.'

Without giving Seb another look, she strides out into the hallway and shuts the door.

He mutters, 'Fuck,' then bends down and ties his shoelaces, vigorously double-knotting them. Through the door, he can hear that Elizabeth's tone of voice is incredulous and even more frustrated.

Seb doesn't relish the prospect of informing Jimmy about him and Elizabeth – what if it comes across like he's trying to even things up because Jimmy had been sleeping with Alice? – but he was being sincere about his concern that it'll be Elizabeth who ends it with him. While he doesn't care that she's six years older than he is, he feels that they are at different stages of their lives, and he's waiting for her to recognise that he's a bad bet for her. He has a revolving door of flatmates because he can't afford his own place, and he's living pay cheque to pay cheque and borrowing money from his parents whenever he's in a bind, which happens with embarrassing regularity. Meanwhile, Elizabeth has her own house and successfully manages a pair of restaurants.

Coming back into the room, with her phone to her ear, she says, 'Tell Dad that I'll cook, but you're on potato-peeling

duty, and you can be in charge of the washing-up too . . .
Yeah, congratulations to all of us.' She hangs up, tosses her
phone on the couch – where a cushion slumps over it – and
says, 'Guess what Tighe's fucking done?'

On Sunday afternoon, Isabel stands outside the Diaz house,
her thumb on the doorbell but not exerting any pressure.

When Jimmy phoned her, it was comforting to hear that
the invitation was Eamon's idea – she'd been anxious that he
might be ashamed of how his prospective grandchild would
be both illegitimate and a reminder of Tighe. Then she awoke
to her first bout of morning sickness in weeks and her rosy
outlook for the day ahead was evacuated along with her meal
from the night before. Lying on her bathroom floor, she
conjured scenarios where everything went wrong. Maybe she
would make an awful impression, or they would deny that
Tighe was really the father and the purpose of the dinner was
to warn her to stay away from the family, with Elizabeth being
drafted in to provide Eamon and Jimmy with moral support.

Searching for a moment of calm, she closes her eyes and
rests her hand on the front door. It gives way and her eyes
open as she lunges into the hallway. Jimmy catches her, then
steps back. 'Whoa! You all right?'

'Sorry, sorry. You must think I'm drunk or something.'

He laughs. 'Not at all – I'm attributing your reeling about
the place to harder drugs than alcohol. I saw you walk up the
driveway from the window. We were wondering what was
taking you so long to ring the bell.'

'I was steeling myself for a big entrance.'

'It's not too late for me to clap.'

'That's okay.' She smiles with semi-mock trepidation. 'Have
I been keeping the three of you waiting?'

'Your arrival has been anticipated, but we're not a tough crowd.'

Jimmy leads her into the living room. Elizabeth, a tea towel in hand, is standing by the other door, connecting to the kitchen. Eamon had been sitting in his armchair, but he stands and puts down his glass of beer. Isabel extends her hand. He ignores it, hugging her instead and thanking her for coming.

She feels a lump in her throat. 'No, thank *you*.'

Elizabeth and Isabel went to the same school, but Isabel was a year ahead and there wasn't much interaction between their classes. Nevertheless, Elizabeth hugs her as if they're old friends. She asks what she can get her to drink and Isabel agrees to an apple juice.

As Elizabeth steps into the kitchen, Jimmy and Isabel sit on the couch and Eamon sits in his armchair. Despite having a fair idea of the answer, Eamon asks Isabel, 'How far along are you?'

She places her hand on her cardigan-and-T-shirt-covered belly. 'Four and a half months. It feels longer, and shorter, if that makes any sense.'

'You've barely begun to show.'

'I suppose I've been keeping myself wrapped up until there's no choice except to make it public. I'm amazed more people haven't put it together that I'm, y'know, knocked up. Maybe they're too polite to say anything in case I might only be getting fat.'

Jimmy says, 'I didn't think you were fat *or* pregnant.'

'Maybe your powers of observation could use some fine-tuning.'

She's alarmed that she might have said the wrong thing, but he doesn't disagree.

Eamon says, 'Just to get my obligatory sentimental speech

out of the way, I want to make sure you understand you're not alone. We consider you to be one of the family now, and even though Tighe can't be by your side as you go through this, if there's anything I, or *we*, can do to help, you only have to say the word. Your child may not have a father at the beginning of his or her life, but you've a grandfather in me and there'll be an uncle and an aunt on hand as well. There won't be a lack of affection, I guarantee you.'

She says, 'You're not going to make me cry,' then, seeing Eamon's eyes moisten, she bursts into tears.

Elizabeth, who had been standing in the doorway as Eamon made his speech, puts a glass of apple juice down in front of Isabel, squeezes her shoulder, and says, 'I'll be right back with some tissues.'

Soon the four of them are sitting around the dining-room table and digging into the roast dinner that Elizabeth prepared. Despite her initial embarrassment, Isabel is glad she became so emotional – it was something of an icebreaker, and the warmth with which Eamon, Elizabeth, and Jimmy treated her emphasised how different they are from Tighe. He doesn't need to be physically present for his shadow to loom over the afternoon, though.

When Elizabeth has nearly finished her second glass of white wine, she says to Isabel, 'I feel like I need to apologise for my brother.'

Looking up from the slice of beef he's cutting a chunk off, Jimmy says, 'What did *I* do?'

'Not you. *Tighe.*'

'I agree that he owes Isabel an apology, but I don't see what good it does coming from you.'

'Well that might be the best she can get.'

Isabel says, 'Elizabeth, I appreciate the sentiment. I really do. But I don't need an apology from anyone. My situation is what it is, and I'm going to make the most of it. Eamon, I hope you understand that while I'd love for all of you to be in my child's life, I'd rather that Tighe never is. I don't want anything from him and I don't want to see him again. I'm sorry to say that. I don't mean to be hurtful.'

Eamon has a chug of his beer, as if to wash down a grimace, then says, 'I love my eldest son, unconditionally, but I think you'll get your wish.'

To fill the ensuing silence, Jimmy says, 'Isabel, your mother and father must be as excited about becoming grandparents as Dad is.'

Putting a smile on it, she says, 'I haven't told them yet. They won't be overjoyed.'

Kindly, Eamon says, 'Maybe they'll respond better than you think.'

'Anything's possible.' She realises from the expressions around the table that she didn't quite sell the line. 'They *do* want to be grandparents, but the circumstances are not what they expect of me and they won't be shy about sharing that. In the end, they'll have to accept it.'

Later on, after dessert, Isabel is ready to head home. Eamon wants to call a taxi, but her flat is only twenty minutes away by foot and she'd prefer to get the exercise. To Eamon's relief, Jimmy says he'll accompany her, to 'stretch my leg'.

He spends most of the walk reassuring her that Eamon and Elizabeth like her, which they do. When they're almost there, he asks about her parents and she says, 'It's not so much their immediate reaction I'm concerned about. It's the aftermath. Mam will be adamant that I move home so that she can help with the pregnancy and then the baby. Inevitably I'll have to give in. At least for a while. Losing my independence, at forty and when my parents have never had much faith in me, well, "demoralising" doesn't quite sum it up.'

It isn't until they're at her place, drinking coffee in her kitchen, that he summons his courage and says, 'I have an unusual proposition for you.'

She gives him a lively grin. 'Oh good. It's been a while since I've had one of those. How unusual is it?'

He smiles, but is serious when he says, 'Maybe not at all. It could make sense, but it's your call. You should probably sleep on it.'

'And *it* is?'

'You shouldn't be forced to move in with your parents. I think *we* should move in together.'

'Wow. Why? I mean, why would you want to do that?' She puts her hand to her belly. 'This isn't your responsibility.'

'I know. But I'm the uncle, and besides, I shouldn't be living with my father indefinitely.'

'Wouldn't your girlfriend mind? Vicky said you were going out with a girl named Alice.'

'That's over. She cut me loose.'

'You say that like you admire her for it.'

'I do. I wasn't good for her.'

'Jimmy, I'd like to be able to say yes.'

'Then do.'

'I can't. It wouldn't be fair to you.'

'I'm not making a selfless gesture. I just need to know that I can be of help to someone.'

She wants to hug him, but restrains herself, knowing it would bring her to tears. She sips her coffee. 'Turns out I am going to need to sleep on it.'

Chapter Thirty-One

Back to Life

I
June 2015

JIMMY ISN'T DEAD. HE'S JUST LYING ON THE FLOOR, motionless. His face is turned to the side, his eyes closed and a drop of blood on his lips. His limbs are sprawled out and his pincer is pointed at the white crib, which nestles Isabel's daughter, Zoe. She's lying on her back, her head on a pillow. Her feet kick the woollen blanket with silk trim that covers her, but it only seems to shrug in response. Her hands grasp at the dreamcatcher hanging out of reach from the ceiling. Her desperate screams are picked up by the walkie-talkie affixed to the top of the crib and emitted by the receiver walkie-talkie on the table in the living room, but there's no one there to hear them. Her head is bright red. Her eyes are only open a slit, hiding their colour; enough, though, for tears to stream into the hollows of her ears and down her cheeks to her gum-baring mouth.

And Jimmy continues to lie there, not budging and not hearing anything.

August 2014

Jimmy, sitting in the snug of the Long Man, grips his pint and, in a resolutely relaxed voice, says, 'I'm *not* nervous.'

Finbar sits across the table wearing a faded Rage Against the Machine T-shirt under an unbuttoned dark-green army shirt he has had since he was a teenager. He has let his hair grow long, styling it to look dishevelled, and he's sporting a layer of stubble. Jimmy guesses that his second-rate-rock-star look is his way of demonstrating that being married doesn't mean he's not a free spirit.

Finbar nods at the beer mat Jimmy has been tearing to pieces. 'It's obvious that you're shitting it from that fucking mess you've made.'

Jimmy swipes his pincer across the table, sending the beer-mat remains fluttering over the edge. 'I don't know what you're talking about.'

'I'm just at a loss for why you're taking responsibility when it isn't yours.'

'I'm not. I'm helping out.'

'But why?'

Jimmy drinks and says, 'Never mind me, how's married life treating you?'

'I expected to feel settled. Instead, I feel like a kid playing house. Y'know, Vicky's the love of my life, but I still see her as my girlfriend more than my wife. Nothing's changed between us, not really.'

'Except for the rings.'

Finbar holds his hand palm out and eyes his ring. He sighs and lets his hand flop on to the table, like a puppet whose strings have been cut. 'Except for those.'

'You need time to adapt. Ten, twenty years should do it. You could fast-track it by getting her knocked up. That'll make you feel like a family man.'

'So that's your game? Playing family man? I don't know which of us to feel more sympathy for. Us married men.'

'There's no ring on my finger.'

'It's more a state of mind, and that makes you as married as me. Only you seem to have bypassed all the perks.'

'Perks?'

'If you're living with the woman, providing for her every whim, and aiming to fill in as daddy to her child, you should be getting the occasional shag out of it.'

'She is nine months pregnant. With my niece or nephew. And about to pop.'

Finbar's grin widens. 'You're biding your time, then?'

'My intentions are purely honourable.'

'I don't get you.'

'I'm not sure I get myself.'

Finbar knocks back his pint, stands, and makes a shooting motion at Jimmy's glass. 'Same again?' Without waiting for a reply, he lodges himself at the section of the bar bordering the snug and pulls a tenner from his wallet as the bartender approaches.

Jimmy takes out and checks his phone, but he hasn't missed any messages.

He and Isabel have been living together for three months now in a three-bedroom flat. He had insisted on her having the largest bedroom, leaving him with one that doesn't have space for a desk, and so he has been working from the living room. During the day, he prepares food for her and does errands, then, during his editing shifts, from early in the evening to late into the night, she's careful not to disturb him. She spends most of this time in bed, watching TV shows on her laptop, usually with a bowl of whatever food she has been craving propped against her belly. When she wants something from the kitchen, she slips, or waddles, by him as quietly as she can, while he sits stooped over his workstation, headset on and his back to her. When she knows he has passed the halfway mark of a shift, she's in the habit of making him coffee. She announces her presence with a hand on his shoulder, setting the thermos next to his laptop. Without removing his headset, he thanks her and tells her she shouldn't have. She smiles as if it's a meaningless gesture and leaves him to work.

Her due date is in two days, so when Finbar arrived on the doorstep earlier demanding that Jimmy join him for a beer, he declined, but Isabel overheard and said, 'Go. I need a break from you.'

He considers texting her, but doesn't want to appear overprotective. He leaves his phone on the table.

When they've resumed drinking, Finbar says, 'Vicky's birthday is coming up and I could do with some advice on a gift. I'm thinking of getting a tattoo.'

'She wants a tattoo?'

'Well, it would be *for* her, but *on* me. Part of it could be her name. It would prove how devoted I am to our future.'

'Is your wedding ring not symbolic enough?'

'Rings come off. Tattoos stay on forever.'

'I won't argue with that.'

'My first thought was to go for a heart with "Vicky" on it, but that seems clichéd, and her name by itself would be boring. I want something to go with it, like her favourite flower, or a bird she likes, something along those lines. What do you reckon?'

'It depends. What's her favourite flower?'

'If she's ever said, she didn't do a great job of getting my attention.'

'Which birds does she like then?'

'Could be a dove. I'm not sure. I'd rather a tougher-looking bird anyway.'

'Like maybe an irate ostrich or a malicious pigeon?'

'Fuck off.'

'You could print her name on a ball and chain.'

'It would be almost worth it to see her face. You're not going to be much help, are you?'

'The more I drink, the better my ideas will get.'

Jimmy gulps his pint. It's then that his phone bleats, giving him a start. Standing, he turns his back to Finbar and to the bar, and answers before the third ring.

Finbar listens to Jimmy's side of the call as he tells Isabel, in a tense but steady voice, to hold on and that he'll be home as fast as he can. He hangs up and states, 'It's time.'

Finbar, his phone already in hand, says, 'No shit,' and dials for a taxi.

III
April 2015

Jimmy wheels a trolley down an aisle, stopping next to the baby-products section. Pressing his forearms against the handlebar and hunching his shoulders, he scans the shelves. He grabs a package of a dozen nappies and tosses it into the trolley, where it bounces on the uneven battlements formed by the assorted groceries then rests. He's reaching for a second package when another trolley bumps into his. He turns to find Alice staring at him with a shy but unrepentant smile. 'You're in my way, stranger.'

'Hey! What are you doing here?'

She waves her hand over her trolley. 'There are clues available to you.'

'My question might be more existential than stupid, like what are you doing in life?'

'Sorry if I underestimated you.'

'I won't hold it against you. You're looking well.'

Glancing over her attire, she says, 'In my raggedy tracksuit bottoms and my shapely jumper.' Her tracksuit bottoms aren't raggedy; her jumper *is* shapely.

'I repeat: you're looking well.'

'You too.'

He nods. 'That's the difference between us. I don't need convincing.'

'That's the difference, huh?'

'Among other things. Probably. Maybe. I don't know.'

'I miss your sense of certainty.' She comes around her trolley to his and looks at what he has: nappies, vegetables, fruit, a six-pack of beer, two bottles of wine. 'You can tell a lot about someone from their shopping.'

'I'm aiming for a balance between healthy living and surviving-the-day vice.'

This is the first time they've met since a few days after Finbar and Vicky's wedding, when he picked up some stuff from her flat. They promised to remain friends and not allow things to get awkward. He feels guilty, but not keeping in touch was a conscious choice – he'd hoped that, with space, it would be obvious to her that harbouring any romantic feelings for him was a mistake. She was often tempted to contact him, but didn't give in to it. She thought she needed space too. When he heard from Seb that she was seeing someone, part of him was relieved. Later on, when he learned of her break-up, part of him was relieved then as well, although he was also annoyed with himself for not wishing her all she deserved.

She says, 'How's that niece of yours? And how's the new mother?'

'They're both very well. Zoe likes to demonstrate just how well she is by waiting for me to fall asleep before she pierces my ears with her wailing.'

'You've taken to uncle-hood then?'

He smiles in spite of himself. 'Generally speaking. Who would have thought it?'

'It's not such a shock.'

There's a silence between them until he says, 'You look like you have something you want to ask me.'

'I guess I'm curious if you and Isabel are together.'

'We're good friends, that's all.'

'I wouldn't freak out if you were more. It would be nice if you found someone.'

'There's no one. You're not the first to ask about me and Isabel, y'know. I don't know where the rumours are springing from.'

She gives him an amused look. 'You're living together and raising a child together.'

'I'm not "raising" anyone. I'm helping out. At some point, I'll go my own way.'

'Does Isabel know that?' Seeing his taken-aback expression, she says, 'Don't answer that. Sorry. It's none of my business.'

'I don't mind. She knows. Neither of us is under any illusion that it's a long-term arrangement.' She's wincing, so he says, 'It's a fair question.'

'Okay, good. I'm glad that . . . we ran into each other.'

'Thanks for smashing your trolley into mine.'

'Any time.'

He watches her as she spins her trolley around, wheels it down the aisle, and turns the corner. He grabs that second package of nappies and chucks it into the trolley, where it rattles against the sides with a more belligerent bounce than the first one.

Ten minutes later, when Alice pushes her trolley, now full of bagged groceries, towards the exit, she discovers him sitting on a bench. He says, 'You're not stalking me, are you?'

She smiles, a bit perplexed. 'You appear to be the one waiting for me.'

'You've got me there.'

She looks about him. 'What happened to your groceries?'

'I'm getting them delivered. I was wondering if you'd like to go for coffee? We could catch up properly.'

'Won't Isabel, and child, be waiting for you?'

'All I'd have to do is let her know I'll be later than expected.'

He thinks she's about to agree, but she says, 'Some other time, okay? I've a lot of stuff to do.'

He doesn't ask what she means by 'stuff' for fear she would have to make something up on the spot. It would be embarrassing for them both if she had to admit to a lie. He stands. 'You can call me sometime.'

'I will.'

They go outside. She says, 'Want a lift?'

'Nah. I need the exercise and you're going in the opposite direction.'

'If you're sure. It was lovely to see you, Jimmy.'

She almost kisses him on the cheek but thinks better of it, waves, and wheels her trolley away.

When Elizabeth arrives in Rathbaile, she drives to Jimmy's place first. She makes the expected comments about how much Zoe has grown since she saw her at Easter, and how she's even more beautiful. Unprompted, Isabel gives her Zoe to hold. She sleeps through Elizabeth apprehensively rocking her. Once Isabel has taken multiple photos of aunt and niece, and promises to post them on Facebook, Elizabeth hands Zoe off to her with great delicacy of movement, as if she's ridding herself of a time bomb. She ignores Jimmy when he heaves with his arms and says, 'Just throw her.'

Elizabeth and Jimmy have dinner in their old house. There's a lull in the otherwise upbeat mood when Eamon comments that Zoe has the same eyes as Tighe. The dejection in his tone is apparent, but he means it as a good thing. Elizabeth agrees that her eyes are a similar shade of brown as Tighe's without conceding that they are the same, considering that his were untrustworthy. Jimmy doesn't voice an opinion.

After Eamon calls it a night. Jimmy invites Elizabeth to have a beer with him on the patio. She puts on Eamon's coat over her purple tank top to keep her arms and shoulders warm, and they go outside. When they're sitting at the patio table, Jimmy waits for her to finish a sip of her can, then says, 'I've learned your secret. Want to come clean?'

Elizabeth, unable to conceal her sudden unease, says, 'No, because maybe it's a bluff, and even if you do have intel, I don't know *which* secret. So you can spill it or not. See if I care.'

Jimmy laughs. 'Yesterday evening, Seb called me.' He pauses to give Elizabeth the chance to speak. She doesn't, so he continues, 'He said that you and him are a couple, and that it's serious.'

'We are. It is.' She drinks. 'What's your take on it?'

'I never saw it coming, but that doesn't mean it wasn't about damn time. I'm overjoyed. Why all the secrecy? Am I such a misery-guts that I seem like I can't bear the happiness of others?'

'It's nothing personal. It was more of a hang-up of Seb's than anything else. If it had been entirely up to me, I would've told you sooner. I'm going to have to give him a clout when I next see him – we spoke this afternoon and he didn't let on that he'd told you.'

'Yeah, well, he said that I should be the one to tell you I'm in on the big secret, because if he did it himself you might not believe him. I'm not sure if it's a relationship you're in, or if the pair of you are adversaries in a game of espionage.'

Last year, not long after Elizabeth heard that Isabel was pregnant, she and Seb broke up. Living on different islands hadn't helped; neither had the tiptoeing-around-Jimmy factor, and their feelings, though strong, had been undermined by their insecurities. What changed it around was that in January, Seb scored a regular part on a gritty TV hospital drama called *Scalpel* – he plays a crack-addicted doctor who cares more about his patients than is healthy for him, hence the crack – and this has been leading to other offers too. He was able to afford his own apartment – renting, which was still a significant step up – and soon after moving in, he asked Elizabeth to come stay for a weekend. When she did, he told her how he hadn't gotten over her and that he wanted to try again. Not being a fan of the 'you complete me' concept of relationships, he'd felt that he needed to become more comfortable in his own skin before he could be right for her, and that meant getting a proper foothold in his career. In bed, she asked him, 'So if you hadn't aced that audition, we probably wouldn't be getting back together?' and he admitted, 'Maybe not, but I put that motivation into the performance the casting director saw. Feel free to take credit for everything.'

Elizabeth shakes her head, but it's a gesture of relief. She tells Jimmy, 'It's so good that you know,' and has a long drink of her beer. 'I could do with a few more of these.'

They drink some more, then, as it's getting colder, they return inside. Jimmy takes the last four cans from the fridge and they retreat to Elizabeth's room because she wants to smoke hash as well.

They share a joint, but after that, he decides to stick to beer. She rolls herself another and smokes it sitting in the middle of her bed, leaning forward against her raised knees with her feet flat on the blanket. He's sitting in a chair that's turned towards her. His elbow is on the windowsill behind him and he has a can in hand. She exhales a puff of smoke and waves it away from in front of her face. Gazing out the window, she says, 'I see so many stars.'

He'd been pondering the faded posters on her wall of the Smiths and the Cure – two moany bands he has always hated – but now he looks over his shoulder at the sky outside. 'It's beautiful, isn't it? I've always thought—'

'Y'know,' she coughs, clears her throat, and says, 'I'm still pissed off at Tighe.'

Jimmy sighs. 'He didn't know about Zoe and that he was leaving Isabel in the lurch.'

'Do you honestly think it would've made a difference?'

'I've no way of knowing.'

'Sure you do. If he thought nothing of screwing over all

the people whose money he stole, and letting Dad down, and me, and you, how can you believe he actually would have stood by Isabel and Zoe?'

'He didn't let *me* down. I get mad at him when I think about what his mess has cost *him* – and yeah, I get mad on behalf of the people he hurt too – but then I remind myself of all he's done for me. People make mistakes.'

'He's not a good guy who slipped up. You have to be a bad person to do what he did.' Elizabeth takes a drag of her joint, inhaling deeply, before stubbing it out in the ashtray on her nightstand. Picking up an already open beer can from next to the ashtray, she says, 'I feel sorry for you that you don't see who he is. Neither does Dad, but he has more of an excuse. He feels responsible because sons are supposed to reflect their fathers somehow, even though Tighe has never had Dad's good heart. Incidentally, you do have it.'

'What gave you that impression?'

'It's where your gullibility towards Tighe comes from.'

'Is that a backhanded compliment?'

'It's more of a criticism that suggests something positive about you.'

'Awesome, thanks.' He swigs from his can. 'So, if Dad expects his sons to reflect him, where does that leave you?'

'I reflect, just not as much. Dad would be upset if I ripped off loads of people, but he wouldn't be as disappointed as he is with the golden boy, and he would be less surprised. Since I was a little girl, I've been handled like I was a danger to myself, destined to fuck up sooner or later. I was supposed to take after Mam and after Granny Dorothy before her.'

'That isn't true. I'm likelier to lose my mind than you are.'

She gives him a hard look. 'Maybe now you have some confidence in my stability, but you used to be afraid of me.

You might as well own up to it. It doesn't get to me any more.'

'Maybe it's fair to say you made me nervous. You were kind of intense.'

'Everyone was so worried about me that I assumed they must have had their reasons and so I used to freak myself out. After Paul, can you blame me for not knowing how to put the people around me at ease?'

He sips his beer and says, 'Okay, you're right. You were sold short. *I* sold you short. When we were growing up, I was too self-absorbed to understand what it must have been like for you. I'm sorry.'

She smiles at him and sets her can back on her nightstand. 'It's nice to hear that from another Diaz. I think it's a first. Cheers. And pass me another beer. I'm empty.'

There are two more cans on the windowsill. Jimmy stands and hands one to Elizabeth. She opens it and sits back against her stack of three pillows, stretching her legs out. Sitting on the chair again, he opens the other can, getting a dab of foam on his thumb, which he wipes off on his jeans. 'Any other grievances you'd like to discuss?'

'I've a list as long as my arm, but I wouldn't want to use them up all at once. They'll keep. I do feel better about a lot of things to do with the past, though, and I have Seb to thank for it. I know our thing has been sprung on you out of nowhere, but whenever I think about it, I'm still surprised by it too. I used to be so determined not to end up like Mam that I had pretty much sworn to myself that I would always be alone. I saw relationships as something that could be fine for other people, but for me they seemed dangerous. If I had one it would mean I was trying to escape who I was so I could pretend to be some kind of "normal" person, whatever that is. If I did have the potential to go crazy, I thought that was the surefire path to it. I had it all wrong. Having someone feels so different to what I expected. It might be an odd way to put it, but I feel more like myself than I ever have before. Hopefully, I haven't jinxed Seb and me by saying all of that.'

'It sounds like you've both found something special, and it's well deserved. In my case, I've been going the other way. I think it genuinely *is* for the best that I'm alone. I'm suited to it and I don't mind. Not everyone should be with someone, but I'm glad that you're not like me.'

She frowns. 'I don't know if you're prepared for me to tell it like it is, with gloves off.'

He grins. 'We've been wearing gloves? Fuck it, whatever you're thinking, lay it on me.'

She puts down her can and sits up straighter. 'The reasons I used to have for being alone aren't like yours. You see, you're like Dad.'

'We've already covered this.'

'No, we haven't. Dad has my respect and devotion, but he's also a sad and lonely old man. So are you.'

His grin stiffens. 'I'm a sad, lonely old man?'

'Yes. And you know what else? I feel like I've been cowardly because of how I've held back from bringing this up with you. You were madly in love with Nicole, but you never mention her name. Before you put up your defences and deny, deny, just know that you can't persuade me she doesn't haunt you.'

Quietly, he says, 'Be careful.'

'What good would that do you, Jimmy?'

'Plenty of people have been through much worse than me.'

'Is that supposed to matter?'

He goes silent. Finally, his voice saturated with exasperation, he says, 'I thought I could save her, and if I could do that, maybe she could save me too.'

'From what?'

'From every stupid thing. I imagined us protecting each other from our worst qualities and from any terrible experiences. At the very least, I believed I could keep her alive, but I couldn't even do that much. Is that enough venting for you?'

'It's sad, just sad, and no, it's not enough.'

'What would be?'

'I think you need to find a way to honour her memory.'

'How – please tell me – am I supposed to do that?'

'If you loved her, and I know you did, you should be doing everything you can to be living your life to the full, and not going through the motions.'

'I've already lost more in my life than I can ever expect to gain.'

'That doesn't mean you can't find a way to be happy.'

He decides not to patronise her with a promise to try to follow her advice.

V
June 2015

One hour ago:

Jimmy and Isabel sit on their couch, trading reassuring glances; he's holding her hand against her knee. She stands. 'I really have to go, but we'll talk about it when I get back.'

'Whatever we end up doing, it'll be okay. I promise.'

She says, 'Great,' and leaves.

Once he hears the door shut, he stamps his palms to his aching head. 'Fuck. Fuck. Fucking fuck.'

Despite all his protests that his friendship with Isabel was platonic, things got weird.

A few weeks ago, they had stayed up late talking and – after she confessed to Jimmy how she felt guilty for visiting Tighe in their house on the day he was attacked by those dogs – they shared a fumbling kiss. The next morning, they laughed about it, blaming it on drunkenness, although neither of them had been more than tipsy. It was a one-off, until it happened again, but there was an explanation for that too. Zoe wouldn't stop crying. Isabel and then Jimmy put a hand to her forehead. They convinced themselves she was burning up, without verifying it with a thermometer, and rushed her to the emergency room. By the time they got there, she was asleep. The doctor patiently checked her over, then said her temperature was only barely above normal and she would be fine with some rest. They felt foolish, but after returning home and putting Zoe to bed, Isabel became teary and Jimmy put his arms around her. Their kiss felt like a natural extension of the embrace, and it was understandable, given the fright they'd shared. He apologised, but she said she'd no regrets – it had made her feel like she wasn't alone in a moment when she needed that, and they didn't have to let it confuse things.

They carried on, still just friends, but they became more physical with each other. They sat closer together. When he walked in on her rocking Zoe, he would put his arm around her waist and she would lean into him. Then there was the night when she came into his room, panicked after having a nightmare – 'Zoe died.' He pulled back his blanket and she got in. They kissed, and groped, and fell asleep entwined. The next day, they didn't discuss it, and later that night she got into bed with him again. Their groping progressed.

Today, he woke with her beside him for the fifth consecutive morning. With her elbow pushed into the pillow, she was propping up her head with her hand and staring at him. 'We should talk.'

He touched the curve of her cool shoulder with his pincer. 'Mind if I shower first? I might need my wits about me.'

'Go ahead. I'll put on the coffee.'

After showering and dressing, he procrastinated a little more by looking in on Zoe. She was fast asleep, so he denied himself his wish to lift her out of the cot and hold her.

While they were eating the eggs and bacon that Isabel made, they talked about Zoe's sleeping patterns and double-checked their itineraries. Once they had cleared their plates, they went into the living room to drink their coffees. Jimmy said, 'Are you going to ask me to move out?'

She put her hand on his. 'No.' They both smiled at the uncertainty in her voice. 'Or that's not exactly what I was going to say. I guess we should consider it.'

They talked, without rushing to any decision, until she had to get going for her shift at the Westbrook Inn.

Alone, he stamps his palms to his aching head. 'Fuck. Fuck. Fucking fuck.'

They've left the platonic-friendship line in the dust, but they don't believe they could ever quite fall in love. Neither wants to be in a relationship where they are stand-ins for someone else, and even if they could make such a compromise, they wouldn't want Zoe to grow up with them as an example for how a couple should be. A withdrawal to friendship, then, is the better option, but living together won't help with that. They don't want to end their arrangement. Yet it might be for the best.

On the walkie-talkie, Jimmy hears Zoe crying, so he goes

to her room and looks in at her. He pinches one of the dream-catcher's feathers and raises it high. He lets go and the dream-catcher swoops down, then wobbles backward and forward. He feels empathy for the flimsy object. Zoe, entranced by the desultory swinging motion, halts her cries. He reaches his pincer into the cot and touches her remarkably soft cheek. She clasps his index finger in her hand.

He waits until she releases it, then puts his hands under her arms and lifts her up against his shoulder. He breathes in the milky smell of her scalp, and thinks that maybe, if he was tougher with himself, he could keep his loneliness from under-mining things with Isabel again and he could stay. Pacing the room, he rocks Zoe in rhythm to his walk. His mind wanders back to ten months ago, when he was in the pub with Finbar and Isabel went into labour, and how it hadn't even occurred to him that he would love Zoe from the moment he set eyes on her: she was hideous and drenched in the slime of afterbirth, but tiny and beautiful too. He thinks back two months to seeing Alice in Tesco. He misses her, but doesn't know if he should call. He thinks about his 'gloves off' conversation with Elizabeth, ten days ago, and how it has probably done him some good; and then about Isabel and what to say to her later.

He returns Zoe to her cot, but when he steps outside the room, she starts crying again. As he goes back inside, he's struck by a sharp pain just behind his forehead that gives way to an overpowering dizziness. His eyes roll, he bites his tongue, and when his knee buckles, he reaches out to grab something, finding only air as he topples face-forward.

Now:
  Zoe is wailing. Jimmy's phone is ringing.
  If someone doesn't come soon and save him, I think he'll

die. In the midst of my terror, a mad idea claws at me, and I wonder if I'm somehow responsible for what has happened. Did I imagine this – because I secretly wanted it – and then it came true?

Maybe the only one who can bring him back to life is me.

Chapter Thirty-Two

Mortality

July 2015

While you've never heard me, Jimmy, I think I've always been telling this story to you, especially in the recent present. You're my ideal reader, for your flaws as much as your strengths.

When Isabel arrived at the Westbrook Inn on the day you collapsed, she had changed her mind. She no longer thought it would be a good idea for you to move out, not before the two of you had tried harder to make it work. When you didn't answer her calls, she got scared that something bad had happened – rationally, she figured you were likelier to be okay, but she wasn't about to take the chance. She rushed home before you were gone forever and saved you by calling an ambulance. Others saved you too: the paramedics, and the neurosurgeon at St John's who cracked open your skull and relieved the pressure on your brain.

You suffered an intracranial haemorrhage due to an aneurysm causing bilateral damage to the reticular formation of your midbrain. It's a mystery why you had an aneurysm, as you don't tick the boxes of the known risk factors. You're not obese or diabetic or a smoker. You're a tense guy, but to say you suffer from hypertension would be a stretch. On occasion you drink too much, but you don't possess the true dedication of an alcoholic.

Your coma has lasted six weeks now. The doctors have run their tests, from peering into your eyes with a torch to taking a more intimate look at your brain via a CT scan. You have no corneal reflex, no papillary response to light, no gag or cough reflex. You react to neither vocal nor painful stimuli, so if someone shouted at you or stabbed you, you would be just as indifferent. For all it has been through, your brain doesn't appear to be permanently damaged. The doctors don't know why your condition persists. If you died today or woke up, they would be equally surprised, yet unsurprised. Assuming the more positive outcome, they say you could make a full recovery. They cannot, however, offer guarantees.

In the meantime, your mind and body aren't on speaking terms. In this ongoing feud, it's as if they've forgotten how they used to get along. Your mind would be interested to know that your body has been fitted out with coma paraphernalia. You have a rectangle of tape on both of your eyelids to keep them closed so they don't dry out. There's an IV in your arm, an endotracheal tube down your throat – in case you forget to breathe – and you have other tubes too, one up your nose, two more inserted in . . . let's just say you're well plugged.

Considering how we're both disembodied these days, you've never been more like me. By some measures, I'm doing a little better than you. I can pay attention to other people and consciously choose which memories I place myself in. I can focus my thoughts and think things through, for all the good that does me. You are lost. Your mind is diluted and you pitch about in a dream state that is, well, dreamy; nightmarish too. Memories flash before you, but you can't slow them. They just ignite and perish, merging with other memories, dissipating as fast as they appear. The details are a convoluted mixture of fact and fiction, like your imagination is fucking with you and more than usual. Then there are all your emotions flailing about, erratic in their variety and intensity – anger and guilt, fear and love, happiness and sadness, and the rest of those hackneyed symptoms of the human condition, coexisting one moment, eclipsing each other the next.

Your body stoically refrains from communicating any of this to the people who have been at your bedside. They've been watching you very intently, taking turns trying to determine what's going on in your head. Sooner or later, they've all wondered if you can hear them when they speak. It's strange how they tend to whisper, as if they're afraid to disturb you when it's something they would be glad of. You'd be amazed at the number of declarations of kinship and friendship made to your body. You're even more popular than when your leg was chopped off, and this time you haven't had to resort to anything as gimmicky as that. Instead, you've adopted what could be called a minimalist approach to charisma. All this entails is abstaining from talking and emoting. That's not as great as it sounds. Yes, they're captivated, but they preferred the old you.

And who are your caring watchers?

The person who has clocked the most hours is Eamon. He has been in your private room every day and many of the nights. He isn't a fan of your shaved-head look. It accentuates your frailty, but more than that, he's bothered by your new scar. It's a nice cruel-looking one that runs across the side of your skull, like you were initialled by Zorro, only he was drunk and employed a hatchet rather than his usual rapier – actually, though, the neurosurgeon used a special type of drill and a special type of saw. During your craniotomy, he removed a section of your skull – what they call the bone flap – and reattached it afterwards with tiny titanium plates, covering the incision with a turban-like dressing. The turban is now gone. The plates have been unscrewed, the stitches have been taken out, and the bone flap has been reintegrated into your skull. Your hair is growing back. Still, Eamon's eyes are drawn to the malevolent leer of your scar.

Throughout your nap, he has looked as depleted as he ever has, but he assures himself that this is your last big test of misfortune. Once you wake up, you'll soldier on and attain emotional and physical rejuvenation, and you'll be successful at whatever you apply yourself to; more importantly, you'll be happy. And he will redouble his own efforts to be happy because he knows you worry and he doesn't want to put any more weight on your back. He's betting on you; the flipside is that if you don't return, he'll give up on everything. You'll doom him. No pressure, mind.

As much as his belief in you has helped him to keep it together, Elizabeth's support has been invaluable to him too. She has taken a break from her work responsibilities to stay with him and make certain he doesn't skip too many meals. She has been dealing directly with the doctors and nurses, informing others about your status, and co-coordinating visits. She discourages people from bringing you flowers. There are limitations on space.

If you don't get back up, it's not lost on her that Eamon will drop next and, with Tighe no longer counting, that would leave her as the last family member standing. But there's a difference between being aware of something and being prepared for it. When no one else was around, she leaned in close and growled into your ear, 'If you dare to even try and die on us, I'll find you in your dreams and strangle you back

427

to life.' She laughed as she folded her arms hard against her body. There were tears in her eyes, but she didn't look away.

Seb came over from London and has been here for four out of the six weekends you've been under. He told you that he's planning on asking Elizabeth to marry him, and he wants you to be his best man. The only thing he's waiting on is for you to wake up. If you die, he'll still ask her – and I expect her to say yes – but you'll have darkened a day that should be a celebration.

Brian came from Dublin. He has decided to settle there indefinitely, in light of how the referendum went the right way, but he wasted no time in reminding you about what a mistake you made in returning to live in Rathbaile, his insinuation being that the town itself bore the blame for your current state.

Finbar came from a few streets away. He had cold feet about getting that tattoo for Vicky's birthday, but now he's contemplating getting one again and has promised to let you make the call. He's even willing to go with the ball and chain.

One afternoon, Seb, Brian, and Finbar were in your room at the same time. You could take credit for the reunion of the old gang – they generously considered you present – but maybe it would be best not to. The atmosphere was dismal. They all silently wondered if the next occasion to bring them together would be your funeral.

Alice has been here frequently. She broke down once when she was holding your pincer in her hands, and said, 'I'm so sorry I didn't go for coffee with you that day when you asked. I wanted to prove I didn't need you in my life, but I could've pulled myself together and been your friend.'

She has somehow persuaded herself that you must have a poor opinion of her. She needs to be set straight. You know *what it's like to live with regret because of a ruptured end to knowing someone. Alice is another reason you have no right to die like this.*

Isabel and Zoe are two more.

Isabel brought Zoe in to you yesterday. She'd kept her away from the hospital before because she didn't want her to pick up any bugs, but she risked it to see if her presence could provoke a reaction from you. She held Zoe against your chest, restraining her hands when she tugged at the tube in your nose. Zoe screamed at you and only calmed down when Isabel walked with her over to the window, blocking you from sight. Isabel touched her cheek to Zoe's head and shut her eyes. She's not a believer in prayer, but she did, with all her will, wish for your recovery. They need you to come back, and that's your fault. You knowingly allowed them to depend on you.

All of these people have been here for you, but the one who appears the most in your fragmented pieces of mind is Nicole.

You used to joke with her that you had a surplus of body parts so you weren't troubled by the loss of your leg and fingers, but, of course, she could tell you were. You once said to her, 'Just because I'm not whole doesn't mean I'm not together.' It was true enough to not be a lie, but then, when she died, you lost all of her. You would no longer claim to be together and you deliberately turned the volume down on your emotions to withstand being deafened. To your thinking, it was necessary to survive. And surviving was important, not because you loved life and wanted to experience more, but because you owed it to those who cared about you. You avoided your grief because it seemed too vast. Instead, you adopted its lesser cousin and nourished your sweet unhappiness, which has been such a reliable companion that you haven't seriously tried to part ways with it. You taught yourself to forget that life is something to be enjoyed, not endured.

I can almost hear you deriding the notion of grieving. You might put the word in quotation marks, and ask me to explain what it is and how someone could possibly go about doing it. Well, I would begin by saying you should acknowledge your grief, and not just for a moment or two. You need to persistently tell yourself: 'I knew Nicole; I have a right to express my sorrow; I loved her.' But you would probably laugh. You'd retort that what you learned about her after she died proved that you didn't really know her; that you lost your right to any sorrow when you failed to save her; as for love, you'd say that if you loved her enough, why did she leave you, why didn't you really know her, and why couldn't you save her?

There are some answers. But they don't neatly fit your questions and they're not easy to accept.

She left you because she thought it was the best way to protect you. She was wrong, but it was an act of love.

She loved you as much as you loved her.

Excluding me – and I cheated – she let you know her better than she had let anyone else know her, and while that might not feel like a great consolation, it should feel like some.

In a sense, it doesn't matter if your impressions of her were accurate or if you created an image of her based on what you wanted to see. Your feelings were real, and they count for something.

I can't give you an adequate explanation for why she told lies. I have an excess of facts at my disposal, reams of her most pressing thoughts, a wealth of her most heartfelt emotions, and I still don't fully get it myself. Even though there's no excuse for that and I should be able to . . . Strike *that; I sound like you. But consider, if I had too much of a blindside to understand her, and I'm psychic, for fuck's sake, isn't it possible you're expecting too much of yourself?*

And that's another answer: you couldn't save her because you're not psychic.

I agree with what Elizabeth said, that you can honour her memory by living your life to the full. Just so you know, the difficulty of that is a big part of what makes it valuable.

To be clear, you're not really living if you aren't open to the idea of falling in love again. I know you don't think you have it in you to love someone as intensely as you loved Nicole. While I don't foresee it happening for you with either Alice or Isabel, you could conceivably meet someone who is as potentially dangerous to you as Nicole was. It's a matter of luck and courage. If the former happened to you, and if you committed yourself to possessing the latter, and if the object of your desire felt the same way – yes, there are a lot of ifs – it would, inevitably, be painful for you to pursue her. Your love would be initially laced with grief, but if you could outlast the grief, one day you might look around and discover you're not unhappy, that you don't feel alone. Is this something you can imagine?

For anything good to be possible – how many times do I have to stress it? – first you have to wake up.

I'm rooting for you. It's just a small aspect of me that struggles with being so supportive. I've never fully shaken my resentment towards you for all you take for granted. It's petty and I'd like to be better than that, but it's there.

Don't get me wrong. You're the only true family I've ever had. You see, I don't feel like Tighe, Elizabeth, or Paul were ever really my siblings, or that Grace and Eamon were really my mother and father – she gave birth to me but had no chance to mother me, and he had no chance to be a father to me – but I think of you as my brother and twin. You're my reflection, my could-have-been, and though you've never known me, I've inhabited you.

I can't help but wonder what I would do if I had your life, with the proviso that I could bring all I've learned to the role. Well, it would depend on whether I was starting from your beginning or whether I was starting from now.

In the first scenario, I would try to save some people. That would include my new self. There would be no jumping into yards with starving dogs and no pissing off gangsters.

I would confront Grace about her suicidal thoughts and attempt to convince her of the effect her death would have on her family. I'd plead with her to hold on for as long as she could. If she felt like her desperation was too great, I'd tell her to leave us all and go somewhere else if there was a chance it could bring her happiness. Save yourself, I'd say. I think I could make a difference to her, if only for a while. Maybe she would end her life anyway, but I'd have tried.

Nicole I believe I could save. To begin with, I would murder Tighe. I'd do it as a child, when my innocence would be most credible. I'd wait for a good opportunity and make it look like an accident. I'd sleep peacefully afterwards. When I finished school, I'd still move to Dublin so I could seek out Nicole and we could fall in love. I'd call her out on any lies and I'd make her trust me. I'd never disappoint her.

I would be a dutiful son, a reliable brother – to Elizabeth – and a loyal friend.

What else would I do? Everything I could think of worth doing. I'd touch and eat and push my body to exhaustion. I'd experience pleasure and pain. I'd meet more people and try more things than you did. I'd never indulge boredom or waste time. I'd travel, with Nicole. On some perfect beach somewhere, I'd ask her to marry me.

In the second scenario, if I possessed your body in the here and now and had to pick up where you've left off, I would tell my family and friends what they mean to me, and thank them. I wouldn't tell them who I really am – they'd think I'm crazy – but everyone needs a secret or two. I could fake it, being you. I could be you better than you ever could.

I would give everyone time to get used to having me back, long enough for them to gain faith in my new-found durability and zeal for life. Eventually I'd move out of Isabel's flat because I'd still want to see the world, even if I couldn't share it with Nicole. I'd return, though. I'd be dependable.

As for Tighe, if he ever showed up, wanting his brother to provide him with refuge, I would say, of course, it's the least I can do for you after all you've done for me. I'd embrace him, and as soon as I had the opportunity, I'd murder him and find somewhere no one would look to dispose of the body. I'd sleep peacefully afterwards.

If I lived, I would follow my dreams no matter what. I'd be someone who doesn't get too scared or complacent to take risks.

I know how simplistic it all sounds, talking about what I would do, and while I can imagine getting things right that you didn't, reality would quickly become more complicated than I could anticipate and I'd be bound to make many mistakes. But bring them on.

And Jimmy, if you don't want your life, then I've no problem admitting I do. Maybe that reveals a coldness in me when all I should be contemplating is your well-being. Maybe I've nothing to apologise for. I didn't choose to exist as whatever it is I am. I've always wanted, and still want, to be something more.

Maybe I can be, at a cost.

I haven't addressed what I said before about the possibility of my being responsible for what has happened to you and how I might be the only one who can bring you back. It's a hunch I've been ignoring because of the decision I have to make if it's true.

I could be wrong – every mind has its delusions – but if I can trust my awareness of my own nature, this is the curse of you and me: the unnatural state of two consciousnesses for one body has always had a termination point. I pushed you out and I can allow you back in by willingly ceasing to exist, or I can suffocate you and have life as my reward. Everything I've been imagining could be attainable.

Could I really be blamed if I acted on this monstrous power? It would be so easy to rationalise it as a form of self-defence. You've had your time to get things right. Surely I should get a chance too.

Or can I vanquish myself forever, for your sake? Can I surrender my identity so you can have yours?

What it ultimately comes down to is whether I love you or myself more. And I love you very much.

I'm done with debating this any further when the outcome will be what it was always going to be.

Jimmy Dice, I wish that you could have known that I was your witness. Your loved ones are calling for you.

15/7/2015
I'm finally and overwhelmingly awake.

Acknowledgements

I'm indebted to more people than I can name here – I would need another book – but I owe particular thanks to:

My parents, Ken and Geraldine Ryan, and my sister, Carolyn Karina, who are the people I look up to, frequently straining my neck, whenever I contemplate 'how to be a better human being'.

My extraordinary agent, Karolina Sutton, who relentlessly championed the book and my outstanding editor, Imogen Taylor, who vastly improved it.

Caoilinn Hughes; David J. Fleming; Anna Jackson; Mark Williams; Rajorshi Chakraborti; Juha, Emily, and Aden Karina; Aisling and David Whitaker; Kate Gleeson; Claire Wren; Amy Perkins; Phoebe Swinburn; Patrick Insole; Nathan Burton; Jane Selley; Melissa Pimentel; Lucy Morris; Alice Dill; everyone at Tinder Press and Curtis Brown.

Anne-Laure Richert was a warm and vibrant soul, and the dearest of friends. She inspired me to pursue becoming a writer and this book wouldn't exist if I hadn't known her.

THE FRACTURED LIFE OF JIMMY DICE

Bonus Material

Why I Write

Why I Read

Q&A

Why I Write

THE FRACTURED LIFE OF JIMMY DICE BEGAN WITH MY ANGRY
hands and, later, a dedication.

Aged eighteen, I had a bad case of eczema on my hands
– whenever I flexed my fingers, the skin would crack and
bleed. I visited an acupuncturist who attributed the affliction
to my 'unexpressed rage', then she held my wrists and discovered an oddity: on my right wrist my pulse was very slow and
on my left it was very fast. She looked at me as if she was
wondering whether I was somehow producing this effect on
purpose, and she asked if I ever felt like I was two people
inhabiting one body.

After a series of acupuncture sessions, and the repeated
application of a gooey seaweed-based salve, my hands healed.
I had only the vaguest idea of trying to be a writer, but the
acupuncturist's question lingered in my mind.

At that time, the most precious thing in my life was my
friendship with a young French woman, Anne-Laure. She had
such a big heart and we were kindred spirits. I simply felt
more alive, and more like my best self, around her than I did
with others.

She died in a senseless accident in Paris, her home city. I
had known myself to be strong, but losing her broke me on

the spot, and I wasn't equipped to verbalise my sorrow to anyone.

A year later, on the day she would have turned twenty-one, I went to a café in Dublin with the intention of committing to paper some memories of her, for my eyes only. It had been just the two of us for most of the time we spent in each other's company so I was worried I might forget something crucial and then it would be gone forever. I expected to fill up a couple of pages, but one bout of writing led to many others and I didn't stop at writing down some of my memories of her; I wrote down all of them. The release it gave me was tremendous and, within months, I had written over two hundred pages.

I soon reckoned that, if I could finish a memoir without really setting out to, I should see if I could write fiction. I got hooked immediately and I vowed to someday get a novel published that I would dedicate to my friend. If it took the rest of my life, so be it.

After completing a pair of learning-curve novels, I thought back to what the acupuncturist had asked me and started to imagine a character who weathers a string of traumas, which are often the unintended consequences of poor decisions, while, unbeknownst to him, his body hosts a witness to his actions – his stillborn twin – who powerlessly longs to be capable of making mistakes.

Writing the first draft of *Jimmy Dice* was at times a euphoric experience, but it was painful too. The story was hyper-personal and, in the telling, I was hit by waves of delayed grief. The goal of the dedication became paralyzing. I felt that if I failed to follow through I would be letting Anne-Laure down and so I equated having a bad writing day with being a bad person. The pressure I was putting on myself was causing me to be frequently sick to my stomach and my hands kept shaking.

To pull out of my meltdown, I had to change my way of thinking. I told myself, again and again until it stuck, that I had been a good friend, and that would remain true regardless of whether I ever published, and I vowed to press on with my wish to build a career as a writer. My primary motivation, however, couldn't continue to be the dedication; my love of writing itself – and I do downright love it – had to take priority.

That first draft was written between 2006 and 2009. I was proud of my efforts, but I hadn't been ready to bring it off – for one thing, at nearly 200,000 words, I had crammed in an excess of narrative and I couldn't figure out how to rein the novel in. So I put it aside.

Six years later, I stalled on another novel and, needing a break, I retrieved *Jimmy Dice* from the drawer, thinking I might tinker around with a few lines. Approaching it fresh, and having spent the intervening time obsessively developing a better writer-brain, I was finally able to identify how I had obscured the story I had been attempting to tell. It was exciting to discover so many missteps because for each of them I conceived potential solutions. Over a feverish ten weeks, I cut reams of material, ruthlessly throwing characters and scenes overboard, and I rewrote almost every sentence, adding more humour and hope.

I submitted my redraft to a shortlist of agents without lofty expectations – although I believed I had instilled new life into the novel, I was conscious of the possibility that it had expired on the operating table the first time around and I just couldn't accept it because it meant too much to me. Then I received four offers of representation in five days.

When I went to London for meetings, I tried to appear as

if I was taking it all in my stride, but it must have been obvious that my head was spinning. I signed with my dream agent, who saw right into the heart of the novel, and she found the perfect editor, whose insights drew out the best in it.

My head is still spinning actually.

The problem of my angry hands has never reoccurred. With the publication of *The Fractured Life of Jimmy Dice*, the dedication is in print at last and so it will endure.

A version of this essay first appeared in the *Irish Times*.

Why I Read

I BELIEVE BOOKS CAN SAVE PEOPLE. WRITING THEM HAS been a lifeline that has pulled me through my most challenging experiences. And my sister, Carolyn, was sustained through debilitating illness by audiobooks.

She has been living with Chronic Lyme Disease for two decades and in the worst years she was forced to endure extreme exhaustion and extreme pain. Because of her acute sensitivity to light and sound, she was confined to spending day after day in her bedroom with the curtains drawn and the lights off. She couldn't watch television, and taking a phone call or using a laptop intensified her pain. Our parents brought her meals – bland ones due to dietary restrictions – and, on good days, she could talk to them, but only for short periods. While she lacked the energy to hold up a book and read it, she could play audiobooks. She listened to about 300 per year and they gave her imaginary worlds to focus on. She wouldn't have made it to the other side of those excruciating years if it wasn't for the depth of her fortitude, as well as the love and support of our parents and of the man she went on to marry, but she has told me that fortitude, and that love and support, probably wouldn't have been enough if it wasn't for the stimulation and solace gifted to her by all those books.

I'm perpetually in awe of the magic of books. Even when I haven't been able to afford to buy any, I can rarely walk by bookshops without stepping inside to breathe them in and to place my hand on a few familiar spines. Every book on the shelves is a writer's dream come true. By the alchemical means of covering paper with a combination of symbols, they've managed to cross space and time to channel their imaginings into the minds of strangers.

Great novels put you in the shoes of people who you wouldn't have thought you had much in common with and yet you can come to recognise your own feelings in their heart of hearts. If you've ever felt vengeful, you'll root for Edmond Dantès in Alexandre Dumas' *The Count of Monte Cristo*; if you've strained to comprehend injustice, you'll sympathise with Scout in Harper Lee's *To Kill a Mockingbird*; if you've had to reinvent yourself time and again, you'll relate to Norma Jeane in Joyce Carol Oates' *Blonde*; and if you've ever found it agonising to express your true emotions, you'll wince in solidarity with Stevens in Kazuo Ishiguro's *The Remains of the Day*. As anyone who has read Vladimir Nabokov's horrifying masterpiece *Lolita*, and caught themselves laughing along with Humbert Humbert, can attest to, sometimes becoming close to a character can be disturbing, but the further you dare to extend your empathy, the more you'll know yourself.

Great novels, and the great writers who write them, make me feel much better about our species. I'm glad to live in a world where Margaret Atwood infuses her novels with crackling intelligence and mordant wit – her Grace Marks from *Alias Grace* is as fascinating a character as I've ever read; where E. L. Doctorow, in standouts like *Ragtime* and *Homer & Langley,* has written of the past with such vitality that it seems even more immediate than the present day; where John

Irving, in the likes of *The World According to Garp*, champions those who might be considered misfits with humanity and exuberance; and where Marilynne Robinson, with her clear-eyed wisdom, is apparently incapable of producing a novel that's less than exceptional. All of these writers, and many more, inspire me with their boundless creativity, and with their willingness to confront dark subjects – the implication is that a deeper understanding can be reached and so it's always an optimistic act.

When a reader is someone who is going through a hard time, and is failing to communicate with or relate to the people around them, the human touch provided by the right book can be immeasurably valuable. Even more extraordinary than how well-drawn characterisation can induce a reader's empathy is that it can feel like the empathy is being directed towards the reader too, and when empathy is being transmitted in both directions simultaneously, that's intimacy, and I don't know of anything more essential.

Q&A

There is a fair amount of tragedy in Jimmy's life – were there any parts you found particularly hard to write?

More often than not, the most torturous parts to write weren't the scenes where something terrible was happening. The bigger struggle was in writing the key moments in which it was still possible for tragedy to be averted if only Jimmy could have been wiser or braver or a better communicator. I wanted to intervene by imbuing him with the foresight to make shrewder decisions or by making him more perceptive about what others were keeping from him, but I stayed my hand. I had a clear and fixed idea of his psychology, and deviating from it would have felt like cheating. As much as I'm aware that Jimmy is a figment of my imagination, and so I should have been able to bend him to my will whenever I had the urge, my emotional investment in the fictions I write are magnified in direct proportion to the degree of agency I ascribe to my characters – their behaviour must ring true to who I think they are. It's a necessary delusion.

Did a 'favourite' character emerge for you as you wrote?

After having spent so much time with them, I have a great deal of affection for almost all of these characters – there are exceptions: I can't think about Tighe without feeling anger – but my favourite is Nicole. That's partly because she was Jimmy's and his twin's favourite person and I was writing about her from their perspectives. Whenever I conceive of a character, Henry David Thoreau's observation, 'The mass of men lead lives of quiet desperation,' tends to hover in the back of my mind – and I update it to include women – but I was especially conscious of the insecurity, pain, and loneliness at Nicole's core. While I divined early on what her fate was likely to be, as I wrote about her I was searching for a recourse. It eluded me.

Reversing the previous question, the most difficult thing for me *not* to write was a scene depicting her final moments. If I had written it, even with the intention of excluding it from the novel, I would have confirmed exactly what happened to her. By denying myself the chance to find out for sure, I could relate more closely to Jimmy's lasting uncertainty and his inability to attain some peace of mind.

What is your writing process like, day to day?

In the morning, I'm a sleepwalker until I've had a mug, or two, of coffee, but my brain ramps up with the passing hours. I'm more creative at midnight than I am at noon.

With first drafts, the target is 1000 words per day and I stop if I hit it, even if I'm in a groove – to have a starting point for tomorrow. On a highly productive day, that might take two hours and I could be done in the afternoon. Or it might take fourteen hours and it's not uncommon for me to be toiling away deep into the night. Most days, I fall short. 3000 words in a week is good, and I can count on 10,000 words per month.

I work from my flat for weeks on end. When I inevitably slip into a rut, I switch to writing in cafés. When I slip into another rut, I switch back to my flat.

Before I sit down to work, I'm always nervous. Sometimes that's nervous-excitement. Sometimes that's nervous-fear. When I'm haunting cafés, I suspect the baristas peg me as being more socially awkward than I really am, but I'm not jittery because I'm battling to overcome a coffee-ordering phobia; it's because I can't anticipate what will happen when I put pen to paper. On the worst days, when the paper remains entirely white, I'm mortified. But then the best days offer pure elation: it seems as if I'm writing sentences faster than they can fully form in my mind's eye and it's as if nothing is inexpressible.

After I'm finished with a session, or a session is finished with me, I need about an hour to decompress before I'm fit for a normal conversation. If I speak to someone too soon, I can appear frantic. My thoughts are still pinballing so everything I say spills out at a mile a minute. Alternatively, if I've come down from that, I'm often so drained that producing better-than-monosyllabic utterances can be akin to rolling a boulder uphill.

If I could rewire my post-writing temperament, I'd like to be able to rejoin the human race in less time. I would never wish for a cure for my pre-writing nerves though. They're critical to how alive writing makes me feel and the more intimidated I am by the demands involved, the more rewarding it is to complete a novel.

The existential comes into play in the novel – is the spiritual a subject you are drawn to?

Yes, it is, and that's despite not being a spiritual person myself, or at least not in a typical way. I don't believe in higher powers, or the supernatural, or an afterlife. While I'm an atheist, I'm not one of the chest-beating variety. Many of the people I'm close to are spiritual and I admire how they can draw strength from their confidence that everything happens for a reason, even if the precise nature of it is hidden. But where they see an order to things, I see chaos. It's not that I think life is meaningless; rather, I think that meaningfulness has to be created from out of chaos and this can be achieved by caring strongly about something. I also don't believe a person has ever existed, myself included, who has perceived the world with anything resembling lucidity. We all have so many biases and, to be frank, I doubt we're clever enough. That said, I aspire to stretch my understanding as far as it will go and a lot of spiritual people seem to share a similar ambition, but they're regarding the world through a different muddied lens to my own.

I didn't choose to narrate *The Fractured Life of Jimmy Dice* from the point of view of a ghost – even when I don't believe in them – because I wanted the story to be a step removed from my take on reality. Instead, I hoped that by introducing a fantastical and juxtapositional layer to the story, I could capture a trace of how unavoidably surreal it is to experience life.

I differentiate between my beliefs, which are constrained by scientific principles, and my irrational feelings, and in relation to the latter there are spiritual aspects to being a writer for me. So while I don't believe for a moment that I've been somehow 'chosen' to be one, nonetheless, it *feels* like a calling and there's an almost religious fervour laced into my approach. When I'm writing, I have a sense like I'm building a bridge across a void and it's imperative to make the leap of faith that, so long as I persist, inch by inch, with my mission, a destination will present itself. I realise that I would tell myself just about anything if it would spur me on to produce another page, but it would be hard to embark on a novel without the conviction that deliverance awaits.

Were you ever tempted to give Jimmy a more emphatically 'happy' ending?

No. If anything, I had to resist the temptation to go darker. This might well be my personal hang-up, but, except perhaps in stories which are primarily light or comic, I find emphatically happy endings to be depressing. They suggest that, no matter what has transpired along the way, there was never really much at stake because unambiguous closure was always around the corner. For me, this kind of reassurance feels contrived and hollow, even anti-life, and I didn't want to sell out the severity of Jimmy's misfortunes by neatly resolving them.

Readers are welcome to form their own interpretations, but I see the novel, and the ending in particular, as being life-affirming. Jimmy's twin has witnessed everything he has undergone and, despite grasping that to live is to suffer, she yearns for it anyway. Fully embracing life, she argues, is worth it.

SEE
WHAT
I
HAVE
DONE

SARAH
SCHMIDT

I yelled 'Someone's killed father.' I breathed
in kerosene air, licked the thickness from my teeth.

Just after 11am on 4th August 1892, the bodies of Andrew and
Abby Borden are discovered. He's found on the sitting room sofa,
she upstairs on the bedroom floor, both murdered with an axe.

It is younger daughter Lizzie who is first on the scene,
so it is Lizzie who the police first question, but there are
others in the household with stories to tell: older sister
Emma, Irish maid Bridget, the girls' Uncle John,
and a boy who knows more than anyone realises.

In a dazzlingly original and chilling reimagining of
this most notorious of unsolved mysteries, Sarah Schmidt
opens the door to the Borden home and leads us into its
murkiest corners, where jealousies, slow-brewed rivalries
and the darkest of thoughts reside.

The clock on the mantel ticked ticked.

'[A] seminal voice of the future . . . a dark, dense visceral ride
that proves that this former librarian could be on course to
become one of the breakout writers of the decade' *Stylist*

'[A] gory and gripping debut' *Observer*

TINDER
PRESS

ISBN 978 1 4722 4087 3

SARAH DAY
Mussolini's
ISLAND

Non mollare. Never give up.

Italy, 1939. Francesco has been imprisoned on the tiny
island of San Domino, among a group of men that
include his lovers, friends and enemies. Certain one of
their number has betrayed them all to the fascist police,
they are determined to find out who.

Before long Francesco meets Elena, a young island
girl desperate to escape her cloistered existence.
Dazzled by the beautiful young man, she
cannot help but pin all her hopes on him.
When Elena discovers the truth about the prisoners,
the fine line between love and hate pulls her towards
an act that can only have terrible consequences for all.

'Impressive . . . Day handles her plot with great dexterity'
The Sunday Times

'A fascinating debut . . . Day is a talent to watch' *The Times*

'A genuine standout amongst literary debuts. This complex,
brave and powerful novel, both tender and hard-hitting,
features fine writing and a transporting sense of place'
Isabel Costello

TINDER
PRESS

ISBN 978 1 4722 3820 7

You are invited to join us behind the scenes at Tinder Press

TINDER
PRESS

To meet our authors, browse our books
and discover exclusive content on our
blog visit us at

www.tinderpress.co.uk

For the latest news and views from the team
Follow us on Twitter

 @TinderPress